A MYSTERY AT CARLTON HOUSE
Copyright © 2017 by Jennifer Ashley / Ashley Gardner

Printed in the USA.

Cover Design and Interior Format

© KILLION
THE
GROUP INC

USA Today Bestselling Author

ASHLEY GARDNER

A *Mystery* at *Carlton House*

CAPTAIN LACEY
REGENCY MYSTERIES

Also by Ashley Gardner

CHAPTER 1

December 1818

"SIR." A HAND SHOOK ME as I dozed fitfully in a chair. I jerked out of a dream of falling from my horse and landing surrounded by French cavalry, their glittering swords aimed straight at my throat. A cry of rage left my mouth as I grabbed the nearest arm coming down at me to haul the black-guard out of the saddle.

I found myself in a frigid hallway of a fine house, my hand locked around the arm of a tall specimen of a footman, his blue eyes round with fright.

"Damn it all, Bartholomew," I growled. My voice was hoarse, my throat parched, and I was chilled to the bone. The blanket Bartholomew had draped over me sometime in the night had fallen to the polished wooden floor.

"Sorry, sir."

Bartholomew knew never to wake me suddenly like this, as the dreams of my past could sometimes be too incredibly real. I didn't want to shove a knife into his chest before I realized he was the footman who'd become my valet and a friend.

I shook off the memories of battling at Ciudad Rodrigo and forced myself to the present. There was only one reason I slept in a stiff chair in the hall and only one reason Bartholomew would risk waking me so abruptly.

"Is she—" I couldn't finish.

Bartholomew's countenance was drawn, eyes worried. "You'd better send for the surgeon, sir."

Ice-cold fear streaked through me, and I was on my feet at once. "Why? What's happened?"

"I don't know, Captain. That's what the midwife says."

The midwife was a stout woman with a mannish brow, a stern glare, and a no-nonsense attitude. She had no good opinion of doctors, and on that point, I agreed with her. Most were quacks who diagnosed a patient without coming near them, gave them a bottle of hideously expensive tonic, and then disappeared, leaving a bill and a chill breeze in their wake.

The midwife wasn't fond of surgeons either but conceded they were good in a pinch. She hadn't objected when I told her I had one standing by in case he was needed. If she had asked for the surgeon, things were not well.

"Want me to run for him?" Bartholomew asked.

It was dark outside, snow stinging the windows of the long, ornate corridor. We were in Oxfordshire, on my wife's father's estate, and a brutal country winter had settled in.

"I'll go," I said. I took a step and was rewarded with a knifing pain in my knee that had grown too stiff as I slept. Bartholomew's large hands caught me before I could fall.

"Rest yourself, sir. I'll be back in a tick."

"No." I wrenched myself away from Bartholomew's well-meaning grip and began thumping down the window-lined passage, hoping the walk would warm my knee and loosen my muscles. Time had healed the injury I'd received four years ago, but my leg would never be what it had been. "I want to go. I can't sit and wait."

It had been too long already, though I could not remember exactly how many hours ago Donata had sent for the midwife. A night and a day at least, and we were on into the next night. Donata had made me promise I'd stay far enough away from her chamber that I wouldn't hear her groans—she'd known I'd never take myself to bed or out to Oxford so my friend Grenville could pour ale and whisky down my throat.

I'd been too worried to pretend it was all women's business and nothing to do with me. Donata had often been ill during the last months, and I'd never forgive myself if I were out of the house or insensible in bed if something happened to her.

Leaving to fetch the surgeon would allow me to do something instead of standing outside the barred door, bowing my head and waiting in terror.

Bartholomew seemed to understand. "Yes, sir." He ran ahead of me down the corridor and had my coat, gloves, and hat ready by the time I reached the side door that led to the path to the stables. Not long after I stepped into whirling whiteness, a groom led a saddled horse to me.

"Had him waiting," the groom said. "In case."

His face was wan beneath the yellow light from his lantern, fear in his eyes. He, like the rest of the servants in the house, who'd watched my wife grow from tiny girl into lovely woman, worried and wondered if this would be her last night on earth.

I couldn't let it be. I thanked the man, allowed Bartholomew to boost me exuberantly upward, steadied myself on the saddle, and turned the horse into the wind.

The surgeon was staying in a small house in Oxford. I'd wanted him to take a room at Donata's father's estate with the rest of us, but he'd refused. I'd decided not to argue—the fact that he'd agreed to come out here at all had been a victory.

Oxford was not far across the fields. A pleasant enough ride on a summer's day, it turned brutal in the darkness of a winter night, and the scarf I'd raised over my nose and mouth barely kept out the blowing snow. Low clouds cut off the moonlight, though the snowy ground seemed to glow with a faint light of its own.

I'd have lost the way if the lights of Oxford hadn't guided me. Warm lamplight on the streets, the glow of candles in windows, and flickering bonfires of those outside trying to stay warm beckoned me on. I had difficulty remembering that only one month ago I'd been hot—stiflingly so—in the embrace of the Egyptian sunshine. I would return to Cairo and Alexandria, I vowed, this time taking Donata and our child with me. This night would end, and we would go.

I had rented a small room over a shop in a back lane for the surgeon, paying much coin to keep the man in comfort and to ensure the landlord would say nothing to his neighbors about his guest. I threw aside all idea of discretion when I reached the shop and pounded on the outside door that led to the rooms above.

The surgeon must have been waiting, because he appeared a few moments later, candle in hand. He looked at me without surprise, cold eyes in an unmoving face, candlelight brushing his shaved head.

Before I could gasp, *For God's sake, you must come,* he'd stepped back inside, snatched up a coat, blew out his candle and set it down, and shut the door. Without a word, he tramped around the corner of the lane, where he banged on another door.

A sleepy, portly man with a thatch of greasy hair yawned but came outside and led us through a tiny passage to the stables. There he saddled up a horse as sleepy-looking as he and handed the surgeon the reins.

"Take mine," I snapped at the surgeon. "He's a bit more lively."

The surgeon—whose name I had never learned— swung easily into my horse's saddle, and clattered through the passage to the street.

"I'll need a leg up," I called to the portly man. He'd moved at a surprisingly quick pace back toward his warm house.

The man turned around, shuffled toward me, cupped his hands so I could step into them, and boosted me upward. I thanked him, turned the horse, and rode out. The man gave me a sour look as I went, no doubt expecting to be paid for his services. I'd have to settle with him later—I'd not take the time even to dig into my pocket for a coin.

I never caught up to the surgeon. On the better horse, he made the estate long before I rode breathlessly into the inner courtyard and swung down. I saw neither horse nor surgeon as I pulled up and a groom came to assist me.

"He did come here?" I asked the groom as I landed on my feet. I had the momentary fear that the surgeon had deserted

Donata and galloped off, and that I'd just handed a transported criminal who'd returned illegally to England one of the Earl of Pembroke's prized horses.

"Aye, he ran inside." The groom looked at me in trepidation. "She'll be all right, won't she? Our young lady?"

"She will," I said, my mouth set. "I'll make certain of it."

"Godspeed, sir," the groom said, and I moved past him into the house.

By the time I reached the upper floors, I felt fear rising until it crackled through me. The beginning of battle was like this, when the fighting began and men started dying. The stench of blood, death, gunpowder, and churned earth overlaid with the noise of guns, horses, men, and steel had sent my blood pounding—not only in fear but in determination that I would survive to the end of it.

Sweat filmed my skin though it was bitterly cold and my heart raced as I hurried to the chamber where my lady wife was trying to give birth to our child.

The noises were different, and the scents. I smelled beeswax, the smoke of hearth fires, and dampness inevitable in old houses. I heard the wind in the eaves and voices behind the door at the far end—a woman arguing, a man's abrupt tones silencing her.

I limped to Donata's chamber, my walking stick ringing on the polished wooden floor. I yanked open one of the double doors that led to her suite, moving straight through the small anteroom to the next room. Many of the chambers in the old part of the house were layered, one leading to another, the most private chamber tucked well away in the back.

I opened the last door and was immediately assaulted by odors—here was the blood, the fear, the stifling heat, the hovering death.

The midwife came at me, arms extended as though trying to shove me out. I barely noticed her.

My wife lay on the bed, uncovered. Donata's body was slick with perspiration, her hair wet with it, her belly hugely swollen. She was limp, her arms and legs puffy, her face ashen, and she never turned her head as I came lumbering in.

She should have opened her eyes, fixed me with a frosty glare, and said, "Really, Gabriel. You promised you'd wait until I sent for you."

I had promised. I'd given my word. My word, my honor, was everything to me, and Donata knew that.

But I refused to let her die alone, refused to be told by a terrified Bartholomew that they'd lost her, and she was gone from me. They would cover her up and trundle her away, not allowing me to see her. She would ask them to do that.

I knew Donata was still alive. I'd seen death in many forms, and I knew the difference between life and the lack of it. Even so, her pallor was bad, and I could barely see the rise of her breath.

The surgeon had his back to me, rinsing his hands in a basin of water, catching up the towel there to dry them. The midwife regarded him in irritation.

"She's dying," she muttered, "and he's groomin' 'imself."

I'd seen surgeons on the Peninsula who made certain they rinsed everything with water before they started, and I'd seen ones who dug in with muddy hands. I preferred cleanliness.

The surgeon dragged a table next to the bed and began laying out his instruments on it, metal things of differing lengths which had various points on them. I did not know what they were for—had no wish to. He put his hand on Donata's abdomen. The touch was competent, professional, assessing. He squeezed, moved his hand, squeezed again.

"When was her last pain?" he asked the midwife.

"Hasn't had any for a while," the midwife said in a hushed voice. She gave me a sideways glance. "I fear the poor bairn is gone."

Bile wedged in my throat. I moved toward the bed—I have no idea why. I could do nothing.

"It isn't dead," the surgeon snapped, and I halted. "But it's turned wrong."

"Then there's not much we can do," the midwife said stubbornly.

The surgeon's glare made her step back. "Either stay quiet and help me or get out," he told her, and then turned to me. "You, Captain. Wait outside."

I didn't want to leave. My feet were fixed to the floor, my voice gone. I couldn't argue, couldn't obey.

The surgeon turned his steely eyes back to the midwife. "When I tell you to do something, you do it. No question, no hesitation. If you want to save her, you'll obey me. If not, find me someone who will."

The midwife flushed in mounting fury. She opened her mouth, no doubt to tell the surgeon exactly what she thought of high-handed males who pushed their way into a woman's chamber, but just then, Donata groaned.

My wife opened her eyes a slit, dark blue gleaming between her lashes. "Gabriel."

My name was barely a whisper. I moved as swiftly as I could to her, bumping into the surgeon on the way. I seized her hand. "Donata."

Her fingers were limp in mine as she looked past me at the surgeon. "Do what you must," she croaked.

Then her eyes slid closed, and her hand relaxed.

"Captain," the surgeon said in a hard voice. "Out."

I swung to him. "Save her," I said clearly. "Whatever it takes. Or you will answer to me."

The surgeon did not move. His dead eyes didn't even flicker.

We stood face-to-face for a long moment before I turned away from him back to the bed. I bent over my wife and kissed her sweat-drenched face. "Be well, Donata," I whispered.

I pressed a light kiss to her lips, brushed her hair from her forehead, and then made myself turn and walk out of the room. I pulled the door closed behind me as I went, shutting off the tableau of the surgeon and midwife regarding each other stonily over my wife's corpselike body.

It was a very long time before I could take my hand off the door handle and walk away. I took three whole steps to a window seat in the antechamber and collapsed numbly to it, never minding the bitter cold at my back.

I don't remember how long I waited there. My breath fogged in the air, the anteroom unheated. It was a square chamber with its high ceiling painted by an artist of the last century, who'd been quite fond of cherubs. Winged infants buzzed about painted meadows, chasing coyly draped goddesses with mad persistence.

The painting was full of sunshine and joy, brightness and summer. The window behind me showed darkness and snow, deep winter night.

I heard little from inside the chamber where Donata lay. The midwife must have decided to cease arguing with the surgeon, because I heard only his low commands and silence in response.

No cries from Donata, nothing of her pain, her fear. She must be deep asleep, which could only be a mercy for her. About our child, I had no idea. Many women died bringing in a babe, and even more often the child itself died, or lived only a while, being too weak to fight in the harsh world. That any of us survived at all was a miracle.

No one came to me. Bartholomew must be keeping everyone away, knowing I needed to be alone. I couldn't bear to face the others in the house—Donata's mother and father, servants, Grenville—and their well-meaning comfort. They were afraid as well, and would look to me to comfort *them*.

I was hunched over, my head in my hands, when the door opened so quietly I almost missed it. Only a chance creak of the hinge made me look up to behold the surgeon standing in front of me. He'd discarded his coat and cravat to reveal a perspiration-beaded throat, and his hands were balled.

I sprang up, but questions died on my lips when I saw his face. It was bleak, empty, nothing in his eyes.

"You must be prepared to tell me," he said. "Which I will save. The mother, or the child."

CHAPTER 2

THE SURGEON'S WORDS WERE MEANINGLESS, syllables falling into silence. I stared at him for a time, wondering what he had said, my mind unable to comprehend his statement.

I wouldn't allow myself to understand. The words buzzed past me like elusive insects, while the surgeon merely stood and waited.

But I had to respond. The world walked on while I stood in my bubble of disbelief, and I had to walk with it. I had no choice.

Animation returned to my body in a rush, and I caught the surgeon by the lapels of his loosened shirt.

"Save them both," I said, my voice holding hard clarity. "Or I will kill you."

Another man might try to berate me. Or reason with me, placate me, firmly try to make me understand. The surgeon only hung in my grip and watched me. I saw a dangerous light deep in his eyes, but also, surprisingly, understanding.

"So be it," he said.

I opened my hands. The surgeon stepped back, never losing his balance, turned, and disappeared into the chamber. The door clicked quietly as it shut.

Time moved forward without me. The window behind me grew gray, the trees black against the snowy horizon. This deep into winter, the sun didn't show itself until midmorning, which meant the household was already awake by then, lighting fires, eating meals, preparing for the day.

And still I waited. I had no sensation of hunger or thirst, weariness or pain. I didn't exist, floating in a place where my fear and grief wouldn't break me. I knew the time would come when I'd have to experience life again, and I dreaded that hour.

The long, long silence at last broke. I heard a faint sob, and then a sharp, unexpectedly strong wail.

I was off the window seat in a flash, yanking open the bedchamber door. I realized dimly they'd locked it, but I'd wrenched so hard the bolt ripped from the doorframe, splinters of wood raining to the floor.

The surgeon held a tiny babe upside down, shaking it by its feet. The infant howled in protest, the howling not ceasing when the surgeon swung it upright and thrust it at the midwife.

Donata's body and the sheets were covered in blood, as were the surgeon's hands and arms. The surgeon looked exhausted. But instead of covering Donata with a sheet, turning to tell me she'd died in the process, he squeezed out a large sponge from the basin and began mopping off her skin. Then he threaded a wicked-looking needle and plunged it through her flesh.

The midwife had turned away, using another sponge to wash off the babe, which she quickly wrapped in a blanket. She'd nearly disappeared out the door to Donata's dressing room when I caught her.

She turned back to me, the bundle in her arms crying its fury. The midwife's eyes were round with fear, which lanced coldness through my heart.

"Her ladyship came through fine," she said in a shaking voice. "She's powerfully strong, like all her mother's family. This one needs a wet nurse."

She was about to swing away, but I caught her arm. "For God's sake, woman," I said. "Let me see my child."

The midwife's look was full of trepidation, but she peeled back the blanket. I saw a face scrunched in rage, eyes closed, a pink mouth opened in a deafening roar. Tiny arms moved, tiny fingers clenching desperately at nothing.

My heart must have stopped beating, because suddenly I was gasping for breath. I reached out and touched the hand, and the fingers closed around mine in a startlingly firm grip.

"He's a Lacey all right," I said, the pride bursting from me before I could dampen it.

"Not he, sir," the midwife said in a terrified whisper. "*She*. It be a little girl. I'm sorry, sir."

Warmth blossomed in my chest like the sun pushing through a dense bank of fog on a winter's day. The heat radiated through my body until my skin began to sear.

"A girl," I said numbly. "I have a daughter?"

"Yes, sir." Again the whisper. The midwife held the baby protectively, as though I might snatch her up and dash her to the ground.

I'd never do anything to hurt her. Never. In my readings about ancient times, I'd learned that in those days a father had had a right to—had been encouraged to—leave a girl child exposed in the wilderness to die alone. The Spartans were made to have their children inspected by their leaders, who would decree whether the babe—male or female—lived or died. While I admired the ancients their courage, I'd never forgive them this barbarity.

"A daughter," I repeated, my voice ringing. I wanted to laugh in triumph. I had told Donata, when I'd first returned from Egypt, that we would have a girl. I'd already bought jewels for her. I'd been so certain, and now a bubble of joy wafted up and came out of my mouth as laughter. "Nothing could be better."

The midwife regarded me round-eyed. "A man wants a son."

"What for?" I asked in true amazement. "We have Peter. Another girl is perfect. She will be a rare beauty, like her mother. Now, let me hold her."

At last the midwife, still uncertain I wouldn't harm a hair on the girl's downy head, put my daughter into my arms.

The babe was so small. I recalled holding Gabriella at her birth, the swelling of my heart, the terror that I was responsible for this little life.

Nothing had changed. I had the same joy, the same fear, the

same incredible love.

My daughter opened dark blue eyes, glared at me, and bellowed.

"Welcome," I said over the noise, then my voice softened. "Anne."

When I returned to Donata after giving tiny Anne to the midwife to take to the wet nurse, my wife was still in the profound slumber I'd seen when I'd burst in. The surgeon had finished whatever stitching he'd done and was again washing her, cleaning away all traces of childbirth. His strokes were methodical and unemotional, a man following a routine.

"Let me do that," I said and reached for the sponge.

The surgeon turned a flinty expression to me, but to my surprise, handed the sopping thing over. "She shouldn't be moved," he said in his cold voice, his Cornish accent odd to my ears. "I had to make a deep incision. It will heal, but it has to be washed and the dressing changed regular. The wound can't get too damp or too dry; don't use oils and don't let it get dirty."

The look he sent me from his usually cold, dead eyes held admonishment. I knew from experience that even small wounds could take sick and send a person to death within hours.

I nodded. "I understand."

He seemed to believe me. "Tend her well, and she'll live. The babe is strong and will thrive, even if it is a girl. It makes no bloody difference." The disgust behind his words told me what he thought of the midwife's anguish that Donata had borne a daughter.

"I know," I agreed. "My first wife brought in a daughter, who is the most beautiful young woman in the world. We'll care for her well."

"Start with your wife," the surgeon snapped. "Nothing wrong with the child." He gave me a severe look. "Guard your wife and don't let anyone try to heal her by bleeding her. She's lost too much already. Draining her will kill her. Understand?"

I felt an icy chill. "Yes," was all I could manage.

"Once she begins to recover, she must have complete rest, no exertion, no picking up or moving heavy things."

I swallowed. "She has servants to do such tasks for her."

"*Complete* rest," the surgeon repeated. "For six weeks at least. That means no asserting your husbandly rights. She must sleep and sleep alone."

Another cold wave. The idea that I could irreparably hurt Donata because I was amorous made me rather ill. "I understand." My voice cracked.

The surgeon studied me a moment, his gaze assessing, as though he wanted to say something more. Then he gave me a nod and turned away.

I found it odd that a man who apparently had taken lives with the same precision he'd used to sew up Donata knew so much about keeping people alive. There was not one ounce of compassion in his eyes, however. He was like a weapon, dangerous and deadly—one only had to point him at an enemy and pay him well.

So James Denis had told me. The surgeon had been employed at one time to kill Mr. Denis himself, and only Denis's powers of persuasion, plus his considerable wealth, had changed that.

"Thank you," I said in sudden gratitude. No matter what the surgeon had done in the past—and I saw no remorse in him for it—he had saved Donata and my daughter. "You must accept a token of—"

"I accept nothing," the surgeon broke in, his weariness with this conversation evident. "Mr. Denis pays me."

"Of course," I said, removing my hand from my pocket where I'd thrust it to find coins. The surgeon did not possess the reactions of a normal human being, I thought, no gratitude, no humility, no simple politeness. It was as though he did not understand such things and could only watch as the rest of us went through the motions.

"I thank you again," I said, and gave him a formal bow.

The surgeon gathered up his bag, which clinked with metal instruments. He brought out a dark vial and handed it to me.

"If she has too much pain when she wakes, give her a few drops of this."

I took it, wondering if it was the same liquid he'd given my bodyguard, Brewster, when he'd been shot nearly a year ago. The surgeon had let on that he'd made it with plants from the Americas but no more than that.

He didn't enlighten me now. He only gave me another nod and abruptly left the room without so much as a good-bye.

I set the bottle carefully on the night table, took up the damp sponge, and wiped it over Donata's abdomen above the bandage the surgeon had wrapped around her. I'd ring the maids to help me settle her in dry, clean bedding, but for the moment, we were alone, husband and wife, though the wife was insensible.

I leaned down and kissed Donata's damp forehead. "She's beautiful," I whispered. "Thank you, my love."

Donata drew a long breath, as though acknowledging her ordeal was over. She let it out again, her body going limp but with the deep tranquility of sleep.

I kissed her hand and rested it by her side. I rang for the maids to carefully change the bedding, then I settled into a chair beside the bed and remained there for the rest of the day and far into the night, thanking God every moment.

Donata recovered slowly, but recover she did. I nursed her through the first weeks, washing and drying her wound and bandaging it as the surgeon had instructed. When she had pain, I fed her some of the medicine he'd left, which she confessed had an odd taste but gave her a pleasing sensation.

"A little bit like the magical gas we enjoyed at Mr. Inglethorpe's," she said as she reclined in her bed, a lacy cap nearly lost in her dark hair. Her color was good, her eyes sharp, and her observations as pointed as ever. "Pity he got himself killed before I could ask where he obtained it."

Donata's bed was littered with newspapers, books, letters, and paper from a writing box. After the first week, she'd begun writing letters like mad, and receiving many in return. I insisted on keeping a close eye on her, nursing her myself, which drove her to distraction, but she hadn't banished me.

Once a day, I went to the nursery, took Anne from the wet nurse and the other maids who doted on her, and carried her down to Donata for a visit.

In those first days, Anne was little more than a small, pink thing wrapped in blankets. She had a shock of black hair and dark blue eyes, a belligerent stare, and a cry that could shatter glass. I believed her the most incredible thing on this earth.

Donata was pleased with her, and she was pleased with me for not fussing because Anne wasn't a boy. Why such importance was placed on having a man-child I couldn't fathom. Girls were lovely, sweet, kind, and gentle. I'd gone to school with boys from the age of eight, and I saw nothing to recommend them. Peter, Donata's son from her first marriage, was the exception, of course.

Peter was welcome to these sessions with Anne as well. He wasn't certain what to make of a sister who did nothing but sleep, belch, or bellow, but I saw fondness and a proprietary look creep into his eyes as he got to know her.

The surgeon vanished from Oxford the day after Anne's birth, not to be seen again. Bartholomew, who'd gone to Oxford at my insistence to satisfy my curiosity, reported that he'd gone. I was grateful to Mr. Denis for persuading the surgeon to come here at all. Denis had never said a word about it, but I knew the surgeon had journeyed here only at his request—all my persuasion could not have done it.

Our friend Lucius Grenville, who'd returned to London after Donata had been safely delivered, turned up again after New Year's, to Donata's delight, to tell her all the important news from Town—who was planning to do what during the social season, and who was having affairs with whom. I left them to gossip while I walked up and down the heated room with my daughter, my heart swelling with pride and affection.

Pride goeth before a fall, they say, and I was due for a hard smash.

Donata wanted to travel back to London as soon as she was able, bringing Anne and Peter with us. I wished her to stay in Oxfordshire for the entire Season and be as well as possible for next year, but she, of course, would have nothing of that.

"I certainly cannot rusticate in the country for six months, Gabriel. I would never live it down," she said, exasperated after arguing with me for days. "The South Audley Street house will be open, and I will begin my musicales. Grenville told me Lady Partington is hosting a tenor, and she has ghastly taste. I cannot let her inflict a young man who screeches like a banshee on my friends and acquaintances. Gabriella will be returning to us in April, and we must continue introducing her to eligible young men. She left too quickly for proposals last summer—which is as I prefer, so we can find the very best prospect for her, not simply a young man who is more eager than sensible. We must be in London."

I had known I'd lose the dispute even before I began. When Donata said *we* would continue presenting Gabriella, she of course did not mean she and *I*. She meant herself and Lady Aline Carrington, her dear friend and confidant. Between the two of them, they had most of London cowed.

I did continue to protest, because I feared for Donata's health, but I had to admit that between her rest at Oxfordshire and the surgeon's elixir, she regained her health fairly rapidly. My anxiousness turned to relief, though I did not relax my vigilance. A person could appear to be on the brink of recovery, only to relapse and slip away with no notice.

I conceded to return with her to London on one condition: That she rest as often as she could and to go out at night only with me or Grenville accompanying her.

Donata smiled at me. "Of course, Gabriel," she said. "I wouldn't have it any other way."

She'd planned all along to recruit us as her escorts, I realized. She'd not have given in so quickly otherwise.

The last week of January saw us traveling up to London in easy stages. We took two coaches—Donata's father's traveling chaise for the nursemaids and children and Grenville's for Donata, Grenville, and myself.

My wife and my closest friend talked incessantly about people I'd never heard of while I dozed against the window. Grenville reposed on his cleverly made bed that pulled out from the seat— he suffered enormously from motion sickness and could not travel more than a mile without having to lie down. I marveled at the fact that he'd journeyed with me all the way to Egypt and back, and indeed, he'd been quite ill on the sea. Grenville, for all his dandified manners, had much courage and even more determination.

We spent the night on the road, not at an inn, but at the home of a friend of Grenville's, an older couple with a large house and plenty of room for us all. The slow journey gave me the opportunity to make a complete fool of myself over Anne, with me carrying her, talking to her, marveling at everything she did. The waving of a fist, she tracking me with her eyes, or a gurgle from her mouth meant she was the cleverest girl in the world, and I never tired of drawing attention to that fact.

Grenville's friends, fortunately, were kind people, and indulged me, as did Grenville himself. Grenville did not even complain when Anne dribbled a long stream of drool down the front of one of his best waistcoats, which told me he was quite taken with her as well.

We arrived at South Audley Street to be welcomed by Donata's staff and then nearly smothered by their coddling. Donata ran them off with good-natured scolding, but out of her hearing I quietly encouraged the servants to keep a sharp eye on her, no matter what she said.

Donata and I had been settled in the South Audley Street house only two weeks, January merging into February, when her butler, Barnstable, who had very black hair and a cool manner, informed me, while I breakfasted alone at an hour Donata called inhuman, that a Bow Street Runner had called to speak to me.

Barnstable's expression was stony as he conveyed the news. He regarded Runners as lowly thief-takers, working for reward, and did not approve of them coming to the house.

I expected Milton Pomeroy, who had been a sergeant in my regiment on the Peninsula. He'd turned Runner when he'd left the army, and prided himself on carrying thieves to the magistrate. He was a large man with a larger voice, not clever but canny and vigorous.

Barnstable had put the Runner into the reception room, a jewel box of a chamber with an inlaid floor, no windows, hard chairs, and painted panels. The Runner hadn't sat down but paced the small room and swung around when I opened the door.

I halted in dismay. The Runner was not my old friend Pomeroy. The man facing me had dark red hair slicked from his forehead, light blue eyes, and a hard, rather pink face on top of a large, fighting-man's body. His name was Timothy Spendlove, and he'd once arrested me for murder. He'd not been pleased when it was proved I had nothing to do with the death and had released me with only the greatest reluctance.

"Good morning, Captain," he said. "I am pleased to see you've returned from foreign parts."

His eyes sparkled with malice—he'd have been more pleased if I'd remained in those foreign parts and perished there. Then again, Spendlove had told me, repeatedly, that he wanted to use me to tie a noose around James Denis's neck, so I suppose he was not merely being polite.

"What do you want?" I asked. I had no patience for banalities with a man I distrusted.

"Pomeroy can be thick sometimes," Spendlove began, keeping his cool eyes on me. "But he's shrewd when it comes to collecting evidence to get convictions. He advised me, if I wanted my conviction and money, to consult with you."

Runners gained rewards for the criminals they arrested only if said criminal was convicted. After the arrest, while the unfortunate kicked his heels in Newgate or some other prison, the Runner did his best to collect evidence to convince a jury that he or she was guilty. The condemned went off to hard labor, to transportation across the seas, to the hulks, or to the gallows, and the Runner swept up the reward.

"To consult with me?" I repeated, uncertain how to respond. I clenched the handle of my walking stick, my fingers pressing its cold golden head.

"I have arrested a man for theft." The corner of Spendlove's eyebrow twitched once, twice. "Pomeroy claims you are diligent as a hound at finding out who has done what. I know the chap did it, but I must have a clear case. The magistrate warned me of that, though he was happy to keep the man for trial." Spendlove looked sour—the current Bow Street magistrate was the same one who'd let me go for lack of evidence when Spendlove had arrested me for murder.

"Theft of what?" I asked. I knew bloody well Spendlove could have banged up a man for no reason but suspicion and dislike. The only thing that kept me in this room asking him questions was the thought that I might rescue a poor innocent from his doom.

"Ah, you will enjoy this, Captain." Spendlove's eyebrow flickered again, faster this time. "The culprit has absconded with priceless pieces of art from under the nose of royalty. None other than the Prince Regent himself has seen things go missing from his most beautiful house down the road from St. James's Palace. The reward for this one will be quite spectacular. And you, Captain Lacey, are going to help me get it."

CHAPTER 3

SPENDLOVE'S EYES GLEAMED WITH BOTH greed and
excitement. He rocked on his heels while his brow went
twitch, twitch, twitch.

I reflected that while the surgeon had no emotions whatsoever, Spendlove had too many. At the moment he'd wrapped
glee, single-mindedness, and self-righteousness into an unsavory
bundle.

My instinct was to tell him to go to the devil—to dismiss him
and have Barnstable throw him out. I had no wish to do any
favors for the man who had broken into my rooms, arrested me
for murder, and tried to blackmail me into giving him evidence
against James Denis.

I did admit to curiosity, however. The Prince Regent had built
the ostentatious Carlton House as his sanctum away from the
formality of St. James's and filled it with treasures, or so Grenville had told me. Grenville had the fortune—or as he sometimes
said, the *mis*fortune—to be accepted into the Regent's "set," and
was often invited to soirees, balls, suppers, and the like at Carlton House as well as the prince's retreat at Brighton.

Any man who would steal from a place like Carlton House
had to be audacious. Would such a man be so easily caught by
Spendlove?

I swallowed my quick response and settled for a cold stare.
"I have many things to do at the moment. A family to look
after. Bow Street has plenty of foot patrollers who do this sort of

thing, don't they?"

"None with your quick wit and your luck, Captain. Pomeroy is right about that." Spendlove cast his eyes around the little room, admiring the gilded trim on the paneled walls, the landscape paintings—my favorite a hay cart in a field under a lowering sky. The painting had been done in Norfolk, and the artist had captured the emotion of the region well, the broad expanse of land that could be frightening or uplifting. "This is a very nice abode, I must say."

"Lady Breckenridge is a woman of good taste," I responded cautiously. Spendlove never threw out a remark without a reason.

He turned back to me with a skewering gaze. "A house a man would enjoy living in. I would, meself. My own rooms are comfortable, but not very splendid."

"What are you working up to?" I asked in a sharp tone. "I told you, I have much to do."

Spendlove laced his hands and stretched his arms then let his hands fall to his sides. "You are correct—I should make my point. Only this, Captain. You *will* help me look into this matter. Else you might not see this tasteful and warm house again. I know you are the confederate of Mr. Denis, a known criminal, and all your connections will not change the fact that if you do not help me sink him, you will fall with him. I have told you this before."

"And I have told you," I said, trying to keep a firm rein on my temper, "that I am *not* his confederate. I have done my damnedest to avoid him for years."

"Yet, you carried out a commission for him in Egypt, going directly to visit him upon your return. You helped him recover a priceless book before that and befriended a man who owed him money to no doubt help squeeze the man dry. Do you recall any of this, Captain? One of Mr. Denis's ruffians nearly paid with his life to keep you from getting yourself shot. Now why would he do that, if you weren't well in with Mr. Denis?"

Every action Spendlove recounted had happened, more or less, but he could put a nasty spin on anything. The ruffian who'd shoved me out of the way of a bullet, Thomas Brewster, had recovered and accompanied me to Egypt at Denis's behest. He'd become a comrade in arms, of a sort, and I thought, a friend.

"Brewster is his own man and does what he will," I said. Not strictly true, but Brewster did not obey orders from anyone blindly. "Any assistance I give Mr. Denis comes at a high cost to myself, and I usually have no choice. If my actions benefit him, it is accidental. He is ever a man who turns an opportunity to his advantage."

"That is something he has in common with me," Spendlove said. "I seize an opportunity, as I am seizing one now." He leaned to me, his expression turning hard. "I know Denis is behind these thefts. The unfortunate man waiting in Newgate for his trial works for him somehow—I can feel it. What I need is evidence, and what better gent to bring it to me than you?"

"Your pursuit of Mr. Denis is your own preoccupation," I said, holding my ground. "I do not like the idea of these thefts, but if it is Denis's scheme and his man carrying it out, I will leave you to discover this on your own."

Spendlove's eyes filled with a chill disapproval, an anger that was dangerous for its unwavering focus. "You walk on a thin edge, sir, a very thin one. I could pull you for many things, Captain, but I don't—I'm mindful you have a lady wife who is unwell and a new child in your household. I'm not an unfeeling man. But you go too far. Help me prove Mr. Denis has committed this crime, and I'll release you from all else. Never to trouble you again."

I did not believe him. Spendlove was the sort of man who liked having people in his pocket, to pull out whenever he needed them.

If he'd been very certain Denis was behind the thefts, he'd have moved on Denis at once and not waited to corner me for my help. There must be some doubt, if not from Spendlove then someone higher up than he was.

I wondered myself. The paintings and sculptures in the prince's collection were certainly worthy of Denis's attention, but would he do something so overt as to send in a man to steal them? If Denis wanted a painting the Regent owned, that painting would move from Carlton House to Denis's house in Curzon Street with no one being the wiser. The Regent would likely hand it over himself, whether he was aware of it or not.

However, I did not turn a scornful back on Spendlove and shout for Barnstable and the able Bartholomew to throw him out for three reasons.

First, I felt sorry for the poor fellow sent to Newgate on Spendlove's say-so. The man might be undeniably guilty, but I could still pity him. If he was innocent of the crime, leaving him to Spendlove's mercy would be cruel in the extreme. My help might free him.

Second, I was undeniably curious as to what artwork had been stolen and how it had been done.

Third, as much as Denis infuriated me, I owed him much. Had he not made certain the surgeon was in Oxford when needed, I'd have lost Anne and likely Donata along with her. Denis had helped my life to change from the circumstances I'd been in when I'd first come to London, letting in hope and happiness. Ironic that I owed so much to him, but I also knew Denis had carefully planned that. If I could prove he had nothing to do with these thefts, I could repay some of my debt.

I would be saving my own skin as well, but that outcome would be consequent to the other three. If I refused, Spendlove might decide to produce evidence that *I* had something to do with this crime, and it was in my own best interest to discover what had really happened.

I hadn't looked away from Spendlove as I'd pondered, but I saw his eyes flare with triumph. He'd known from the beginning I wouldn't be able to resist, known I would now be nodding my head and agreeing.

Damn the man.

Spendlove went away without telling me much more, not even

the name of the man he'd arrested. Apparently I was to prove he'd done the crime without knowing anything of him. I asked to visit the man in question, but Spendlove refused.

To cool my temper and also to think, I took myself to the nursery. I liked the room at the top of the house, sheltered from the world, decorated in creams and whites, and filled with the sounds, loud and soft, of children.

The wet nurse, a plump young woman with fiery red hair, had a babe of her own. She often had both her son and my daughter at her bosom when I went up, the children quietly suckling while she sat in lazy contentment. The ancients believed that two children nursed by the same woman, regardless of parents, would have a special bond, like brothers, or brother and sister in this case. I would have to pay attention as the children grew, to see whether this transpired.

Peter was with his tutor in a separate chamber, the boy staring into space as the tutor droned on about something or other. Cyril Roth, Peter's new tutor, was a thin young man from King's College, Cambridge, apparently brilliant, but as usually happened with men of intelligence, completely out of pocket. The third son of an untitled gentleman of not much means, though his lineage was impeccable, he'd had a place at Cambridge with certainty from the day he was born.

Many well-educated third sons went into the clergy, but young Mr. Roth had declared to me he had no calling or aptitude for it, so he'd settled for tutoring instead. That he was well qualified to teach young Lord Breckenridge, I had no doubt, because Donata would not have let him join the household otherwise.

Mr. Roth sprang to his feet when he saw me, and Peter looked around, his eyes lighting with sudden hope when he beheld me in the doorway.

"Sir." Mr. Roth had some awe of the fact that I'd been a soldier in the recent wars against Napoleon. One of his older brothers was an officer of a regiment in Buckinghamshire, but apparently, he merely swanned about in his uniform and had never seen action. "How are you, sir?"

"Very well, thank you," I replied. Mr. Roth's formality amused me. "Sit. I am not here to interrupt."

Peter looked disappointed. Sometimes I'd burst in, certain he'd been penned up with lessons long enough, and take him on a tramp or a ride. Usually this happened when *I'd* been penned up too long.

At the moment, I was absently wandering the house while contemplating what Spendlove had told me. I'd heard nothing about thefts from Carlton House—every morning I read every word of several newspapers, and I'd seen no mention at all of artwork going missing from the Regent's house or, indeed, of anyone arrested for it. Journalists usually knew about these things before the rest of us mortals did.

"Mr. Roth," I said, sitting down abruptly. I caught him standing, off guard, and the young man plopped back into his chair. His hair was wheat-colored, which he'd tried to tame with pomade, but wisps resisted lying flat and straggled to his face. "What can you tell me about the artwork in Carlton House? Paintings, statuary? The Regent is a great collector, I have heard."

The newspapers loved to go on and on about *that*, either praising his taste or bemoaning his extravagance.

Mr. Roth's mouth hung open. "Oh, sir, I've never been to Carlton House ..."

I cut off his modest bleating with a wave of my hand. "But you're a scholar, a good one, my wife says. A historian. Surely you have some idea of the things he's bought to decorate his mansion."

Mr. Roth was nervous and shy—from what I understood, his father was a martinet—but I didn't have the patience to ease him into the question. He cleared his throat, scratched his head, which scattered pomade droplets to the book on the table, and sniffled.

"A good many things," he said, and then I watched this thin, nervous, twitchy young man transform. He sat up straighter, his color rose, and his eyes took on a sparkle of interest. "He's sent men far and wide to bring him items, haunts the catalogs of the antiquities auctioneers, and lavishes a fortune on his paintings. He has things from Roman times—how I'd love to see those, sir. Touch them ... like reaching into the past, it is. There are bronzes from Flanders in the fifteen hundreds, paintings by Dutch masters and beautiful modern paintings as well—Mr. Stubbs and the like. Gold cups and vases from the ancients ... it would be worth my life to see it."

Mr. Roth sat in happy contemplation a moment, then the light faded from his eyes, and he returned to the present. He looked around the prosaic nursery of his young charge and let out a small sigh.

Peter had listened with rapt attention—he liked historic things, especially the bits of pottery, gold, and tablets with writing on them I'd brought him from Egypt. He and I had been going over the writing together on these winter nights, trying to figure out what they said. The decipherment of the hieroglyphs, even with the stone Napoleon's officer had found, still eluded even the best scholars.

"Why do you ask?" Mr. Roth said. "Sir."

I rubbed my left knee, the one that had sustained injury on the Peninsula, courtesy of French soldiers in need of entertainment. I thought of Spendlove's threats to coerce me into helping him, coupled with the lack of information in the newspapers—the thefts were being kept quiet, I surmised, Spendlove working frantically to have the culprit convicted and condemned before the world knew of the situation. The magistrates must want to present a fait accompli, not have the newspapers rubbish them for letting a member of the royal family be robbed.

"Curiosity," I extemporized, which was true. "Carry on with your lessons. I apologize for interrupting."

"Not at all. We always welcome you, Captain." Mr. Roth rose when I did. Peter got up too, already painfully polite at age seven.

Peter gave me an imploring look. I could never resist the look, especially as I remembered myself at his age, confined to a room with a tedious tutor, beaten if my attention wandered—not that

Mr. Roth would dare with Peter—while all the world called to me.

"Half an hour," I told Peter. "And then we'll go riding. All right, Mr. Roth?"

Mr. Roth nodded, looking unhappy to cease lessons, but he acknowledged that I was the head of the house now. Donata would be annoyed with me, as she did not want Peter to grow up to be an ignorant lout like his now-deceased father, but I had far more sympathy with Peter than his mother on this matter.

Peter brightened, and I left them. I heard Mr. Roth's voice take on its authoritative drone behind the closed door. "Now then, your lordship, let us try the passage again ..."

True to my word, in thirty minutes' time, I returned to the nursery and took Peter out of the house and to Hyde Park, along with a young lad called Philip Preston. Philip ought to have been back at his school, since it was Hilary term, but his mother often kept him home, fearing for his health. Philip had grown from the thin stripling I'd met two and a half years ago to a robust boy who'd become quite a good rider. He was a few years older than Peter and protective of the lad. They were already good friends.

I turned the ride into a lesson so Philip's father could justify allowing him to come with us. Today we learned to sit a hard gallop and how to give the horse his head while still maintaining control.

The lads enjoyed themselves letting their horses burst down the Row, yelling like hellions. Fortunately, at this early hour, not many people were about, so most of fashionable London was not there to be shocked.

After the lesson, I sent the boys and horses home with their respective grooms, Peter's groom riding my horse and leading Peter back to the mews. I walked from Hyde Park alone, out through Grosvenor Gate and up Park Lane to Grosvenor Street.

Grosvenor Square, its four streets lined with mansions and surrounding a large green park, was filled with carts and other vehicles, drivers making deliveries to the many households.

Like a great machine, London was never dormant for long. The wealthy in this square bought clothing, food, and drink from the finest shops in Bond Street and other lanes, passed last year's clothing down to the servants, who wore them until they sold them to secondhand merchants or tore them up to use for rags. The empty bottles and bones from last night's roast and wine went to the rag and bone men, as well as the cloth that could no longer be used for anything else. The rag and bone men would sell the bottles to those who would reuse them or melt them for the glass, the rags were beaten and pulped to form paper, the bones crushed for meal to raise the crops or feed the animals who would be next year's feast. The cycle went around without end. Comforting or dreary—however one chose to look at it.

It was ten o'clock in the morning, and the great Lucius Grenville would hardly be awake. He was one of the wealthiest men in Britain, obtaining his money by inheriting several fortunes from male relatives who'd died without issue as well was from wise investment of said fortunes.

Grenville's tastes were envied and copied, including by the Prince Regent, and his fame had spread throughout England to the Continent. Grenville had once told me he valued my company because it was refreshing. "You do not say what you are supposed to say, or anticipate what I wish to hear," he'd explained.

In other words, I was blunt and rude. I suppose, to a man surrounded by fawning sycophants, my blatant opinions could be considered a novelty.

It was the height of rudeness to call without warning so early in the morning, but I knew Grenville would never forgive me if I kept the problem Spendlove had thrust upon me from him. We'd quarreled in the past about that very thing, and truth to tell, I knew I'd need his help. He'd know about the artwork in Carlton House and how it might be stolen, and by whom.

I stepped up to his door and rapped smartly on it, to have it wrenched open by a haughty footman. I had hoped for Matthias, brother to my valet, Bartholomew, but this was not to be. Matthias would have greeted me warmly, admitted me to the foyer, and then rushed up the stairs to see if Grenville was awake.

This footman gazed stiffly down his nose at me. "Mr. Grenville is not at home, sir."

I gave him an impatient frown. "Mr. Grenville can hardly be out at this hour. He's shocked at my heartiness for even being dressed at ten in the morning."

"Nevertheless, sir. He is out."

I peered into the young man's eyes but found no deception. Grenville, for reasons of his own, must truly have pried himself from bed and left the house.

"Who the devil is that? Never tell me it's Captain Lacey."

A woman's voice floated down the stairs, followed by the personage of Marianne Simmons. Marianne had at one time been an actress and had lived in the rooms above mine in the narrow street of Grimpen Lane near Covent Garden. She'd given up the stage to become Grenville's mistress, sending tongues wagging across the world.

I stepped past the disapproving footman and bowed to Marianne as she halted halfway down Grenville's magnificent staircase with its arched landing, resting one hand on the railing. Her golden hair poured from under a lace cap to tumble over a peignoir of exquisite silk, a gift from Grenville. Softly lit by the windows above her, she was poised and beautiful.

"Good morning," I said to her. "Grenville is truly out?"

"He is." Marianne remained where she was, not coming down to greet me. "He ran off at an excruciatingly early hour when Matthias brought him a message. He'd tell me nothing about it."

She sounded annoyed but not unduly worried. Grenville was prone to dashing about on a whim, though rarely this early.

"Come up and have coffee," Marianne said. "It's bloody cold down here, but I've got a nice fire in the morning room. You can watch me have breakfast, if you've already eaten."

I wouldn't have minded warm coffee and a chat with Marianne, who was a mine of London gossip, but I was aware of the footman's chill stare.

"It would hardly do for the close friend of Mr. Grenville to sit alone with his paramour while he is out," I remarked.

"That is absolute nonsense, and you know it. Everyone is aware you live in the pocket of your lady and that I wouldn't touch you even if you did not."

"Your art of persuasion needs polishing," I said, amused rather than irritated. "You are to flatter, not insult."

"Flattering you would only raise your suspicions. You know this, Lacey, so do not bother to argue. Forget about scandal and come up. I need to ask you a question."

"Fire away," I said.

"In private." Marianne's tone turned icy. The footman was listening while pretending not to, and I knew many of Grenville's servants would be lingering in the shadows. They didn't spy, exactly; they simply had a healthy curiosity about everything involving Grenville.

I knew, however, that if I ascended and closeted myself with Marianne, no matter how innocently, the fact would be all over Mayfair in a few hours. Plenty on the street had seen me arrive, which probably included a few journalists passing by to discover what sorts of stories they could tell. I wanted the reports of my visit to say I'd stepped indoors for a only a few moments, could be seen at all times through the door the footman had pointedly left open, and that I'd barely had time to remove my hat.

I also knew Marianne would not want to ask me a question she did not consider important, especially one she did not want the servants to hear.

"I will meet you," I said. "Somewhere public. Send me a note when you are ready with a time and place. I will be there. With the full knowledge of my wife."

"Bring her along," Marianne said. "She's a wise lady, and her opinions will be welcome. Good morning, Lacey."

With that, she turned and skimmed up the stairs. She was already slamming a door above by the time I made my polite bow. It was to the footman that I said my good-byes, and then I stepped into the crisp, bright morning and settled my hat upon my head.

As I could not put my hands on Grenville, I made my way to a hackney stand in Oxford Street and directed the driver who stopped for me to take me to St. Giles.

The coachman did not want to go. I could not blame him, though at this time of the morning the worst of the St. Giles's denizens would be asleep, exhausted after a night's hard thieving and violence. I persuaded the driver with the promise of extra coin and told him he could let me off before we reached the warren itself.

After a jostling ride down the length of Oxford Street, the driver pulled up at the junction of it and Tottenham Court Road, refusing to go any farther. I paid over my shillings and walked the rest of the way through the rookeries to the narrow street of my destination.

I'd been to the house I sought only once, but I remembered the narrow lane, its dwellings rammed together as though a giant had put great hands on either end of the row and pushed.

I was partly correct that the denizens of the area were sleeping off the night, some slumped in doorways or lying on the street itself. I wasn't foolish enough to simply step over bodies in my way—one could rise up, knife in hand, to relieve me off all I possessed, and possibly my life.

The smells of gin, fire, and waste lingered in the air, the stench the worst when I hobbled past a gaping hole in the road. This was a forgotten part of London, where people lived ten to a room, where water wasn't clean, and the Watch and even intrepid Runners feared to come.

Why Mr. Denis allowed one of his most trusted retainers to live in such a place I did not understand, but neither Denis nor the man I came in search of seemed to think anything of it.

The front door of the house I wanted stood open. The first two landings were covered with grime, but the floor where my quarry lay was clean and a bit damp, as though it had been recently scrubbed. I scraped the dirt from my boots before I dared tramp there.

All was silent in the stairwell until I knocked, the sound of which set off voices that rose behind the door.

"Whoever that is, Tommy, run 'im off," a woman shouted. "I need to get on."

"Run 'im off yourself." The male growl was irritated but not angry. "I'm asleep."

"How can ye be asleep if you're talking t' me, ye lazy sot? Heave your arse off the chair and open the door."

I leaned as close to the wooden panels as I dared. "It's Captain Lacey," I called.

There was a moment of silence, and then the woman cried, "Well, why didn't ye say so?"

The door swung open, emitting scents of ale and scalded tea. A middle-aged woman with brown hair laced with gray, a sharp face that managed to be pleasing, and rouge rubbed heavily on each cheek stood on the threshold, beaming at me.

"Come in, come in, Captain, and see if ye can shift me husband. He's been morose as an old dog without you to look after."

I had not seen Thomas Brewster since our return from Egypt in late November—I'd left abruptly for Oxfordshire and Donata, while Brewster had remained in London. Brewster had endured much following me to Alexandria and Cairo and back, and surprisingly, Mr. Denis had been compassionate enough to let him take a rest.

Brewster was a large man of solid build. He'd once been a pugilist, until he grew tired of the sport, and then took up a post to be bodyguard and all around lackey to James Denis. Brewster had also been a thief and a good one but could read and write as well as any educated man and knew when a thing was worth stealing and when it wasn't. He eschewed the trinkets pickpockets took—watches, handkerchiefs, coins—and cast his eye on silver, rare books, paintings, and the like. I had the feeling he'd know more about the Prince Regent's collection of art than the prince himself.

I accepted Brewster's wife's delighted invitation to sit, and she ducked into another room to brew coffee. I reposed on a surprisingly soft chair in the cozy parlor as the lady bustled about, while Brewster, in shirtsleeves with his stockinged feet propped on an ottoman, only gave me a belligerent look.

"How have you been keeping yourself?" I asked him.

The inquiry, made in a friendly tone, earned me a glare.

"Well, I ain't been keeping at all, have I?" Brewster rumbled as Mrs. Brewster, whom Brewster affectionately referred to as "My Em," returned from her tiny kitchen with a tray of cups and a tall pot. "Have done sod all, and you know it."

I took the full cup Mrs. Brewster poured for me, curbing a start of surprise. "I know nothing of what you've been doing," I said. "I've been in the country, watching my wife recover from her ordeal and dandling my beautiful daughter."

"Aw," Mrs. Brewster broke in. "We heard about the little mite. Good on yer, Captain."

"Aye," Brewster said. "Felicitations." He snarled the word.

"What the devil is the matter with you?" I asked him in bewilderment.

Brewster had been angry with me before we'd left Egypt because I hadn't trusted him completely—and he'd been right. I still owed him a few pints of ale for that. But Brewster usually wasn't one to hold a grudge, not out loud and not for three months, anyway.

"Never mind him," Mrs. Brewster said. She shoved a cup of coffee under her husband's nose and turned back to me. "He's put out because Mr. Denis has given him the sack, hasn't he? And Tommy blames ye for it, the daft man."

CHAPTER 4

ISTARED AT BREWSTER IN SHOCK. "Sacked? What the devil for?"

Mrs. Brewster's response was lost in the grumbling noise that issued from her husband's mouth. "For going soft," he said.

"Soft?" I blinked.

Brewster was not a person with whom I associated the adjective *soft*. This was a man who'd thought me mad to return stolen silver to a church, who'd coolly purloined a book worth thousands of guineas, and had nearly killed a man with his bare hands before I'd stopped him, not to mention the dangers he'd faced without a qualm in Egypt. He'd worked for Denis for years, trusted to carry out tasks that would make most men blench.

Mrs. Brewster took a chair next to me. "Mr. Denis says Tommy is more loyal to *you* now than he is to *him*. Said Tommy ought to stay home quiet and cause no trouble for a while." She shook her head, brows pinched, but I noticed she didn't say she disagreed with Denis.

"Meaning he don't trust me to do you over if 'e tells me," Brewster growled. "Finks I'd protect you from him."

"And would you?" I asked in curiosity.

Brewster pinned me with a hard stare. "I don't know. 'Aven't decided."

"But it's why he's home," Mrs. Brewster put in. "Because he couldn't argue that Mr. Denis was wrong."

I sat back, resting a heavy hand on my walking stick. "Then I shall speak to Mr. Denis."

The idea of me admonishing one criminal for sacking another might seem strange, but Tommy Brewster had done me many good turns. He'd pushed me out of the way of a bullet, kept me from harm during the dangerous journey through Egypt, and had lent me his good sense to help solve puzzles in the past. He didn't deserve to be shunted aside.

If Denis no longer employed him, would Brewster return to thieving to make ends meet? Men like Brewster didn't always reform—they fell back on what they knew. Without Denis to protect him, he would quickly find himself in Newgate if he were caught stealing, finishing his life dangling at the end of a rope. I did not want that to happen to Brewster, who was, underneath it all, a good man.

"I wish you wouldn't," Brewster said wearily. "If you go talking to his nibs, you'll only cause more trouble. Leave it."

"I feel responsible for your dilemma," I argued. "Let me at least try to fix it."

"You *are* responsible. But leave it, for God's sake." I wouldn't, and Brewster and I both knew it. Brewster heaved a sigh, looking resigned. "Drink your coffee, then, and bugger off."

"Tommy," Mrs. Brewster admonished. "The Captain's come all this way, to St. Giles of all places, to see yer. At least let him tell ye what he wants." She turned back to me, avidly curious.

The simple way I could help Brewster struck me. "Indeed, I came for your expertise," I said. "If you are at a loose end, then *I'll* employ you."

Brewster's eyes narrowed in suspicion, but he looked a bit less belligerent than before. "Employ me to do what?"

"Help me learn about what sorts of things would be found in Carlton House, the prince's residence. And how and why a man might steal what's there."

Brewster's eyes flickered with interest. "Aye, I heard about a chap arrested for nicking from royalty. Bloody fool, is all I can say. Good luck to 'im. 'E'll need it."

"You heard?" I sipped the coffee Mrs. Brewster gave me,

wincing as I burned my tongue. "I saw nothing in the newspapers, have heard nothing through gossip."

Brewster unbent enough to chuckle. "Don't need no newspapers, Captain. These things get told, like. Everyone wants to nick a priceless bit of art and not get caught. Set you up for life, that would. Much more respectable than nicking apples off a cart. Moves a bloke up in the world."

"Do you know what he took?" I asked, my interest growing.

"That I do not. But it could have been any number of things, couldn't it? Gold cups are easiest to shift. Can be walked out with in a bag, painted over to look like bronze, sold to a collector what loves historical things and ain't too particular about where a thing comes from. Or, in a pinch, melted down for its gold. A snuffbox all over gems is easy too—slides into a pocket, no one the wiser. Much harder to walk a great square of a painting out of a house, innit? Have to cut it out of a frame, fold it up without cracking the paint. Hard to shift too—have to prove it's real or the buyer thinks you're having him on. Who do they have banged up for the job?"

"I don't know," I answered. "Mr. Spendlove wouldn't tell me."

Brewster's face puckered. "Spendlove? He's a right bastard—don't do noffink for the likes of 'im."

"I agree with you. Spendlove wants me to find evidence the man is the thief, or I shall see *myself* in the dock for whatever crime he can pin on me. Besides, I want to make sure the scapegoat he's arrested is truly guilty. I don't wish to see an innocent hang."

Brewster's expression didn't change. "Spendlove's a bastard but he's also clever, Captain. He wouldn't pull a man if he weren't guilty of *some*fink. Stay clear of it, that's my advice. Ye can get around his threats. Your lady wife has plenty of blunt to hire fancy lawyers to keep you free."

I wouldn't stay clear, and Brewster knew that. I shook my head. "I cannot in all good conscience let Spendlove send a man to the gallows for something he didn't do. Also, I can't help wondering what this theft has to do with Spendlove's pursuit of Mr. Denis—why he's commanded *me* to help him and no other."

Brewster nodded sagely. "He wants his nibs to have somefink to do with it and you to hand him the evidence. Sodding bugger."

"It's why I need your help," I said truthfully. "I'm out of my depth."

"Ha. You need someone to lead you around the world of art thieves— that's what you're telling me. Someone *not* his nibs." Brewster stretched back in his chair, crossing his giant feet in worsted socks. "It might not be a brilliant thief at all, you know, but an under-footman what saw a chance to make a bit of coin. Not everyone is like Mr. Denis, or in his employ."

"True, but I am beginning at a disadvantage. If Pomeroy had asked for my help, he'd have told me all he knew. Spendlove plays a closer game. Will you ask about for me—discreetly—if anything's come on the market, or even a rumor of such things? And who brought it there? We can negotiate a fee for your services."

Brewster's scowl returned. "Don't give me no charity, Captain. His nibs sacked me, but he gave me a pension. I worked for him near twenty years."

"Even so." I set aside my cup and rose, giving Mrs. Brewster a nod of thanks for her hospitality. "I wouldn't ask you to do a dangerous job without compensation. I appreciate your help—I owe you a night of imbibing."

Brewster eyed me with his usual surly stare, then his lips twitched. "You're still remorseful about what ye said to me in the tomb, ain't ye? That the only reason I'd not rob ye is because of what his nibs would say? Ye did hurt me feelings, Captain, that is true."

I gave him a bow. "I know. It was rude of me."

"Aye, it was. I forgave ye for getting me out of that grave we were in alive, ye know. But if ye want to pour ale into me down the pub, I'll not stop ye."

As I walked back through St. Giles to find another hackney, I felt eyes upon me. I might have been in deep woods, with wolves circling beyond sight in the trees. The wolves were leaving me be for the moment, but just for the moment. Those here would have known I'd gone to see Brewster, likely the only thing that kept them in check.

I moved as quickly as I could, my walking stick ringing, my awareness prickling. A jaunt through enemy territory on the Peninsula hadn't made me this uneasy.

I'd nearly made it to Great Russell Street when an unsavory person stepped out in front of me. He wore shabby clothes covered by a threadbare greatcoat, gloves whose fingertips had worn through, and a battered hat that once had been a tricorn. He had few teeth and a face covered with grizzled whiskers through which sores shone red.

He was a sad specimen, one fit for charity, but he planted himself in front of me and would not move. Attempting to step around him did no good, as he swiftly put himself before me again.

"Give us a coin," he said, bathing me in breath foul with gin. "Give us a toll, and I'll let ye pass."

I had no intention of reaching into my pocket and pulling out anything. These days, I had a few more shillings with which to pay my hackney coach fares, but I wasn't foolish enough to go walking about London jingling with gold. I had enough to get home, but I didn't dare bring out my meager purse to give this man a farthing.

My advantages over the reeling gentleman were that I was sober, a trained fighter, and had a sword sheathed in my sturdy walking stick. His advantage was that he wasn't lame in one leg, and he had friends.

These emerged from doorways and passageways as I stood face-to-face with the gentleman, my fingers tight on my walking stick.

Someone came to my side, and I felt a prick at my armpit. I turned to see a man a head shorter than I, hard-faced, and definitely not drunk. He held a knife poised to go straight into my lung.

"Give 'im the lot," this man said quietly. "Tell ye what—just 'and over your coat and waistcoat with all what's in 'em. We'll let ye go 'ome to your missus in your shirt and trousers." He glanced at my walking stick. "Your prop stays wiv us too."

The walking stick was a gift from Donata, the first gift she'd ever given me. Likewise she'd bestowed upon me the watch that was tucked into my waistcoat pocket, and my daughter Gabriella had supplied the chain that dangled from it.

"I'll gladly give you my purse," I said, "if you want four shillings that badly. But I'm going with the rest. It's chilly today."

The knife point dug a little harder. "You're amusing, you are. Ye fink this is an argument? Ye fink being a pal of Tommy's will help ye? 'E's not from around 'ere, and 'e ain't got his old mate to 'elp him no more, 'as 'e?"

I would definitely have to speak to Denis about his decision to dismiss Brewster. Perhaps Denis hadn't realized he might put Brewster in danger ... Then again, Denis made no action he hadn't thought through clearly. I doubted he'd sacked Brewster in a fit of pique.

"The purse," I said. "It is in my inner pocket. Enjoy that, or I fight you."

"And die," the man said without worry. "I've got many mates between me and your way out. And we know 'ow to keep a body from being found for a long, long time."

I did see a flicker of interest in his eyes that I wasn't afraid. I wasn't. I had no intention of leaving my belongings with this man, treasure that meant more to me than the cost of them.

Perhaps battling every day of my life for years had sent me into a state of resignation—this would simply be one more battle. Perhaps being thoroughly beaten by highly skilled Turkish toughs in Egypt had also inured me. And absolutely nothing could compare to being walled alive in a tomb under the desert floor.

I caught the man with the knife in the gut with my elbow and swung around with my walking stick to slam it into the stomach of a confederate who'd been creeping up on my left. The gap-toothed man who'd originally stopped me faded quickly out of sight, whether dismayed his quarry fought back or to summon help, I could not know.

Or perhaps I wasn't afraid because I knew bloody well that Denis would not let me wander about in St. Giles without some-one to watch over me. As I fought, this watcher, a giant of a man, emerged from the shadows, cudgel in hand.

He went at the St. Giles men with ruthless professionalism—only one of him and five—no, six—of them. Three turned and fled without hesitation, two fought and then retreated, leaving only my assailant with the knife. That man bent into a fighting crouch, rage in his eyes. Denis's thug brought his cudgel down toward the man's head, then danced back when the knife nearly swiped off his privates.

Snarling, Denis's man straightened up, drawing his own knife, a wicked-looking thing about a foot long.

The other man glared at it, then swung around, his long coat flying. "Don't let me see you back 'ere," he said to me, his spittle glinting in the morning sunlight. "Or you're for it."

With that, he twisted away, sprinting hard as Denis's man went for him, and disappeared into a noisome passageway.

I straightened up, breathing hard. I expected Denis's thug to sheath his knife and escort me from the rookeries, but instead, he balled up the hand that held the blade and swung his fist at me.

I ducked before his blow could connect with my face and grabbed his arm. In return he smacked his cudgel into my side and kicked my leg out from under me. I went down on my bad knee, pain banging through me and making my teeth rattle.

"Bloody hell!" I shouted at him. "Enough!"

"Ye need t' be taught your place, Captain," the man said with-out contrition. "'E's tired of ye waltzing into danger, knowing 'e'll pull ye back out of it."

"You beating me to a pulp will assist with that, will it?" The words barely came out as I struggled to breathe. Rage kept the worst of the agony at bay, but I knew I'd pay later.

"It'll teach ye manners," the man said, his scarred face unmoving. "I'm not your minder. This'll 'urt but not leave ye where ye can't do what you're told."

If Denis had ordered this man to pummel me into submission, no wonder he'd accused Brewster of going soft. Not that I planned to kneel in the muck and tamely take my punishment. I brought up my walking stick as the man's cudgel came down again, ready to fight him weapon to weapon.

The cudgel never struck. It was ripped out of the man's beefy hand by another hand equally as large. Then Brewster's huge fist landed on the thug's face, snapping his head sideways.

Denis's ruffian danced back, shaking his head, but swung around, his knife ready. I struggled to my feet. Brewster advanced on the thug with the nabbed cudgel held ready, murder on his face. The man studied him then me as I drew my sword, gave us both a look of disgust, and turned and tramped away, his knife still in his hand as he faded into the shadows.

Brewster lowered the cudgel and steadied me as I sheathed the sword and planted my walking stick on the cobbles to regain my balance.

"My Em has the right of it," Brewster said. He was fully dressed, coat, hat, boots, and all, and breathing hard, as though he'd run swiftly after me. "Ye get into too much trouble left on your own. I suppose I'm working for you now. Let's get ye home."

I'd managed to come through the scuffle with only a bruise and cut on my left cheekbone. Barnstable, who'd ministered to me in the past when I'd arrived at this elegant house looking like a prizefighter, did not flick an eyebrow over my appearance. He did, however, suggest I retire to my chamber where I might wish to tidy myself before entering the sitting room.

"Her ladyship is there, sir, as well as Mr. Grenville."

So, Grenville had reappeared. "An excellent suggestion, Barnstable," I said and made to move past him and up the stairs.

"I beg your pardon, sir." Barnstable held out a folded piece of paper he'd extracted from his waistcoat pocket. "This came for you while you were out."

I took the paper, neatly torn from a larger sheet, and found Marianne's handwriting telling me where and when she wanted to meet to ask her question. I thanked Barnstable, who made certain he looked in no way curious as to what was on the missive, and I continued upstairs.

Brewster, who had ridden with me in the hackney, had already descended to the kitchen. Donata rather liked Mr. Brewster, and so did Grenville, and Brewster had been privy to many of our discussions, but he had no wish to accompany me to an upstairs sitting room. A former pugilist and thief hired to watch over me belonged below stairs, and only below stairs, so Brewster said.

Bartholomew did comment on my wound when I entered my chamber to wash up. "Mr. Denis's man did that?" he asked, outraged. "Even after he drove off the other ruffians?" He shook his head. "Bloody bastard has no honor. I hope you'll speak to Mr. Denis, Captain. It ain't right for him to sack Mr. Brewster." Our sojourn in Egypt had softened Bartholomew a long way toward Brewster.

"I will have a word with Mr. Denis," I said as Bartholomew helped me into a fresh coat. "But don't tell Brewster about it. He has his pride, and my protests may do no good."

"Try anyway, sir." Bartholomew brushed down the back of the coat with a soft-bristled brush, smoothed the cloth across my shoulders one more time, then stepped back and nodded that I'd passed his inspection.

"I intend to," I said, and left him.

The sitting room one floor below me overlooked the garden and was relatively quiet, shutting out the rumble of traffic on the street. Donata had decorated it with her usual taste in creams and yellows, the woodwork white, the fireplace and windows done in the style of the Adam brothers. A painting of Donata and Peter hung on one wall—she stood regally, one hand on the back of a chair, while her very young son lolled on the chair seat.

The painting was ostensibly a portrait of young Lord Peter Matthew St. John, now Lord Breckenridge, but the painter had captured Donata's essence. Her head was lifted, her dark blue eyes watching the viewer, the slight tilt of her lips a mark of her intelligence and her biting sense of humor. At any moment she might make a quip that reduced the viewer to an apologetic mass of bewilderment.

The background in the painting was filled with a floor vase of flowers, a drapery that revealed nothing, and a pillar in the Greek style. Against these props, Donata was vibrant, her beauty singular.

Today she reposed on a cream-upholstered chaise, her legs covered by a deep blue shawl that went well with her lighter blue gown and brought out her eyes. Knowing my wife, this color combination was not by chance.

Grenville, who'd been speaking animatedly with her from the green-and-gold striped Bergere chair near the crackling fire, sprang up as I entered.

Marianne had said he'd departed abruptly from his Grosvenor Street house at an unusual hour, but even so, Grenville had taken time to dress for his outing. His coat of black cashmere could have graced a ballroom, though he would protest he wore a simple morning suit. His waistcoat was a subdued gray-and-ivory stripe, rising to a cravat tied in a fairly simple knot—simple for Grenville, that is—and his skintight buckskin pantaloons fitted well into his top boots.

"There you are," Grenville said. "Where the devil did you get to?"

It spoke of his agitation and excitement that he made no formal bow, no friendly salutation, no inquiry about my health. He simply quivered with whatever it was he wished to tell me.

"Looking for you, as it happens," I said. I lifted a Louis XV chair from the writing table and carried it to the chaise so I could sit next to Donata without disturbing her. Her look was welcoming, but no less eager than Grenville's.

"Grenville's been summoned to the palace," Donata said. "He is agog with it."

Grenville shot her an admonishing look. "Not exactly." He resumed his seat as I took my place, and leaned forward, the tails of his coat falling to brush his boots. "I was indeed summoned, but to Carlton House, early this morning."

He waited, no doubt hoping I'd widen my eyes in astonishment. "About the thefts there?" I asked without changing expression.

Grenville's dismay was comical. "Damn it all, Lacey. You might let me surprise you *once* in my life."

I relented. "It is why I went in search of you. Mr. Spendlove has asked me to look into things."

Grenville's brows rose, as did Donata's. "Spendlove?" Grenville repeated.

"That detestable man," Donata said with rancor. "I hope you refused him."

"I wished to." I spoke slowly, resting my hand on my walking stick. I did not want to tell Donata about his threats, not yet. "But—"

"But you had to see what it was all about," Grenville finished for me. I let out a breath, happy I was spared an explanation. "Yes, I heard all about the arrest. The majordomo at Carlton House told me about it. And the Regent himself. The prince wrested himself out of bed at that early hour to ask me—indeed, beg me—to bring 'that clever captain' to visit him and discover everything you can. The Regent wants me to cart you to him so he can implore you himself to find out what is happening to his collection, and have you put it right."

Another man might be flattered that the monarch-in-waiting had requested his advice, but the announcement only bewildered me.

"Does he expect me to stride in, identify the culprit without doubt, and sail out again, a good deed done?" I asked in astonishment.

Grenville nodded. "That is likely. I told him it was not so

simple as that, but the Regent is adamant to meet you. You have become rather famous."

The most popular man in England explained this without resentment. I shook my head. "Infamous, is more likely. *Infamis* as the Romans said, and they did not mean it as a compliment."

"Nonsense." Donata cut through my ramblings in a clear tone. "I will go with you to this appointment, as will Grenville, and we will explain things. My father was one of the prince's advisors before Papa decided country life was more to his taste. Not that the Regent listened to Papa much, another reason he'd had enough. The prince used to praise my riding. I was eight years old and already thought him a fool."

And Donata did not suffer those gladly. However, she knew what to say and not say to anyone at any level of society, and I'd welcome her help.

"He expects us at two o'clock," Grenville said, rising. "A cheek, I know, but if we set off soon, we'll arrive in time."

"Ah." I remained seated, closing my hand more firmly on the walking stick. Marianne's note had asked me to meet her at two at Egyptian Hall. "I cannot go on the moment. I am afraid I have another engagement."

CHAPTER 5

GRENVILLE GAVE ME A DUMBFOUNDED look. He stood in silence while the porcelain clock behind him ticked at least a dozen times. For once in my life, I'd caught Lucius Grenville at a loss for words.

Donata filled them in for him as she fixed me with her shrewd gaze. "What he means, Gabriel, is that the king's son has sent for you, and you say you are too busy to attend? Grenville is trying not to be rude and ask what *you* could possibly have to do that is more important."

By the flush on Grenville's face, Donata had the right of it.

"I beg your pardon," Grenville said, his voice subdued. "Of course I will make your apologies and fix the appointment for another time."

He was angry at me and striving not to show it. He'd be angrier still if he knew with whom I'd be meeting. I had the strong suspicion Marianne wished to speak with me on a topic she'd not shared with Grenville and would not be happy if I imparted it to him.

I kept my countenance neutral, unwilling to satisfy his curiosity. At last Grenville heaved an exasperated sigh and gave us both a formal bow.

"Very well, then. I will hie to Carlton House and explain things."

"If he can wait but an hour," I began, but Grenville shook his head.

"Even our frivolous prince's time is tightly scheduled. I will ask for another appointment. He is sufficiently agitated enough to accommodate you."

I rose. "My sincere apologies," I said. "But I made a promise."

"Yes, indeed." Grenville went to Donata and lifted her hand to his lips. "I am happy to see you looking so well, Mrs. Lacey. Motherhood suits you—again. Good afternoon."

Donata graciously accepted the compliment and the kiss. She watched Grenville depart with his usual agile step but didn't speak until we heard him descend the stairs and Barnstable greet him to politely see him out.

My wife gave me a severe look as I turned back to her. "Good heavens, Gabriel, you are cool as ice on a winter's day. Grenville might be too polite to ask what you could have planned that's more important than visiting Carlton House, but I am not. Even if you do not think much of the Regent as a person, I know you are intrigued by this theft."

"I am." We heard the front door close below, Grenville gone. I moved the chair in which I'd been reposing in front of the chaise and sat down so I could hold Donata's hands in mine. "How are you?" I asked her.

"Anxious to know what you've been getting up to," was her immediate reply before her dark blue eyes softened. "I am well, Gabriel. Truly. Better every day."

I closed my fingers tightly over hers. "Good."

We shared a look. She knew how grieved I'd been, how certain I would lose her. I'd tried, once we'd arrived in London, to hunt up the surgeon and press on him a reward for saving the life of my wife and child, but he'd vanished. I hadn't been very surprised that I could not find him.

Donata had not at first understood my concern for her. I do not believe she realized my depth of feeling. But I am not a man who loves by halves—it is everything or not at all. After a time, she'd ceased admonishing me for fussing and now answered my inquiries with seriousness.

She returned the squeeze of my hands then withdrew, caressing the backs of my fingers as she went. I saw a flicker of deep worry in her eyes, however, which I did not like. But she'd fought to live, and I could well understand her not wanting to relax her vigilance too early.

Her voice became brisk again, the anxiety banished. "Now that we have established that I am robust as can be expected, tell me what you are up to, blast you." My dear wife bent me a glare.

"Of course," I said. "You are invited to my appointment as well, and in fact, we should leave soon. We will be spending an hour at Egyptian Hall."

Donata's brows rose. "Will we? It's rather passé, isn't it? Captain Cook's voyages, armor, and natural history? We've seen it."

"Ah, the ennui of the very rich." I gave her a faint smile. "I quite enjoyed the displays. Napoleon's coach and camp bed and so forth."

"Only because you defeated the man." Donata reached to the inlaid table beside her then arrested the movement. She used to keep her cigarillos there, but she'd given them up while she'd been with child, convinced they'd not be good for the baby's health. She was waiting until she fully recovered to enjoy them again, but I saw the pucker of frustration between her brows.

"I did not defeat him by myself," I said with faux modesty, then dropped the pretense. "I fought his soldiers but never saw the Corsican. He stayed well off the Peninsula. Had more pressing business elsewhere. He didn't need to be there, in any case. His generals were top notch."

Donata drummed her fingers on the empty table. "You sound as though you admire them."

"One can fight a man and commend his skill," I said. "Will it cause too much damage to your reputation to be seen entering a building whose popularity has waned?"

Donata unwrapped the shawl from around her and swung her feet to the floor. She put her hand in mine so I could steady her while she stood.

"I will risk it," she said. "But only because I am so bloody curious. Give me a moment to don something appropriate, and we will be off."

Donata met me downstairs in only a quarter of an hour in a straight-skirted cream-colored gown with appliquéd roses on its hem, covering this with a long coat of red and green vertical stripes, its collar and cuffs lined with fur against the cold weather. A hat with five ostrich feathers standing stiffly from its crown completed the costume.

My plain suit of black with a subdued waistcoat of yellow and ivory contrasted it nicely, I thought. We made a fine pair.

Donata, however, looked me up and down with a critical eye. The ensemble had been made for me last winter and therefore was now a year out of fashion.

I saw no reason to throw away or hand down a perfectly good suit of clothing because a season had passed. Quite wasteful, I thought, though I suppose an argument could be made that having a new suit every sixmonth kept the tailor and his family fed.

I said nothing to her silent assessment—it was an old argument—and we walked out to the carriage that one of her footmen had run to fetch. The crest of Viscount Breckenridge was on the door, so we would not be moving about the city anonymously. I told Donata what the errand was as we journeyed the short distance through Mayfair, and her disapproval vanished as her curiosity grew.

Egyptian Hall was so named because of its façade. Unlike its fellow houses on Piccadilly, this one had three large pylons that reached from its second to third stories, with two giant figures intended to represent Isis and Osiris above the doors. Above those, over the window Isis and Osiris flanked, two sphinxes sat back to back around a winged scarab. The door itself was flanked by fat pillars. Very eye-catching when one hurried to and fro along the busy road of Piccadilly, but now that I'd seen the reality of Egypt I knew this façade for a fantasy.

The interior showed nothing of the Egyptian exterior—the building's large rooms had plain walls filled with shelves and cases devoted to curiosities collected by William and George

Bullock. There were displays of plants, pressed and preserved, shells, insects, and other things from the South Seas, an enclosure in the middle of the room holding stuffed beasts of fearsome proportions—ostriches, a zebra, even an elephant. One wall was covered with breastplates, pikes, and swords of faraway lands and past centuries.

I'd heard that the interior of this museum was to be redesigned this year to house the things Mr. Belzoni was collecting from Egypt, and I certainly hoped so. I'd met the huge Belzoni, who'd been a strongman in entertainments throughout England, in my last weeks in Cairo. I'd found him personable—he'd been happy to show me what he was busy digging up around the massive pyramids and discuss with me his previous finds. I was humble enough to acknowledge that part of the reason he shared these things with me is so I could spread the tales of his greatness when I returned to London.

Donata glanced about the collections with interest, in spite of her declaration that the museum was becoming outdated. We strolled from room to room, arm in arm, studying the curiosities as any married couple would. Donata paused to scrutinize the insects and flowers from the tiny islands in the middle of the Pacific, and I wondered out loud what it must be like to journey to such an exotic place.

"Grenville will surely go there one day," I said. "If he has his way. He will tell us."

Donata flashed me an amused look that also had some anxiousness, as though she thought I'd leap onto a ship with Grenville and sail off into nowhere. Not now, I could assure her. For now I was perfectly contented with my domestic arrangements and had no wish to leave England unless Donata accompanied me.

A group of Grenville's cronies, gentlemen I'd seen at White's and Brooks's, had decided to visit today as well, but by the way they pointed disparagingly at the exhibitions or waltzed with each other around the open spaces, they'd come here for a lark, I saw, not serious contemplation. They were younger than Grenville, though dressed in imitation of him. One or two had intelligence and wit, I knew from brief acquaintance; the rest were hangers-on and rather ridiculous.

One gentleman gave a polite nod as he caught sight of us, though I suspected that if I hadn't been with Donata, he'd have pretended not to notice me.

London society was sharply divided in its opinion of me and my marriage to Donata. Half the *ton* thought me an upstart, brought in by Grenville to pinch the best women for myself. The other half acknowledged that I had an old name, though my family's wealth had dwindled, and more or less accepted me in my own right.

All envied me Donata. She had been born into one vastly wealthy family and had made her first marriage into another, not to mention she was young, popular, and lovely. Those against me muttered that I would try to heavily influence Peter as he grew, so the boy would favor me above all others, perhaps facilitating a way to get my hands on much of the Breckenridge money. Not directly, of course but through gifts, trusts, and other legal twists.

I was attempting to counter these beliefs by refusing to touch any of Peter's or Donata's money at all, and living on my half pay, which Donata said was absolute nonsense. I had at least consented to take an allowance which was more than adequate for my needs, annoying Donata by not letting her man of business make it larger. It was a point upon which my wife and I'd had words about off and on for much of the year.

The dandies parading before us now, their elegant black suits worth my entire quarterly allowance, had come to Egyptian Hall out of that ennui I'd jested about with Donata. Not to learn something of the world, of course, but to be as exasperating to others as they could. They were loud and annoying, two of the most unruly following patrons around the room and aping them.

One of the dandies, Lord Lucas Parnell, son of a marquess, I considered had more intelligence and better manners than the others. He frowned in disapproval at the two who were mocking the museum's visitors and barked an order at them to cease.

The two young men looked slightly abashed as they rejoined their friends, but not very contrite.

Another member of the group was Rafe Godwin, a gentleman whose goal in life was to supplant Grenville. I'd become acquainted with Rafe during a visit to Norfolk shortly before my marriage—he'd been the guest at an estate not far from mine. He'd been rude and condescending at the same time trying desperately to gain Grenville's approval.

Lord Lucas was the man who'd nodded at Donata and me, and as our wanderings brought us closer together, he made a gracious bow. Rafe also made a bow, a fraction of a second after Lucas. I bowed in return, and Donata gave both gentlemen an acknowledging bend of the head.

We would have to speak to them, of course, being acquainted, though I chafed at the interruption. What I had not seen since I'd entered Egyptian Hall was any sign of Marianne.

"Good afternoon, Captain," Lord Lucas said. We met halfway between a display of brightly plumed birds and a case of odd sea creatures. He hesitated before he addressed Donata, as though debating what to call her. "Mrs. Lacey," he chose.

Rafe gave Donata a broad smile. "*Mrs. Lacey,*" he said, and extended a hand to her.

"How charming to see you, Mr. Godwin," Donata said as she allowed Rafe to raise her fingers to his lips. Her ostrich feathers quivered. "Lucas, what a surprise."

She'd known Lord Lucas Parnell since childhood, I understood. Lucas flushed and bowed again. His hair was a rich brown, styled in the disheveled curls that were the rage, his coat and waistcoat fitted to his trim body. His trousers, in contrast, were loose and baggy, as was becoming the fashion—Rafe's positively ballooned. Lucas had hazel eyes that took in Donata and rested on her, his look turning wistful.

I had no sympathy. Donata told me he'd always been fond of her, but if Lucas had wished to marry her, he'd had a chance between her first husband's death and my proposal nearly a year later. If Donata had been interested in Lord Lucas as a suitor, she'd have encouraged him. My wife was not shy about going after what she wanted.

"I came on a mission," Lord Lucas said once our greetings were over. "I have a message for you, Captain Lacey."

"For me?" I asked, surprised. "What message?"

"I have no idea." Lucas sounded pained. "I was only instructed to deliver it." He took from his smooth black coat a folded and sealed sheet of paper, which he handed to me. My name, *Captain Gabriel Lacey,* was on the outside of it, and nothing else. I did not recognize the seal, and the name had been written in no hand I knew.

"Thank you," I said. I slid the missive into the pocket of my coat, much to the disappointment of the half dozen gentlemen surrounding us. I suppose they meant me to open it, read it, and clutch my hair at its contents while they sniggered. I was burning with curiosity but I refused to perform for them.

"Shall we visit the Napoleon room?" Donata asked me, also feigning indifference. "Give my regards to your mother, Lucas. I hope she is doing well."

"She is in very good health," Lucas said. "I will pass on your wishes."

"Excellent. Good day, gentlemen," Donata said. She gave Rafe a nod. "Mr. Godwin."

Rafe returned the nod with a bow, but his eyes sparkled in annoyance. He'd be wondering whether she hadn't included him under the sobriquet of "gentlemen" with intent to insult him or whether she'd been singling him out as a compliment. He'd chew on the problem for days. I decided I adored my wife.

As we walked away from the group, Donata's fingers tightened on my arm. "How tedious. I apologize, Gabriel."

I looked at her in surprise. "You have nothing to apologize for. Godwin's behavior is his own fault."

She sent me a faint smile. "I know that. I mean for having to interrupt your errand. Lucas is an old friend. He's out of pocket, poor man, as his father gambles away every farthing as soon as it comes in, and Lucas will inherit a bankrupt estate. I feel the

CHAPTER 6

EGYPTIAN HALL WAS HARDLY A place to discuss the matter. Donata led the way out, as I was too stunned to do so, summoning the doorman to call her carriage.

Rain spattered outside, clouds having rolled in as we'd rambled through the museum. Our carriage approached through the crush of Piccadilly, drivers growling and cursing as Donata's coach shoved its way to Egyptian Hall's front door. Hagan, her large coachman, shouted back at those who railed at him—his snarl and huge fist made the curses trail off.

Once I had climbed stiffly in beside Donata, the damp making my knee throb, the rain began to come down hard. Brewster himself slammed the door then climbed onto the back of the coach, shifting his weight for balance as the vehicle moved forward.

Donata had stuffed the letter into her reticule but now withdrew it to read again. "Miss Simmons can't have gone off of her own free will," she declared as she scanned the lines.

"Why not?" I asked. "Marianne runs off all the time." But I argued without conviction, because I had the feeling she was correct.

Donata smoothed out the paper. "First, she calls him *Lucius*, a name I've never before heard Miss Simmons utter. Whenever she condescends to speak his name, it is *Grenville*."

"True." I had observed the same thing. "But this note is in her hand." Though it did not match the writing on the outside—not uncommon; some people had their secretaries write directions on letters for them. A duke would be lofty enough to keep a secretary at his beck and call who would be instructed to assist even his mistress.

"Never mind that for now," Donata said impatiently. "Second, and more importantly, why on earth should Miss Simmons throw over Grenville for *Dunmarron*? It is inconceivable from every side." Her eyes snapped with adamancy.

"Why do you say so?" I asked. "I don't know Dunmarron—never met him."

Donata sniffed. "Consider yourself fortunate. The Duke of Dunces keeps to his estate most of the time, thank God. He is very hearty, talks only of the hunt and shooting, whatever he can kill—anything his servants more or less hand him to destroy, anyway. He has a houseful of art and eagerly buys it but can't tell a Botticelli from something his footman painted on his day out. He sits through a conversation mostly looking baffled then asks for all the jokes to be explained to him, regardless of whether anyone made a witticism or not. In short, he is a tedious excuse for a gentleman, an argument for not marrying too close to the bloodline if there ever was one."

"A mistress might overlook his conversation for the fact that he is a wealthy duke on a large estate," I pointed out.

"Not a woman who'd been the mistress of Lucius Grenville. Grenville outshines Dunmarron in all ways—Grenville has more wealth, more influence, better taste, better manners, far more intelligent conversation, and much more kindness than Dunmarron ever will. For a woman to run from Grenville to the Duke of Dunces is beyond belief. Therefore, she must not have gone willingly."

"I take your point," I said, my alarm increasing.

Donata's eyes were sapphire hard. "Miss Simmons has common sense, I have seen, and she cares for Grenville. If she were one of the silly sopranos or bits of fluff Grenville has taken up with from time to time, then I'd conclude that she leapt at the chance to be mistress of a duke, but Miss Simmons is not the sort who would let a title turn her head."

"I agree with you," I said, convinced. "Where can we find this duke? If Marianne has been carried off by him, we must bring her back."

"He will not be in London. His house is in Bedfordshire, and you can be certain he will remain ensconced there among what he thinks is his fine collection until he has business in London. By *business*, I mean to go to the 'Change and the bank and make certain his money and investments are all in order. Not that he understands much about them. He comes in once a quarter to hound all those who work for him until they wish him at the devil."

"Then we will go to Bedfordshire," I said. "I'd rather make a journey than break the news to Grenville. I'll bring Marianne home and we'll tell the tale once she is safe and sound."

Donata gave me the look she reserved for simpletons. "Dunmarron will hardly take Marianne to his estate. He has a wife and six children. Do not pity his wife—it was a marriage for the convenience of their families, and she has a house in Town and plenty of paramours of her own. There is some doubt the two youngest children are the duke's, a quite justified doubt. No, he will have put Miss Simmons into a house in London. I will find out which, and we will speak to her and have her return with us to Grenville."

She sat back with a thump that sent her feathers oscillating. I saw the look on her face and decided not to argue. When my wife set her mind on something, the might of the entire Austrian Empire would not be able to stop her.

"There is subterfuge here, Gabriel," she said. "I'll not sit by and see Grenville shamed or Miss Simmons hurt."

I warmed. "Nor will I." I slid my hand over her clenched fist that rested on the seat. "I will leave it to you to find her." Donata knew everyone in London and would no doubt locate the duke's house quickly. And then I'd hunt up this Dunmarron and make him explain himself.

"Thank you," Donata said. "I will begin at once. But I do

expect you to take me with you when you speak with the Regent. He will be out of temper with you for making him wait, and you will need me to soothe him over."

Our new appointment at Carlton House was for eight in the evening. Grenville sent a note saying his carriage would arrive for us at half past seven and we'd make the short journey together. The missive was brief and terse, Grenville annoyed with me.

Donata was a long time in her dressing room with her maid, and Bartholomew worked himself into a state trying to get me ready. I saw no reason to dress as though I were being presented at court—I acknowledged that I would be meeting a royal prince and so should look well, but this was a private consultation, not a public display. Bartholomew only gave me his long-suffering look and continued to try to coax me into my most formal suit.

Soon after I'd married, Grenville had dragged me to his tailor to have a wardrobe made for me, with Donata supplying the funds. I conceded to have suits made that would not embarrass Donata with their plainness but also would not embarrass me with extravagance. No quilted waistcoats or puffed pantaloons or other such nonsense. What I'd come away with were several suits of black superfine and several of wool, silk waistcoats in muted colors, trousers that balanced between the extreme of skin tight and excessively baggy, two redingotes that complemented the suits, and crisp cravats.

Bartholomew might mutter that his talents were wasted on me, but I was firm. I'd dress respectably—not like a Puritan but also not as a wastrel and a fop.

I finally agreed to climb into my best suit, if only to silence Bartholomew. When he'd finished with me, I had on one of the superfine coats and cashmere trousers, an ivory moiré waistcoat, and a cravat tied with a fairly plain knot. I thought I looked well and ignored the pained expression on Bartholomew's face over the cravat.

Donata, on the other hand, when I met her at the top of the stairs, outshone me in every way. Her ensemble was a study of elegance in velvet mixed with silk—a dark green bodice with contrasting sleeves of ivory silk buttoned over a green velvet skirt, the skirt's hem decorated with two rows of light green rosettes with ivory centers.

While women's costumes this year seemed to have gained more froufrou decorations than ever, Donata carried off the gown with aplomb. Her regal neck lifted from the low scooped décolletage, and her dark brown hair was pulled up off her face and gathered in a subdued knot of curls on top of her head. Rather than the garish items replete with feathers she'd worn in previous seasons, tonight she had a simple circlet of diamonds around her top-knot. Diamond earrings that had been in her mother's family for generations adorned her ears—since her husband's death Donata had refused to wear any of the Breckenridge jewels or anything her husband had given her.

When she made certain the gown's skirt swirled back to reveal her ankle, I saw that she'd put on the thin gold chain with the tiny bell I'd once bought her.

I tugged Donata back into the shadows of the upper hall before she could start down the stairs. I said not a word, only leaned down and pressed my lips to the warm curve between her neck and shoulder that the dress bared to me. I straightened up again, taking her hand to lead her forth.

Donata flushed at my attentions, but sent me a pleased look.

Donata's first husband had never paid her any attention at all, preferring his paramours without bothering to hide his infidelity. Many husbands of the *haut ton* took mistresses, but it was understood that they were to be discreet. Lord Breckenridge had not been, and Donata had borne the brunt of that humiliation.

My wife squeezed my hand a little more than strictly necessary when I assisted her into Grenville's carriage, and her smile was warm.

Grenville waited in the carriage, vacating the forward-facing seat so Donata could take it. I heaved myself in with Bartholomew's help and landed on the seat next to Grenville, watching Donata spread her cloak across the empty cushions to either side of her so it wouldn't be wrinkled.

Donata and I had agreed not to spring Marianne's news on Grenville until after our meeting with the Regent. Grenville would be furious, and he'd want to rush off on the moment to find Marianne or Dunmarron. Donata had been of the opinion that Marianne would be in no physical danger from the Duke of Dunces; he had the reputation of being rather cowed by his mistresses even as he complained about their demands on his purse. The game he was playing, or attempting to play, likely had to do with debts owed or the duke wanting to embarrass Grenville for his own reasons.

Even if Donata could persuade Grenville to keep the meeting with the Regent once he knew about Dunmarron, he would be most agitated, and when Grenville lost his sangfroid—a rare thing—the world suffered. His anger manifested in either viciously cutting remarks or cold silence, and the prince was already put out with us for moving the appointment. I disliked to think how the Regent would take out his wrath on Grenville if Grenville told the Regent exactly what he thought of him and his petty difficulties. Thus, we'd keep Marianne's note to ourselves until later.

We moved down South Audley Street to Curzon Street, past Chesterfield House and the austere facade of James Denis's abode then turned on Half Moon Street to Piccadilly. The carriage rolled along Piccadilly almost to Egyptian Hall before we turned off to St. James's Street and made our way south, the pile of St. James's Palace just visible at the end of it.

St. James's Street was the demesne of gentlemen's clubs—first White's on the left, then Brook's and Boodle's on the right and left respectively, nearly opposite each other. Ladies never walked down St. James's Street without a mar to their reputation, and Donata leaned to the window to blatantly look her fill.

We hadn't quite reached St. James's palace before Grenville's coachman turned onto Pall Mall and took us to the gates of Carlton House.

The residence had begun modestly, so I'd heard, before it

was given to the Prince of Wales upon his twenty-first birth-
day, more than thirty-five years ago. Since then the house had
been remodeled, expanded, redesigned, and rebuilt, with thousands and thousands of guineas lavished upon it. Fortunately,
the prince had chosen architects of taste in later years to take
the place in hand: Henry Holland, Mr. Wyatt, Mr. Hopper, and
John Nash, who had turned their skills to make the house a
thing of beauty.

I'd learned all this from Grenville and from books he lent
me—much of the controversy and construction of Carlton
House had occurred when I was far away, fighting wars on the
king's behalf.

The carriage went through an arched opening in the long line
of Greek-looking columns that separated the house from the
road. Grenville, who had been a guest at Carlton House many
times, didn't pay the building much attention, but I stared like a
tourist. What I'd seen of it had only been what I could glimpse as
I'd trundled down Pall Mall in a hackney, but then only through
a crush of vehicles and the grease-stained windows of the coach.

The house's exterior was not as ostentatious as I'd expected,
but instead had been designed with classical symmetry. Two
identical wings jutted out from either side of the main house,
which was built to pleasing proportions. Columns supported a
pediment over the front door, and the windows were evenly
spaced along the façade—full-length windows on the ground
floor, smaller ones on the upper stories.

As we descended at the entrance, I could see how a thief might
easily get into and out of this house—it was a showplace rather
than a fortress. The window nearest the coach was at least eight
feet high, the latch visible from the outside. The many-paned
windows were framed with heavy wood and set into stone, but
any thief could break the glass—quietly even—and swing open
the window to admit himself.

There were plenty of footmen about the place, beefy young
men who could double as guards, but a clever thief would know
how to bypass them. Brewster had not accompanied us tonight,

saying he wanted to go home to his wife, and I let him, assuming a jaunt to visit the Prince Regent would be safe enough, especially with Grenville's coachman, Jackson, and Grenville's footmen to protect us. When I spoke to Brewster again I would share my speculations with him about how a thief could go about robbing the place. No doubt he'd come up with many more methods.

The famed ostentation of Carlton House began as soon as we were inside. A footman in a blue coat and satin knee breeches led us from the courtyard into a wide hall whose upper walls were lined with friezes of gold against a ceiling painted to resemble a summer sky brushed with clouds. The ceiling was exquisitely done, filling what could have been a dark chamber with light. Green marble pillars divided the hall from the rooms on either side, continuing the feel of airiness. Huge marble urns stood here and there atop gold-leafed tables whose supports were in the form of standing golden birds—phoenixes, I thought.

The footman took us around another set of pillars and into an octagonal hall with walls of cream and green, the room accented with long red and gold upholstered divans against four of the walls. Red draperies had been pulled back from arched openings on the other four walls, which led to the staircase and other rooms. A gallery encircled this vestibule from the next floor, the banister made of beautifully gilded wrought iron. A fantastic, Turkish-looking chandelier hung from the ceiling three stories above us.

Squares of marble tile covered the floor, and busts of men in Roman togas—one of them the Prince Regent himself—rested on bracket shelves above the divans. Long, horizontal paintings of classical gods and goddesses framed the walls under the gallery.

Donata glanced about with sharp-eyed assessment. She, like Grenville, had a keen interest in architecture and the design of interior spaces. Her own house was a model of taste—she'd had a free rein on the decoration of the South Audley Street house and had employed the best of the modern masters to redo it exactly as she wished.

Having lived with her for nearly a year now, I could appreciate what Donata and her architects had done, which helped me see the clever touches in *this* house. In spite of the overabundance of velvet and gilding, the lines of Carlton House's rooms had a pleasant symmetry, the use of light filtering into enclosed spaces ingenious. In this room, which must be in the center of the building, a lead glass octagonal skylight right at the top of the house would let in a flood of sunshine during the day.

The footman, without speaking, led us through one of the red-draped arches to the staircase. We descended, which was a pity, because I would have liked to climb to the very top and look back down through the octagon. With a silent reminder that I was not there to indulge myself I walked obediently down the stairs, my walking stick and Donata's hand on my arm keeping me steady.

At the bottom of the stairs, we were taken through another equally lavish vestibule to the rear of the house. Here the huge rooms stretched the long distance from one end of the house to the other, the doors in a line. I could stand in the exact center of one doorway and look all the way down to what Grenville told me was the Gothic dining room, and then turn in place and gaze the other way to the equally Gothic arches of the conservatory.

The footman gestured for us to follow him toward the conservatory. I marveled as we went how casual the house was. Not in decoration—each chamber we passed through was more ornamented than the last. I mean it was casual in that it encouraged the visitor to move, unrestricted, from room to room and, here on the ground floor, from house to garden. Every chamber was lined with long French doors that gave directly out to the park beyond, which was dark now but would be sunny and inviting on a summer's day.

I stopped to peer out one of the doors. It wasn't latched, allowing me to swing it open.

Just outside was a paved walk that led around the house itself; the moon shining through a rent in the clouds illuminated the path like lamplight. One could stroll from room to room along this walk if one wished.

Beyond the path was a lawn. No stairs, no veranda, no impediments to block the garden. A guest might simply step from the splendor of the house to the cool outdoors, to enjoy a vast park studded with trees. There were no stylized gardens here as at Versailles, just a rolling green, an oasis in the middle of the city. This could be a country house of some wealthy squire, rather than a prince's city retreat.

I would have enjoyed walking along the outside path, no matter the night's chill, but I was recalled to my errand by the footman's voice. "It is *this* way, sir."

He was polite yet firm, so I stepped back inside and closed the door, but not before I spied a shadow under the trees in the park. I stared at the shadow for a time before I turned around and followed the others.

Grenville walked directly behind the footman as we moved through a huge dining room done in gold and red velvets to the conservatory. We seemed to be the only guests. Indeed, I wondered where the horde of servants, which would be needed to tend this house, were hiding. Aside from the footmen guarding the front door and this footman who was our guide, I'd seen no one.

The footman took us into the conservatory, and I halted in astonishment.

The place was a wonder to behold. For a moment, I wasn't certain whether I was in a private house or a cathedral, or perhaps a Turkish mosque in Constantinople.

The floor was pale marble, black tiles accenting the corners of each larger white one. Pointed arches lined the walls, and fan vaulting supported the ceiling. Plaster ornaments reached down like ornate stalactites from circular decorations that marched down the middle of the high room. Between the curved spokes of the fan vaulting was glass, which would let in sunshine during the daylight hours—what there was of it in a cloudy London February.

Square red and gold Turkish-looking lamps hung from between each arch, casting a soft light over the glittering room. At the far end, a glass door led out to the park, conservatory and outdoors blending into each other. The lamps sparkled on all the glass above us, making it seem as though we stood inside a jewel.

"I have not been here since the year of Waterloo," Donata stated as she craned her head to take in the ceiling. "There were celebrations all year, one after the next, lasting for days. All the world seemed to be crammed into this house."

"They certainly did," Grenville answered. "Some fellows were in mourning that Emperor Napoleon had lost—wore black bands on their arms. They regarded him as the embodiment of liberty, which had now been crushed by the despots of Russia, Prussia, and Britain."

I regarded him in amazement. "The embodiment of liberty? He had a bloody odd way of showing it, then. Taking over the world is more what Napoleon had in mind."

Grenville shrugged. "Apparently, he was to bring enlightenment to benighted Britain, which was under the sway of tyrants."

A rather thin, overly cultured voice broke in above the faint rattle of a wheeled vehicle. "I believe *I* was one of those tyrants in question."

A man rose from the Bath chair another footman pushed to a halt before us. The gentleman's fleshy face and red nose beneath graying dark hair held a rather foolish expression, but his eyes were wary.

"Or a despot, if you prefer," he went on. "Good evening, Lady Donata. How splendid to see you. Grenville." The Prince Regent of Britain, Ireland, and Hanover, turned the full force of his watery gaze on me. "Is this your captain? Good heavens, I had no idea he was lame."

CHAPTER 7

THE REGENT LOOKED UP AT me, not realizing I was tall, either. His irritation turned to glee as he observed the heavy way I leaned on my walking stick.

Donata curtseyed with a formality that would make any governess proud. She knew exactly how deeply to go, how to gracefully sweep her skirt to one side so it would skim the carpet.

The movement took the Regent's attention from me, delight entering his eyes as he beheld my wife. "As I say, it is a fine thing to see you, Lady Donata."

She returned the greeting with a polite nod. "You appear to be well, Highness."

The prince looked more as though he was recovering from a bad cold, but I held my tongue.

The Regent stepped shakily forward and took Donata's hand, raising it to his rather effeminate mouth. "You appear more than well." He lowered her hand but kept it clasped loosely in his fingers. "My felicitations."

He did not make clear what he congratulated her for—her marriage, the birth of our daughter, looking well, or all three. I strove to remain still and silent. The Regent had the reputation of taking up with strong-willed women, making mistresses of them for years. His current paramour was Lady Hertford, who was a few years his senior—the Regent had always preferred older women. Donata, if anything, was too young for his taste.

All the same, I did not like the way the man gazed so fondly at my wife. The Regent was reputed to be growing tired of Lady Hertford and looking for her replacement.

Grenville spoke into the awkward silence. "Can you tell us, Highness, what sorts of things have gone missing? The captain is most curious."

"Better still, I will show you." The prince turned to his Bath chair, wincing as he put weight on a gouty foot. "Walk with me, my dear."

He did not release Donata's hand. She, who could freeze a man cold at ten paces, only smiled and helped the prince back into his chair.

Grenville shot me a warning look, as though waiting for me to explode into one of my famous rages. But I could hardly call out the Prince Regent in his Bath chair or shoot the heir to the throne of Britain dead. I only gave Grenville a weary nod and followed him as the Regent waved a hand in front of him, indicating the direction he wanted to go.

He insisted Donata push his chair. She did so without argument and without a glance at me. She gave the footman who had brought the prince in a serene look, took hold of the back of the chair, and guided it onward.

The prince weighed much, but Donata was strong. My only worry was her recent ordeal, only eight weeks ago now—I remembered the surgeon's warning that she must not lift or push heavy things. He'd indicated she'd be well at six weeks, but I watched her with concern, ready to rush in and pull her away at the first sign of fatigue.

Donata hooked her shawl more firmly around her arms and rolled the chair over the marble floor. It went easily on the smooth tile, and then I began to fear she'd give it too hard a shove. I imagined it skittering down the vaulted room with the prince waving his arms in alarm.

Such a vision comforted me, and my lips twitched. Grenville shot me a puzzled glance.

We emerged from the conservatory then journeyed along

the lower floor—to the Bow Room with its large bay window, through the anteroom we'd arrived in via the staircase, and finally into a library.

Five French windows lined this long room, which held a vaulted ceiling painted with a cloud-strewn sky—all the rooms I'd seen so far except the conservatory had this feature. Bookcases lined the three windowless walls, filled with books reaching to the ceiling. The vast floor of the library contained two desks and several tables, and a soft chair rested near one of the windows as though put there so a reader could sit in the sunshine of an afternoon.

The Regent twirled his hand, indicating he wanted to be stopped in the exact center of the chamber, under the massive chandelier. Donata complied then leaned down and spoke to him, the two of them laughing at some joke.

By the time Grenville and I reached them, they were finished with the jest and the Regent looked up at me sideways, like a naughty schoolboy.

"Tell him," he said to Donata.

My wife lifted her head and gazed at me with clear eyes. "He wants you to have a look at the figure on that table." She pointed, her slender finger steady.

Grenville and I obediently departed for the table. I heard whispers—mostly the prince's—and laughter behind me.

"His father is still king," Grenville murmured to me. "So it would not be called, as the French say, *régicide.*"

"I am certain it will not come to that," I answered. "My wife is not fool enough to have her head turned by all this." I indicated the room and the house above us.

I knew so in my heart. I also noted that, even after a year, I swelled with pride every time I uttered the words *my wife.*

The table to which we'd been directed reposed about six feet in front of a bookcase and had no chairs around it, the better to be able to see the objects on it from all sides. The octagonal marble-topped table, supported by gilded legs, bore two items. The first was a clock, recently made in what is called the Egyptian style, the second a bronze statue about two feet high that spoke of earlier centuries.

The bronze was of two figures together, a man holding aloft a woman who had a longbow in her upraised hand. Both of them were blatantly nude, every proportion of their bodies exact and exquisitely done in gleaming, polished bronze. The man in the scene was clearly carrying off the woman, whose long legs were crowded against his side. The figures were so lifelike I thought at any moment I'd see the woman kick out, the man struggle to hold her.

"Theseus and Antiope," I said after studying the statue a few moments.

"Ah," Grenville said. "Of course."

I had been an indifferent pupil during my years at Harrow—my Latin declensions had left much to be desired, my Greek pronunciation worse. However, I'd been fascinated by the stories buried in the texts we had to memorize, the more lurid and adventurous, the better. I'd followed Hercules to battle with the Amazon women, where Theseus had carried off one of them, Antiope; later the two had fallen in love, their tale ending happily, which had been a bit unusual in ancient mythology.

This bronze was the moment of the abduction—Antiope, who'd been a warrior as much as Theseus, was blatantly furious. The artist had caught them so well I waited for her to bludgeon him with her bow.

"Beautiful, is it not?" the prince called to us. "Sixteenth century Flemish, so I'm told."

It was beautiful indeed. I did not know enough about antiquities to identify who'd sculpted it or when or where, but I recognized superb artistry.

"Excellent," Grenville said with genuine enthusiasm. "De Vries?"

"Indeed." The Regent sounded pleased. "What do you think of it, Captain Lacey?"

I turned to him and gave him a polite bow. "It is quite well done, Your Highness."

"And the clock. Is it not divine?"

The clock sitting incongruously next to the statue was long and squat, with four ebony sphinxes facing outward on a gold base. The clock face that rose from the base was surprisingly plain, though done in silver and gold gilt. The clock must have been very expensive, and it was well made, lovely in its own garish way.

"An interesting piece," I said, since the Regent was waiting for my answer.

"I saw one like it in Egypt," the prince said. "And so I commissioned it to be made. I was there, you know, when the French were driven out."

I forbore to look at Grenville or do anything but keep my expression neutral. During the long wars with France, the Regent had never left England. He'd been put in charge of a regiment that had drilled on fields in the country, and then the men had returned to London to drink themselves into a stupor. Apparently he had declared that his regiment had been what kept the Corsican from the shores of England, and later began to put about that he'd gone to the Continent and Africa himself and engaged in actual battle.

I had no idea if he told these stories to make himself look noble, or if he'd begun to believe them. His father was by all accounts now completely mad, and madness in a parent often showed itself in the offspring.

I'd seen absolutely nothing like this clock in Egypt, and I knew Grenville had not either—and he'd traveled Egypt far more extensively than I had. The clock was no more Egyptian than the lamps in the conservatory were Turkish or the chinoiserie chairs and cabinets we'd passed in an anteroom were Chinese.

Grenville's response was diplomatic. "An excellent addition to your collection, sir."

"Indeed," the prince responded with satisfaction. "Now for the unnerving part." He made a show of shivering. His footman, who'd followed Donata and the chair, started forward with a rug, but the prince waved him away. "Those two pieces are not meant to be here."

Grenville frowned. "Not meant to be here? What do you mean?"

The Regent lowered his voice to dramatic tones. "The de Vries belongs in the Golden Drawing Room. The clock, in the upper vestibule. So why are they here, eh?"

Grenville and I exchanged a glance. "Perhaps one of the staff …" I began.

"No, no." The prince's voice strengthened as he interrupted me. "Push me over there, my dear, do. My servants know never to move any object, either from room to room or even to a different place within the room. Higgs won't allow it. It would spoil everything."

The chair drew closer. Donata's gaze met mine over the top of the prince's head, and I read in the depths of her eyes good-humored glee.

Knots inside me loosened and I suppressed the urge to laugh. "Higgs?" I asked.

"Mr. Higgs, who is in charge of my collection," the Regent returned impatiently. He snapped his fingers and pointed to the footman who'd originally led us downstairs. "*You*, go find Higgsie. Tell him to bring himself here, at once."

The footman, though he looked icily disapproving, bowed. He moved to one of the bookcases, swung open a door that had been made to look like another column of books, and disappeared through it.

As we waited, Grenville and I wandered to another table to examine the treasures there. A gold chalice with a tiny serpent woven around the lid rested next to an inkwell also in the Egyptian style. It looked much like the clock on the other table, with sphinxes flanking the main bronze urn that would hold the ink. A frieze along the bottom depicted winged lions and eagles.

"Vulliamy," Grenville murmured to me, indicating the inkstand. "The clock as well. He was the king's clockmaker before his death—designed the clock that keeps the official time for the Prime Meridian."

"I bought that for the Blue Velvet Room upstairs," the prince's querulous voice came to us. "The inkstand, I mean. But then suddenly it was in the Bow Room, and now it's here. Very odd, is it not? And my servants have noted uncanny noises, shadows in the corners." The Regent covered his face. "It has so unnerved me, gentlemen. I cannot tell you how much."

Grenville cleared his throat. "Begging your pardon, sir, but my footmen move things about all the time, in spite of instructions. My valet as well—he is always telling me a thing would be more suited to this place or that. He believes I have deplorable taste."

The prince lowered his hands and gave a high-pitched laugh. "*You*, Grenville? I'd give him the sack."

"No, indeed," Grenville said, looking mournful. "He is correct. What would we do without our valets, eh?"

"Very amusing," the prince said. "But you do not have a Higgs in your house, that is certain. He keeps inventories, you see. He knows where everything is and should be, and he is vastly displeased if something moves."

Donata leaned down and whispered into the prince's ear. He smiled and patted her hand.

Grenville gave me another quick glance, as though ready to stop me lunging at the prince, but my anger and worry had vanished. Donata was playing her part and enjoying herself.

Their conversation was interrupted by the return of the footman. He was followed by a gentleman in a subdued black suit, the restraint of color incongruous in this room of garish reds and golds.

"Ah, Higgsie, there you are." The prince began to heave himself out of his chair. He struggled but Donata and his footman were instantly at his side to steady him. "Tell Captain Lacey and Grenville what I mean. *Things are moving about my house on their own.*"

"Hardly that, Your Highness," the man who must be Higgs replied. He had dark hair combed flat against his head and shadows on his cheeks and jaw as though his whiskers grew as soon as he could shave them. "But it is decidedly odd—that is certain."

"I refuse to sleep in this house," the Regent went on. "My nerves are not conditioned to these upsetting occurrences. You must discover what is going on and put a stop to it, Captain." He pointed a pudgy finger at me. "You must, do you hear me?" He poked the air dramatically, then he coughed and gently collapsed backward into the chair. "John, I need my tonic."

The footman at the chair instantly produced a small silver flask, which he held to the prince's lips. The Regent snatched it from him, upended the flask, and drank a long swallow. When he finished and wiped his mouth with a large handkerchief, his color did look better, and his breath became less wheezing.

"Carry on, Higgsie," the prince said, his voice a croak. "Lady Donata will keep me company, won't you, my dear?"

"Of course, Highness," Donata said promptly.

"Good. Take me out of these rooms at once. It is cold down here."

No fires had been lit in the fireplaces we'd passed, and indeed, we hadn't removed our wraps. John the footman immediately turned the chair and glided it out toward the anteroom, Donata walking with the prince a step away from the chair.

I wondered how on earth they'd lever the prince and his chair up the long flight of stairs— perhaps they'd go outside and walk around the building to the shallow steps in front, or perhaps he had a lift of some kind behind the walls. Whichever was the solution, I knew Donata would tell me, so I turned back to Mr. Higgs and shut off my curiosity on that point.

Higgs bowed to us, giving us an apologetic look for the prince's rudeness. "I am Cedric Fletcher Higgs, cataloger of the prince's collection. I have been instructed to answer any questions you have."

Grenville returned the bow. "Lucius Grenville, at your service, sir. And my friend, Captain Gabriel Lacey." We shook hands all around, very civil. "Tell us the whole sad story, my dear fellow. Things have gone missing—a man arrested—items moving from room to room ... What the devil has been happening here?"

Mr. Higgs let out a long breath. "Would I understood it, Mr. Grenville. But please, shall we move to more comfortable surroundings? And I will explain."

We followed him through the door disguised as a bookcase—the false books were realistic in a bookcase six inches deep—into the bowels of the house. The walls in the hall we traversed were whitewashed, the corridors wide, stone staircases curving up to the main floors with shallow steps. For a servants' passage below stairs, it was quite regal. I'd been down to Donata's kitchen and servants' hall a few times since our marriage, and while the white-paneled rooms were cozy, they were also rather cramped. This servants' area was airy and far more pleasant than some of the rooms in which I'd lived at various times of my life.

Mr. Higgs took us to a black-painted door that led to an office. A true office, with bookcases overflowing with books and papers, catalogs open on tables or marked with cards depicting antiquities, letters strewn about seemingly from all over the world. I saw writing in French, German, Italian, Greek, and some languages I didn't know.

A fire burned on a small hearth, enough to keep the cluttered room heated. A brandy decanter with several glasses stood on one table, the decanter half full.

Mr. Higgs encouraged us to sit, though we had to move books and papers to do so. I lifted a tome on Michelangelo's work and one on Bernini, plus a catalog from an auction in Amsterdam.

Higgs glided to his desk with the quiet movements of a cat and sat down. He rested his hands on the desk's top and gave us a neutral look as Grenville and I settled ourselves.

"Gentlemen," he began once Grenville and I were ready. "I fear the matter is more serious than even the prince understands. He is not wrong that objects have been moving about the house with no explanation—statuettes, clocks, urns, even small paintings. This has been going on for some months now. The servants have been questioned, but all are adamant they have nothing to do with it. They are well trained and know not to disturb anything by even one inch. Every piece has been precisely placed for the look of that room, and changing things arbitrarily would mar the grouping."

I understood what he meant. In Donata's house, the objects d'art had been chosen not only for their beauty but to match others in her collection. The style of each chamber was slightly different; an item that went well in one room would be out of place in another. Barnstable was very particular about it.

Grenville asked, "Things have gone missing, have they not? A man is in Newgate because of it."

Higgs shook his head, distressed. He had blue eyes in a curiously light shade, almost gray. "The man they have arrested, Mr. Floyd, is no thief. He is a librarian." Higgs' tone conveyed both amazement and disgust.

"Tell me about him," I said.

Higgs blinked his light eyes at me. "I beg your pardon?"

I realized belatedly that Spendlove had likely not told anyone in Carlton House he'd asked me to gather evidence against Mr. Floyd. We were here tonight because the Regent had begged Grenville to bring me to tell him who'd been taking and moving his things.

"You say Mr. Floyd is not the sort of man who would steal?" I amended. "Did the magistrate not take your word for his character?"

Higgs made a noise of impatience. "I never saw the magistrate. The Runners spirited Mr. Floyd away before anyone knew what happened, and the magistrate speedily decided to hold him for trial. I doubt he had anyone to speak for him."

Curious. The Bow Street magistrate, Sir Nathaniel Conant, was a reasonable man, in my opinion, and careful. He liked indisputable evidence that a person had committed a crime before he sent him to Newgate to await trial. Spendlove must have had Floyd up before a different magistrate.

"When is the trial?" I asked. Spendlove hadn't bothered to tell me that either.

"One week," Higgs said. "If I cannot lay my hands on the missing objects or show that Mr. Floyd had nothing to do with it, I fear he will hang. What is gone is so very valuable the judge is certain to send him to the noose."

"What has been taken?" Grenville asked.

Higgs let out a long sigh, one that climbed from the bottom of his plain leather shoes. "It will be easier if I show you."

He rose, moved to a glass-fronted bookcase, unlocked it with a key on his watch fob, and removed a ledger from the clutter. He didn't have to search for the ledger—his hand went directly to it.

He brought it to us, lifting a small triangular table on his way, and spread the ledger open on top of it. The page he pointed to listed a dozen entries. Each entry had a line drawing depicting an object, followed by the name of the object, where it had been acquired, and its worth. After that came a series of letters that meant nothing I could discern.

I saw a drawing of a silver cup similar to the one I'd observed in the library, another clock by Benjamin Vulliamy, this one porcelain and in the French style, and two miniature paintings by Richard Cosway—one of the Princess Charlotte as a child, the other that of a smiling woman, her breasts bared for the viewer. Whoever had made the line drawings was a master, as the details of the objects were clear.

"These are definitely gone?" I asked after I'd looked over the list. "Not moved as the others have been?"

"We believe so." Mr. Higgs leaned back against his desk and crossed his feet. "We have searched high and low, though this is a large house full of many things, so they might turn up eventually. I have been keeping a record of where the things move to instead of simply putting them back—I have the notion that if I wait and watch, I'll catch the culprit."

It was not a bad plan. I pointed to the letters I couldn't make out. "And these?"

"A note of where the thing was and where it is now." Higgs tapped the entry for the porcelain clock. "Was in the Golden Drawing Room—GR—then the Blue Velvet Room—BV. Gone from there now, but I'll make a note when it turns up again. If it does."

I studied the page. "Would you allow me to copy this out?" I asked. "It might help me make sense of what is happening."

Higgs gave me a hesitant look, which I returned without expression. The reason I wanted the list was to show it to Brewster. He would know, in five minutes, I was certain, where I'd be likely to find these things if they'd been stolen. Perhaps he'd even know who'd purchased them from the thieves and where they were now.

However, I hardly wanted to tell Higgs that I wished to show a sheet describing valuable objects from Carlton House to a known thief. I simply waited patiently for his answer.

"An excellent idea," Grenville said. "We would guard the list and return it to you, Mr. Higgs, I give you my word. It would help us to know, if we find any of the items, whether we have the right things to return to you."

Higgs's expression softened. "Of course, Mr. Grenville. I have a great admiration for your own collections, sir. I'd be honored if someday I'd be able to see them."

"Of course," Grenville looked surprised the man felt he had to ask. "I'd be delighted to know your opinion. It is only a small assemblage, I must warn you. I haven't the space to acquire much. But I pick up trinkets as I travel."

I hid a smile at his notion of "trinkets." In Alexandria and Cairo, he'd bought a hookah; a necklace of large beaten squares of gold for Marianne; a solid silver statuette of a cat-headed god; and several scarabs made of gold and jewels that now held pride of place in his collection room in the upper story of his house.

"I will have the page copied for you at once," Higgs said. "The drawings on it possibly not, however. Those were done by Mr. Cosway himself, from memory—his sight is not what it was. He's fallen out of favor with the prince, but he is still interested in what goes on at Carlton House."

Another person I might speak to, I decided. "And Mr. Floyd," I said. "Would it be possible for me to see him?"

Higgs heaved another sigh, lifting the ledger from the table. "I have no idea, Captain Lacey. I have not been granted permission to visit him. I have sent letters, but who knows if they have been given to him? If you can speak to him Captain, please do. I would like to know how he fares."

There was not much more we could say. Higgs closed the ledger, promising to have the page copied and delivered to Grenville. We thanked him for his time and help, Grenville saying he'd arrange an appointment for Higgs to view his personal collection. We departed, another footman appearing to lead us up a back staircase to the main floor.

We found Donata in an anteroom near the hall to the front door. She stood by a red velvet draped window that looked out into the dark garden, and was quite alone, no sign of the Prince Regent.

She turned as we entered, statuesque in her velvet gown and cloak, the candlelight of the immense gold and crystal chandelier glittering on the diamonds in her hair. Again I marveled that such an exquisite woman had taken up with a broken soldier like me.

"Imagine," Donata said, as she glided to join us, "lighting all these rooms when no one is using them. Such a waste. No wonder the Regent's finances are constantly in threat of being cut off. Did you learn anything useful?"

Donata took my arm as she reached me, but she gave me a quiet look, not an impatient one. She knew I'd tell her all.

The same haughty footman who'd let us in ushered us out, Jackson and Grenville's coach waiting at the bottom of the steps. I handed in Donata myself but hung back and let Grenville ascend after her.

"Go on with your evening," I said, looking in at them as Grenville took his seat. "I need to speak to someone."

Grenville raised his brows, but Donata gave me a nod. "Yes, I saw him lurking about. I'm off to Lady Featherstone's for a rout, but Grenville can escort me. *You* dislike routs."

"Grenville would be honored to," that man said, pressing his hand to his chest. "We shall be the envy of all who enter, my lady."

They would be, two people at the height of elegance, both dressed in the very latest fashion. I, on the other hand, would be skulking through a park in the darkness, searching for a criminal.

"We will speak when I return home," Donata promised, and then sent me a steely look. "You will fill in anything Grenville leaves out, will you not? Good night, Gabriel."

One of the prince's footmen shut the heavy carriage door, the youngish man keeping his expression carefully neutral. I imagined he'd seen many an odd person come and go from this mansion, could tell many tales if he saw fit. The conversation below stairs at Carlton House must be very interesting.

I walked through the columned gate after the departing coach and turned left, making my slow way down Pall Mall toward St. James's Palace and beyond to Green Park at the end.

While this part of St. James's had become very fashionable, Green Park could be a dark and unsavory place at night. If no public entertainment was going on in the vast expanse of lawn and trees, the forlorn park filled with those up to no good.

I'd concluded Brewster wanted to meet me here, because when I'd seen him in the gardens at Carlton House, he'd jabbed his fingers to his left, pointing toward this park, before he'd disappeared from the moonlight, back under the shadows of the trees.

I disliked wandering the area by myself, so I kept to the edge of the park, where I could dive back into the lighted streets of St. James's if necessary. Highwaymen used to lurk in the park, so Lady Aline, who knew everything there was to know about London, had told me. In her day even, she'd said, when she'd been a little girl, which meant about forty years ago.

"Guv." Brewster's voice came out of the pitch dark, and an instant later he was beside me.

I suppressed my start and frowned at him. "You could have come with us," I said. "And not pretended to hurry off home. Londoners are used to seeing me with a guard."

"Didn't fink ye wanted me seen by His Royal Highness's servants." Brewster sniffled, drew out a giant handkerchief, and wiped his nose. "In case ye wanted me following anyone at some time."

"Good thought," I said. "But I hope you haven't caught a cold for it."

"Naw. The air just makes me sniffle, is all. Em will see that right. Did you find out what was nicked?"

"Yes—the curator will send me a list. Although, I wonder ..." I trailed off but felt the weight of Brewster's stare.

"'S too cold out here to wait for you to wonder, Captain," he said. "If ye tell me what was nicked, I can help ye look for it."

I let out a breath, which fogged in the air. "I was pondering the fact that small items have been moved from room to room and not actually stolen. I wonder if the missing things have left the palace at all."

Brewster sent me his long-suffering look. "If you was to cease speaking in ponderings and wonderings, and tell me exactly what you need to find, I can tell ye where to start looking."

"I did not memorize the list exactly—but a silver gilt cup with a lid, a porcelain table clock by a master clockmaker, and a miniature painting of a nude woman in a gold frame."

"When was they nabbed?"

"Recently," I said. "I can't be more specific, because I do not know. Mr. Floyd was arrested a few days ago, but things have gone missing or have been moving about for months, so Mr. Higgs says."

"Right." Brewster didn't linger to mull over my information. "Come with me, Captain. I suppose we can get a hackney—it's a bit of a walk and it's bloody cold."

"Certainly," I said. "I'll be happy to get out of the wind myself. Where are you taking me?"

Though I would swear that no one stood near us—the entire park looked deserted on this chilly, windy night—Brewster stepped very close to me and spoke quietly into my ear.

"To a Nazareth," he said. "One for pretty trinkets. Only ye can't breathe a word of where ye've been or what ye've seen. Understand me?"

CHAPTER 8

THE THREAT UNDERLYING THE WORDS was clear. Brewster and I had become friends of a sort, but I never doubted that he'd break my neck if I endangered him, his friends, and most especially, his wife. Because he liked me, he might kill me as painlessly as possible, but he'd kill me all the same.

"I do understand," I said. "I give you my word, I shall not tell a living soul what I see tonight."

Brewster studied me a moment longer before making up his mind. "All right then," he said, and motioned for me to follow him out of the park, back to the light.

I found a hackney at a stand in St. James's Street. A crowd of young dandies wove drunkenly through the road, never minding vehicles or horses that nearly ran them down. They were moving from the gentlemen's clubs to the hells, those secret dens where fortunes were lost on the turn of a dice. Plenty of wealth changed hands in the clubs as well, but at least in the hells a man could take his ladybird with him for comfort.

Brewster rode inside the hackney, warming his big gloved hands under his armpits as he sat across from me.

"Ye ruined me taking me to foreign parts," he growled. "It was godawful hot, but I grew used to it, like. There's no sun in London, is there?"

"We can make another journey to Egypt next winter," I suggested. "Stay longer, bring our wives."

"Bit hard on the ladies, wouldn't it be? And you're thinking

I'll be working for you that long, are ye?"

"I merely mention it," I said, not taking offense.

Brewster grunted and fell silent. I always found him a good companion, because he didn't expect witty conversation from me—no conversation at all, in fact.

He'd given the driver a direction, which I hadn't heard, so I watched out the window, curious, as we moved down Pall Mall to Charing Cross, and thence to Whitehall.

We passed the grand buildings that housed the Horse Guards, the Admiralty, the Treasury. The gentlemen who sat all day in these offices running the kingdom would soon turn their steps to join their sons and nephews in the clubs and hells just up the street in St. James's.

Not long later, we crossed Westminster Bridge, the bulk of Lambeth Palace to our right as we reached the other side of the river. A little way past this, Brewster thumped on the hackney's roof and bade the driver to stop.

The coachman pulled to a halt, and Brewster climbed down, automatically reaching back to steady me to my feet. We did this ritual seamlessly now, Brewster knowing exactly how much support to give me to both help me stand and save my dignity.

When I hobbled forward to pay the fare, Brewster stopped me. "Don't bring out your coin in a place like this. I already settled it."

The coachman, not waiting for our debate, slapped his reins on his horse's back and rattled away from us toward the bridge. We were left on a quiet street that was very dark, the buildings on either side of us close and unlit.

"Keep to my heels," Brewster said. "Don't stray. I don't want to explain to your lady wife why I carried you home full of knife holes."

I nodded and kept my hand firmly on my walking stick, the cane within it comforting. My other hand went to my coat and the small knife tucked inside it. London, especially at night, was a dangerous place, its pockets of civilization few and far between.

Brewster took me along the narrow lane and out into a wider

street that sloped down to the river. The noisome smell of the
Thames came strongly to us, though it was not as bad here as it
would grow farther downstream, after it passed the bulk of the
city. Upriver was Chelsea, Richmond, and open country.

Even so, the air was rank with the odors of fish and sewage. Brewster kept a steady pace as though he didn't notice the
stench, until we were under the end arches of the bridge itself.
Shingle crunched beneath my boots, the gravel extending from
the sluggish river.

Brewster guided me onward around the bridge and through a
tiny lane that ended in a large door. The door opened not to a
building, to my surprise, but to another street. London, a very
old city, was constantly shifting, roads and buildings moving and
occasionally merging into one another. The lanes back here had
obviously been built over at some point, houses rising through
and over them instead of bothering to go around.

No doors opened from the brick passage, but it was wide
enough for us to walk side by side had we wished to. I followed
Brewster, however, trying to keep the thump of my walking
stick quiet.

Another turn led us into open air, but we were enclosed by
walls so I wasn't certain there was another way out. Here I saw
market stalls, or at least tables with men and women behind
them, goods on top. The tables were thin and rickety, as though
they could be taken apart and carried off at a moment's notice.

"Mind." Brewster hung back to speak into my ear. "Not a
word."

I nodded, but in any case, I was too interested in what I saw
to speak.

Some of the stalls held fairly ordinary items—bowls and plates
a housewife might buy for her kitchen, garden tools, bolts of
cloth, cooking utensils.

Another table contained mirrors of all shapes and sizes; another,
empty frames for pictures or the mirrors at the last table; another,
porcelain cups and saucers, mixed and matched; and another,
cutlery. Very fine cutlery, if I were any judge. The heavy forks

and knives with which I ate food at Donata's table had taught me about quality silver, and these were that.

I would have thought a market for stolen goods would be frequented by only a few people, sales taking place in whispers, but the place was thronged. Respectable-looking women with maids or cooks in tow shopped among the stalls, and men of all sorts, from gentlemen in City suits to laborers, browsed the stalls, picking up things and haggling over the price.

I was familiar with vendors from Covent Garden and other markets who hawked their wares with a cross between good-natured banter and volatile abuse, and here they were no different.

"That is perfectly good silk, madam—never turn up your nose and walk away from it. You're a fool if you do. You'll never see better. Naw, don't look over there—*his* things are foul imitation. If ye want real silk, ye'll take mine. Tell ye what, love—I'll throw in these handkerchiefs, softest linen, woven in the Low Countries, I swear on my grave. Can't say fairer than that."

"I can see you've got a few coins to spend, sir," another called out to me. "Buy a trinket for your ladylove. Look at these little boxes, best from France for her snuff or her buttons. Or these lockets—beautiful paintings to wear 'round her lovely neck."

I glanced at the wares on his table, spying miniatures of beautiful people enclosed in delicate ovals, snuffboxes of enamel and gilt, and gold vinaigrettes studded with tiny jewels. These lovely things had no doubt come from a lady's or gentleman's dressing table. That lady or gentleman might have been robbed of them, or they might have sold the things to raise money on the sly. So many in polite society needed extra coin to pay gambling debts, and so many feared to tell the husband or wife, father or mother, guardian aunt and uncle, that they were up to their ears in debt. Hence the lucrative market in trinkets.

I passed on, and the vendor called after me. "Won't see better, nor cheaper. Make it up to your lady for being out all hours—do!"

I continued walking, the only way to counter persistent vendors.

Brewster had halted at another stall by the time I caught up to him, this one with the finest fichus and caps I'd ever seen. Donata liked caps of very thin linen to wear about the house, and fichus for her day dresses. I would be tempted to purchase one for her if I didn't highly suspect they'd been filched from one of her neighbors.

The wizened man behind the linen table was a tiny fellow, and it took me a moment to realize he wasn't sitting down. He stood perhaps five feet high, his small limbs matching his size. His suit almost swallowed him, his cravat covering the bottom of his chin. He had gray hair and small black eyes, but a large smile and a matching voice.

"Tommy, me dear old darling! Been donkey's years since I've seen ye. How's the missus?"

"Em's well," Brewster answered, his voice more friendly than usual. "How's your Violet?"

"Keeping. Keeping. The old girl has plenty of life in her yet. What brings ye here of all places, me old sweetheart? I thought ye'd left us for the higher life. Apprentice, is 'e?" The man jerked his chin at me, laughing silently.

"This 'ere's the captain," Brewster said.

This simple statement made the man's dark eyes widen. "*That* captain? Good gawd, don't we run in 'igh circles? Pleased t'meet ye, Captain. I'm Billy. Billy Boxall, but don't go telling everyone ye know me."

Billy Boxall. The name had a familiar ring. "Aren't you …?"

"A world-famous jockey, that's me." Billy chuckled, the cravat moving. "Had the finest racers between me legs at one time in me life. Won many a Derby, haven't I, Tommy?"

"Aye, Billy's a dab hand with the gee-gees, Captain," Tommy said generously. "Can't stand the beasts meself. The captain here was a cavalry officer."

"So I've heard," Billy said, looking me up and down. "I don't envy you there. Too many horses killed in battle. Would break me heart."

"It did." I had lost two fine horses, brave lads, both of them. I had grieved a long time when I'd had to put them down—still did when I thought of it. "But that's behind me."

"Heard ye fight battles of a different nature now," Billy said. "Pulling murderers and handing them to the Runners. Good on ye, Captain."

He gave me a nod of approval, a likely receiver of stolen goods admiring me for having men arrested. I had already learned, however, running errands for James Denis, that there were different levels of morality among the criminal classes. A cold-blooded murderer was a far different thing from a petty thief.

"Poppy about?" Brewster asked Billy.

Billy mulled this over. "Saw her a few weeks back, I fink. Now, where was it?"

Brewster gave him an impatient look. "De ye know or not?"

"Try the Ox's Head," Billy said. "She ever liked that house."

"Right." Brewster gave him a nod but didn't seem ready to rush off. "Anything new about?"

Again, Billy considered, taking his time. "Egyptians is the rage. And kettles, but they're fetching less than they used to. A few gewgaws, some pretties. What'cha looking for?" *Kettles*, I'd come to know from Brewster, meant watch fobs, which rhymed with *kettles and hobs*.

"Gilders, maybe some tickers and kettles," Brewster said. "From high places."

Billy straightened up. "Sorry, mate. Don't know nuffink about that."

Brewster scowled. "Who does know? Come on, lad."

"Only one man nicks from 'igh places lately," Billy said.

"Who's that then?"

Billy gave him a pitying look. "You ought to know. You work for 'im."

"Work for the captain now. You mean his nibs? He don't nick from royalty, old son. He's not that daft."

"Well, I can't help that. You ought to be talking to '*im* somewhere cozy, not me in the cold and dark."

Brewster rumbled his annoyance. "Never mind. You sure

Poppy's at the Ox?"

"I don't know, do I? I ain't seen 'er. I just know she likes the place. Now, 'ave a look at me wares. If I don't go home with at least a pony, my missus'll not be pleased."

Brewster grunted something under his breath and cast his gaze across the linens. His blunt finger rested on a cap. "'S fine."

"A lovely thing, ain't it?" Billy gave us a beatific smile. "Look pretty on your Em's hair. Yours for a quid."

Brewster withdrew, sending him an outraged look. "A quid? Bloody hell. You're having me on."

"That's quality, that is," Billy said, sounding hurt. "Woven across the water in the fair city of Brussels."

"Huh. Woven in South London more like."

"You've lost your touch, Tommy, if you don't know hand-em-broidered linen from sackcloth. Quid's giving it away."

"Give you a tanner for it," Brewster said.

Billy took on a sorrowful look. "Now, Tommy, what do I tell my missus if I let you walk away with this for sixpence?"

"Tell her I didn't pay you with me fists. All right then, I'll go as high as a shilling, no more."

"Aw, Tommy, ye break my heart."

I, impatient with the haggling, cut in, a coin in my hand. "Here's a half crown. If you hear anything, you'll tell Mr. Brewster, won't you?"

Billy had the coin out of my hand, testing it between his teeth before I could draw another breath. His teeth were brown, but strong enough to make a light indent in the silver.

He looked at the coin and the tiny mark, nodded in satisfaction, and slid the half crown into his pocket. "Very generous of you, sir. Now, how about you take something for your lovely lady?"

"Better not," I said. "She might arrive at a supper hosted by its former owner."

Billy gave me an indignant look, and then he burst into laughter. "Nice one, Captain." He guffawed, his eyes lost in his crinkled face. "I forgot you took a toff to wife. You're a fine one, sir. Thank ye. For you, I'll keep my eyes and ears peeled. 'Ow's that?"

Brewster regarded both of us sourly as Billy wrapped the cap in paper as tenderly as would a proprietor in a Bond Street shop.

"There ye are then, Tommy," Billy said, handing the paper-wrapped cap over. "Love to the missus."

"Aye," Brewster said, unbending now that business was done. "And yours, Billy. Keep this to yourself, mind."

Billy touched his finger to the side of his nose. "I can keep a secret for an old mate. You'll see, guv," he said to me. "I won't fail ye."

"Thank you," I answered, giving him a polite bow, which sent Billy into paroxysms of laughter again.

"See that ye don't," Brewster growled at Billy, and then he ushered me away.

We traversed other stalls in the market, though Brewster asked the vendors no questions. At each table, I looked for signs of the goods stolen from Carlton House but saw nothing.

After a time, Brewster led me out of the market and the narrow lanes outside it, back along the riverbank, and then across streets again, moving through the dark until I had no idea where we were. I certainly would not be able to find my way back to the bridge without him.

Brewster halted at long last outside a public house whose sign bore the faded picture of an ox's head.

I realized as I entered, that while I'd been to taverns and public houses with Brewster near St. Giles and Covent Garden, I'd never been to one as foul as this. The fire smoked, lending a pall to the air, the fug increased by the pipes men smoked in all corners. The floor was gritty, and the whitewashed walls were blackened with soot, greasy handprints, and stains I did not want to know the origin of. The air was fetid from the unwashed bodies of the house's many patrons, the reek of river and sewage strong behind the smoke. The landlord's nose was red and veiny, his shock of dirty hair sliding on his forehead as he sent Brewster an acknowledging nod.

I hated to think what the ale would be like, but Brewster ordered a pint, wiping the edge of the tankard with his handkerchief before he drank. The landlord did not seem to find this offensive.

Brewster did not ask for anything for me or indicate I should ask for myself. He moved purposefully through the crush toward an open door in the back of the taproom. I surmised that so many were packed into this alehouse because at least it was warm. I saw no other reason to come.

The door through which Brewster exited opened to a passage that led to a long, narrow room, this one with fewer people in it. Women sat here with men, either husbands and wives together or ladies of the streets offering their wares.

One end of the room contained a bench that bent around three walls, a table in the middle. A lady sat by herself at this table, several empty glasses strewn across it, but she was writing in a notebook and looked in no way inebriated. The glasses must have been from those who'd sat with her and since gone away.

Brewster went straight to the table. He stopped in front of it but said nothing as the lady went on writing in her notebook.

The woman was of middle years, her hair where it peeked from her mourning bonnet brown touched with silver. Her gown was a rather plain dark gray trimmed with black, covered with a high-waisted black jacket. She wore fingerless gloves with jet beads on their backs, and matching jet beads trimmed the jacket. Her mourning bonnet held an ostrich feather, dyed black, which drooped over her left shoulder.

She continued to write, not words, I saw, but numbers. Her hand moved rapidly but carefully, no ink blotting her page. An ink bottle stood at her elbow, and she dipped her pen into it from time to time with efficient quickness.

The woman never lifted her head or acknowledged our presence. Brewster continued to stand in silence, presumably would have stood so all night had I not decided to pointedly clear my throat.

The pen slowed then halted, and the lady lifted her head. I found myself pinned by cold hazel eyes in the sort of gaze I'd seen on a French soldier as he'd looked over a pistol at me. The eyes took me in then flicked to Brewster.

"Mr. Brewster," the woman said in the tone of an admonishing governess. She laid down her pen, slid her notebook aside, and rested her hands on the table. She spoke no more, only waited.

Brewster sketched a respectful salute. "Poppy," he said. "This here's Captain Lacey. We just want a moment, love, I promise."

"Your friend has no manners," Poppy said sternly as she waved an imperious hand for us to sit. "What do you want? Make it sharpish. I have appointments."

I gave Poppy a bow and seated myself on the bench to her left while Brewster plopped himself to her right. I noted he kept his ale jar clenched in his hand instead of plunking it to the table.

"The Prince Regent's collection," Brewster said without pre-amble. "Things have gone missing. Know about it?"

Poppy sent him a patient look. She continued to regard him in silence until Brewster fished into his pocket and laid a few coins on the table. Silver, I noted, not copper. Poppy put out a calm hand and slid the coins to her, dropping them into her palm under the table. She said nothing even then, only watched Brewster expectantly.

Brewster sighed and turned to me. "I'm cleaned out, Captain," he said. "A sovereign wouldn't come amiss."

If I took out a gold sovereign in a public house like this one, I'd likely never leave here alive, or at least not with my purse. In any case, I rarely walked about with such money, knowing the talents of London's pickpockets.

I pulled out the small drawstring pouch I'd buttoned into a pocket inside the lining of my coat and opened it. I let the few crowns and half crowns inside clatter to the table, keeping back only enough shillings so Brewster and I might ride back across the river.

Poppy glanced at the pile then at me, her scorn evident.

"No manners at all," she said to Brewster. "Some gentlemen

have no idea how to behave to a lady. Try the market, Mr. Brewster. Though it's probably too late."

"Ye seen any of it about?" Brewster asked without moving. "Certain things? Say, a silver cup with a snake around its lid. Clocks like a gent would put on his mantel. Small paintings, done on ivory and the like."

"I wouldn't touch 'em," Poppy said. She drew her notebook to her, ignoring the money on the table, and turned a page. "I don't fancy dancing on the wind for stealing from the king. Sounds like small things anyone could tuck into a bag or his coat and waltz out the door with, but only if he's a fool."

She spoke without much of a London cant, nor working-class cheerfulness. I'd never seen the woman before or heard of her, but I was reminded of Mr. Denis, who spoke with a smooth, neutral voice, betraying nothing of the fact that as a child, he'd sometimes had nowhere to sleep but a dung cart.

Denis had never mentioned Poppy, but I could not doubt that he knew about her. Brewster seemed well acquainted with her, and Denis kept his finger on anyone who might either be useful, or a rival. I wondered which this woman was to him.

"Any idea who would take them?" I broke in.

Poppy turned her cool eyes to me. Her face had pleasant proportions, nothing unsightly about her, but she was not what I'd called pretty. She was not plain either—rather, she was neutral, like her voice, as though she'd striven to become the most harmless-looking and -sounding woman she could possibly be. When she walked down a London street, few would notice anything unusual about her. She only stood out here, in this incongruous setting.

"A man has been arrested, has he not?" she asked me.

"True, but that does not mean he is guilty," I returned. "He has a right to prove himself innocent before a jury. It might have been someone else."

"I see." Poppy watched me as though trying to decide what to make of me. "You are a very fair-minded person, Captain, as I have heard. I have also heard you have a rotten temper and often take matters into your own hands. What would you do to this thief, once you caught him?"

"Make him return what he stole," I said. "And tell me why he'd done it."

"Ah, so *you* can be his judge and jury. Very ambitious of you, Captain. But then, I hear you are ambitious. Your marriage has certainly raised you up, giving you the ability to fling silver coins at respectable widows. London should be wary of you. A man who acts as the law who now has money and connections among the highborn is a frightening thing. The guilty shall tremble."

I was growing annoyed with this lady, whoever she might be. "I assure you, ambitious is the last thing I am."

"I see. Forgive me if I do not take you at your word." Poppy closed her notebook. "At the risk of you dragging *me* to the magistrate, I will tell you what I know, which I warn you is little. I have heard that certain pieces similar to what are found in Carlton House have found their ways to stalls in Southwark and other markets. I know that a man was arrested for convenience and that inquiring too closely about this matter is dangerous. I'd heed the warning, Captain Lacey."

Poppy at last put out her gloved hand and drew the coins to her with neat efficiency. They disappeared under the table with the others.

"Now, gentlemen, I truly do have appointments," Poppy said, switching her stare to Brewster. "Good evening to you."

Brewster immediately rose to his feet, and I stood as well. "Thank you for taking the time, Poppy, love," Brewster said.

Her eyes flickered the slightest bit at the endearment. "Not at all. I am always happy to speak to old friends." Her icy glance my way told me she did not include me in this category.

I could not leave without one final request. "If you hear anything, will you send me word? Or Brewster?"

"No," Poppy said promptly. "I don't convey messages. You are welcome to return after sufficient time has passed, but I advise you not to visit without Mr. Brewster."

She gave me a severe look then she opened the notebook once

more, dipped her pen, and returned to making notations.

Brewster flicked his fingers at me, indicating we were leaving. He strolled across the room, depositing his tankard on a table in passing as we went. The men sitting at that particular table wasted no time pouring the tankard's contents into glasses of their own.

From the door I looked back to where Poppy sat, but she never glanced up, never watched us go. She'd returned to her notebook, blissfully ignoring the world around her. I noticed the men at nearby tables carefully did not look at her.

I said nothing as Brewster and I made our way back through the passage and the crowded taproom, he nodding at the landlord on his way out. We emerged into the street, which had quite a number of people on it despite the late hour and the cold.

I began to speak, but Brewster held his finger to his lips and led me on through the warren of streets until we were well away from the tavern.

"We'll have to walk a bit to find a hackney," he told me. "Coachmen don't like to come hereabouts."

I didn't blame them. A hackney driver could be pulled down and robbed unless he was quick enough and ruthless enough to run the horse and coach over his attackers.

"Where are we?" I asked.

"Southwark. We'll head for a bridge and back across to streets where you belong."

"I certainly seem to have a bad reputation here," I remarked as we went. I felt eyes watching me, as I had in St. Giles, but if anything, the men behind the stares here were more hostile.

"That's Mr. Denis's fault," Brewster said, sounding apologetic. "He likes to put about that his agents are not men to be trifled with. It helps us walk down streets like this one without being waylaid."

I did not at all like being thought of as Mr. Denis's agent, but I realized that protesting about it here and now would be rather foolish, especially if that misapprehension was keeping both me and Brewster whole and well.

"Tell me who the devil that woman was," I said as we wound through the lanes. Brewster, who'd lived in London most of his life, he'd told me, after his father brought him down from Lancashire to escape the black smoke there, moved swiftly and confidently. "What was she doing in that wreck of a tavern, of all places?"

Brewster shrugged. "She turns up here and there, where she wants, and she's not bothered. No one would dare. Her husband was king of the streets around here, until he passed. Some say she killed him, but I don't hold much with that rumor. She was sweet on him, from all accounts. She took over his business the moment he were gone. She hands out money to those who need it, but ye have to be desperate to take it from her. She wants payment back when she demands it, and it's a brave man who stands up and says he don't have her money. She's not quite a usurer, but she does charge a fee for giving the money to ye. A hefty one, if you take my meaning. Woe to you if ye don't pay it to her."

"She's a woman," I said, pointing out the obvious. "She might have a cold eye and a sharp tongue, but I doubt she could beat a man into submission."

"Oh, she has plenty to do it for her. Like I say, she took over her husband's business, and it was extensive. She runs South London just as Mr. Denis runs everything north of the river. Only she's not as genteel, like. 'Sides, those around 'ere respect her. She helps them out of binds, as no one else will. There are plenty who'd be in the workhouse if not for her, and they know it."

"I see." I fell silent. I disliked what Brewster was telling me, but I might have to bend my principles a little and allow this Poppy to help me save a man from Spendlove's ruthlessness, if she could. And perhaps save me from him into the bargain.

A shadow slipped past us. I saw it and halted, my breath coming faster, my encounter in St. Giles too fresh. I had no wish to battle for my life again today.

Brewster stepped into the darkness and returned with a tall youth in his clutches. The youth was swearing hard at Brewster, the cap on his head knocked askew.

Brewster shook him to silence. "What are you following us about for?" he demanded.

The youth yanked himself from Brewster's grasp, though I knew Brewster let him go. "I was sent, wasn't I? 'E wants to see '*im*."

I knew who without asking. I recognized the larger shadow that waited farther down a side street as one of Denis's stronger ruffians. A hackney waited for us on the bridge, almost lost in the darkness and lowering fog.

"Very well," I said without hesitation. "I want to find out what he knows of all this. You do not have to accompany me," I told Brewster as he followed me toward the hackney. "If you feel it would be awkward for you, I'll make the visit and have the coachman take you on home."

"Chance would be a fine thing," Brewster growled. He put his hand on my shoulder and more or less shoved me into the hackney. "If you're charging into the lion's den, Captain, I'm going right in with ye. Your lady wife would be that angry with me if ye didn't come out again."

CHAPTER 9

THE HOUSE AT NUMBER 45, Curzon Street, a place I frequently vowed never to set foot in again, had become quite familiar to me.

The cold-eyed butler took my greatcoat and hat and ushered me up the white-paneled staircase. We passed the painting of the milkmaid standing in a flood of sunlight, the only action in the picture the stream of cream trickling from her jug. On we went up to the white-paneled upper hall and into the study that opened to the back of the house. None of Denis's private rooms faced the street.

The study I entered was austere. It had been repaired and repainted since an incident the previous winter had wrecked it, but no evidence remained of the problem. A painting hung above the fireplace, dark with years, but from it peered the eyes of an artist who'd dressed himself in Arab costume. His face was round, somber, ingenuous, as though he wasn't certain why he was wearing the garments, except that it was required for the picture. The artist gazed down at me in sympathy as I was taken to my usual chair in front of the desk, a table next to it bearing a glass of brandy.

I sat, stretching out my leg, waiting for Denis to finish whatever he was writing and give me his attention. I was reminded of Poppy, making notes in her book, indicating she had no interest in the person who sought her until she was ready.

Brewster had followed me inside and upstairs. He now stood

uncomfortably by the door, he and the butler eying each other warily. Another guard—not the one who'd accosted me in St. Giles—stood next to the window, his gaze never leaving me.

Denis's pen ceased scratching, and he set it aside and looked up. James Denis, a fairly young man with dark hair, was in his thirties now, but his face had not changed at all since I'd met him nearly three years ago. He, like his house, remained unaltered.

His eyes, blue, were as chill as Poppy's but with a spark more of strength and confidence. The confidence was understandable. After all, Denis sat here in this comfortable, elegant house surrounded by guards who'd fight to the death for him, while Poppy worked out of the back room of a grubby pub.

Denis looked from me to Brewster, his eyes becoming colder than ever. "Mr. Brewster," he said. "Wait downstairs."

Brewster drew a quick breath. "Can't do that, sir, begging your pardon. Captain's hired me to look after him. That means watching over him, including when he's with you. Especially when he's with you. Sir."

Denis looked in no way surprised or outraged at Brewster's response. "I am aware you have taken new employment. I will give you my word that no harm will come to the captain while he is in this room."

"What if he loses his temper as he does and attacks ye? Or tries. I should be here to hold him back and keep Robbie there from cudgeling him."

Robbie, the thug at the window, let his lips twitch. His fingers did as well, as though he anticipated reaching for said cudgel.

"I will call for you," Denis said, his voice hard. "If you prefer to wait on the upper landing, you may, but on no account will you disturb us until you're sent for."

Brewster frowned and looked to me, waiting for me to tell him what to do. He was nervous with the situation, but he was taking refuge in the fact that he was not in charge. No matter what was decided, Brewster could claim he'd only done what he was told.

I spread my hands. "It is evident that Mr. Denis will not speak to me until you go. Please wait downstairs, Mr. Brewster. I will endeavor to keep my temper in check."

Brewster did not like this, I could see, but he nodded, glared at Robbie and the butler, and then departed the room. His large boots made much noise on the stairs as he descended.

Denis opened his desk drawer, slid the paper he'd been writing on inside, and closed the drawer again. The butler came forward and took the inkstand—a heavy silver base that housed an ink-well and a cup for holding pens. It was less ornate than any of those the prince had, but likely more valuable. Ornamentation did not mean worth.

The butler shut the inkstand into a cupboard across the room, and Denis rested his hands on the now empty desk.

"I am pleased Mr. Brewster has decided to look after you," he said. "He is the sort of man who likes being useful."

I'd have more faith in Denis's compassion for Brewster if he'd changed the inflection of his voice. "I had no choice after your man let me be nearly beaten to a pulp in St. Giles," I said. "And then continued the beating. If not for Brewster, I might be dead or senseless somewhere, my family searching for me."

"I know." Denis's voice was icy. "I have replaced the man who was watching over you. He seemed to not understand I prefer to have you whole."

There was a silence. Even Robbie at the window and the but-ler were utterly still. I did not like to think what had become of the men he'd "replaced."

I decided to end the uncomfortable conversation. "What did you wish to speak to me about? In the middle of the night that could not wait for a more convenient time of day?"

"Your appointment at Carlton House," Denis said without hesitation. "I know you have been asked to look into the thefts there. I have called you in to tell you that I wish you to have nothing to do with it."

He finished the statement with a neutral look, as though what he said was perfectly reasonable, and I should have no trouble granting his wish.

"Why?" I settled into my chair. "Have the thefts been made by you?"

What might have been amusement flickered across his face. "I assure you, Captain, that if I chose to rob the Prince Regent, I would have the entire collection, not a few trinkets, and he would be none the wiser. But I wish you to leave it be. I should not like to see you come to harm because of it, as you already nearly have. You have a new daughter to think of."

I did. Anne would be fast asleep in her cot, the nurse snoring on the bed beside her. Thinking of my daughter made my heart turn over. She was tiny, vulnerable, and nearly hadn't made it into the world at all.

"You raise more questions than you answer," I said. "Why should looking into these thefts be dangerous to me? Other than from tramping about illegal markets in the dark, I mean. Besides, I have no choice. Mr. Spendlove will not accept my refusal."

"In any case, you must make it. Mr. Spendlove will have to do without your assistance."

I frowned. "Mr. Spendlove has made clear that he'll hang me—alongside you—if I do not help him with this problem. If I do not, he will find a way to arrest me for something and link it to you. I'd think you'd wish me to placate him."

"Mr. Spendlove does not concern me," Denis said in clipped tones. "You have friends who are far more powerful than Mr. Spendlove, and who can protect you. Please do as I say and leave this problem alone."

"The Prince Regent himself has asked me," I pointed out. "I rather think he'll make it a command if he must. And I am not happy about the wretch Spendlove has arrested. He should not go to the dock for something he did not do. There is more going on here, I am certain, than first appears."

"Certainly there is. Which is why *I* will clear it up, and you will not. I will ensure this wretch as you call him, is not tried for the crime."

He had my interest. "How would you ensure that?"

Denis's fingers moved the slightest bit. "You know I will not answer such a question. I will have him withdrawn from New-gate very soon and back home with his family. But I will perform this deed only if you agree to cease looking into the matter."

I had opened my mouth to continue arguing, but as he fin-ished, my hot words died on my lips.

He handed me a dilemma. If I abandoned the quest, a man I suspected was innocent would go free. I knew Denis could have him released from Newgate if he truly wanted to—he had a hold over many magistrates in London.

However, if I obeyed Denis, Spendlove would close his fist around me. He'd more or less told me I'd be in Newgate with the man he'd arrested—or in place of him—and I would be the one who needed to clear my name. Donata had solicitors to help me, but even they could do nothing if a magistrate and then a jury and judge decided I had assisted Mr. Denis in his crimes. They might not be able to put their hands on Denis, but Spend-love would enjoy making me pay in his stead.

I would also be angering the Prince Regent if I walked away from the problem, a man known for holding a grudge. Would the prince retaliate somehow against Grenville and Donata if I disappointed him? Grenville and my wife had the birth and fam-ily connections to protect them, but even so, being shunned by the man who'd one day be king might have dire consequences for my friends.

"What you ask is difficult," I said sharply.

"Not difficult. Stay home and advise Mr. Grenville to do the same, and Mr. Floyd will be released."

"Grenville too? Bloody hell—it hardly matters if the Regent looks with ill favor upon me, but Grenville has more to lose than I do."

"On the contrary." Denis spread his hands on the desk. "*You* have much more to lose."

Spendlove had insinuated the same. He'd looked around the splendid reception room of Donata's house and told me all I'd gained could so easily be taken away from me.

Spendlove had erroneously thought I'd longed for luxury, but he was wrong. I married Donata for herself—whether we lived in a mansion or a hovel was of no consequence to me. I had no doubt Donata could brighten up even a hovel; she'd receive her friends there as regally as a queen.

My heart squeezed again as I thought of Anne, her tiny face, how she could hold my finger in her hand with surprising strength.

"If you touch my wife or daughter," I said, savagery in my voice. "I cannot answer for what I do. All your men will not be able to stop me."

Denis gave me a calm nod. "I know this. Your daughter is safe from me, Captain—she is an innocent and should be given every comfort. As is your wife. Her ladyship is a highly intelligent woman and not without connections herself. I was thinking more of your cousin, at whom I remain angry for his violence. I could have so many things happen to him for that—arrest and conviction for shooting at Brewster, or I can simply mete out my own justice. I have already told him so."

I was on my feet at once. "Marcus was here?"

During my sojourn in Egypt, I discovered I had a cousin, one raised in Canada. We shared a mutual grandfather, and in fact, he was the rightful heir to my house in Norfolk, or so he claimed. Donata's man of business was even now trying to verify that this was the case. Donata had been horrified when I'd suggested Marcus simply take over the house—I felt I had enough homes to live in now between South Audley Street, Oxfordshire, and the Breckenridge estate in Hampshire. Donata had told me tartly not to be a fool and had summoned her man of business.

"I asked him to call upon me," Denis said without alarm. "He shot at you and nearly fatally wounded Mr. Brewster. He needed to answer."

My temper rose. "Why did I not hear of this?"

"Because it was none of your affair. It was private business between myself and Mr. Lacey. He apologized to me and agreed to do me one or two favors."

Marcus had been coerced into doing favors, Denis meant, just as I was being coerced now. "I'd be grateful if you would leave be members of my family," I said, tight-lipped.

"Whether he is truly a member of your family remains to be seen. However, he bears a remarkable resemblance to you, which could be useful."

I took a step forward. "I risked my life to carry out your wishes in Egypt, when all the while you were playing your own game. I have indebted myself to you, and I acknowledge that, but I have paid and paid. Do not use my cousin to make me pay more."

One day I would get myself across the desk and put my hands around Denis's throat. Tonight would not be that night however. Robbie from the window was in front of me quickly, blocking my way like a stone wall.

"Please sit down, Captain," Denis said without moving. "I am not finished."

"*I* am." I swung around to face the door, only to find the butler in front of me. I turned back to Denis. "To hell with you. You barter with Mr. Floyd's life to force me to do your bidding. You dangle your hold on my cousin over me for the same."

Denis said nothing, made no move. I turned to charge out, ready to shove the butler aside if necessary, but the man stepped out of my way, his face impassive. I snatched up my walking stick and strode for the door, my anger making my pain negligible.

I knew I'd never have left that room had not Denis allowed it. The thought made me angrier still. I slammed myself out and plunged down the stairs to where Brewster waited at the bottom, a scowl on his face. Another of Denis's men next to him held my coat and hat.

I grabbed the coat and thrust it on as I strode out of the house, nearly forgetting my hat in the process. It was cold enough that I was glad to jam the hat on my head, but not so cold to prevent me walking home, too agitated to look for a coach.

Brewster lumbered after me. "I knew ye'd never keep yourself calm. What happened?"

"You are well rid of your old master," I said with a growl. "I vow to be rid of him too. Only now I must extricate my cousin along with me."

"Ah," Brewster said, suddenly subdued. "Ye heard of that?"

"Yes, just now." I halted and eyed him narrowly. "What do you know of it?" We stood near the intersection of Curzon Street and South Audley, next to Chesterfield House, a mansion with a huge garden stuck like an island amidst the narrow townhouses around it.

Brewster cleared his throat. "It's what made Mr. Denis tell me to go. He had Mr. Lacey in, giving him the evil eye about shooting me and making our lives such hell in foreign parts. I stepped up and said I wasn't bothered any more about it, that me and Mr. Lacey had made it up. Ye ain't stuck alive in a grave with a man without thinking over a thing or two."

I gave Brewster a look of new respect. "Did you? That was good of you."

"Huh. It were stupid of me. His nibs looks at me in that cold way of his and says that I'd be better off taking a rest at home with me wife. What he truly meant was I weren't to interrupt him when he were closing his hand around someone. So off I went." Brewster heaved a long sigh.

I stared at him in bafflement. "Why did you not say so? You told me he sacked you for going soft, for him knowing you wouldn't pummel me if he ordered it."

"I didn't like to say," Brewster said, scowl in place. "And he did tell me I were going soft, that I was 'developing a strange affection' for the Lacey family. So I took meself home, not wanting anything to do with any of you."

And probably Brewster had not told me about Marcus being interviewed by Denis, knowing I'd storm to Denis and confront him about it, possibly getting myself hurt for my trouble. Denis also wouldn't thank Brewster for spilling the tale.

"I am sorry," I said, heartfelt. "I promised to stand you many an ale—you deserve them. I mean somewhere better than that pub in Southwark that Poppy likes."

"Aye, I think they make horses piss in a barrel and call it

drink," Brewster muttered. "I will take your kind offer. But first we'll send you home so your lady wife will know I haven't got you killed. No matter how much ye try to do it to yourself."

I assumed Donata would still be out when I returned home, as one in the morning was an early hour for the fashionable world, but to my surprise, I found her there. She waited for me, alone, in her boudoir, a room of golds and greens and comfortable furniture. This chamber had sustained damage during one of my investigations—by the same kind of incendiary device that had burned Denis's study, but repairs had been done to restore it to its former splendor.

A portrait of young Peter Breckenridge hung on the wall next to the fireplace, painted last summer, the lad standing straight and tall, a hound lounging at his feet. If anyone doubted Donata's fondness for her children, the painting, hung where she could look at it every day, would dispel the doubt. A blank space on the other side of the fireplace waited for the portrait of Anne when she was old enough.

Donata had not yet put off her evening finery of green velvet and ivory silk. I thought the room complemented her nicely.

I could not have brought in the most pleasant odors, but my wife came to me and kissed me on the cheek. She did so absently, as though worried about more than what her husband had been getting up to.

"I would have thought you still at the rout," I said when she released me. "Ensconced with your friends and talking over those not fortunate enough to be there."

Donata heaved a sigh. She hadn't removed the diamonds in her hair, and they sparkled in the candlelight.

"We never went to the rout. I told Grenville about Marianne." Donata's words were flat and uninflected. "I thought it kinder to give him the news baldly and not have him hear about it from some evil-minded person while we were at Lady Featherstone's."

"Ah." I imagined Grenville becoming cool and still while Donata broke the news. "Is he all right? Has he gone home?"

Donata's eyes flashed with irritation and anxiousness. "No, he has not gone home. He was dumbfounded, as I was, to learn Marianne had left him for Dunmarron. He didn't believe me, I am afraid—though why he'd think I'd invent such a story, I have no idea. But he did not go home. He went off to find Dunmarron, and I fear what might come of it."

CHAPTER 10

I LISTENED IN ALARM. "DO YOU mean to tell me that Grenville has gone to storm the house of a duke? He'll be up before a magistrate before he can blink."

"No," Donata said through my last words. "The Duke of Dunces, it turns out, is staying at his club while he's in London. As I told you, he only comes up for business, but apparently a bill is being debated in the Lords he has taken a keen interest in. He holes himself up at Brooks's when he's not sitting on his rump in debate, or wenching. So I am told."

"Damn and blast." I had to go after Grenville before he did something irrevocable. "I have not set him the best precedent with my own behavior in Brooks's. They'll throw him to the pavement."

"I doubt it," Donata said. "If you refer to what you did to Mr. Alandale, he deserved your wrath, and you did what so many wished they could. Most gentlemen couldn't stick Alandale. Most don't like Dunmarron either."

"Even so. Bloody hell."

If Grenville began to beat on a duke in the middle of Brooks's subscription room, he might not escape arrest, even if it was only for disturbing the other members of the club.

But no, I told myself. Grenville wasn't likely to fly into a man with his fists—his temperament was different from mine. Grenville would call him out instead.

I opened the door and put my head out. "Barnstable!" I'd

never grown used to bell pulls, and I knew Barnstable would be lurking somewhere close. When he appeared on the landing, I continued, "Summon her ladyship's carriage. I am going out."

"And I am going with you," Donata said at once.

"Not to Brooks's," I said. "If a woman rushes inside, the entire building will fall down, I am certain. Or at least all the gentlemen in it will expire from apoplexy."

"Don't be ridiculous. I do not intend to do anything so tasteless as to darken the door of a gentlemen's club. I will wait in the coach. Grenville will need soothing down when you bring him out. He was most distraught."

"Could you not have kept him here?" I asked. "Had Barnstable sit on him if nothing else?"

Barnstable had arrived in time to hear this statement. "I assure you, sir, her ladyship and I tried to dissuade Mr. Grenville from leaving."

"He did not tear out of here in a fury," Donata said. "More in disbelief. He said very much what I did when we saw the letter. The Duke of Dunces? It is unbelievable. I imagine he is off to see whether the story is true or a bizarre joke."

"Well, we had better go and make certain," I said. "Thank you, Barnstable."

"I would have sat on him if I'd thought it would do any good, sir," Barnstable answered. "I would have called your large valet as well, but he is out visiting his brother."

I had a small but only flickering hope that Bartholomew and Matthias had noted Grenville departing from here and accompanied him. But we would soon see.

By the time the carriage rumbled to the front door, Donata's maid had helped her don her wraps, and Brewster had come up from the kitchen where he'd been warming himself. I told Brewster he ought to go home, but he shook his head stubbornly and said I wouldn't be traipsing around London without him. He climbed onto the footman's perch on the back of the coach, his considerable bulk making the vehicle list.

Hagen drove us down South Audley Street the way I'd tramped

up, reminding me of my anger at Denis. Spendlove, in my opinion, was more ruthless than Denis, and so I'd have to let Mr. Floyd sit in Newgate until I could find evidence to clear him.

I tried to push aside this worry to focus on Grenville. I'd extract him from Brooks's by any means necessary and then return to the problem of Denis's orders. I needed Grenville's cool and steady head to help me, but at this moment, his mind would be anything but clear. I wondered briefly if discomposing Grenville was Dunmarron's intention.

Brooks's club faced St. James's Street, its imposing facade lined with lofty columns and tall windows. The building was topped with a Greek pediment, making it look as though a temple had been transported from the Aegean Sea and dropped in the middle of prosaic London houses. This particular temple was dedicated to the goddess Fortuna—or might as well have been from the fierce gaming that took place inside. The Whig party was also worshipped here, its well-established members alternately venerated or despised by the younger men.

If Dunmarron took a room here on occasion, he must be ensconced within the Whigs. I took little enough notice of politics these days—spending most of my grown years out of the country had made me lose interest in it. Whatever hot air was talked in Parliament decided whether I went to battle in India or Portugal, and it seemed to make no difference which party held the reins.

I knew enough to understand that the Prince Regent had been a great friend to the Whigs in his youth, throwing in his lot with Mr. Fox and others against the Tory bastions and his father, who had a decidedly Tory bent. As the prince aged, however, coming closer to the throne as the king grew more enfeebled, the Regent had begun outraging his Whig ties by becoming more Tory by the day. He looked with approval upon lords Castlereagh and Liverpool, telling his old friends it would upset his father if he did not support the Tory end of government. Grenville could go on for some time about why the Regent had shifted his alliances, longer than I listened to him, truth to tell.

In any case, Dunmarron was inside Brooks's, and Grenville presumably was with him. I descended, Brewster climbing down to wait on the pavement near the door. I had no doubt he'd shoulder his way inside if he thought I'd be in any danger.

The doorman whose task it was to allow or deny entrance to those seeking this lofty edifice, stood squarely in the middle of the vestibule as I walked inside. His name was Richards, and he knew me well.

"Good evening, Captain Lacey," he said, his voice more cultured than those of many of the members. "Do you seek Mr. Grenville? He has been here and gone."

I gave him a nod, making myself contain my impatience. "Thank you. What about Dunmarron? Might I have a word with him?"

"His Grace is not here either, sir."

Whether Dunmarron was truly out, had never come in, or was simply not receiving visitors I could not tell, but there was little else I could do. As long as Grenville hadn't strangled him, all was well.

"Did Mr. Grenville leave alone?" I asked.

Richards's nose rose a little higher. "Yes, sir."

"Hmm." I would have to think on where the devil he'd gone. "If he returns, will you tell him I am looking for him? He may send me word at home."

"Yes, sir," Richards said, looking relieved I wouldn't be pushing my way in. "May I offer my congratulations, sir, on the arrival of your daughter."

I instantly softened. "You may, Richards. You may. Thank you."

Richards looked upon me a touch more kindly. "I will convey the message if Mr. Grenville returns. Good night, Captain."

I took the hint, gave him another nod, and retreated.

I went back to the carriage, Brewster coming out of the shadows to boost me in. "Grenville's not here," I said to Donata. "According to Richards. Now to decide where he's got to."

"The theatre at Haymarket." Brewster looked inside at us, his hand on the door handle.

I blinked at him. "How the devil do you know that?"

"Asked the lad what sweeps the street. Says Mr. Grenville came out of the club and into a hackney, telling the driver to take him to Haymarket. Not storming, not angry—cool as you please, as per usual."

I glanced past Brewster to see the lad in question quickly approach a man who was stepping into the street, the boy's treble voice coming to us. "Clear your path, milord?" The gentleman rumbled something and tossed him a coin, which the lad caught with expertise. The boy scrambled to sweep the horse dung and mud from the cobbles so the gentleman could walk across the road, keeping his fashionable boots somewhat cleaner than they otherwise might have been.

"Very well," I said, trying to be calm. "Tell Hagen to take us to Haymarket."

Brewster slammed the door and shouted up to Donata's coachman, and we were off.

"This time I *shall* enter with you," Donata said in a determined voice. "Even if I am hardly dressed for the theatre."

I raised my brows as I glanced over her ensemble, her velvet cloak soft against my shoulder. "You are beautiful."

She smiled and gave my leg a squeeze with her gloved hand. "You are a comforting person to have near, Gabriel. More so because I know you mean your flattery."

Her tone held a tinge of pity—I, a poor deluded army captain, had no idea of the difference between a gown for a rout and one for the theatre—but her thanks was no less warm.

"If you can bear to be seen with a crusty old thing like me," I said, "I welcome your company."

Another squeeze. "Of course. I enjoy showing the world that you and I continue to live in each other's pockets, even after a year of marriage and a child. Speculation was that we would not last a sixmonth."

I laid my hand on hers. "Speculation is wrong."

"I know, and you cannot understand how much I love making

all of polite society eat their words. I believe there was even a wager about my fidelity to you when you were gone to Egypt."

I stilled. "I beg your pardon? A wager? About you?"

"Oh, yes. So many gentlemen lost their money on it. It was delicious."

I stared at Donata and her pleased flush for so long that she became exasperated. "I knew I should not have told you—for heaven's sake, do not fight a duel over this, Gabriel. You barely escaped arrest for your last one. It is done, and I was highly amused. Those who disparage us look like fools."

"A man does not make a wager about another man's wife." My body had gone rigid, my anger rising. "Especially when that man is not there to defend her."

Donata gazed at me, coolness entering her eyes. My first wife, when she'd sensed my transition to rage, would begin to babble, trying to soothe me down, and then break into nervous laughter and then into tears.

My second wife only gave me a look of disdain, annoyed I was going on about a matter when that matter was closed. "Take no notice," she said. "Those fool enough to wager have had their comeuppance. Take a leaf from Grenville's book and let the world see that you care nothing for them."

"That is the secret to surviving among the aristocracy, is it?" I asked stiffly.

"Of course." Her coolness increased and she withdrew her touch, laying her hand on her lap. "Give way, and you drown."

She was angry. When Donata lost her temper, she never raged, never shouted. Instead she retreated behind a wall of ice, waiting until others sorted out the problem. She became haughty, disdainful, and utterly unapproachable.

"Forgive me," I said, trying to climb down from my mountain of pride. "I know I can be an embarrassment to you. I will endeavor to keep this unfortunate tendency to a minimum."

She shot me a scornful look. "Please, Gabriel, do not give yourself airs. My husband with his boorish manners, foul tongue, and blatant debauchery was embarrassing. You are hardly in his league." She sat forward as the carriage halted. "Escort me inside, and do try to look as though we've not had a row."

I gripped her elbow, supporting her as the door opened, letting in a wave of chill wind. "Is this a row?" I asked in her ear. "I look forward to making it up later."

Every so often, I said the right thing to my wife—entirely by accident. Donata sent me a smile that promised many things, before she descended, Brewster helping her down.

Grenville was indeed at the theatre. He had a box there, a private alcove high above the stage that was decorated with a gold frieze and red velvet curtains that could be pulled closed for privacy. The box held eight chairs, all of which were full tonight.

I heard a man speaking on the stage, though in a measured voice rather than a dramatic shout. No actors answered him, but there were a few bellowed questions from the audience. A lecture, I concluded, not a play.

Grenville reposed in a chair in the front of the box, a lady to either side of him. All the occupants of the box rose as Donata and I entered, turning to greet us, never mind what was happening on the stage below.

I recognized the lady on Grenville's arm as the Austrian violinist, Mrs. Anastasia Froehm, who made the occasional journey to London to play and dazzle us all. She had a round face that was plain but open and friendly, soft eyes, and an engaging smile. Grenville had introduced me to her on one of her previous visits, and she held out her hand to me as I bowed.

"So pleasant to meet you again, Captain Lacey," she said in her richly accented English. She curtseyed deferentially to Donata, who acknowledged her with a regal bow.

Grenville gazed at me, his eyes still, but I knew he was asking me to keep my silence while we were in public. I gave him a steady look in return, my signal that I would.

Grenville had explained to me during Mrs. Froehm's last visit that there was nothing more than friendship between them. They'd known each other a long time, and Grenville's presence at her side prevented Mrs. Froehm from having to fend off too-persistent admirers. Gossip and newspapers enjoyed themselves pairing their names, however, and Grenville never bothered to dispute the claims.

I understood why Grenville had sought out Mrs. Froehm tonight and brought her to his box in front of all of London. He was saving his reputation. If Grenville's mistress had slipped from him at the beckoning of the man referred to as the Duke of Dunces, he'd be a laughingstock. Grenville was changing the story.

No doubt it was already common knowledge that Marianne was with Dunmarron. But, if Grenville behaved as though he'd simply tired of one mistress and had returned to another, this cast Dunmarron in the role of a man taking a famous man's leavings, not one successfully luring away Grenville's beloved.

After we had greeted Mrs. Froehm, we were obliged to exchange good evenings with the rest of the people in the box, some of whom I hadn't met before. Therefore, introductions had to be made. Finally, Grenville ordered a footman to drag in two more chairs so that we could squeeze ourselves in to watch the performance.

Donata managed a seat in the front with the ladies and Grenville, while I was relegated to the back among the gentlemen. One of the gentlemen had a grudging respect for me since I'd been an army man, and offered me snuff. I took it politely though I didn't particularly like snuff, but one didn't refuse without snubbing the offerer.

The gentleman on my other side wore sagging cashmere trousers and a scarlet waistcoat, a large cravat and perfume. He'd even rouged his cheeks. I thought he looked a perfect fool, but I said nothing. The fellow beyond him completely ignored me.

All the conversation concentrated in the front row among the ladies and Grenville, while we gentlemen sat in silence. When I was finally able to focus my attention on the stage, I saw that we were in the middle of a lecture on astronomy—the sun, moon, and planets.

A giant orrery had been erected on the stage, the sun a huge ball in its center, with wires and levers to send the earth and other planets around the sun. Just as I turned to listen, a fiery ball shot from the outer reaches of the theatre and sizzled around the sun—a comet. The audience burst into applause, as did I. The gentleman who'd given me the snuff looked sideways at me and then followed my lead to clap.

I leaned forward, trying to hear what the fellow said. I knew I'd find this lecture fascinating and was sorry I'd missed the first of it. I was also a bit surprised Grenville had surrounded himself with rather dull company, but it made sense if he'd wanted to prove himself not pining for Marianne, and to prove this in a hurry. He'd gathered hangers-on who would report what a splendid time he was having with Mrs. Froehm, never mind what was going on around them. *Grenville* was the entertainment, not the lecture.

I tried to shut out the ladies' chatter and the rude remarks of the two gentlemen on my right. The rather portly man on the stage, dressed in a subdued black suit except for his waistcoat, which sported large stars on it, went on in an authoritative tone about the movement of the planets in their dance, and how total eclipses of the sun happened, which could be predicted almost down to the minute.

It was very interesting—I would have to return to this lecture at a later date, perhaps alone with Donata. She had a keen interest in higher matters and would probably enjoy it as well.

At the moment, Donata was raising her lorgnette to gaze about her and make remarks on those she saw. She had the ladies in the front row laughing and hanging on her words, in the way Donata could. My wife knew all about saving a reputation and holding one's head up when one was being publicly humiliated.

Before the end of the lecture, Grenville executed his grand exit. He rose to his feet, making a show of being finished with this entertainment. Mrs. Froehm rose with him, smiling and pleasant. Grenville invited Donata and me to journey on with him to his next destination, a supper ball of some sort. Donata gladly accepted—she and I had tickets to the same, she claimed, though this was the first I'd heard of it.

The others in the box looked disappointed Grenville was leaving—apparently they hadn't been invited to this supper ball—and Grenville told them to remain and enjoy themselves as long as they liked. That perked them up—the use of Grenville's private box would raise their standing.

We made our way down the stairs, Donata on Grenville's arm, Mrs. Froehm on mine. Heaven help us that we gentlemen should escort the ladies we actually wanted to be with.

Plenty of people were making their way downstairs as well. If one remained to the end of the performance, one would miss so many more events of the night. London always had something on.

The foyer was crammed with those going out and those coming in. I caught sight of Rafe Godwin with Lord Lucas Parnell and hoped our paths would not cross, but it was not to be. Rafe deliberately moved upstream so that we would meet near the doors to the street. Between Rafe and Lord Lucas was a man I didn't know, but by his bullish air and the fact that people moved quickly out of his way, I decided who he had to be.

Mrs. Froehm halted at my side. "*Also*," she said in a low voice. "Is this the man Herr Grenville names the Duke of the Dunces?"

"It must be," I said. "A well-orchestrated encounter."

"*Vielleicht*," she said.

Rafe Godwin steered his friends directly for us. The foyer grew more chaotic as he did, because of course everyone wanted to watch the encounter. Grenville continued to stroll with Donata, speaking to her as though having no idea Dunmarron was anywhere near.

Rafe stepped in front of Grenville, quite rudely, but the excitement in his eyes told me he'd decided to let manners fly out the window. "Grenville," he said heartily. "Well met."

Mrs. Froehm and I were a few yards from Grenville, but cut off from assisting him by others who squeezed between us. Fortunately he had Donata with him, though I was not happy to see her being accosted by Rafe and the Duke of Dunmarron.

Grenville raised his brows at Rafe, conveying his disapproval of the man's behavior. "Godwin. Parnell," he said politely then, "Good Lord." Grenville's quizzing glass came out and he ran it over the man between Rafe Godwin and Lord Lucas. "Is it Dunmarron? In a theatre? You are a long way from home, Your Grace. What brings you to Town? It cannot be the fine weather."

The Duke of Dunmarron gazed back at Grenville with more intelligence in his eyes than I'd expected. He was a fairly tall man, not quite as tall as I was but had half a head over Grenville. He was about my age, forty-odd, with black hair cut short as though showing his disapproval of the flowing poetic curls now the rage. His suit was subdued and well tailored, no flopping trousers and definitely no rouge.

He was a beefy man, stocky and not athletic of figure, although not rotund either. When he bowed over Donata's hand, he moved with ease. In short, he was a country man who counteracted the effects of beef and port by riding and hunting, an old-style squire who happened to be a lofty duke.

His eyes were small and dark, and I saw in them a flicker of anger so deep it alarmed me. This was not a man simply stealing another's mistress to tweak his nose, I realized. There was something else behind this matter, and despite Donata's earlier reassurances, I felt a sudden and profound qualm of fear for Marianne.

CHAPTER 11

BEFORE DUNMARRON COULD RESPOND TO Grenville's question as to why he'd come to town, Rafe broke in.

"Are you looking for something, Grenville?" he said with false joviality. "Something you've lost, perhaps?"

Irritation crossed Dunmarron's face, though a few around us strove to hide laughter. The encounter had been paced to the moment, and now Rafe had ruined it by being obvious.

Grenville won the round by ignoring Rafe utterly. "Good evening, Lucas," he said. "Did you enjoy the lecture? The phases of the moon were fascinating—I must look up more often at night. If we can see anything through London's wretched fog and smoke, that is."

Dunmarron finally spoke. "The lecture," he said, his voice a booming baritone. "Yes, that is why I came out tonight. I heard it was most instructive."

"A pleasure after a day of sitting," Grenville said to him.

His words meant sitting in Parliament, but his tone conveyed *sitting* as in on his arse. More titters surrounded us.

"Indeed," Dunmarron said.

My wife's voice cut in. "How tedious for you, Dunmarron. And how fortunate that London is rife with entertainment."

Dunmarron was obviously not skilled at verbal sparring. He only rumbled uncomfortably, "Yes. Of course."

"Quite a lot of entertainment this evening, in fact," Donata went on. "If you will excuse me, we are moving forward. So much to do. Give my best wishes to your wife—dear Olympia, I see too little of her." She gave Dunmarron a nod of dismissal.

Dunmarron was a duke, outranking Donata's father on the aristocratic scale, and far outranking her first husband and now her son, but she was refusing to unbend with a curtsey or a "Your Grace." She knew everything there was to know about everyone, including their family trees. No doubt she'd explain to me later that Dunmarron's family were merchants or some such from a hundred years ago, while her ancestors—and mine—had been gently born for centuries. It was not a title that made a man for Donata, but breeding.

Dunmarron nodded back. He fixed Grenville with a freezing stare then moved around him toward the doors to the boxes.

Donata smiled, said a "Good Evening" to Lord Lucas and Rafe, and turned to wave at another lady in greeting. She and Grenville floated on toward the doors, and I followed with Mrs. Froehm.

Grenville kept his aplomb until we were in the carriage, he handing in Donata, then Mrs. Froehm, and climbing in after them. Grenville's footman assisted me inside while Brewster stood by on the lookout for pickpockets and other thieves.

As soon as I was in and the carriage jerked forward, Grenville snarled, "What the bloody hell is he playing at?" He threw his walking stick to the floor, a display of temper rarely seen in him.

Mrs. Froehm apparently was aware of what had happened with Marianne, because she showed no surprise at his anger. "He has come to goad you," she said to Grenville with sympathy. "To see how you will respond."

"He expected me to fly at him," Grenville snapped. "Shout at him, call him out. Make a boor of myself. To what end? What have *I* done to incur the wrath of the Duke of Dunces?"

"Perhaps he is madly in love with Miss Simmons," Donata suggested in a neutral voice.

Grenville gave her a cold look. "Hardly a matter for jokes, dear lady."

"Hardly a matter for letting him, as Mrs. Froehm says, goad

you," Donata said.

I broke in. "He wants you angry."

"Do you suppose?" Grenville returned, opening his eyes wide. "Well, he has succeeded. I can only hope that my outburst will be kept private among friends?"

"Of course," I said at once. "But when you have calmed yourself, I want you to think of these facts." I waited until Grenville had focused on me, ready to listen, before I continued. "Marianne did not rush to him in delight, as we concluded from the note. She asked to meet Mrs. Lacey and me and then did not keep the appointment, from which we suppose she was prevented. As Mrs. Lacey remarked, even if Marianne had been staying with you purely for the love of material comfort, she would lose money, luxury, and esteem by going to Dunmarron. Therefore, there is a more sinister reason Dunmarron has taken her from you." I let out a breath as I finished. "I am worried for her."

Grenville's anger slowly drained from him as I spoke. "The question remains, Lacey, why should he do this?"

"That I do not know. I believe we should find Marianne as soon as possible and *then* try to understand Dunmarron's motive."

Before Grenville could respond, Donata said, "I have been asking all my acquaintance about Dunmarron, but so far I have not been able to discover where he is keeping her. I am awaiting a few more responses, but it seems odd."

"Blast and bloody hell." Grenville clenched his hands, stretching his kid gloves over his slim fingers. "Damn the Regent for dragging me out of the house—I was listening to him wail about his treasures while *my* greatest treasure was stolen from under my nose."

Mrs. Froehm looked distressed for him. Donata and I shared a glance. Never had Grenville come so close to admitting how much he cared for Marianne.

I said to him, "We will find her. Never fear that."

"I too will look," Mrs. Froehm said. "Many from the aristocracy, they speak to me, as do the musicians. We will find where he has her."

Grenville heaved a sigh, though his hands remained fisted. "I beg your pardon, Anastasia. I do not mean to spoil our friendship by dragging you into my troubles. I will take you back to your hotel, and you can pay me no mind."

"No, indeed, *mein freund*, I wish to help you, as you have helped me in the past. I can be—how is it in English?—discreet."

Grenville let out another breath then gazed about him as though becoming aware of his surroundings. "I see I have commandeered your coach, Donata. I have spent all evening abusing my friends, and you are being cloyingly kind to me."

Donata leaned forward and patted his knee. "Nothing is more touching to your female acquaintances than to see you concerned for a lady, Grenville. We shall be nothing but rude to you once you are happy again."

Grenville was not mollified, but he fell silent as we continued across St. James's and back to Mayfair.

We devised plans for how to search for Marianne before taking Mrs. Froehm to her hotel and Grenville home.

Marianne and I had not always seen eye to eye—in fact, she'd driven me to distraction when she'd lived above me in Covent Garden, but I'd come to care for her in my own way. She was to me like a wayward sister who had to be looked after, even if she didn't like me doing any such thing.

Then there was her child. Marianne had a son who dwelled in Berkshire—no one knew this secret except me, Grenville, and Donata, and a few of Marianne's oldest and most trusted friends. If Dunmarron had somehow learned of this, he might have threatened to harm young David to make Marianne behave. If so, I would return to his club and beat the man, never mind he was a duke and possibly a lord lieutenant.

I knew a man who could put his hands on Marianne if he wanted to and wouldn't give a tinker's damn about Dunmarron's power. That would mean returning to Curzon Street, apologizing for my outburst, and pledging my obedience in return for

Denis's help, but I would if necessary.

When we reached home, Donata bade me come to bed. We could not tear around London looking in every house in the middle of the night, and she assured me she'd cast a wide net to discover where Dunmarron might have hidden Marianne.

Truth to tell, it was a relief to sink down into my bed, Donata at my side. She rested her hand on my chest and whispered that she was feeling quite well, mended once again.

I understood what she meant, and in my agitation, I fell upon her hungrily. I had not been with her since before Anne was born, indeed, before I'd gone to Egypt. Donata laughed at me, but I tried to keep myself gentle, the surgeon's warning whispering in my head, fearing she might not be as recovered as she claimed.

But Donata was as lively as she'd ever been. For a time, I forgot my troubles, forgot Spendlove and his threats, Denis and his constant presence in my life, and my fears for Marianne. I reminded myself why I'd taken this courageous lady to wife, for her beauty and intelligence, and above all for the incredible tenderness she showed to very few.

She showed it to me tonight, and afterward I sank down into oblivion, my body wrapped around hers, and fell into a powerful sleep.

It was still dark when Bartholomew shook me awake, a candle in his hand.

"What the devil?" I growled, coming out of slumber. I had not wanted to waken from my deep sleep, and I became doubly unhappy when I realized Donata was no longer beside me. She must have retreated to her own chamber, not wanting a snoring lump of a husband next to her all night.

"Mr. Brewster, sir," Bartholomew said. His six-foot frame towered over the bed, the candle throwing a monstrous shadow onto the wall behind him. "He says it's time."

"Time for what?"

"I don't know, do I, sir? Mr. Brewster ain't one to encourage questions, if you take my meaning."

"I understand." Brewster had likely grunted at Bartholomew to run up and fetch me and expected to be obeyed.

I heaved myself out of bed and reached for a shirt. Bartholomew had a clean one ready for me as well as freshly pressed trousers, and clean undergarments, stockings, and boots. I didn't bother with a cravat, but Bartholomew persuaded me to a stock, a stiff cloth that could be simply tied and at least cover my throat.

I was downstairs in less than a quarter of an hour, unshaved, but that couldn't be helped. Wherever Brewster was dragging me, I doubted anyone would care about the state of my dress.

"Time for what?" I barked at him when I met him in the street.

Brewster gave me a puzzled look. "For the market, guv. The one Poppy told us about."

"It's bloody early for a bit of shopping," I said. I was groggy, barely awake in spite of Bartholomew splashing water into my face upstairs. If a few hours with my wife could lay me out like this, I knew I was not a young man anymore.

"Best to get there before sunrise," Brewster said.

He put his hand on my shoulder and more or less pushed me along the road to Mount Street, where he led me to a hackney stand. The driver was yawning but he tapped his horse awake as we climbed aboard, and he clattered us down the street.

We drove through Berkley Square and from there to Piccadilly. The length of this led us to Leicester Square, and then the hackney navigated narrow streets to St. Martin's Lane and down to the Strand. My old rooms were not far from here, just off Covent Garden. I gave them a passing thought as we rolled by Southampton Street, thanking the Lord for Donata's warm, snug house this chill February. I'd spent too many nights shivering and alone.

At the moment, I was shivering again and in no mood to pursue the Prince Regent's lost trinkets. But Brewster was correct that we should get an early start. It was four in the morning, and the streets were already teeming with carts trundling goods to market.

We crossed the river on the London Bridge, a span of arches marching its way across the Thames. The quaint houses and shops that had been perched along the bridge's length were long gone, abolished half a century ago; only paintings and drawings survived to tell us what they'd looked like. Likewise the heads of traitors and murderers were no longer affixed at its ends, for which I could only be thankful. The bridge itself would not be with us much longer—plans for it to be pulled down and replaced were already in the works. London ever remade itself.

On the other side of the river, we plunged into darker streets, until we reached the place Brewster looked for, a wide square of open ground that had not yet been filled in by buildings. Areas south of the Thames could open to fields and meadows without notice, as I'd discovered on a previous journey to Bermondsey. The hackney driver let us out where Brewster indicated, and departed.

The open field Brewster steered me to was covered with market stalls jumbled with goods, much as the Nazareth had been, but with far less elegant wares. I saw for sale battered tin buckets, iron rods that had seen better days, chipped porcelain tea sets missing a few cups, pretty pictures in frames of tarnished brass, clock parts, broken children's toys, and dinged cutlery. A larger muddle of junk I'd never seen in my life. Anything that hadn't been melted down and repurposed, it seemed, had found its way to these stalls.

There were gems among the dross, I discovered before long. I found an ell of silk in a glorious blend of red and orange among piles of threadbare muslin and worn wool, the silk unmarred and shining in the stall's lamplight. The large woman who ran the stall, muffled to her ears against the cold, mumbled that she wanted a shilling for the silk. I bought it.

"How could the prince's things end up *here*?" I asked Brewster in his ear. "It's a motley mess."

"Because this is a market overt," Brewster said. "Know what that is?"

I did. A *marché ouvert* was a place in which the goods, once sold, became the legal property of the buyer without question, no matter where the stall owner had obtained them. In other words, if a vendor wanted to sell me a piece of silk stolen from a warehouse on the Thames, once I purchased it, that cloth was mine without argument. The warehouse owner or shipper, or shop owner who'd ordered it, had no more claim on it.

The *marché ouvert* was a quaint holdover from medieval times, but from the crowd at this market, I saw that its popularity was alive and well.

We walked about the place for a long time, looking over every table. The vendors watched us carefully, though many recognized Brewster, which did not surprise me. I imagined many goods had passed from his hands to the vendors here, likely for a split of the price.

At a stall filled with cogs and wheels that looked like spare parts for milling machines, I found the statue of Theseus and Antiope.

The bronze had been coated with white paint, making it resemble a cheap plaster replica of a wealthy man's object d'art. I nearly missed it, buried among the rubbish, but the raised bow in Antiope's hand caught my attention.

I paused, my heart beating swiftly, as I pretended to flip through the junk around it. Casually, I rested my finger on the bronze. "Pretty thing."

The vendor, a small woman with wiry hair sticking out from under a wool cap scowled at me. "Venus and Mars," she said. "If you like that sort of thing. Give me a quid for it."

This statue must be worth thousands of guineas, but I did not need to appear too eager. "A crown," I said, offhand.

She gave me a look a disgust. "A quid, and that's givin' it to ye."

She wasn't wrong. "Six shillings," I said, pretending to be annoyed. "The paint's chipped. I'll have to restore it."

"Don't make no never mind to me what ye do with it. Give me half a guinea, and it's yours."

Half a guinea was ten shillings and sixpence. An amazing bargain, but I frowned at her. "Ten shillings," I said, firming my voice. "I still have to buy my breakfast."

The woman shrugged. "Let's see your coin then."

I reached into my drawstring bag and extracted two crown coins, laying them on the table in front of her. They disappeared quickly.

"Go on then," she said. "Take it and get on with ye."

I lifted the statuette, which was heavy, and carried it back to Brewster. He raised his brows when he saw it. "You have the devil's own luck. I ain't seen nothing. You sure that's what you're looking for?"

"Very certain. But one man will know better than I."

Brewster shrugged, not wanting to talk too much or name names while we were in the middle of a *marché ouvert*. We ambled along like two men interested in the wares, Brewster purchasing a small porcelain bowl he liked the look of for tuppence.

"Your wife will be pleased with all these gifts you're buying her," I remarked as we climbed into another hackney.

"Oh, aye. I like to surprise her now and again. She deserves it, the old girl, for putting up with me."

I rested the statuette on the seat beside me, the two striking nudes incongruous against the battered leather seat of the hackney. Brewster gave them a critical eye.

"His Highness likes to look at a bit of flesh, don't he?"

Considering the number of nude figures and paintings I'd seen both in Carlton House and on the list Higgs had showed us, I had to agree. The prince's appetites for ladies was well known—he rarely had been without a mistress since he'd come of age, and likely he'd had them before that.

"Not what I'd want in my front room," Brewster said decidedly. "This will be more to my Em's taste."

I leaned forward to peer at the bowl he turned around in his fingers. "May I look?"

Brewster gave me a sudden grin and handed it over. The bowl was small, shallow, and well formed, if covered with grime. I rubbed at the dirt encrusting its rim until a translucent glow of porcelain greeted me. Rubbing a little more showed me the green tail of a stylized dragon.

"Brewster," I said half in admiration, half in exasperation.

Brewster had a knowing sparkle in his eyes. With the expertise of a man who'd learned the worth of everything he touched, he'd found what was likely the most valuable object kicking about the *marché ouvert*.

"Tuppence, you paid for this?" I said, turning it around in my hands.

"Aye." Brewster reached for the bowl, and I reluctantly gave it back.

I'd seen a bowl very like this one in a collection of the Duke of Devonshire when I'd viewed a display of ancient Chinese porcelain at Chatsworth with Grenville. I wasn't certain what period the bowl Brewster held came from, but I knew it was old. I hoped this was *not* one of those I'd seen in the duke's house.

Even if so, it belonged to Brewster now under the odd laws of the *marché ouvert*. I reconciled my conscience with the thought that the bowl had likely been stolen from China itself, probably long ago.

Likewise, I was the proud possessor of a piece of silk and a painted-over bronze from the sixteenth century. I would take it to Mr. Higgs to confirm it was the prince's, but I was certain it would be.

The most interesting thing about me finding the Theseus and Antiope statue is that it hadn't been listed as missing. I'd seen it yesterday evening, sitting on a table in the prince's library. So how had it journeyed from there to the *marché ouvert* in the few hours since I'd seen it last?

When I returned home, Donata was still abed. It was her habit not to rise until noon and sometimes later. I was tired yet my body knew it was meant to be awake at this hour and it had no desire to sleep.

I instead deposited my statue in my dressing room and left for

Hyde Park to ride, exercising the excellent horse Donata kept for my use. He was a hunter of about sixteen hands, a large gelding, quite powerful. I had missed any hunting this autumn by running off to Egypt, but I looked forward to taking him out across country in Oxfordshire.

It was so early that I was the only gentleman riding, almost the only person on the Row at all. I found it refreshing.

I rode back to the mews and dismounted, taking my walking stick from the groom and giving the horse a pat. He was a good animal.

I had persuaded Brewster to go home, telling him I would be returning to bed, but that had been before I'd decided to ride instead. He'd be incensed that I'd gone to the park alone, but I would point out that even he had to sleep sometime. Besides, riding through Hyde Park was not as dangerous as strolling through St. Giles—usually.

Barnstable looked sour when I clattered back into the house, removing my muddy boots for the shoes Bartholomew always made certain were waiting when I finished riding.

"He's here again, sir," Barnstable said, his face so stiff I thought it might crack.

"Who is?" I planted my heel in the boot jack and dragged the boot from my leg.

"The Runner, sir. I tried to tell him you were out, but he insisted on waiting. He's in the reception room. Sir."

CHAPTER 12

"**B**LOODY HELL." I DID NOT care if Spendlove heard my words. "Thank you, Barnstable. Make certain her ladyship does *not* come down until he's gone."

"Of course, sir." Barnstable looked surprised I thought I had to tell him this.

Growling to myself, I shoved my feet into the sturdy shoes I liked to wear inside the house. Bartholomew was always trying to persuade me into a pair of pumps, low-cut slippers for indoor wear, but I told him that with my large feet and hard legs I'd look a damned fool in them.

Spendlove wore a pair of thick-soled boots that he'd thrust toward the grate in the reception room, as he lounged back in one of the gilded, leopard print chairs. He unfolded to his feet as I tramped in, the big man dwarfing the room.

"Well, Captain," he boomed. "What have you found out? You went to Carlton House and tore about London all night, did you not? Can you prove Mr. Floyd guilty?"

"By no means," I said, my jaw tight. "I have had hardly any time to pursue the matter."

"You must have learned *something*," Spendlove returned impatiently. "You're an inquisitive gent, Captain. What have people told you? How did he spirit the things out, what did he take, and how—?"

"What I did learn of interest," I said, cutting through his words, "was that small pieces in the prince's collection are trans-

porting themselves about the house. What is meant to be in one room ends up in another and no one knows how or why."

Spendlove waved a large, black-gloved hand. "Servants. So many things about they can't remember where it all should be. I'm not concerned with things that *haven't* been nicked."

"You ought to be. There is something odd going on here. I can tell you that I did find a piece that might be the prince's on a market stall in Southwark."

"Ah, so that's where you went. Well, give it to me, Captain. I need evidence."

Without hurry, I went to the door and instructed the disapproving Barnstable, when he came to me, to bring the statuette from my dressing room.

"While we wait," I said after Barnstable had bowed and closed the door. "Tell me, do you know anything of the Duke of Dunmarron?"

Spendlove's brows rose. "Dunmarron? Why?"

"I met him last night at the theatre," I extemporized. "I take it he rarely comes to town. I wondered, that is all. Runners hear so much."

"True." Spendlove shrugged with false modesty. "From all accounts, his dad were a fine gentleman, but the son—the man what's duke now—was a bad 'un in his youth. Did daft things like stand on the streets with his friends and turn up ladies' skirts with his walking stick, trap watchmen in their boxes, that sort of thing. He also beat one of his servants near to death and wasn't above a spot of blackmail. Couldn't touch him, him being son of a peer. His da' always got him off. He ran with another bloke, name of Peterson, bad lot, the devil who tempted him into sin. Then Peterson died—broke his neck falling off a horse—and Dunmarron married, inherited a year later when his da' finally fell off the twig, and has been quiet since. Lives to ride hunters and revel in dross he buys and nothing more." Spendlove bent me a wise look. "You want to know because Mr. Grenville's ladybird ran off to him. It was in the newspaper this morning, a rag Pomeroy reads."

"Yes, unfortunately," I said. "I was trying to discover why, is all."

Spendlove gave me a sharp look. "If I find Dunmarron dead, a bullet through his heart, I'll know where to start looking for his murderer. Tell Mr. Grenville to keep his head, will you?"

"Thank you for the warning," I said without changing expression. "And the information."

"I give it to you to show you I am not ungenerous. But I expect information in return. Soon."

The door opened for the arrival of the statuette, borne by Bartholomew instead of Barnstable, large hands to carry the heavy bronze. Bartholomew set it on an octagonal table in the middle of the room and departed. I noted that the latch on the door did not click all the way closed.

Spendlove flicked his finger over the peeling white paint. "You sure this is one of the prince's?"

"Not entirely. He has one very like it, in his library. At least it was there last night. If a thief managed to get it out of Carlton House, slap a coat of paint on it, and take it down to Southwark to be sold to me at five this morning, then that should indicate Mr. Floyd had nothing to do with it."

"Unless he has an accomplice," Spendlove said at once. "And yes, a thief can work that quickly. Them markets are notorious for getting goods out in a flash." He closed his hand around Theseus's head. "Thank you, Captain. I'll let you know if it does any good. But I want more."

I grasped the statuette by Antiope and the base. "I believe this is my property now," I said. "By the right of the *marché ouvert*."

Spendlove didn't move. "It's evidence for a trial."

"That remains to be seen. I might be mistaken that this is from Carlton House. In any case, it belongs to me, no matter what its provenance. I paid ten shillings for it."

Spendlove scowled at me, his anger mounting. "You walk a thin line with me, Captain. You don't want your little daughter growing up knowing her dad was hanged for conspiracy in heinous crimes, do you?"

"I have not said I refused to find evidence for you," I said. "I will continue to look for the answer to this puzzle if only to help Mr. Floyd. But we don't know if this bronze is the prince's or not. I will take it to his curator, Mr. Higgs, and ask him. If it was stolen last night, then we will advance in our investigation."

Spendlove released the statue but gave me a scowl. "A fair point, Captain. Tell you what—you keep this indecent piece of art and take it to Mr. Higgs. In fact, I'll come with you. Save you the trouble of journeying all the way to Bow Street to report to me later."

Barnstable insisted that I return to Carlton House in Donata's coach with the Breckenridge arms on the door and hinted that Spendlove should sit with the coachman. I overruled him and motioned for Spendlove to ride inside with me.

Bartholomew, on the other hand, climbed to the box after he'd assisted me in, not about to let me journey through London alone with Spendlove. Bartholomew had deposited the statue, wrapped in paper, on the seat by my side, and I rested my hand on it as we rode.

Spendlove said nothing about the sumptuous carriage with its well-cushioned seats and marquetry walls, velvet curtains to shut out the cold and prying eyes. He sat quietly, his large feet planted opposite mine as we rolled to St. James's and Carlton House.

I had no appointment, and the doorman at Carlton House did not want to let me in. He did not want to admit Spendlove either, even when that man descended from the coach and demanded entrance.

"I will inquire, sir," the footman said. He was a different man from the one on the door last evening, but he wore similar knee breeches and blue coat, his hair covered with a powdered wig. "Please have your coachman drive you 'round to the side."

The tradesman's entrance. I wanted to laugh. Spendlove scowled at the footman. "The door's right there." He jabbed his finger at the wide entrance beyond the columns. "Just move, lad."

"I will *inquire*, sir," the footman said with stubborn rigidity. Spendlove stepped forward, but the footman moved to block his way.

A footman to a member of the royal family clearly outranked a Bow Street Runner. However, Spendlove was not above arresting anyone who got in his way, and this young man would not do well in the common room at Newgate in his wig and satin breeches.

I planted my walking stick with a loud thump. "We are here to see Mr. Higgs," I said to the footman. "No need to trouble His Highness. We are happy to wait in the coach."

The footman turned a relieved look upon me. At least *I* knew how to behave, that look said.

"We found one of his bloody statues," Spendlove growled. "Fetch Higgs. Now."

The footman's expression did not change. He gave me a bow and Spendlove a frigid look, and walked into the house, leaving us under the grim guard of several larger footmen.

We waited. The footman was a long time in returning, then even longer. A half hour passed. Forty-five minutes. I had returned to the carriage and its tin box of coal to get warm, though Spendlove remained pacing outside. The coachman, Hagen, descended to see that the horses were all right. I saw him through the window as he moved about, warming himself with nips from a flask.

Just as Spendlove threatened to push past the burly men at the door and shove his way inside, another footman came out to us. He headed straight for Spendlove, agitation on his face.

I couldn't hear what the footman babbled at him, as the coach windows were shut. I did catch the phrase *sent for you at once, sir,* and a moment later, Bartholomew was flinging open the carriage door.

I had been reaching for the handle at the same time, and it burned my fingers as Bartholomew wrenched the door open. Bartholomew helped me down so hastily I lost my balance and had to clutch at him.

"What the devil happened?" I demanded.

"Mr. Higgs has been hurt, sir," Bartholomew said rapidly. "That's what the footman says anyway. He'd been sent to fetch Mr. Spendlove."

Bartholomew took a few quick steps to the house then turned back as though waiting for me to approve. I motioned him on with my stick.

"See what you can. I will be right behind you."

Hagen watched sharply as I took the statue from the seat, tucked it under my arm, and hobbled along in Bartholomew's wake. I was glad now that Barnstable had insisted Hagen drive us—he would fetch help if it was needed.

The ostentatious interior of Carlton House swallowed me into itself as I entered. Its light and decor guided me through the house to the vestibule and staircase.

This time I did not descend the stairs but followed the sounds of voices to an anteroom in the rear of the house. The anteroom's windows overlooked the park and gardens, pleasant on this sunny day. I turned to my left, continuing through another room with an oriental design—green wallpaper covered with bamboo-like plants, cabinets of black lacquer, and chinoiserie vases perched on top of the cabinets.

The room beyond this was decorated in rich blue, the color most evident in the massive velvet draperies at the long windows and the silk of the divans. Gilded molding marched around the top of the room, framing paintings within it, the entire frieze enclosing a broad ceiling with a painted sky.

A gigantic chandelier hung from the exact center of the ceiling, glittering with what must be a thousand and more crystals that caught the midmorning sunshine. A large painting on the wall depicted a man and woman in the dress of the Low Countries two centuries past—the white ruffs around their necks a stark contrast to their black clothes. The man was glancing up from a paper on which was a drawing that looked like a ship's hull, his pen in hand, while the woman bent to him with another paper.

I noted every detail of the room in abstraction, as though I stood inside a painting myself, every facet etched upon my mind. Spendlove, Bartholomew, and the palace footmen were grouped below the painting. At a desk in the middle of the floor was Mr. Higgs, who sat in a gilded Bergere chair with a rounded back and silk upholstery. Higgs had fallen forward to the desktop, which now bore a large stain of blackish-red—blood and ink. The substance had dried, its spread arrested, though the ink in the middle of it still glistened.

Higgs was dead, his body unmoving, the hands that were clenched on the desktop gray. He was facedown, his pomaded black hair unmoving. On the desk, next to his hand, was an elegant equestrian bronze statuette with a match of the black stain coating the hindquarters of the horse and its unfortunate rider.

CHAPTER 13

"DON'T TOUCH HIM, CAPTAIN," SPENDLOVE commanded.

I had no intention of doing so. Not answering, I set the paper-wrapped statue on a table and moved to the desk and Higgs.

The poor man had a large dent in the back of his neck, courtesy of the bronze next to him, but there was nothing else on the desk. Not a scrap of paper to show he'd been writing or reading, not a pen, no bottle of ink to account for the puddle of it amidst the blood, no books. Nothing. He'd simply sat down and was killed.

His fists were clenched so hard his nails had driven themselves into his skin. A tiny bit of blood had leaked to the desk and also dried.

"He's cold," Spendlove said, his words abrupt.

"It is a cold room," I remarked. No fire had been lit, the chamber obviously not intended for use today.

"Means he was bashed on the head some hours ago." Spendlove focused a sharp eye on me. "Where did *you* get to this morning? I had to wait for you to return."

"Riding," I answered, impatient. "I always ride early in the day."

"Anyone see you?"

I thought of how empty Hyde Park had been, stretches of wilted grass under cold winter sky. "No," I said. "I was quite alone."

"You sound proud of it."

"Look here," Bartholomew broke in, indignant. "You can't accuse the captain of killing this man. He never did. Why should he?"

Spendlove shrugged. "I never worry about why, lad. I only know the who and the how. *Why* don't come into it. You were out most of the night, Captain, weren't you? I lost track of you—or my patrollers did. When I arrived at your house this morning, your butler says you came in very late and left again very early. He told me, because he was explaining why he didn't want you disturbed. He didn't know he was helping me keep track of you." He sounded smug.

"I told you where I'd been," I said without heat. "South of the river looking for stolen property. I'm used to rising early, no matter how late I retire, so upon my return I was fully awake and went riding. As usual. Instead of interrogating me, perhaps you should roam the house making certain nothing else is missing. Mr. Higgs was the curator for the collection."

"You're quick to speak of him in the past tense, Captain," Spendlove said, his blue eyes hard.

"The poor man is dead," I said, though I was numb. I'd liked Higgs, found his cluttered office interesting and oddly cozy. I'd observed that he'd been quite organized in spite of the seeming disorder.

Why the devil should someone wish to kill him? Answer, because with all his lists and knowledge of the collection, he must have discovered who had been making the thefts. Perhaps he'd come into this room to confront the thief, or perhaps he'd been checking the whereabouts of an object and surprised the thief in question. For whatever reason, that person had murdered him.

"Coshed." Spendlove rocked on his heels. "Nasty."

"No." I pointed to the wound on the back of Higgs's head. "This did not bleed much, and there is little bruising. I believe he was hit after he was dead. This, on the other hand ..." I moved my finger to indicate his clenched fists. "He did this as he died."

I put my hands on Higgs's shoulders. I did not like handling him, as I had done this far too often before—turning over comrades and friends on the battlefield to see whether they were beyond help. I'd looked into the lifeless faces of men I'd drunk with the night before too many times to want to see another.

But we needed to know as much as we could if we were to find who had done this terrible deed. I eased Higgs back into his chair and immediately saw why his fists had been clenched.

The man's face was black with death, his eyes wide, his tongue protruding. Around his neck was a deep line, dark red with blood. The puddle had come from that wound, from the veins that had been severed.

"He's been garroted," I said in a grim voice.

Spendlove was next to me in an instant, bringing with him his scents of sweat, smoke, and stale breath. "Bugger me," he said in a near whisper.

The footman who'd brought us in turned away, retching. Bartholomew stared, his mouth open.

Spendlove recovered quickly and snapped his fingers. *"You,"* he said to Bartholomew. "Run to Bow Street. I need patrollers here. *You*—" This to the footman. "I want anyone working in this house rounded up and brought upstairs. Put them in the next room and do not let them leave. Where is His Royal Highness?"

"Not here," the footman answered in a wheezing breath. "He was at the house of a friend late and stayed there."

I suspected he was with Lady Hertford, whether at her own house or in a secret love nest, I could not know, but I wondered. The Regent was reputed to have a temper, and his brother, the Duke of Cumberland, was widely thought to have murdered his valet one night about ten years ago. The valet's throat had been cut, and Higgs had been strangled—not quite the same, but close. And why had the murderer then struck Higgs over the head?

Bartholomew, at a nod from me, made to depart, but the footman stood his ground. He was a sturdy young man, perhaps twenty-five years in age, tall, handsome of face, and stubborn.

"You'll not be bringing in the patrollers," he said. "The journalists can't get wind of this." He sent me a look of appeal, his dark eyes wide. "You see how it is, sir."

Spendlove scowled at him. "What I see is a dead man that someone in this house killed, maybe the captain standing right next to me, maybe even your master. I need to put my hands on someone I can bring up before the magistrate. Want it to be you?"

The footman continued to address me. "We can't have the journalists, sir."

"It will get out sooner or later," I answered, keeping my voice gentle. "You know that. Who is in charge of the household?"

The footman gulped but looked relieved he could pass the problem higher. "The majordomo, sir. I'll fetch him." He ran off before Spendlove could stop him.

"Shall I go, sir?" Bartholomew, who'd paused at the door, asked me.

"Yes," I said heavily. "This is a murder. Have Hagen drive you and bring the patrollers back with you. Keep the location secret until they get here. The journalists can wait."

"Yes, sir." Bartholomew was gone in a flash, looking happy to have something to do.

Spendlove eyed me in annoyance, but he didn't try to countermand my orders. He bent over Higgs, running a careful gaze over his hands, his throat, and the statue used to bash him on the back of the head. I realized, as I glanced at the statuette, that it was a bronze of Louis XIV of France on horseback.

"He didn't fight," Spendlove declared.

I looked at Higgs again, not liking to. He'd been a modest, efficient man, and as I said, I'd liked him.

My ire at his killer stirred through my numbness. Higgs had not deserved this.

"No bruising on his hands," I said, following Spendlove's reasoning. "No ripped nails, no sign he struggled for his life."

"Someone walked right up behind him and ..." Spendlove waved his hand to indicate the rest. "Either they were very, very quiet, or he knew the man and didn't fear him."

"That man was *not* me," I said emphatically. "I had every reason to want Mr. Higgs alive—he was helping me find out who was stealing things from the Regent, helping me fulfill your commission. I needed him, and I thought well of him. Unless you believe I ran mad, gained entry to the palace last night, lured Mr. Higgs to this room, and strangled him with a garrote."

As I rambled, I wondered again why he'd come to this room at all. Had he found something odd here? The desk was bare as I'd observed, no books or papers in sight. Then where had the ink come from?

Higgs might have been making notes in one of his ledgers and discovered something that had uncovered the thefts. The killer could have been with him, realized he'd been unmasked, killed Higgs, and taken away the ledger, pen and ink bottle. Higgs no doubt had knocked over the bottle in his struggle. The killer would not have been able to clean up the spill or the blood without getting either on himself. There would have been plenty of time for the killer to take the things away and be halfway to Dover by now.

Spendlove studied me in irritation. "I know you visited your Mr. Denis sometime in the night. Yes, I keep a careful eye on him and know who comes and goes at his house. Maybe *you* had no reason to kill this man, but perhaps Mr. Denis did. He tells you to do it, and you obey."

"I am not a hired killer," I said impatiently. Denis had those at his disposal, but I did not mention that fact. "Mr. Denis summoned me to ask me to cease investigating the thefts. I told him to go to the devil. If he'd instructed me to kill a man for him, I would refuse, no matter how much he threatened me. He'd have to choose a better man for the task anyway." I tapped my injured knee with my walking stick. "I'm hardly fit to run about murdering people."

"You're an army man," Spendlove pointed out. "Do not tell

me you are not used to killing."

I clenched the stick. "Fighting for my life on a battlefield and strangling a man as he sits at a desk are two different things. I'd only ever face a man honorably—if I wanted to kill someone, I'd give him an even chance."

"Such as fighting duels in Hyde Park of a March morning?" Spendlove grunted. "You're lucky Lord Stubbins recovered from his wound."

I said nothing. Last year, I'd potted a man called Stubby Stubbins, the son of a marquess, for beating a game girl. The man was disgusting and had deserved every bit of fear I'd seen in his eyes over the barrel of my pistol. But I'd given him a fighting chance, and Stubbins had survived. He'd made himself scarce from London and had not tried to prosecute me for wounding him.

However, I was not foolish enough to acknowledge to Spendlove even now that I'd been involved in a very illegal duel. I did not trust what he'd do with such an admission.

"I give you my word I did Mr. Higgs no harm," I said. "Why would I let you come here with me if I had? I needed his expertise to tell me if the statuette I recovered indeed belonged to His Highness."

Spendlove only gave me another grunt.

I moved to the statuette and peeled away the paper. A few bits of paint had flaked off, revealing the bronze beneath. I was fairly sure the statue was the same but I needed to be certain.

I picked it up, wrapped it in the paper again, and strode the length of the large room for the door.

Naturally, Spendlove followed. "Where are you taking that?"

"To see if my ten shillings were wasted."

Spendlove could move faster than I and he reached the door before me. He did not try to stop me, however, but led the way out.

I hobbled with some difficulty through the japanned room and the anteroom to the stairs, hampered both by my walking stick and the statuette. Spendlove made no offer to carry the bronze for me, though I'd refuse if he did.

The footman must have roused the house, or his frantic mood had alerted the other servants, because they had emerged from the woodwork and were now rushing about trying to understand what was happening.

I saw distress on all faces, murmurs of, "Mr. Higgs? Is he really dead? Lord love him, sir."

Spendlove stood aside as we reached the grand staircase, he clearly unsure where I was going. I went down, with no one attempting to stop us, and at the bottom, made my way through to the library. Spendlove followed in silence, his tread heavy.

Light from the long windows spilled into the library, glittering on the gilding, dancing on the facets of the crystal chandelier and wall sconces. This chamber and the others along the floor were rooms made to catch the light and play with it, sending it back over the inhabitants for their delight.

The library, with its soaring ceiling and bookcases awaited us in silence. So did the bronze of Theseus and Antiope, sitting proudly on the table where I'd seen it last.

I shoved the clock next to it aside, plunked my statuette down on the table, and stripped off the paper.

The statues were identical. Except for the white paint, hastily applied, the size, poses, and artistry were the same.

"Bloody hell," Spendlove said. "Which is the real one?"

"I have no idea." They looked exactly alike to me. "I am no expert. I know a man who is, though. His opinion could possibly tell us what the devil has happened here."

"Yes." Spendlove gave me a hard nod. "Have him fetched at once."

"Grenville?" I asked, surprised he'd agreed so easily.

The smile Spendlove gave me was unfriendly. "No, Captain. Mr. Denis."

I argued but to no avail. Spendlove stood firm.

He said, "If Mr. Denis didn't have a copy of this statue made himself, he'll know who did. I know he is the man behind these thefts—everything about it speaks of him. I want him standing here to explain himself."

"He will never come." Denis wasn't such a fool as to rush to Carlton House and calmly explain that he'd stolen a statue and had it copied. "In any case, why go to the trouble to steal an expensive piece of artwork and then let me purchase it for ten shillings at a market?"

Spendlove's eyes glittered as much as the sun-dappled chandelier. "No doubt he sent you to retrieve it for him—you'd be the owner fair and square—and hand it over to him." He gestured in imitation. "Get him here, Captain. You are persuasive. He listens to you."

"As I have said, I told him to go to the devil."

Spendlove didn't look worried. "You will find your neck in a noose for this murder fast enough if you do not assist. You know I can make it happen, and what the shame will do to your lady wife. I'd wager she'd abandon you in a trice if it meant keeping disgrace from her son."

Meaning if I were to be condemned, Donata would do everything in her power and her father's power to distance herself from me, perhaps even attempt to have our marriage annulled. After all, my first wife was still alive and our divorce had been kept very quiet. Donata's wily solicitors could concoct something to free her from me, whether strictly legal or not.

I also knew Spendlove would hound her, perhaps making things difficult for Peter and my daughter—both my daughters—as well. Though I knew Donata was capable of fighting back, Spendlove could make Donata's existence hell if he chose.

This was not the life I wanted for her or for Anne. I did not want Donata to constantly have to defend herself against Spendlove's attacks because I'd decided to defy him.

Denis had threatened Marcus if I continued my investigation. Spendlove threatened Donata and my young family if I didn't.

My decision, I was sorry to say, came easily. I would throw Marcus to the wolves. He was my kin—I firmly believed that—and I felt responsibility for him, plus I'd been growing to like

him. But he would have to stand on his own. I would be cour-
teous enough to send him a warning, but I would do what
Spendlove wanted and disobey Denis's wishes.

"Very well," I said tightly. "I'll need a hackney."

Carlton House's staff was at such sixes and sevens none could
run to fetch a hackney for me. Indeed, they seemed to completely ignore my presence and Spendlove's to deal with this
crisis in their midst.

I strolled out of the house and beyond the columned screen to
the street, the statuette once again wrapped and under my arm.
I had no intention of leaving it with Spendlove, who would
probably pinch it in the name of evidence.

I'd paid over my own money for the bronze, not Donata's,
using the few coins I allowed myself from my half-pay packet.
This statuette was mine until I decided otherwise. Nor would
I tamely turn it over to Denis as Spendlove implied. I'd keep it
and put it up in the library to mull over on a rainy afternoon.

I walked the length of Pall Mall but found no coaches to hire—
St. James's was full of vehicles by this hour, but no hackneys
awaited. I set off walking up St. James's Street. With determination, despite my protesting knee, I could make my way to
Piccadilly and then north to Curzon Street. I'd be exhausted by
the time I reached Denis's house, but so be it.

A plain black coach pulled alongside me as I walked past the
narrow opening to the lane called St. James's Place. A man leapt
out and seized me by the arm. Without worry, I thrust the statuette into his hands.

"I'm too weary to carry that any longer," I said. "How did you
know I needed a hackney?"

Brewster glowered at me over the paper-wrapped Theseus.
"Your butler peached," he rumbled. "Said you ran off with the
Robin to the prince's house. Should have waited for me."

"He gave me no choice. As I have no choice now. We're off to
beard the lion in his den—that is, call upon Mr. Denis when he
is not expecting us."

Brewster's brows lowered further. "You, guv, are like a compass for danger."

"I agree with you." I reached for the door of the hackney. "Higgs is dead."

The way Brewster's eyes widened in pure astonishment told me he knew nothing about it. He kept quiet, though, until he'd laid the statuette on the hackney's seat and boosted me inside.

"Did the prince kill him?" Brewster asked from the seat opposite me as the hackney started. "His brother murdered his valet they say. *And* His Royal Highness is taking his wife to court to try and rid himself of her. Fine lot they are. A shame to their dad."

"I don't believe the Regent killed him," I said, though I'd reserve judgment. Who knew what sort of relationship the prince had had with his curator?

"Who did, then?" Brewster asked.

"Who indeed?" I replied, annoyed I could not answer.

We soon arrived at Denis's house in Curzon Street. I descended, as did Brewster, who was determined not to let me walk inside alone.

I often wondered whether, if I turned up unexpectedly at Denis's home, I could catch him doing something astoundingly human, such as just rising from a bath, his hair a wet mess, or wiping a runny nose, or slipping back inside from the privy.

I was to be disappointed today, because when the doorman admitted us, Denis was walking down the stairs, fully dressed in suit, greatcoat, and hat, pulling on his gloves—on his way out.

Denis halted in the middle of the last flight and cast a cold look over myself and Brewster. I saw his eyes stray to my open greatcoat and my hands, as though he looked for a sign of a weapon.

The place he'd stopped had been well chosen. If I'd brought a knife or intended to use the sword in my cane, he'd have plenty of space and men between us. I'd never reach him before I was stopped. If I pulled out a pistol, he could dash back up the stairs while his men knocked the gun from my hand and me to the ground.

As Denis continued to stare at me coldly, I announced, "I need you to come with me to Carlton House."

I enjoyed the flicker of surprise in his eyes before he answered in his cool tones.

"I have an appointment. An important one."

He might be leaving to intimidate one of the magistrates he had in his power, or he might be off to view antiquities at the British Museum. Anything Denis did was equally important to him.

"Let me tell you why, and then you can decide," I said. "I need to know whether this is real or not. And the same for its twin."

Brewster, cued, tore the paper from the bronze and set it on a table in the hall. Denis leaned over the balustrade to peer at it.

I saw when his interest was caught. Denis's expression did not change but what was in his eyes changed from annoyance to attentiveness.

He slowly descended the stairs, his two bodyguards flanking him so that neither I nor Brewster could come too close. Denis removed his hat as he approached the statue on the table, handed the hat to one of his lackeys, and ran his gaze over the statue.

He bent to study it carefully, and then rubbed his finger over a bit of paint. "Hmm," he said, his brows drawing together.

"What does that mean?" I asked in irritation.

Denis straightened, brushed a fleck of paint off his glove, and reached for the hat his lackey handed him. "It means I will not know until I look at the other one. Shall we go, Captain?"

CHAPTER 14

IWAS SURPRISED SPENDLOVE WOULD LET James Denis anywhere near a treasure trove like Carlton House, but Spendlove looked satisfied when Denis stepped out of his carriage at the front steps.

Brewster and I had ridden in the hackney whose driver had been persuaded to wait—Denis had not asked us to join him in his own coach, and neither Brewster nor I wanted to insist. I'd ridden in Denis's carriage before, and though it was luxurious, being confined in its splendor with him was not always comfortable.

As I descended, I saw that Spendlove's patrollers had arrived, driven by Hagen, who apparently had insisted they ride on the outside. There were three men, two young and strong of limb, rather like Bartholomew, and a hard-faced, middle-aged man who looked like an army sergeant and probably had been one in the recent wars.

The sergeant scowled fiercely when Denis emerged from his carriage, carefully timed so that his guards would already be on the ground before he descended. The tails of Denis's greatcoat swept around him as wind blew down the tunnel made by the house and columned screen, and he walked past the sergeant without so much as glancing at him.

I fell into step with Denis, and Brewster came along close beside me.

We went up the steps into the house. Denis walked on through the vestibules and anterooms without pausing, as though he'd been here before and was not impressed with their opulence. I could imagine Denis striding through the Louvre without turning his head to admire the splendid paintings Napoleon had looted from the far corners of the world, at the same time calculating their exact worth and how he could obtain them.

We went down the staircase and through to the library, me striding along and pretending my knee didn't hurt like hell. Spendlove brought up the rear with his patrollers. If Denis was unnerved by having the law of Bow Street behind him, he made no sign.

It was now past noon, and the day was as bright as it ever would be. Bands of sunlight made warm patterns on the carpet and shone on the library's gilded walls.

Denis made his way to the table I indicated. Brewster stripped the paper from my statue and set the two side by side.

Denis dipped his hand into his pocket and brought out a knife. Immediately Spendlove and the sergeant started forward, but Denis only showed us that it was a short-bladed thing with a mother-of-pearl handle, something that might be used to open letters.

He touched the blade to the statue and delicately scraped white paint from Theseus's shoulder. A beautiful bronze sheen came through.

Denis stood back to study my statue then touched his gloved hand to the one next to it. He turned that statue the slightest bit so that it aligned perfectly with the painted one and leaned down to study them both.

I saw his interest pique. Like Grenville, Denis was a connoisseur of art, acquiring pieces for his private collection not so much because of their price as for their beauty. Unlike Grenville, however, Denis procured his artwork by any means possible and often obtained it for others, again by methods that I did not want to examine too closely.

Denis had once justified his means to me by stating that all artwork was stolen, often from the original artist who was promised payment but never received it. Monarchs, aristocrats, and military men went through the world taking what they wanted, never compensating anyone for it. Denis claimed that he at least made sure the things were appreciated for their own sakes.

I had not argued with him. Denis's idea of right and mine were different and always would be, but I could sometimes see his point.

Denis slid his knife back into his pocket and circled the table, his quick eyes taking in every facet of each statue. He completed the circuit and returned to stand in front of the bronzes, his hands now at his sides.

When he turned to look at me, I tensed, as I noticed did Spendlove. All eyes were on Denis, awaiting his pronouncement.

"It is interesting," he said. He gazed down at the clock with the gilded sphinxes guarding the clock face. "As is this."

"Why?" I asked sharply, my patience never the best. "Which bronze is the real one?"

Denis faced me again. He looked solely at me, not Spendlove, or the sergeant or his patrollers, as though only he and I stood in the room.

"Neither of them, Captain," he said, his voice clear. "They are both copies."

As I stared at him, stunned, Denis moved his gloved hand to the clock. "As is this," he said.

"Bloody hell," I managed.

"What?" Spendlove asked abruptly. "What are you talking about? These things weren't even nicked."

"No," I said slowly, beginning to understand. "They *were* stolen, and copies returned. That is why they were in the wrong places. Whoever was sent to replace them didn't know their exact location and assumed anywhere was fine. Or the pieces were put into the wrong rooms to make it look as though they'd been mislaid by careless staff, if anyone had worried when they'd gone missing."

"Then where are the real ones?" Spendlove demanded, as close to panic as I'd ever seen him.

Denis answered. "Likely with new owners, probably on the Continent." He returned his focus to the items on the table. "Exquisitely done. A master talent made these."

"A master *forging* talent," Spendlove snapped. "And why two copies? Ain't one enough?"

Denis lifted his shoulders in a shrug. "Perhaps the copier wanted to make a few bob on the side. Perhaps he decided to tell two different people they'd purchased the original, and so double his profits."

"Why stop at two?" I put in. "The forger might have made three, or four."

Spendlove glared at the statues. "Bloody cheek."

"A miscalculation," Denis said. He gave me a nod. "I have an appointment. Good day, gentlemen."

"You are not leaving yet." Spendlove's color was high. "Come upstairs with me."

Denis's eyes flashed a deep anger, which he quickly masked. He made no move to obey or disobey, only gave Spendlove his cold look.

Spendlove, as though there was no question, stormed from the room, heading for the stairs. I followed, saying nothing, giving Denis no indication as to my own feelings on Spendlove's orders. After a moment, I heard the heavy footfalls of Denis's men on the carpet behind me, and the lighter steps of Denis himself.

We went up to the rooms above us, making for the Blue Velvet Room. Higgs's body had been removed from it while I'd been gone—where Spendlove had put it, I could not know. I hoped Higgs's family, if he had one, had been told. The blood was still there with the ink, the stain now black and dry. Denis glanced at it in some disapproval.

Spendlove waved his arm to indicate the room. "Are these copies? Is that?" He pointed to the smaller statue that had struck Higgs, still reposing on the desk. "That?" His finger went to the large painting on the wall.

Denis bent to study the equestrian statue, King Louis of old upright and proud on the steed's back. "No," Denis said. "See how the bronze has darkened with time, the glint of it almost red?" His hand hovered just above the statue's surface. "The Theseus statues gleam gold, a new casting. *That* is also real." He jabbed his forefinger at the painting of the man and wife in black, with ruffs about their necks. "A Rembrandt van Rijn. Far too large for a man to carry off and have copied—even the dullest servant would note its absence."

Denis gave the painting an almost fond look before turning away. "And now I am quite late." He bowed in his detached manner. "Good afternoon." Without waiting for Spendlove to try to stop him, he turned and walked to the open door, again paying his opulent surroundings no heed.

Before he departed, Denis turned aside to Brewster, who had remained near the doorway. They exchanged a few sentences, speaking too quietly for me to hear, then Denis turned and glided out. I watched his slim back in his elegant tailcoat move through the anterooms and then turn and disappear into the vestibule.

Spendlove watched him too, his stance rigid. I knew the man would like nothing better than to arrest Denis for something—anything—just to get him before a magistrate and then shut into Newgate. He'd find it difficult to keep him there, however. Denis had too many gentlemen among the magistrates and law courts cowed.

I lifted my statue again, wrapped in its paper. Was I a little more careless knowing it was *not* four hundred years old?

"You can leave that, Captain," Spendlove said in a churlish tone.

"Why?" I tucked the statue under my arm, the paper crackling, its weight now familiar. "It's a worthless copy—or at least it is worth ten shillings."

I had nothing more to say to him, so I made for the door. Donata would be waking now, and I wanted to return home and impart to her all that had happened.

Truth to tell, I wanted to go home and hold on to her until I no longer saw poor Higgs slumped over the desk or the terrible look death had imprinted on his face.

Spendlove followed me but his next demand was to Brewster. "What did he say to you? Your master? As he went?"

Brewster gave Spendlove his best bland stare. "I don't work for his nibs no more, guv. He was giving his best to me wife. Being polite."

Lies came easily to Brewster—he could swear the sun was dark all the while it shone brightly, and look innocent as a babe while saying it.

Spendlove growled. "If you killed this man, Captain, I'll have you. You too, Mr. Brewster."

Brewster held out his very broad hands. "I might be a villain, guv, but I ain't a killer. Neither is the captain."

Spendlove's eyes glinted. "Ah, you were with the captain while this man died? Wandering about London and then riding in the park, was it? You can vouch for him?"

"Of course." Brewster's gaze didn't waver. "We looked for the stolen things, he went home to bed with his wife, we went to Southwark and bought our statue this morning, then the captain went riding and I went to bed with *me* wife. Ask Mr. Denis. He always has a man watching the captain, even if it ain't me now."

Spendlove listened, skepticism in every line of his body. He gave me a knowing stare. "Be where I can find you, Captain," he said, then he turned away, bellowing to his sergeant.

Brewster was quiet as we made our way through the house and out into the afternoon. The air was crisp but the sun felt good on my face, and I was glad to be outside. The Regent's house was beautiful, but there was too much of it. The soaring, glittering grandeur pressed too much on my senses.

The hackney was still waiting—the driver probably decided he could get a heftier tip from a gent who walked straight into Carlton House than from a casual fare on the road.

I sank wearily to the hackney's hard seat, facing Brewster who had climbed in with me. But I was not to rest for long, it seemed.

"His nibs has a message for ye," Brewster said.

"Indeed." I closed my eyes, trying to ignore him. My long

night and short sleep had begun to take its toll. I needed to go home and let Barnstable fuss over me. Donata never fussed—she came straight to the point.

"It's that surgeon." Brewster sounded uneasy. "He wants a word with ye. I didn't like to say in front of Mr. Spendlove."

I abruptly opened my eyes. "The surgeon? Why?"

"If he told Mr. Denis why, Mr. Denis did not tell me. His nibs only said the surgeon wants to see you and told me where that gent was."

I sighed. I was tired and wanted my bed, preferably with my wife in it, though I knew she would have her own events to attend this afternoon and evening. Donata was seldom idle. The glow I'd carried with me from being with her in the night had died swiftly when we'd found Higgs, and I desperately wanted to renew it.

"Direct me to him," I said, resigned. I did not particularly want to see the surgeon at the moment, but I was certain he would not ask for me were it not important. If I refused to meet him, he might vanish into the mist again, and I'd never know what he needed to tell me.

I worried it was something about Donata's or Anne's health, though I told myself he would not wait three months to convey something like that. But my niggling fear would not leave me.

"I'll go with you," Brewster said stubbornly. "I already gave the driver the direction."

I nodded, leaning back in my seat and closing my eyes again, trying not to speculate. Speculating and worrying led to nothing and only lost me sleep.

Brewster spoke again awhile later. "I'll take that off your hands if you want."

I did not open my eyes but knew he meant the statue. "No," I said. "I rather like it. It will look nice in the library, once we scrape the paint off."

"Suit yourself."

I had no doubt that Brewster, getting his hands on the thing, would clean it up and then turn around and try to sell it as the original. I believed Brewster when he'd told Spendlove stoutly that he was no killer. He was a thief, though, and what he didn't know about stealing things and selling them on wasn't worth the trouble.

I opened my eyes a slit. "How would you steal things from Carlton House if you wanted to? And make copies and return them?"

Brewster stared off into space a moment, his lips pursed, but his answer came quickly. "Get a post in the place," he said. "Do what you said—switch things around for a while so that when I smuggled something out to have the forger copy it, they'd assume a stupid servant moved it to another room. Return the copy to the wrong place—and everyone finks, *aha, stupid servant put it here.*"

"How would you get the original out of the house at all?" I asked. "Some of the things are small, but this is too big to slip into your pocket." I patted the paper-wrapped bronze.

"Down the stairs in the night, out a back window. They lead right out to the park. Have a confederate—if I could find one I'd trust—waiting under the trees. Hand it off to him. Have that confederate return the copy when it's ready in the same way."

"The trees you were lurking under yesterday evening?"

Brewster's lips twitched. "The same. But I can't think of a man I'd trust to take the original and not run off with it to the Continent. Except maybe you."

"Thank you," I said, unsmiling. "You could trust Denis. He'd carry through the plan and pay you well."

Brewster shook his head. "Mr. Denis didn't do this thieving. Not his way."

I agreed. If Mr. Denis robbed Carlton House, the inhabitants would never know anything had been taken. He'd stated as much to me when I'd asked him.

I glanced out the window to see that we were deep into London, rolling along Holborn. I was not surprised to see us turn to a narrow lane off Holborn to a small but respectable house at its end.

I'd been here before, on a terrible night nearly a year ago, and I knew the house belonged to Denis. I was a little surprised he'd tucked the surgeon here, as several people, including me and a few of my friends, knew of the place. I reasoned, though, that if Denis hadn't thought it safe, he'd not have offered it.

I descended from the coach while Brewster handed the patient driver extra coin to wait again, and approached the door to knock upon it. Brewster, with the statue in his firm grip, pushed past me and opened the door himself.

"He'll know we're here," he told me in a low voice.

The surgeon was making his way down the stairs, his stride neither brisk nor slow. He looked us over, noted we were alone, and motioned for me to enter the front room.

Brewster gave us a nod. "I'll just go have a cup of tea. Shout when you're ready, guv."

"Please don't run off and sell my worthless artwork," I told him. "I like it."

Brewster looked hurt. "As if I would, guv." He shut the front door and strode heavily toward the back stairs.

The surgeon had already entered the sitting room, not one for ceremony. I followed and closed the door, finding him standing near the fireplace, holding his hands toward the blaze. He looked neither nervous nor content, but was simply warming himself while he waited for me.

His utter lack of emotion always puzzled me, although I supposed it helped him in his profession. Surgeons lost patients all the time, which could either make them hard or break their hearts. A man who knew how to keep his emotions suppressed could get on with his work.

"You asked to see me," I reminded the man when he didn't speak for a time.

The surgeon rubbed his hands, which were long fingered, almost delicate, like a musician's, and turned to me.

"I've been in the Low Countries," he said. "Amsterdam, mostly, for the last few months."

I did not know how he wanted me to respond to that, so I said nothing.

"I have only just returned," he went on. "This is why I have not had the opportunity to tell you before, though I probably would not have anyway, in case it hampered her convalescence."

"Tell me what?" I asked, my voice going hard as coldness flowed over me. "Explain yourself at once, if you please."

The surgeon took in my threatening tone without a blink. "Your wife might have recovered from her ordeal," he said. "But she will bear you no more children."

CHAPTER 15

IHAVE NO RECOLLECTION OF WHAT I did. I seem to remember standing, stupefied, in the middle of the dark room—dark because the curtains had been drawn, the only light the red-orange glow from the fire.

The surgeon continued in his inflectionless manner. "I had to remove part of her womb to save her. I cauterized and cleaned her, so she'd heal without taking sick. Mr. Denis tells me she has recovered as well as can be expected, but if I had not acted as I'd done, she would have died."

His words were even and neutral, no apology and no superiority behind them. He stated facts. He hadn't paused before he'd broken the news or tried to prepare me gently. The man showed no emotions at all. None. He'd moved beyond stoicism to something I didn't understand.

I swallowed, my throat so tight I could scarcely breathe. "Does she know?"

"I told her, but she was half insensible with pain and my tonic. She might not have understood me."

If Donata had heard, she'd not said one word to me. In my relief that both she and Anne were alive and thriving, I hadn't taken time to note her composure, or lack of it, during her recovery. Both of us had been taken up with Anne, and still were, bursting with pride every time the tiny girl so much as twitched a finger.

I'd been caught up in the return to normal life once we'd arrived in London—whatever my normal life was now—and

I hadn't paid attention to the state of Donata's happiness. She'd thrown herself into her social circle as much as she could and I had not stopped her, knowing her interest in her friends would speed her healing.

She'd told me whenever I'd asked, that she was well, but had she been drawn and preoccupied? Worried or despondent? I did not think so, but I was ashamed to say I had not noticed.

I coughed to dislodge the lump in my throat. "It was good of you to tell me." My voice was a croak.

Something like surprise flickered in the surgeon's eyes. "It is my duty to tell you."

Not a wish to help me, to gently explain to a proud man that he'd never have a son. No thought that it might be easier to understand coming from a man of medicine than from my own wife. He was simply doing his job.

"In any case, I thank you." The words barely came out. I drew another breath. "You were in Amsterdam, you say?"

I was making conversation, babbling anything to force my mind to return to familiar paths. If nothing else, a man could talk about his travels and the horrible London weather.

"Yes," the surgeon said, and closed his mouth.

He had no intention of telling me what he'd done in Amsterdam, no hint he'd walked along picturesque canals or paused to admire Dam Square. No intention of saying why he'd gone or why he'd returned. Why on earth *had* he come back to England, a country he'd been banished from, when returning would mean his death?

I knew I should leave. Rush home and face Donata, discover whether she'd known and hidden it from me, or whether I'd have the unpleasant task to tell her she'd bear no more children.

I couldn't move. My feet remained in place, my walking stick planted on the carpet.

I should hate the man and his equanimity. I'd begged him to save Donata and Anne, no matter what it took, and he'd obeyed me precisely at my word. I'd threatened to kill him if he didn't. He'd mutilated her to save her, but save her he had.

Donata would be dead otherwise, and I knew it, and possibly Anne with her. I'd be alone, having had only a taste of happiness to sustain me the rest of my life. I'd been bloody grateful to the surgeon and underneath my turmoil, I still was.

I envied him his lack of feeling. My own emotions were roiling and bubbling inside me, giving me no answers.

The door banged open behind me, and Brewster strode in without apology. "Guv? Be ye well?"

He gave the surgeon a belligerent glare. Brewster obviously had grown worried by the silence and time that had passed and decided to burst in, hang the consequences. The surgeon had once saved Brewster's life, but Brewster knew the man's history and did not trust him one whit.

"Yes," I managed to say. "I am well. I'll return home now."

Brewster's hostile stare gave me the impetus to rotate my body and make my feet take me to the door. I sent no more thanks behind me, or a good-bye, and the surgeon said nothing either.

I don't remember how I managed to leave the house and climb into the hackney. The sun was beginning to sink, the winter day short. Clouds were building on the northern horizon, boding poorly for the sunny weather. From the cold bite and the dampness in the air, the morning would bring rain.

Brewster peered at me as he ascended behind me, still clutching the paper-wrapped statue. My gaze fell on it, but at the moment I was unable to recall what it was and why it mattered.

"Ye all right, guv?" Brewster asked with more concern. "What did he say to ye?"

I shook my head. Even if I'd wanted to tell him I couldn't. I couldn't speak.

"You're white as a sheet," Brewster said. "Here."

Something pungent was waved under my nose. I had enough presence of mind to grasp the metal flask Brewster handed me and pour a stream of liquid into my mouth.

I coughed. It was whisky, and a good one, but it burned my throat all the way down. I handed the flask back.

"Do you have children, Brewster?" I asked.

Brewster's brows rose as he took the flask, having a nip out of it before he answered me. "Nah. Me and Em, we never. She had a boy a while before she met me, and he's never been no good. He's doing a stretch of hard labor, not that it will bring him 'round. She has nothing to do wiv him anymore."

"I'm sorry," I said. "I suppose it's never easy."

"Your wife's lad, now, he's a sturdy fellow. But I see the spark of mutiny in his eyes, guv. You'd better watch him."

True, though Peter was well behaved, I would not call him a docile child. His father had been a boorish brute, and Peter, without wisdom to guide him, could go the same way.

"I do my best," I said. If I kept my sentences short, I could wheeze them out.

"And ye have daughters," Brewster went on. "I'd be terrified. Your oldest one is in France, is she? With all those Frenchies? Better get her over here again and lock her up quick."

"She is returning in April," I said. The thought of Gabriella in my house again—her musical voice, her light step, her laughter—eased the tightness in my heart. "She is a sensible girl and her stepfather keeps a close eye on her."

"Huh," Brewster rumbled. "Don't you believe it. Some rakehell will turn her head, and off she'll go. Lasses want to believe they'll be the saint who reforms the rake, but mostly the poor girl is crushed underfoot. How do you think my Em ended up in a bawdy house? Trusting a liar, that's how. Good thing she's down-to-earth and didn't let it break her."

I drew another breath, my heart beating somewhat normally again. "If you are trying to cheer me up, Brewster, I wish you would cease."

"Just warning ye," Brewster said. He took another sip from his flask but did not offer any to me. "Your daughter is a pretty thing—I'd hate to see her ruined. Thank God your new daughter is still in the cradle. Ye won't have to worry about her running off with a wrong 'un for a few years yet."

"You're a very comforting person, you know, Brewster."

He frowned at my sarcasm but at least he went quiet for the

rest of the way to South Audley Street.

When I entered the house, I handed the statue to Barnstable and told him to find somewhere safe for it. I heard the strains of music, which I followed to the large drawing room where Donata liked to host musicales and poetry readings.

No one was there today but Donata, who sat at the pianoforte, a trickle of music coming from her fingers. Her back was to me, perfectly straight, her dark hair pulled up to reveal her long neck.

The gown was new—I had not seen her wear it before. It was an ivory-and-gold striped silk, the gold shimmering in the light of the candles she'd lit against the gloom. The bodice's sleeves ended at her elbows, Donata's strong arms moving as her hands competently picked out a Mozart air. She'd lost some of her plumpness after childbirth, no matter how much her servants had tried to stuff her with food, but her flesh was returning now, and she was pink with health.

I closed the door, telling Barnstable quietly that no, we would not be needing coffee or tea. I gave him a pointed look, at which he nodded, understanding I did not want anyone to disturb us.

I shut the door with a click. Donata's piece abruptly halted, and she swung around on her stool.

"There you are, Gabriel. I was wondering about you."

Her expression was serene, even happy, and she had an excited light in her eyes.

"You did not have to stop," I said, the lump in my throat expanding once more. "I like listening to you play."

Donata shrugged and rose gracefully from the stool. "I enjoy music of the most talented composers in the world, but I play only indifferently, I am afraid. I have some excellent news." She came to me, her eyes shining in triumph. "I found out which house Dunmarron has hired for the Season. I knew Aline would be able to put her finger on it. Dunmarron is not being very discreet, but then he never is. Aline says he'd put Miss Simmons into a house in Portland Place."

Donata halted three steps away, smiling in delight. She looked up at me when I did not respond, taking in my frozen face, and her smile faded. She touched my arm. "What is it, Gabriel? Has something happened?"

Something terrible *had* happened today—Mr. Higgs had been murdered—but I could not speak of that now. I cleared my throat.

"I went to see the surgeon."

Donata looked bewildered a moment, and then as I stood in silence, her face changed. She backed a step, her hand falling from me, and all the light went out of her eyes.

She knew. She had known, and she'd said not a word.

Donata turned away from me without speaking, gliding back across the room to the pianoforte. She touched its keys, but it made no sound.

I swallowed and said with difficulty, "He told you."

"Yes." Donata would not turn around, would not look at me. "While I was prostrate with pain and exhaustion, uncertain whether I would live or die. For a time, I thought perhaps I'd dreamed it, but no."

"You did not think to share this burden with me?" My voice was strained, each word barely audible.

Donata at last swung to me, the gold stripes on her gown shimmering like the tears in her eyes. "How could I, Gabriel? How could I tell you such a thing?"

"By speaking," I said. "By saying one word, and the next, and the next."

"And explain to a man that I could never give him a son?" Her voice rang, the strings of the open pianoforte vibrating with it. "A man who put aside his first wife so he could court and marry me? I know that is why you did it—you told me as much. What is to say this man will not simply put aside his second wife when he is displeased with *her?*"

"I divorced Carlotta because she deserted me." My words grew in strength as I spoke. "She deserted me and took my only child with her. And it was no easy matter. I do not put aside wives for my convenience."

Donata straightened, her temper rising to match mine. "Every man wants a son and heir. Was I to rush to you and confess my weakness?"

"Not a weakness. It was done to save your life. And Anne's."

For a moment, Donata wavered, thinking, as I was, of our daughter safe in her nursery.

"Very well, then." Donata's color rose. "I didn't tell you, because I was afraid. Bloody afraid. If I said nothing, we could go on, and when no child came, well, I am getting on a bit. It would be only natural … No, that is not altogether true. I am selfish, and I didn't want you rushing from me to the first woman who smiled at you, trying first one then another until you had a son."

My eyes widened as she went through the speech, my hand clenching the walking stick I still held. "Is this what you believe of me?" I asked as she finished. "That I am a debaucher who rolls happily among female flesh and can barely be bothered coming home? I am surprised you had the courage to marry me at all."

Her mouth firmed in the stubborn way Donata had, the proud aristocrat emerging. "I believe you agreed to marry *me*. I planned to give you plenty of children before I grew too old, but I suppose I was deluding myself. I am already too old."

"Absolute bloody nonsense. You're a stripling."

Donata gave me an impatient look. "In the eyes of the world, I am past it. Obviously the body knows when it is time to stop, sit down in a soft chair, and take up knitting."

"For God's sake, Donata."

"You are a man of great pride, Gabriel. Do not tell me you are not. Every gentleman wants an heir of his body."

What came out of my mouth was a derisive snort. Inelegant but I could not stop it. "Every gentleman is a conceited idiot, then. I have an heir—there is Marcus, my cousin. In fact, he is the true heir, grandson of the oldest Lacey son."

Donata gave me the exasperated look she always assumed when we spoke of Marcus. She'd given it to me when she'd been too weak and ill to move in Oxfordshire, and still we'd argued about him. "*If* his story is true, which you are too quick to believe. My man of business is checking into the evidence. It will take time."

Time to send people to Canada to discover if Gabriel Marcus Lacey was indeed the grandson of my grandfather's older brother, as he claimed. It made my head spin.

"It doesn't bloody matter," I said, my voice rising. "If he's family, I'm happy to give him a leaky house on a patch of land if he wants it. I don't give a damn about heirs and houses and estates, Donata. I give a damn about *you*, and my daughters, and Peter. *He's* my son, you foolish woman—you handed him to me on a platter."

Donata's mouth was open in anger and bewilderment. My fury at her dead husband rose—he was the one who'd made her believe herself worthless if she didn't provide an heir, who'd made her believe she had no beauty or character to keep him from rushing off to other ladies—any lady would do. He'd made Donata believe *I* could not want her for her own sake, that a man would not say to hell with the rest of the world if it meant he could close all the doors and be with *her*.

"Every day I wish more it had been *my* hand that struck down your vile husband," I said, my voice hard with rage. "I did not marry you in hopes for an heir of my body, as you put it. I did not see you as a mill wheel to grind out one child after another. I married you so I could live in the same house with you and sleep in your bed and look upon you day after day. Hell, and shout at you whenever we like. I don't give a rotting damn if we never have another child. What I give a damn about is *you*."

Her shock as I roared gave way to stunned surprise and then to remorse and pain. Tears returned to her eyes.

When she spoke, her voice was broken. "How is it that I could give the man I loathed a wonderful son, but the man I love more than my own life nothing at all?"

Her words cut through my shouts and right through my anger into my heart. *The man I love more than my own life …*

She could not mean that. I wasn't worth such a thing. Not at all.

My next words came out a near whisper. "How can you say you gave me nothing? Have you looked at Anne? Is she not the most beautiful person in the entire world? Next to her mother, of course. Donata—you gave me *you*."

My wife was crying, my noble Donata, she who never gave way. The next moment, I had my arms around her, drawing her into me, kissing her hair.

"Forgive me," I said. "My bloody rages. But you're wrong. I treasure every moment with you, and I'd never throw that away."

Donata looked at me, unable to speak. It didn't matter. I drew her into my arms and then no more words were possible.

My hunger for her had not abated, in spite of our passion in the early hours of this morning. The drawing room had no bed, not even wide couches, but it had a perfectly thick carpet. We were down on that in no time at all, the leg of the pianoforte sticking me uncomfortably in the hip. I tore Donata's pretty new gold and ivory frock in the process, but by the look in her eyes, she did not mind one bit.

My wife had to ring for her maid to bring her another gown, while I lounged on a narrow divan by the fire and tried not to look like too much of a libertine.

Donata took the gown through the cracked-open door but did not admit her maid, and I helped her dress. Then, by tacit agreement, we went up to the nursery to see Anne.

Peter was there, finished with his lessons—the hour had grown late as Donata and I lolled. Peter and I had a chat, man-to-man, about what he'd learned today, and I promised to be up to his bedchamber later to read with him. We were making our way through Tacitus, shaking our heads at the excesses of the emperors. Nero had just taken over after the death by poisoning of Claudius. Peter enjoyed the stories, and I was ashamed to say his Latin was far better than mine had been at his age. Sometimes better than mine now.

I held Anne in my arms after that, breathing in her scent and her presence. She was a tiny miracle, brought in by sacrifice and by a dispassionate genius. We played Grab Papa's Nose then Drool on Mama's Shoulder before the nanny took her away to put to bed.

Anne was a lively child, following us with her eyes, burbling and trying to stuff her fists into her mouth when we said good night and kissed her downy head.

I bade Peter a more formal good night, but Donata caught the boy in her arms and kissed him soundly on the cheek. "There's my bonny lad," she said. "Good night, my lovely."

Peter pretended not to like the female fluttering but I could tell he was pleased.

Back downstairs in the drawing room, I unwrapped the bronze statue and told Donata about Higgs's death and Denis pronouncing both statues to be copies. I also gave her the silk I'd bought for her at the *marché ouvert*.

Donata ran her hand over the deep red and orange gloss of the fabric, the threads changing color in the candlelight. "Gabriel," she said in a stunned voice. "This is an astonishing gift."

"I thought it pretty," I said modestly. I'd had no idea of the worth of the thing.

"You found it in this *marché ouvert*?" she asked, her eyes gleaming. "Hmm, perhaps I could …"

"No, you could not," I said abruptly. "A darker, more insalubrious place I've never been. The things were a jumble, rusting chains next to silver necklaces probably stolen from your neighbor next door."

"Possibly." Donata laid the silk across her lap, looking in no way distressed. "Now, what are you going to do? Who do you think killed poor Mr. Higgs?"

"As to that, I have no idea." We both turned to the topic, clinging to it so we would not resume our earlier discussion. "The thief caught in the act? The prince himself? A rival for Higgs's position? A lover in a quarrel? It could have been anyone."

"Not anyone," Donata said. "Only those who would be admitted to Carlton House. That means the staff, the prince and his entourage, his close acquaintance, and anyone he invited in."

"As I said," I answered glumly. "Anyone."

"Well, we will think about that," Donata finished, her brisk self once more. "Now we must go to Dunmarron and rescue Marianne."

"Have you told Grenville where he is keeping her?" I asked.

"No, indeed. I've not had the chance, and also I am not certain what Grenville would do with the information. Let us spare him his dignity, fetch her home, and send Dunmarron scuttling back to his country estate to rusticate."

"He is a duke," I pointed out. "At the top of society. He will do as he pleases."

My wife gave me a pitying look. "You underestimate the power of disapproval. Gentlemen exchange mistresses all the time, but abducting a mistress to humiliate a man is not done. Not at all. Especially in so blatant a fashion that everyone is talking. Dunmarron might have his estate and his lofty title, but no one will stick him. He's an upstart."

I leaned back on the divan, where earlier I'd waited in dishabille for her fresh clothes to arrive. "You are a snob, Donata. You married me for my name, I see. What if I'd been lower than your lowest footman, raised from the gutter through the ranks, promoted in the field to captain? That last bit is true, in fact. Would you have married me then?"

"Of course not." My wife sat down very close beside me, the silk still in her hands. "We would have had a clandestine and very delicious affair."

I might have preferred that. It was difficult to grow used to the servants in this house following me about and people expecting me in and out at certain hours.

"Very delicious," I agreed.

Donata began to lean to me, but she straightened up with a decided nod. "None of that. We must find Marianne and retrieve her from the clutches of the Dunce."

"*I* must," I said. "I don't want you near the man."

Donata gave me one of her looks that said I was too slow for words. "Don't be silly. You cannot dash up to Dunmarron's door and demand admittance. You've not been introduced."

CHAPTER 16

THE HOUSE IN WHICH THE Duke of Dunmarron had sequestered Marianne was in Portland Place, part of what was to be the grand sweep of road that would lead from a new royal park south, all the way to Carlton House. Swallow Street was in the process of being redone into an elegant crescent of tall houses and shops, the entire plan designed by John Nash. Several of the buildings on the new street were finished, the shops drawing a wealthy clientele.

Portland Place was already full of fine houses. The tall one Hagen stopped us before had a black-painted door surrounded by white marble Ionic columns. The curtains were drawn over every window, all the way to the top of the structure.

I had only agreed to let Donata come because she was correct that this was a matter of her world. I storming into a duke's house, threatening all in my path, would only get me brought up before a magistrate, with Spendlove gloating behind me. I also believed that this situation was more sinister than it seemed, else I'd have let Grenville sort out his own troubles while I continued with mine.

Bartholomew still had not returned from Carlton House, and so one of Donata's footmen—a lad called Jeremy—had accompanied us to Dunmarron's house. Jeremy now descended from the back of the carriage to rap on the front door on our behalf. We would wait in the coach until we were invited inside or bade to leave a card.

Jeremy conferred with the servant in Dunmarron's vestibule for a time and then returned to the coach.

"His Grace ain't home, my lady," Jeremy said through the carriage door I'd opened for him. Cold wind blew in on us, accompanied by a splash of rain. "Footman was surprised I'd even think so. Cheeky about it, if you'll pardon me, my lady. The young lady brought to live here ain't in either. Footman says she's run off, and His Grace is very angry. Boiling mad, apparently."

Jeremy looked delighted. I knew servants prided themselves on their places and looked down on one another if their masters weren't quite up to snuff. I imagined those who worked for a man known as the Duke of Dunces were maligned by all.

"Do you believe him?" I asked Jeremy. "I mean, footmen are trained to say someone is not at home when that is not strictly true."

Jeremy nodded. "I know the difference. This lad is rather disgusted by it all. Says the lady is only an actress. He can't understand why His Grace is bothered and says good riddance to her."

"Does he have any idea where she's gone?"

"He don't. I asked him. His Grace gave them all a flea in their ears when he found out she'd scarpered."

So Marianne had made her own way out of the situation. I could not be very astonished. Marianne was never one to be a helpless victim.

"Does the footman know where His Grace is?" I asked.

"At his club, so he thinks." Jeremy shook his head. "Lad rather gives himself airs, but I think he's truthful."

"Good. Well done, Jeremy. Thank you."

Jeremy again looked pleased. "Yes, sir. Shall I give Hagen a direction, sir?"

"Brooks's club. I believe I'll have a conversation with His Grace."

Jeremy gave me a nod. "Sir." He slammed the door and shouted up to Hagen, waiting until the coach had lurched forward before leaping to his post on the back.

Donata gave me a long look, her eyes appraising. "I believe I told you that you hadn't been introduced."

"Then find someone to introduce me," I growled. "I will end this nonsense for once and for all."

"Oh, dear, you are not going to call him out, are you? I might have lost you to that awful Stubby Stubbins—I certainly refuse to lose you to the Duke of Dunces."

"I was in no danger from Stubbins." I took in the alarm Donata was trying to hide and relented. "I give you my word I will not call Dunmarron out. What *he* does, I cannot help."

We rode in silence down Portland Place, across Oxford Street, and through the arteries to the broad expanse of Piccadilly. From there, Hagen turned the coach down St. James's Street and came to a halt in front of Brooks's.

When I went inside, Richards the doorman did confess, uncomfortably, that the duke was indeed present. Richards was in a quandary whether to admit me, but his dilemma was solved when Lord Lucas, Donata's friend, entered through the front door behind me.

"Captain Lacey?" Lucas asked, the wind he let in cutting off as a footman shut the door. "Good afternoon. I saw Donat—er, your wife—in her coach. She asked me to rush here and meet you. What is it all about?"

I admired Donata's percipience and her ability to grasp opportunities. "She wishes you to introduce me to His Grace of Dunmarron," I said. "I believe you know why. I cannot compel you to."

Lucas, unlike his friend Rafe Godwin, seemed unhappy about the state of affairs. He gave me a nod. "Of course, Captain. I will have to warn you that if you've come on behalf of Grenville to call Dunmarron out, I will be one of his seconds. You can speak to me if you wish to take things that far."

"I promised my wife I'd do no such thing." I shifted my weight to my good leg, impatient to get on with it. "I only wish to speak to him."

Lucas looked me up and down, sighed, shrugged, and thrust his hat and coat at the footman. He waved the footman away, however, as the young man approached me for the same purpose. "Captain Lacey will not be staying. Is His Grace in the dining room, Richards? Good. Follow me, Captain."

Lord Lucas led me up a flight of stairs to the main floor, where I'd been several times with Grenville. From the subscription room came the sound of voices—it was here that men gathered around gaming tables and won and lost fortunes. The noise was subdued now but would swell and grow as the night went on.

The dining room was far more quiet. No gaming was allowed here, and members tucked in for a quick meal before returning to the excitement down the hall.

His Grace of Dunmarron dined alone at a large square table, a footman just taking away the remains of soup and setting before him a plate holding a slender fish.

Lucas halted at the table so that he faced Dunmarron, and I took a stance by his side. Lucas cleared his throat apologetically.

Dunmarron shoveled a large forkful of fish into his wide mouth and looked up at us as he chewed. "Lucas," he said around white flakes of sole. "Captain Lacey. What'ye want?"

I'd likened him to a country squire when I'd met him before. Donata had called him an upstart. The man reminded me of my father, if not in looks, then in manners.

I spoke before Lucas could. Lord Lucas was supposed to have introduced us, but Dunmarron had already addressed me, so I didn't bother with the formality. "I want to ask you, sir, rudely, what you meant by shutting Miss Simmons into your house."

"You may ask." Dunmarron swallowed noisily and took another gulp of fish. "Sit down, for God's sake. You make my neck ache."

I had no wish to sit with him, but I realized he wouldn't talk to me if I did not. Lucas politely waited until I'd lowered myself to a chair before taking the one next to me. Lucas spoke before I could. "Yes, Dunmarron, what is this all about?"

Dunmarron shot Lucas a look of annoyed rage. "Ask Grenville. He knows."

I reined in my temper with effort. It irritated me when people said in that dark tone—*He knows*—because very often the knowledge was only in the speaker's imagination.

"I assure you, Grenville is baffled," I said. "If there is bad blood between you and Mr. Grenville, please confront him yourself and leave Miss Simmons out of it."

"Miss Simmons." Dunmarron spat the name. "She is a termagant and a tart, and he's welcome to her. What does he want with a bitch like that?"

Marianne had put him in his place it seemed, but my ire rose. "I will remonstrate with you later for calling my friend such names, but at the moment, I only wish to know where she is. She's no longer at your house, so where has she gone?"

"Damned if I know." Dunmarron shoveled in another mouthful of fish, splotches of it staining his lips. "She's there one moment, gone the next. My bloody fool servants admit that a delivery boy they'd never seen before went in and out of the kitchen, but they didn't try to stop him. Too snooty to talk to a street boy, the lot of them. The woman is an actress—she dressed up and slipped past them, the—" He now called Marianne a name far worse than the others, a single syllable that had my fist balling.

"One more, Your Grace," I said in a quiet voice. "And we meet."

Dunmarron snorted, unfortunately for us, since he was still chewing his fish. "I'll not shoot a man over the likes of *her*. She was yours, I heard, before Grenville came along and pinched her. He does it to all of us. I thought you'd have some sympathy."

Lucas leaned to me and said in a quiet voice. "Grenville once poached a young woman Dunmarron was fond of, you see. This was before he became duke."

"Silly cow could have been a duke's mistress." Dunmarron destroyed the rest of his fish by raking it with his heavy fork. "I'm only getting back a bit of my own."

"It was twenty years ago," Lucas said to him.

"You may scoff." Dunmarron dropped his fork on top of the ruined fish. "Grenville has walked straight through the rest of us to become the most intimate friend of the prince, and has the so-called polite world eating out of his hand. He's nobody, the son of a whoremonger father who put by-blows in the nursery alongside his one and only true child. But who knows? Perhaps Grenville is one of those by-blows himself."

Lucas grew alarmed. "Now Dunmarron, you can't slander a man, especially when he isn't here to answer. He'll have a law-suit on you."

"I said *perhaps*," Dunmarron said, unabashed. "You take things too seriously, Lucas, old friend."

Lucas looked a bit pained at being called *old friend*. I'd already had enough of him in ten minutes—I wondered how Lord Lucas and Rafe Godwin and others had put up with him for so long.

I rose. "Thank you for speaking with me, Your Grace. I'll give Miss Simmons your regards."

Whenever I found her. I decided, however, that I should leave now before I punched the man in the face and did end up in a duel, despite what I'd promised Donata.

Dunmarron gave me a disparaging look. "Do not be too smug, Captain Lacey. You may have snared the beautiful Lady Breck-enridge, but only for now. *La Breckenridge* craves novelty. I do say *you* are quite novel." Another scornful once-over. "But she wants entertainment. Be careful or you'll have plenty of cuckoos in your nest. Probably you already do."

"Dear God," Lucas said, aghast. "Hold your tongue, Dunmar-ron, do. Lady Donata is a dear friend."

I said nothing. I thought of Donata facing me in the drawing room, her eyes filled with anguish when she admitted she knew she'd have no more children. My strong Donata, broken by what the surgeon had told her and having to face that heartbreak anew when I'd taxed her with it.

Dunmarron's pig-like mouth, stained with bits of fish and the sauce it was poached in, saying so much as Donata's name was an insult. Talking about her bearing me bastard children was beyond the pale. Talking about it on top of what Donata and I had been through, unthinkable. Though Dunmarron had no idea of our private pain, he had no bloody business even speaking of her.

"Name your seconds," I told him. "Or, you can meet me alone, and I will explain to you why you should stay far from me, my wife, and my friends."

Another snort. "I've already told you, I will not fight you. Not over ladies no better than they ought to be. I'm sorry, Lucas. Don't give me your priggishness. Anyway, *la Breckenridge* is well known for her interests. Her name is in the betting book of this very club, with much speculation on how many affairs she'd have when you were off in the Orient."

I remembered how Donata and I had snipped at each other in the carriage on the way to the Haymarket, when she had told me gentlemen had wagered on her fidelity to me. I'd let her believe I'd dropped the matter, but I did plan to speak to those who'd had the audacity to make the wager.

I turned to Lucas. "I would like to see the book."

Lucas flinched. "Now, Captain, do not. I understand why you want to box Dunmarron's ears, but let us depart and say no more about it. Dunmarron is a boor and always will be."

Dunmarron nodded, happy to agree. He seemed to know about his own bad manners and delight in them. Perhaps that was how *he* survived life among the aristocracy.

"The book," I repeated.

Lucas heaved a long sigh. He rose and rang a bell, and we waited in silence until a servant answered. Lucas spoke to the footman in a low voice and returned to us once he'd departed.

Another footman set a plate of beef and potatoes in front of Dunmarron, and we were privileged to watch him noisily masticate them.

Richards himself carried in the book, a ledger with a leather cover, a bit worn on the edges from years of use. Grenville, who'd been a member of Brooks's since his majority, had told me amusing tales of wagers in the past, such as one gentleman

wagering five hundred guineas that his friend would not fornicate with a woman in a balloon a thousand yards in the sky. The
word they used was not *fornicate*, but a shorter and more direct
one.

Richards opened the book with as much reverence as he would
a Bible. Dunmarron looked on while Lucas leafed through it.
"Ah," Lucas said.

I looked to where his finger pointed. *A pool has been collected to
be paid out to the gentleman who guesses the closest number of affairs the
lady of the deceased Ld Breckenridge enjoys while her captain is in the
land of the pharaohs.*

The names of the gentlemen who'd wagered were laid out,
along with the number they'd chosen. Dunmarron had put
himself down for three. Rafe Godwin, five. Lucas, I was pleased
to see, had not wagered at all.

At the top of the list, however, one name blazed out. Lucius
Grenville. At least, I saw through my haze, he'd been kind
enough to enter for the number of affairs—none at all.

Dunmarron said with his mouth full, "You going to call all of
us out, Lacey?"

"Yes," I said with conviction. "Please put it about that if anyone in this club so much as mentions my wife again, they will
answer to me."

Dunmarron laughed. Red wine sauce stained his cravat. "Keep
her home and tamed, and you won't have to worry."

I could not stop myself. Lucas could not stop me either—he
only folded his hands and looked distressed. But I think he
understood.

I walked around the table, took up Dunmarron's plate of half
finished beef and roasted potatoes, and dumped the whole of it
in his lap.

He jumped and swore, his chair skittering backward as the very
wet sauce splashed all over his crotch. I followed the beef and
potatoes with his full glass of hock, which had been moments
ago topped off by the footman.

The other gentlemen dining, about a dozen across the large

chamber, all swiveled to watch. A few burst out laughing, others guffawed. I had the feeling I'd done what so many of them had longed to.

"Damn you, you bloody ..." Dunmarron trailed off as he scrubbed his trousers with a handkerchief. He turned his snarls to the two footmen who'd raced to help him, the two lads going red as they strove to hide their own laughter.

Lucas had his hand on my arm. "Captain? I suggest we depart."

I did not argue. I walked stiffly at his side, the thump of my stick covered by the jeers of gentlemen who ran the British Empire. "Your mouth ran ahead of your brains again, did they, Dunmarron? Or are they in your lap?" "Watch that captain, Dunmarron. He's quite a cut-up."

They whooped at their own wit, or lack thereof, and Lucas and I walked out. Richards followed us, holding the now-closed book and giving us raised brows as Lucas called for his wraps and we left the club for the winter evening. As Richards closed the door behind us, I reflected that I'd likely never be admitted to Brooks's again.

Lord Lucas tipped his hat to Donata where she waited in the carriage, accepting her regal nod for a good-bye. He took his leave from me and hurried up St. James's toward Jermyn Street, putting distance between himself and us very quickly.

Donata's footman Jeremy assisted me into the carriage. She quietly took in my stiff movements and heated face as I sat down beside her and Jeremy slammed the door.

"How many did you challenge?" she asked me in a calm voice.

"Fifteen." I winced as the carriage jerked, my bad knee jolting. We swayed into traffic, which pressed me against Donata, no bad thing. "At least, that is my intention. I did not actually speak to fifteen gentlemen there. Dunmarron dismissed my command to name his seconds but no doubt they will be calling on mine soon to issue *his* challenge."

Donata listened, her amusement fading as she realized I was serious. "Gabriel—what the devil did you do to him?"

I explained about the beefsteak and wine. Donata's eyes widened as I went on, then her stunned look fled and she burst into laughter.

My wife did not laugh heartily very often, but now she lay back against the cushions, put her hand across her belly, and laughed loud and long.

By the time we reached South Audley Street, Donata had ceased laughing, but she wore a satisfied expression.

Bartholomew was home, looking ready to burst with news, but he composed himself to tell us that Grenville had arrived and was waiting for us upstairs. Donata thrust her bonnet and wraps at the maid and glided up ahead of me.

We found Grenville in the sitting room at the front of the house, the fire built high to warm the place. Grenville often met with us in Donata's boudoir or my own chambers above this one, but Barnstable, a stickler for propriety, would never have let anyone, even a close friend of the family, up to our private rooms when we were not home.

Grenville was dressed in black trousers and a coat that contrasted his gold damask waistcoat and very white cravat. Tonight's cravat pin was a sapphire surrounded by a ring of tastefully small diamonds.

His suit was subdued, but Grenville himself was not. Any other evening, he'd have waited for us comfortably in a chair, reading a book from Donata's extensive library. Tonight he was pacing, and he swung around in exasperation when we at last appeared.

"I've spoken to Mr. Cosway," he began, but Donata cut him off with a wave of her hand.

"Miss Simmons is no longer with the Dunce," she said triumphantly. "She foiled him by dressing like a delivery boy and walking out past his servants."

Grenville's words died away, and he stared at her a moment before he gave an impatient nod. "Yes, gossips have already cornered me to tell me she is no longer in his house. I've spent the day tearing through my acquaintance, asking for information far and wide, and this is the latest news. I had not heard *how* she'd left—the utter cheek of the girl." A note of pride entered his voice. "I'd rejoice if I knew where the devil she was. She hasn't come home."

"We'll find her," I said with confidence. "Marianne is a resourceful young woman, and is probably lounging in a luxurious hotel, pretending to be a foreign princess or some such. You and I will look under every stone until we make certain she is well."

Grenville gave me a dark look. "Not tonight, we won't. We're commanded to be at Carlton House. The prince is having a soiree—for about a thousand from what I gather, and we must be among them, according to His High-handed Highness."

I stared in perplexity. "Mr. Higgs has been killed. Did you know?"

"Oh, yes, I know. The Regent himself told me." Grenville's expression turned to disgust. "Why should the death of a lackey prevent him from a gathering he's planned for weeks? My news will wait. If we refuse the prince, I am certain he'll send the army after us, so do put on your best suit and attend with me, there's a good fellow."

CHAPTER 17

I HAD SEEN CARLTON HOUSE EMPTY and gray in the night and then sunny and lofty on a fine-weathered morning. At ten that evening, I saw it as its architects had meant it to be enjoyed— ablaze with light and overflowing with splendor.

Every candle in every chandelier was lit, their glow illuminating the fortunate guests from the grand entrance to the east and west antechambers or down the staircase and through the magnificent rooms below. The conservatory was no less ablaze than the rest of the mansion, its gothic columns illuminated by the Turkish lanterns, which made the windows glitter like black jewels.

Those who'd come to the soiree were as glittering. Ladies wore fine silks and yards of diamonds, gentlemen as opulent in suits set off by jeweled cravat pins, watch chains dangling with gold seals or fobs encrusted with precious stones or mother-of-pearl.

This was the first large outing Donata had attended since her confinement—the routs and journeys to the theatre had been small affairs, she said. Tonight she'd spent hours locked with her maids preparing; that is, once she'd ceased cursing at the short notice and at being included as a last-minute guest. A snub, she proclaimed.

Her maids' work produced excellent results. The gown Donata chose had an underdress of deep sapphire blue with a waist so high it scooped under her breasts and left the skirt to flow unimpeded to her ankles. The long-sleeved overdress was a net of the same blue spun with gold threads, with net bunched at the shoulders of the bodice. The underdress left her arms bare, and the overdress' net sleeves clung to her skin.

The décolletage scooped low, which let her show off a necklace of thick gold from which dangled a diamond pendant, a gift from her father. Her dark hair, on the other hand, shone with the gold and lapis lazuli diadem I'd brought home from Egypt—cleaned, it blazed with beauty. The blue of it exactly complemented her gown, which I knew was no coincidence. Donata would have had the gown made to match.

The earrings that dangled from her earlobes were small and delicate gold, my New Year's gift to her last year. The short hem of the gown allowed her to show off smooth black slippers with cross ties around her ankles, and again the slim gold chain I'd bought her on a whim one day after we'd first become regular lovers.

She'd thrown over this ensemble a long shawl of rich gold with a wide paisley border, which she relinquished to her maid after we entered Carlton House so the shimmering hues of her gown could catch the light. Donata Lacey was a beautiful sight, and I could not help my pride as I viewed her.

I had decided to wear my regimentals, as had several military gentlemen, I saw when we entered the conservatory. These gentlemen had been generals on the battlefield, and I'd been a mere lieutenant for most of the war, not receiving my captaincy until Talavera. Even so, they spoke politely to me, and we were soon reliving the slog of fighting on the Peninsula, in great detail.

Donata left me to it and sailed off on Grenville's arm. Grenville had changed his suit for the soiree, his black cashmere trousers flowing over elegant boots. His waistcoat was of subtle gold and green stripes, his white cravat tied in one of the complicated knots he was famous for. The only thing he had not changed for the evening was his diamond and sapphire cravat pin, which went well with Donata's gown.

I watched the two of them, well matched, as I spoke to the generals and admirals, saw Donata blossom into brilliance under the light of the gigantic chandeliers.

She knew exactly why I'd dumped Dunmarron's dinner in his lap, because I'd told her. I'd left out no sordid detail. Rather than being embarrassed that the wager about her fidelity had been the object of a near brawl, Donata seemed determined to live up to the club gentlemen's estimation of her as a vibrant lady.

As the uniformed men and I relived the noise and blood of Ciudad Rodrigo and the horrors after Badajoz, Donata flirted madly with every gentleman present. She hung on to Grenville's arm, Grenville laughing with her as she became the coquette of the evening.

She and Grenville made a compelling pair, both in the latest fashion tempered by good taste, both matched in wit and manners. I'd once remarked to Donata I was surprised she hadn't chosen Grenville to be her husband. She'd only given me her stare that said I was an ignorant fool and declared such a match would run aground quickly.

I suppose two high-spirited, very determined people would smash into each other with heartbreaking consequences. Perhaps she'd been wise to remain friends with Grenville and marry a rather less complex gentleman, who asked only for an early ride in the park, a warm bed, and a book to read in the evenings.

I enjoyed watching Donata confound the gentlemen of the *ton*—they were enchanted with her, as well as wondering at her ebullience, as the story of my behavior at Brooks's had reached the far ends of Town by now. I suppose they'd expected her to break down and weep in mortification at her eccentric husband or in shame that she'd been the center of a tawdry quarrel.

No, my wife used it as fuel to show her resilience and self-confidence all the more.

As much as I enjoyed watching her, I knew we were here for other reasons. I had not seen the Regent, but eventually, the house's majordomo sought me out and beckoned me aside.

The majordomo was as haughty as any guest here, likely gentleman-born and given the honor of being in charge of the prince's household. His eyes flickered coolly as he took in my regimentals which were showing wear, no matter how carefully Bartholomew looked after them, and then plunged into his reason for summoning me.

"His Highness wishes you to look about the house for signs of other missing objects, or copies of them. *Discreetly,* please, Captain."

"Of course," I answered at once.

The majordomo gave me a nod. "He said you could roam at will, but I would be pleased if you did not disturb the servants at their tasks. So please avoid the kitchens or the pages' room and the back stairs."

"I understand." I agreed with Brewster that the best way to get things in and out of the house was through the back stairs and the kitchens, but I said nothing.

The majordomo bowed and left me to it.

Grenville was busy entertaining the fashionable ladies and gentlemen as only he knew how, as well as keeping the more exuberant bloods away from my wife. No matter. Grenville and Donata distracting the prince's guests gave me the ability to slip away with no one noticing me.

Not that there was anywhere to slip to in Carlton House tonight. Every room was filled with people, though the house did absorb a thousand guests very well. The conservatory, eighty feet long, already drank in many.

I drifted with the crowd to the Gothic dining room at the other end of the long suite of ground-level rooms. The Gothic dining room was a sort of mirror of the conservatory in its architecture, and held an enormous table heaped with food for any to sample.

I passed endless plates of macaroons and more appalling tidbits like bowls of live tiny fish or very small birds on a skewer as I scanned the walls and side tables for anything that looked unusual or out of place.

Though how I'd know what ought to be there and what should not without Higgs's list, I had no idea. I decided to make my way to his office and look through his ledgers, in spite of the majordomo's warning about staying out of the back halls. I would avoid the kitchens, true to my word.

As I made my way through the crowd to the library, I noted that while the rooms were packed with the cream of society, this gathering certainly did not represent all of it. There were no debutantes, no respectable ladies and gentlemen of quiet families, no kindhearted reformers like my friend Sir Gideon Derwent and his son, Leland. Instead the guests were Corinthians—sport-mad gentlemen with unsavory reputations—the Regent's more dissolute friends, ladies of the *ton* whose virtues were far more often called into question than Donata's, and wits, roués, and dandies. A debutante wouldn't be safe here.

Rafe Godwin had come, wearing one of his usual loud waist-coats, Lord Lucas by his side, not looking entirely comfortable. Lucas gave me a benign nod but did not attempt to strike up a conversation. I noted that Dunmarron was very notably *not* present.

His absence did not prevent the wits from talking him over, however. Ignoring me—if they even noticed me—they specu-lated on his attempt to steal Grenville's mistress, and how easily she'd foiled him.

"She ought to do pantomime," one gentleman in the library said. "Beautiful actress, showing her legs in knee breeches. I'd be in the front of the theatre, right under the stage to see it."

"Dunmarron didn't notice that the legs leaving his house belonged to a woman," another man chortled. "No wonder they call him the Duke of Dunces."

"He didn't actually see her in the breeches," Rafe corrected him disdainfully. "Though you're probably right he wouldn't notice. He'd be too busy cleaning the beef off his *own* breeches. His joint got sauced, I would say, my friends."

More laughter. Rafe was hardly a loyal friend to Dunmarron, I observed, though I would not expect him to be. Rafe was the sort who attached himself to a gentleman only when the weather was fair. One hint of a squall, and he was gone.

I stole a candle from a crystal and bronze candle stand and

moved quickly through the door disguised as a bookcase in the back wall of the library. No one observed me go. I drew a breath of relief as I shut the door and found myself in quieter halls.

Higgs's office was unchanged, except that the fireplace was cold. I didn't much mind—the public rooms had become stifling. I used my borrowed candle to light the sconces in the office, flooding it with warm yellow light. I then stuck the candle into a heavy silver candlestick on the desk and sat down.

I had liked Higgs's office the first time I'd seen it, and I admired it anew. Books and catalogs overflowed from shelves onto tables, and sheafs of notes lay everywhere. The chaos was somewhat organized, however. Books in French, German, and Russian had their own shelves, as did tomes on sculpture, painting, and objects d'art.

Grenville might be flattered to learn that a book of drawings of his house's interior reposed with those on objects d'art, the book collected from a series of articles in the *Gentleman's Magazine*. These articles about Grenville's art and curios, complete with colored drawings, had been bound into a slim volume that was now sold in bookshops.

Though I would have loved to browse the fascinating books the office contained, I was at the moment more interested in Higgs's personal notes.

I hunted through ledgers until I found the list of moved and missing items Higgs had shown us before. He, or someone, had been copying it out, as I found the copy on a loose page, half-finished. I set the lists aside and began leafing through the ledgers, examining the inventory of the prince's entire collection.

I became absorbed in the inventory, which had been very neatly done. Each object had been labeled, along with notes about where it had been acquired and when, how much had been spent on it, and where it now lay in the house. I found older lists from the previous curator, Mr. Cosway, with his notations and initials. Then I began to compare Cosway's lists with Higgs's.

It was tedious going, and I had to find pen and paper to make notes of my own, but by the time the door opened and I heard Grenville's step, I had grown quite animated.

Grenville had mentioned he'd spoken to Mr. Cosway earlier today—hunted up the old artist in his house and had quite a chinwag with him. He'd not had time to tell us the details before he'd gone home to ready himself for this outing—we'd planned to compare notes after the soiree. I was now more anxious than ever to hear what the man had said.

Grenville paused in the doorway while I continued scratching notes, running my fingers along entries to make sure I saw what I thought I did.

"You always manage to find comfortable retreats at these things," Grenville said as he closed the door. "And interesting bits to read."

I tore my eyes from the paper and looked up to see that he was quite alone. I rose in alarm. I did not mind Donata taunting the bloods and Corinthians, but only while she had Grenville at her side to protect her.

"You abandoned my wife to every rakehell in London?" I demanded.

Grenville raised his brows. "Hardly. I left her with Lady Aline and her friend Lucas. You do not have to worry about Donata, you know. She is formidable, and her father has much power. No one will touch her."

I let out my breath, trying to assuage my instincts to rush out and protect her. "They worry about her father, not her husband, do they?" I asked, making myself sit back down.

"The earl is a powerful man. Most are amazed you do not tremble before him. Or, they suspect you do, only in private."

"He is quite personable," I said in surprise. I liked Pembroke, a gentleman I could sit in silence with while we read newspapers. He never pushed me into conversation unless he truly wanted to hear what I had to say. "Truth to tell, it is Lady Pembroke I'm never certain about."

"Yes, Donata's mother is quite a woman." Grenville gave me a fervent nod. "She can make the great and powerful feel about three inches tall without ever opening her mouth. But enough. What have you found? You have the look you get when you're interested in a thing."

"Tell me about Mr. Cosway," I countered. "It might be important."

Grenville pulled a Sheraton chair to the desk so he could look at what had me so intrigued. "Quite an interesting chap. He has not much good to say about the prince, except that the Regent gave Cosway fairly free rein in finding and acquiring pieces for him. Cosway would locate a thing and then advise the Regent on whether to buy it. The most beautiful paintings were chosen by him, and much of Carlton House's decor."

"I have many of Cosway's notes here," I said. "Of pieces he acquired. Then Higgs's. Higgs acquired next to nothing, only a few pieces, but he made an inventory of what he found here when he arrived."

Grenville shrugged. "Perhaps Higgs did not have the eye Cosway did. Cosway told me tales of bartering with kings, finding paintings looted by Napoleon from all over the Continent. Napoleon swept through the Italian states pretty thoroughly, you know, destroyed the centuries-old Venetian Republic overnight, and stole from there, Florence, Rome … Much of that artwork is still floating about, claimed by first one city then the other. According to Cosway, Europe is one big *marché ouvert* these days."

"Exactly. With the confusion, who is to say what on the market is real and what is a copy?" I swept my hand over the ledgers. "Higgs was keeping careful track of every piece in the collection, starting with Cosway's notes and then making his own. *Here,* I found another inventory indicating which pieces in the collection might be fakes. There are whole pages about what might be questionable items." I pulled a ledger to the top of the pile as I spoke and leafed through it. "Except this handwriting is not Higgs's, or Cosway's."

"No?" Grenville leaned forward to examine what I pointed at. "Whose then?"

I did not answer directly. "These ledgers were hidden in a drawer with a false bottom. If Higgs had discovered that someone was slowly stealing the collection, he might want to keep it quiet until he was sure, yet keep track of what was coming and going—asking a trusted person to make the notes for him."

"Or Higgs was stealing it himself." Grenville voiced the words I did not want to say. "But he didn't seem the sort. Besides, Cosway told me Higgs did not work directly for the prince. The king employed him—Higgs worked most of his life at Windsor. He was sent to Carlton House to take over from Cosway and more or less keep an eye on the prince's extravagance."

"Which he did quite well," I said. "His books from a few years ago are impeccable, and he has not spent much money on the collection. But a man can be tempted. Higgs had his finger on every piece, and here he is, working for a presumably modest salary alone in the bowels of this house, surrounded by brilliant works of art worth a bloody fortune."

"You make me quite worry about my own collection," Grenville said uneasily. "I have a man help me keep inventory of it. But why would Higgs do this, Lacey? He seemed most distressed about the thefts. And, someone killed him."

I sat back. "Before I came in here tonight, I thought he'd been killed because he'd realized that the prince's artwork was slowly being replaced by copies. But if you examine the list in this ledger, made by someone *not* Higgs, these things have been missing or moving for the last eight months. Why, then, did Higgs wait so long to send for the Runners? I suspect that once the prince finally noticed something odd was happening, Higgs was forced to bring in the Runners—and you—at the Regent's behest. He didn't dare refuse."

"I suppose." Grenville looked unhappy. "I hate to think it, though. I liked Higgs. He seemed a competent, capable man."

"So did I, and I hope I am wrong. But then I found this letter, tucked into the lining of one of the ledgers."

I reached for the paper I'd left on the desk and smoothed it out. The letter was to Higgs and dated October of last year.

Mr. Higgs—I write to you in a hurry from my lodgings in Amsterdam and apologize for my brevity. But I have found here in a house the exact copy of a painting that hangs in the west antechamber in Carlton House. I was looking for the sculpture the Regent wanted, and I was directed to a collector, a wealthy merchant who has warehouses all over the world. The painting is on his wall.

He claims it is authentic, so I thought to ask you whether the prince's had been sold to him. I thought not, but I have been gone some weeks in my travels. Please advise me whether this is the case.

I do not like to tell this gentleman his painting is a forgery when I am trying to flatter him into selling the sculpture, but I likewise cringe at the thought of telling His Highness that his is the forgery. I leave this matter in your hands and will await your instruction.

My hasty regards,
Sebastian Floyd

CHAPTER 18

"MR. FLOYD." GRENVILLE BLINKED AT the page. "Good God."

"The very man sitting in Newgate waiting to go to trial," I said.

Grenville looked at me, his dark eyes distressed. "You will have to tell Spendlove. At once, before the poor fellow is hanged."

I folded the letter and thrust it into my pocket. "I intend to. Also to interview the man. I have to wonder why Spendlove has been reluctant to take me to see him."

"Because he knows Floyd is not guilty?"

I wondered. Spendlove must know I'd discover the truth of Floyd's innocence or guilt—he could not believe I'd suppress evidence that showed the man had done nothing.

"No matter," I said. "I will talk to Pomeroy and convince him to take me to Newgate."

Grenville huffed a laugh. "Be careful how you phrase that. And by *convince*, I assume you mean *bully*, as captain to sergeant."

"If I must. Pomeroy has little liking for Spendlove. He will not mind if Spendlove has no suspect to put in the dock."

"Mr. Floyd is innocent of murdering Mr. Higgs, at least," Grenville said. "Who did that, I wonder?" He glanced about as though worried the person would spring in and have a go at us.

"If Higgs had nothing to do with the thefts but had found out who did, and decided to confront the thief himself, that might explain his death. Or, if he truly was in on the thefts, perhaps he had a falling out with another thief, or perhaps he was having a crisis of conscience." I sighed and closed the ledgers. "I will know more when I speak to Mr. Floyd. I believe I'll take these with me."

I stacked the ledger that contained speculation that certain pieces were copies on top of the one with lists of the missing or moved objects. Higgs had not bothered to show us the list of objects believed to be copies, nor had he mentioned Floyd's letter. That sang of his guilt, or at least his complicity, quite loudly.

Grenville gave me a hesitant look. "Would you mind interviewing Mr. Floyd alone? I want to spend the rest of the night and on into tomorrow looking for Marianne. I want to assure myself the dear girl is all right, no matter whether she wants to come home with me or not. I thought she might return to her old rooms in Covent Garden, but she is not there. I've sent a letter to Berkshire, in case she fled *there*, though I don't believe she'd wish to lead Dunmarron to David."

I shook my head, recalling the snippet of conversation I'd overheard between Rafe Godwin and his cronies in the library. "I have an idea of where she is. I might be wrong, but it's worth a look."

Grenville blinked at me. "Good Lord, Lacey. Where?"

I told him. Grenville looked surprised, then thoughtful. "It is possible. I shall go there, then."

He made ready to spring up on the moment but I lifted my hand. "I believe *I* should go," I said. "Even if she's not there, I may gain a better idea of where she's hiding."

Grenville sank down again. "You mean I should not be seen rushing about London chasing my escaped ladybird? I hardly care about such things at the moment—I only want to make sure she is well."

"No, I mean because she might be afraid Dunmarron will find her again, if he follows you. Let me speak to her and see that she is safe."

"If she *is* safe," Grenville said unhappily. "What is Dunmarron playing at?"

"I'm not certain." On our way here tonight, I'd told Grenville about my encounter with Dunmarron at Brooks's, with Donata filling in the more interesting details. "He seemed very annoyed Marianne had foiled him but showed no intent of pursuing her. But I don't know the duke well, so he might have been feigning his dismissal of the game."

"I doubt it," Grenville said. "Dunmarron is not a subtle man. There's a reason we call him the Duke of Dunces."

"I believe he has more intelligence than you credit him. Cunning, rather, if he is as dull as you say."

"Possibly." Grenville moved restlessly in the chair. "Why on earth should he try to take his revenge on me *now* for relieving him of a dancer when we were just down from university? I hardly stole her—she'd had enough of him, and I offered an escape."

"Biding his time?" I suggested. "Awaiting an opportunity to humiliate you? It is well known that you are more fond of Marianne than your other mistresses."

"More fond ..." Grenville turned a look of astonishment on me. "Is that your assessment?"

"The world's assessment," I said gently. I had long ago recognized in Grenville the symptoms of a man helpless.

"Do not mock me, Lacey. You know I've fallen in love with the wretched woman. Cupid's arrow strikes where it will."

"It struck me," I admitted. "I decided not to resist."

"Not to resist?" Grenville's eyes flashed amusement. "My dear friend, Donata would not let you resist." He heaved a sigh. "As the Bard says, *The course of true love never did run smooth.*"

"He had the right of it," I answered with conviction.

I need not have worried about Donata. When I went upstairs, she was surrounded by admirers, ladies and gentlemen both, guarded by the dragon of Lady Aline Carrington, who'd known her from babyhood.

I did not like to tear Donata away when she was enjoying herself, and Grenville was immediately pulled into conversation, so I walked about looking for the items Mr. Floyd had listed as suspected copies. Damned good copies as far as I could see, as I studied them. I wondered who the forger was, and wondered if Denis knew. Talent like this would draw his notice.

At three in the morning, I fell asleep in the large round room on the first floor, a beautiful chamber of precise proportions. A crowd had gathered here as well, but my chair faced the window, and I allowed myself to doze off.

Grenville found and woke me, and we adjourned to Donata's carriage. He was going on, he said, to another do, accompanying Lady Aline in her coach. I saw in Grenville's eyes that he longed to rush out and discover if Marianne was where I believed her to be, but he was trusting my judgment in the situation.

He said good night to us and departed. Donata had also been invited to the next entertainment, but she'd made her excuses and chosen to return home with me.

Once our carriage started, Donata drooped against my shoulder, the Egyptian diadem in her hair scratching my cheek. "Heavens," she said. "When I was at my father's house this winter, I thought I'd die of ennui, but at the moment, Pembroke Court seems a quiet and peaceful retreat."

I reached to her lap and clasped the hand she'd laid on it. "I thought you were having a fine time playing merry hell with the prince's friends."

"Yes, but I enjoyed such things much more when I was younger. Then, I was defying Breckenridge. I feel no need to defy *you*."

"That is a mercy." I caressed her gloved hand. "We never finished our quarrel," I reminded her in a low voice.

"No?" She turned her head to look up at me, her shawl, which she'd resumed, rustling. "I thought we had. Which quarrel do you mean?"

I lifted her hand and pressed it to my lips. "Do we have so many we must differentiate them? The one this afternoon. I grew distracted at the end. What I wanted to say in conclusion was that I am happy with Anne, and Gabriella, and Peter, and do not need a horde of male children worshiping at my feet to feel whole. From the way my own father and I went at it, and from the bullying the lads did at school—not to mention in the army—I conclude male children are horrible creatures and not worth the trouble. Peter excepted, of course."

I'd had time now and a calmer mind to compose the speech. Donata's eyes glittered with unshed tears.

"Gentlemen can be fairly horrible, can they not?" she said. "That lot tonight would try a saint's patience."

"Ladies are much more to my taste." I pressed another kiss to her hand. "I want to assure you, my wife, that you can tell me anything, especially when it is of this importance. I have no wish to put you aside, no wish to blame you for something that is not at all your fault. I am not Breckenridge. I know it is difficult for you to grant me your trust, but I ask it."

Donata drew a long breath. "I ought to have given it to you. But I was ashamed and afraid, and I hoped—I so hoped—the surgeon was wrong." Her voice became faint. "But he is not, is he?"

"I do not think so." I gentled my tone. "I am sorry."

"As am I, Gabriel. I was a coward."

"Never a coward, my love," I said. "You are as brave as a lion."

Donata turned her face up to me and touched my cheek, and we ceased speaking for a long and interesting moment.

The next morning I forwent my early ride to take a hackney to Bow Street.

Brewster appeared as soon as I walked out of the South Audley Street house. He accompanied me across the city, but he elected to wait in my old rooms in Grimpen Lane while I went around the corner to the Bow Street magistrate's house.

"Not going in there," Brewster said firmly as he descended from the hackney at the top of the cul-de-sac that was Grimpen Lane. "Not Newgate neither. 'Tis bad luck."

"I understand." I gave him a nod.

A wise decision—I could imagine the patrollers or Runners

deciding to hold Brewster at the magistrate's house in case they could pin an unsolved theft on him.

Brewster gave me a warning look from where he stood on the ground, his hand on the carriage door. The coach rolled a bit, the horses and driver impatient. "You don't need to be going to Newgate neither, guv. Mr. Spendlove is too anxious to see you there. He'll have the turnkey lock you in and not let you out."

"I will have to risk it," I said.

Brewster growled something, slammed the door, and waved the coach on.

A short way up Russell Street, the hackney turned to Bow Street and let me off before numbers 3 and 4, the magistrate's house for this area.

I found Pomeroy easily upon entering by the bellow of his voice. Milton Pomeroy had been a sergeant under my command on the Peninsula—fearless, hard on his men, and adamant about bringing those men through battle alive.

He had blond hair that this past year had begun to darken, wide blue eyes, and a muscular body now showing a bit of fat in the belly. Pomeroy liked his meat and drink.

"You want to go to Newgate?" The question boomed through the lower hall where the unfortunate were waiting to stand before the magistrate. Pomeroy's eyes twinkled. "I can accommodate you there, Captain."

"I'd hoped to keep it quiet," I said, pained.

"Not to worry. Spendlove ain't here. Was out all night chasing down thieves and had to take to his bed in exhaustion once he brought them in. Let me finish a task or two, and we'll go."

I did not have to wait long. Pomeroy let me sit in his room upstairs where I paged through the *Hue and Cry*, looking at the notices for criminals wanted far and wide.

One entry caught my eye: *Stolen. Three small paintings of ladies, ovals on ivory with gold frames, taken from a market stall in Southwark last Thursday week.*

I thought of the market where I'd found my statue and wondered if these paintings mentioned were the missing ones from

Carlton House—or forgeries of them. And if so, why should someone steal them from the market stall? Or did this have nothing to do with the prince's collection?

Pomeroy came to fetch me while I was pondering and waved at me to follow him. When we were out on the street, Pomeroy striding for a hackney, I asked, "Where does the information come from for the *Hue and Cry*?"

Pomeroy turned to look at me in puzzlement, saw that I was lagging, and slowed his pace. "All over. We take reports from patrollers, and the magistrate turns in a list. Then it's sent to whoever collects the lot and it's printed. Why do you ask? Want to find someone?"

"Not at the moment. Does it do any good? The newspaper?"

Pomeroy shrugged. "Sometimes. Informs chief constables all over the country about who we're looking for so they can bang them up and let us come for them. Or stolen goods. Or missing persons, gone for whatever reason."

"If there were Runners and patrollers in every city, people might get found faster, wouldn't they?"

Pomeroy snorted. "There's nothing wrong with things as they are. Reformers will have us living with police everywhere, a man afraid to go out of his house in case he'll be arrested for the smallest thing. Not what we need in England."

Reform of the existing establishment or creating a new system of policing came up in every Parliamentary session. So far, the idea had been met with resistance. Most men did not want a regular police force, such as they had in France and other Continental regimes, treating every citizen as a potential criminal, they said, curtailing liberty.

Pomeroy was correct that the Runner system was effective—a small body of men to investigate crimes and travel outside of London to retrieve a suspect—aided by patrollers who could chase a villain or help those in need. I doubted there would ever be much change. Overarching police reform bills had been killed again and again, and I imagined they always would be.

A hackney took us along Drury Lane up to Holborn. From

there we dropped down Holborn Hill, which segued into Skinner Street and Snow Hill, and stopped near the corner of the Old Bailey and Newgate Street. Here Newgate prison stood.

I never liked coming here. Prisoners were executed in the yard on Mondays, so that Sunday they could repent and pray for their souls. Those stuck here awaiting their trials could watch the sinner be led out to the scaffold, hear the final words of the condemned, and the creak of the gears and the rope as he dropped to his doom.

Thankfully, it was not a Monday and the scaffold was empty. Even so, its reminder chilled me as we walked inside, Pomeroy cheerfully greeting all and sundry.

The turnkey, a sullen man I remembered from when I'd visited my regimental colonel after his arrest, trundled up a flight of stairs, bidding us to follow. His keys clanked as he let us into one of the more commodious private cells. The chairs in it were old but upholstered, the bed thick with covers, and a fire blazed in the hearth. The desk was heaped with books and papers, and an inkwell and pen tray lay neatly among them. Not the best surroundings, but a man would not freeze here in the February cold.

The gentleman inside, seated at the desk and writing on a sheet of paper, looked up, then came abruptly to his feet, his face creasing in dismay.

"Mr. Floyd," Pomeroy sang out. "This is Captain Lacey. He's here to interrogate you about the goings-on at Carlton House."

Mr. Floyd looked familiar to me, but I couldn't place him. He was no ruffian but a slender gentleman in a decent suit, his dark hair pulled back in an old-fashioned queue. He was on the small side, about half a foot shorter than I was, with eyes of light blue. Mr. Floyd was not young, but not old either—I put him at about forty or so. At the moment, the left side of his face sported some colorful bruises fading to purple but he kept his head up, undaunted.

I had no idea where I'd seen the man before; I only knew I had.

He obviously recognized *me*. As the turnkey left us, locking us into the room as Brewster had predicted, Mr. Floyd groaned and covered his eyes.

"This is it; the end. I am done for."

CHAPTER 19

"YOU KNOW ME?" I ASKED in bewilderment. "I have not met you ... have I?"

Sebastian Floyd lowered his hands and looked me up and down with eyes that held cynicism. "We have never been introduced, but I have seen you often. You have a short memory, Captain."

"Tell me, then," I said impatiently. "So that my failing faculties might be reminded."

Floyd sent a sharp glance at Pomeroy. "I am allowed a private meeting, Mr. Pomeroy—I have not been condemned yet. I believe I am innocent until proven guilty."

Pomeroy looked in no way offended. "Right you are. I'll leave you to it. Sing out when you're ready, Captain." He knocked on the door, and the turnkey let him out and locked us in again.

I tried not to flinch when I heard the scrape of the key, and Floyd nodded. "You grow used to it. Or so they tell me. Of course you know me, Captain, though we've never spoken. He's not much keen that we grow chummy and lift ales to one another down the pub. Do think hard. I believe you own a miniature painting, a gift for your lady. Where did you obtain that?"

I remembered perfectly well. James Denis had given me a miniature of a young woman, painted by Hans Holbein the Younger, as a reward for helping him—more or less a bribe for my silence about events in Norfolk before my marriage.

Denis had allowed me to choose the miniature from a myriad of beautiful paintings spread across a dining room table, artwork that had been stolen from him. Denis had been busy recovering and cataloging it …

"Of course," I said. I remembered a small man who looked like a clerk roaming the house and making notes in a ledger. I'd barely noticed him in my overwhelmed state and forgotten him right away.

Denis did not only employ former pugilists to guard him and commit crimes for him. He also used clerks, patrollers, magistrates, men of business, cits, merchants, moneylenders, money changers, shippers, stallholders, and half-pay captains.

Floyd gave me a nod. "Now that we understand each other, you see my dismay. One word from you, and I'm finished. Short trial, scaffold waiting."

He thought I'd send for Spendlove, announce that Floyd had once worked for Denis, or still did. This would be all the evidence Spendlove needed to fit him up for the thefts.

I wondered if Spendlove already knew the man's history and had wanted me to independently confirm it. Was that why he'd been reluctant to let me see Mr. Floyd? Because we might collude, since we were both followers of our master, Denis?

"I found your letter to Mr. Higgs," I said, producing it from my pocket. "You discovered a copy of one of the prince's paintings in Amsterdam in October. Did anything come of it?"

"What do you think?" Floyd indicated our surroundings. "Higgs did nothing. He dismissed the idea. That is when I began keeping a closer eye on things. The painting was in the prince's private closet when I returned to Carlton House, an exact replica of the one I'd seen in Holland. I'm not expert enough to spot a well-done forgery, so I still do not know which is the right one. Higgs decided the man in Amsterdam had a copy, and we never spoke of it again."

"And then more odd things began happening in Carlton House," I said. "And you kept notes in your own ledger. I have that as well, by the way."

"Good." Floyd's blue eyes snapped in anger. "I tell you this in truth, Captain Lacey, I was not at Carlton House to steal. I was there to help care for the collection, inventory it, make sure all was well. Several pieces had been acquired through our—er—mutual acquaintance, and that mutual acquaintance hoped to sell still more to the Regent. It's much more lucrative to sell to the prince than steal from him. The Regent does not hesitate to pay for what he wants. He'll hand over princely sums, if you'll pardon the pun."

True, the Regent had the reputation for being a profligate, a spoiled one at that. If he desired something, he'd give over the money, no matter what the amount. Denis likely made a large profit obtaining paintings or sculptures for him. I imagined Denis had arranged for Mr. Floyd to be employed in Carlton House in order to steer the prince toward more purchases via Mr. Denis.

"Nothing illegal in that," Floyd said in a loud voice. "I have committed no crime."

"I believe you," I said. "I know you are not guilty of the thefts, or the death of Mr. Higgs."

"I was told about that." Floyd's tone softened. "Poor old Higgs. He meant well, but there was something strange going on, and his hand must have been far into it. When the prince's major-domo insisted we report the thefts, the Runner was quick to pin it on me, and Higgs did nothing to stop him. Only stood about looking shocked, blast the man. And here I am."

I indicated that we should sit and be more comfortable—as comfortable as a cell in Newgate could be. Floyd took the chair behind the desk as I scraped another from the wall.

"If what you say is true, which I believe it is," I said. "I'll convince Spendlove he has the wrong man and to let you go."

Floyd gave me a stern look as he sat down. "No need. Our mutual acquaintance is taking care of things, so I implore you to say nothing at all. Though with Higgs dead, the thefts and forgeries might dry up of their own accord. But who knows? I don't believe Higgs was acting alone—he was not the sort to orchestrate a scheme, if you understand me. He could organize the world down to the threads in his stockings, but he was no good if no one told him what to do. I don't know what man *is* pulling the marionette strings, or I'd have alerted others by now."

By *others*, I knew he meant Denis and his thugs, who would go explain to the villain that Denis did not like men who got his trusted clerks arrested.

Of course, I was assuming the villain was a man. I realized there was no reason why it should be. Poppy, with her sharp tongue and sharper eyes, had men trembling in their boots because they owed her money. I'd also a few years ago met one of Denis's rivals called Lady Jane, a fiftyish matron who ran bawdy houses and the most notorious gaming hells in London. I could see either of them having a hand in robbing the prince.

"I found a forgery myself," I said. "Of the Theseus statue. A very good one. I had to have an expert's opinion on it, and it turns out the statue in the prince's house is a forgery as well. What I have concluded is that the objects are being taken from Carlton House and copied, the copies returned, the originals presumably sold."

Why a second copy had been there for me to buy in the *marché ouvert*, I was not certain. As Denis had suggested, the forger could have made several copies, thinking he might as well make a few extra bob. Someone could have purchased the fake from him, realized it was a forgery, and given it to the stallholder to be rid of the thing.

If I could lay my hands on the forger, he could explain many things.

"Do you know who they could be using to make the copies?" I asked. Higgs would have had access to artists from whom the prince commissioned paintings, from the great to the new and not-yet-known. He might have asked one of them to secretly copy the artworks. I wagered that an unknown artist would have leapt at the chance to earn a fee.

Floyd gave me a level stare. "I know nothing about forgers, Captain Lacey. I am a man of business."

So said his lips. His fingers lifted a pen and scratched a few lines on a piece of paper. He blew on the ink to dry it, blotted it with another paper, and folded the page before he handed it to me. Then he rose and thrust the ink-smeared paper he'd used to blot his words into the fire.

I understood his precautions—the turnkey or another spy could be listening at the door, noting every word to report to Spendlove. No doubt they went through Mr. Floyd's correspondence and every jot he wrote.

I tucked the paper into my pocket. "Ah, well. Thank you for seeing me, Mr. Floyd."

"Not at all, Captain. I am sorry I could not be of more help."

I rose. Floyd remained seated, as though he had much work to do and couldn't be bothered to escort me to the door.

"I am trying to find the true culprit," I said, wanting to reassure him. "And quickly, so you will be released."

Floyd gave me a nod. "Quite decent of you. But do not worry overmuch about me. I will be well. I am writing a treatise on the works of Mr. Caravaggio, and I welcome the time to get on with it."

Though Denis had told me he would not help Mr. Floyd if I continued pursuing the thefts, I no longer believed him. Denis would never let such a useful employee be hanged. No doubt he was even now working to have Mr. Floyd released. I remembered how impatient Denis had been to reach an appointment when he'd accompanied me to Carlton House, and I wondered if that appointment had to do with Mr. Floyd.

"I wish you good day then." I knocked on the door for the turnkey to let me out.

The turnkey did, thankfully, and after exchanging good-byes with Mr. Floyd, I left him taking up his pen and bending once more over his papers.

Pomeroy was in the courtyard, crouching down to speak to a man through a grating in the lower wall—one of the condemned who could not afford a comfortable chamber like Mr. Floyd's. Pomeroy and the prisoner were having a lively chat, and Pomeroy bade the man a cheerful good day before he turned away with me.

"Chap stabbed his wife a dozen times," Pomeroy told me as we walked through the yard to the street. "She'd been carrying on with his brother *and* his father—can you credit it? And she tried to off this poor gent herself. So he waits for her one night and goes at her. Jury has sympathy but gent couldn't prove he was fighting her in self-defense, as he tried to claim, so he's for the noose. He's resigned, though. Wants me to send his farewells to his mum. Poor sod."

So saying, Pomeroy walked along the Old Bailey south toward Ludgate and a hackney stand, his stride brisk, his merry look in place.

As we waited for the coach that lumbered toward us, I said, "Thank you for letting me speak to Mr. Floyd alone."

"No matter." Pomeroy waved at the hackney driver, though the man had already seen us. "I hope you get him off, Captain. I'd love to see Spendlove robbed of another conviction."

"Another?" I asked in surprise. The rumble of wheels and the clop of horses' hooves grew louder, several wagons running by at the same time the coach reached us.

Pomeroy yelled up at the driver over the noise that he wanted to go to Bow Street, and obligingly handed me into the carriage. Unfortunately, he shoved me with such enthusiasm that I had to catch myself before I went toppling out the other door.

Pomeroy climbed up behind me and slammed the door, falling into the opposite seat as the coach jerked forward. "Oh, yes," he said, continuing the conversation. "Spendlove is desperate for a conviction. Five men he sent to trial in December—for five separate crimes of theft—were all acquitted because Spendlove couldn't bring in enough evidence to please the jury. I think one of the men he'd arrested was guilty in truth, but the others could prove they were elsewhere at the time in question of whatever he said they did. The jury was so annoyed with Spendlove by the end of the trials that they let off the man who was actually guilty just to get up his nose. He's looking bad, Spendlove is. Magistrate is tired of his arresting absolutely anyone, trying to make money from convictions. That's why Spendlove wants *your* help. You can make a conviction stick."

"You recommended me to him," I said, puzzled. "He told me."

"I did." Pomeroy nodded and laughed. "If anyone can prove that chap Floyd *didn't* do anything, it will be you. Floyd isn't guilty—not of *this* crime, anyway. Ain't no one more truthful and indignant than one of the criminal classes wrongly accused."

"Spendlove won't thank me," I said with certainty.

"Very true. But you also won't hand Spendlove false evidence because he threatens you. You are a man of honor, sir. Not much of that about these days."

"You flatter me," I answered in a dry voice.

Pomeroy chuckled and let the conversation drop.

I descended with Pomeroy at Bow Street, thanked him again, and walked to Grimpen Lane alone after Pomeroy sailed back into the magistrate's court.

Not until I reached the bakeshop downstairs from my rooms did I open the note Floyd had given me.

Only one man does work so neat, it read. *A former racehorse jockey, Billy Boxall.*

Before I could storm upstairs and shout for Brewster, Mrs. Beltan, my landlady, who owned the bakeshop below my rooms, intercepted me. "Boy brought this for you," she said, handing me a folded paper. "All's well with you, Captain? How's the wee one?"

My anger dropped away like an avalanche at the mention of Anne, and I felt myself smiling. "She is beautiful, Mrs. Beltan. When she's ready to go out and about, I'll bring her by."

"I'd enjoy that," Mrs. Beltan said, nodding her mobcapped head and beaming me genuine good will. "Now I must get on."

We said our good-byes and I entered the stairwell covered with its familiar worn wallpaper and faded gilt. It was too dark here to read the note so I made my way upstairs as quickly as I could, my walking stick tapping.

Brewster sat in my wing chair, his feet on a footstool as he read one of my books, a well-thumbed copy of Defoe's *Crusoe*. Nothing priceless or worth stealing. Brewster did not spring up when I entered but continued reading, his eyes moving across the page. He emitted a laugh but didn't elaborate on what he found amusing.

I opened the note, which, like Floyd's, was simple.

I am safe. Don't look for me. M.S.

The handwriting was Marianne's. I sagged in relief and had to sit down, choosing the well-carved chair from the seventeenth century at the writing table. I had decided I knew where Marianne was, but to learn for certain that she was well released a tension in my body I hadn't realized I'd held.

I pocketed her note and drew out Mr. Floyd's. I rose, stalked to Brewster, and thrust the paper onto the pages of his book.

Brewster dropped the book to his lap and snatched up the note. He read the words, and his brows went up. "What's this about old Billy? What's it mean—*work so neat?*"

"Forgery," I said crisply. "He's the one who made the Theseus statue and the other copies—so Mr. Floyd speculates. Why did you not tell me Boxall was a forger?"

Brewster blinked at me. "I didn't know. I tell no lie, Captain, I had no idea. I don't go in for that sort of fing." I must have showed my skepticism because he plunged on. "I'm a simple man, me. I take things, and I sell them on. Used to, I mean," he added, looking virtuous. "Forging things, flogging them to gullible punters—that's too complicated for me, guv."

"But you would know about such things. Mr. Denis must deal in forgeries."

"He don't, and I'm telling you true. His nibs would lose his reputation if he passed off fakes for the real thing when gents hired him to find paintings and the like. How he gets them is sometimes not in line with what magistrates call the law, but none of the things he sells are bent. Can't trust a man what passes one thing off for another." He looked distressed. "Old Billy? A faker? Naw, Mr. Floyd's having you on."

"I intend to ask Old Billy straight out. And, if Boxall *is* in on this, I'll make him cough up the names of those who employed him. Higgs was killed either because he discovered who was doing the thefts and the forging, or he had a falling out with whomever he worked with. Perhaps Billy himself."

Brewster's eyes widened, and he rose swiftly, dropping the book to the chair. "Now don't be slandering me friends. If Billy's a faker, I can grow used to it, but he ain't no murderer. It's not in the same league, is it? Forgery and murder?"

I held my ground, not backing from his anger. "No, but Billy might have become alarmed that Higgs was about to spill everything to me and to Grenville. A man in a panic can kill."

Brewster shook his head. "Not Billy. I promise you. Besides, he's only about five foot tall. Higgs was much bigger, and Higgs didn't try to fight, you said."

"Higgs was sitting down, and Billy could have crept behind him, strangling him before he was aware. Why he bothered to bash him afterward … that I don't know."

Crashing the small bronze into a man already dead did not fit with the killing, and I did not know how to make it fit. Unless two men had been in the room with Higgs, and each of them had a different idea how to shut him up. But why bother striking him after he was dead? To make certain? Or had it been done in a fit of pique?

"A man panicking and smashing another over the head, that I can fathom," Brewster said. "But Billy Boxall garroting a chap? That smacks of a cruelty he don't have. He was ever so gentle with his horses, was Billy. Never whipped them, even when he needed them to go faster. They did it to please him."

"A man can be kind to animals and not to humans," I said. "I knew a cavalryman who'd never hurt an enemy's horse but had no qualm about slicing a French soldier's throat or disemboweling him and leaving him for dead. All the while trying to comfort the horse."

"Battle's different, and I am bloody glad I never saw any. London's battlefield enough." Brewster shuddered. "We'll go see Billy, and he'll tell ye."

Brewster was ready to charge out and hunt down the man on the spot. I stepped in front of him. "By all means, find out where Billy is, but send for him, don't confront him. Have him meet you here. Send word to Grenville as well. At the moment, I need to find Miss Simmons, so we will go our separate ways. Meet me back here in two hours—tell Grenville and Billy the same."

Brewster shook his head. "I should go with you, guv. Have Mrs. Beltan send one of her errand boys with your messages."

"You will not want to come with me, trust me," I said, giving him a wry look. "When you're finished sending messages, I'll be in Great Wild Street if you decide to walk that way."

Brewster drew back. "You're right. I don't fancy a stroll there." His eyes narrowed and he emphasized his next words with a jabbing finger. "You be careful, guv. Just because the place is full of mollies don't mean they're peaceful. They'll cosh you for tuppence, they will, *and* likely have a go at you while you're down."

"I will be on the lookout," I said, and left him.

My destination was not far, and the weather, though the sky had clouded over again, remained dry. I made my way down Russel Street past the pile of Drury Lane Theatre, across Drury Lane to Prince's Street, and so to Great Wild Street.

Brewster had not been wrong about danger. Past the theatre and bustling Drury Lane, the roads were quieter, with shadows in narrow passages. When I turned into a lane off Great Wild Street, a man leaning against a wall gave me a sharp look, as though he considered me a choice morsel.

This was molly territory, home to those men who enjoyed the pleasure of other men and boys, and sometimes weren't too choosy about whether the gentleman they had in their sights was of the same mind. Gentlemen of Mayfair came here to enjoy forbidden and illegal delights, usually in the dead of night and in secret.

I gave the man a warning glance but to no avail. After I passed him, he pushed off the wall and followed me.

The ruffian was as big as Brewster, and I didn't think much of my chances against him. I shouldn't have left Brewster behind, I realized, but nothing I could do now.

When I knocked on the door of my destination, I heard the man's heavy footsteps stop, and when the door opened, they reversed and faded.

A sullen youth stood in the doorway, a look of utter disgust in his eyes as he ran his gaze over me. "Yes?"

"I am here to speak to Mr. Hilliard," I said. "Is he in?"

The lad drew a breath to tell me to bugger off. Before he could, a very strong, very male voice thundered over him. "Captain Lacey! How wonderful. I've been expecting you."

Freddy Hilliard, actor and *travesti* of Drury Lane, strode from a room down the passage, his hand extended to me. Freddy was a tall man, broad of shoulder, with a thundering voice that could rise to a trilling falsetto when he dressed in skirts and sang in comedies and the pantomimes. He had deep brown hair cropped close, a square face, dark eyes, and a hard body that spoke of athleticism.

I shook his hand—the grip on mine could have crushed my bones.

"Pleased to see you, Mr. Hilliard," I said warmly. "Is Miss Simmons here?"

"Marianne?" Freddy boomed. "Of course she is. A wonder it took you so long to find her. Come in, come in. Henry, lad, don't look so disapproving. The Captain is a friend and welcome."

CHAPTER 20

FREDDY LED ME THROUGH A narrow but snug passageway with rugs on the polished floor, taper-legged furniture,
and tasteful paintings on the walls. The dining room a few steps
down this hall was also cozy, with a fireplace lending its warmth
and a table of rich golden wood that could seat six. A sideboard
held several decanters and a bowl overflowing with lemons and
oranges.

Marianne Simmons sat at the foot of the table, a glass of
brandy between her hands, the remains of a repast at her elbow.
She wore the clothes in which she must have escaped—a coarse
woolen jacket, breeches, and a plain linen shirt. Her hair was
unbound, flowing in a wave of gold over her shoulders.

She raised her head as I entered, her eyes red-rimmed with
tears and exhaustion. "I told you not to look for me," she said,
her brows coming together. "I ought to have known you would
not listen."

"I had concluded where you were before I received your message." I thanked Freddy, who'd pulled out a chair for me, and
sank down to face Marianne. "Of course I would search for
you."

Marianne determinedly studied her glass of brandy. "Do not
be kind to me, Lacey. Freddy has been very kind, and I cannot
cease weeping like a fool."

Freddy patted her arm before he sat down. "She's had an
ordeal, the dear girl. Brandy, Lacey?"

"No—thank you."

"Coffee, then. It's a cold day. Henry!" Freddy bellowed into the hall. "Bring coffee—hot, with a bowlful of sugar. And don't be all day about it."

Henry, the young man who'd answered the door, peered into the room, curled his lip, and scuttled away.

"Don't mind him," Freddy said. "He's a bloody Methodist. Doesn't approve of actors, especially actors like me."

"Why does he work for you then?" I asked in curiosity.

Freddy barked a laugh. "He wants to reform me, of course. He's on a crusade. Keeps my silver shined something wonderful, though, so I keep him on."

Freddy's aside had been calculated, I saw, to give Marianne a chance to draw a calming breath. That was a characteristic of a great actor, I realized, the ability to divert attention at precisely the time it was needed.

"Can you tell me what happened?" I asked Marianne. I curled my fist on the table an inch from her hand. "If you are up to it, I mean. I do not wish to tax you."

"For heaven's sake." Marianne let out an exasperated breath. "If the two of you continue to look upon me as fragile porcelain, I shall scream. Dunmarron is a brute—I am so worried for Grenville." The face she turned to me was frightened, her cornflower blue eyes wide. "Please tell him to have a care."

"Of Dunmarron?" I stared. "He's a boor, I grant you, but I am certain Grenville can hold his own against him."

"No, you do not understand at all." Marianne shook her head, her hair dancing. "Dunmarron is a dangerous man. He might act the dullard and let the *ton* laugh at him, but underneath, he is horrible."

Freddy rose and patted her shoulders. "Better tell him the whole, sordid story, love. I'll go see about the coffee."

He strode out with energy, growling for Henry. Marianne lifted her glass to pour a large quantity of brandy into her mouth. "He is right," she said after she swallowed. "You need to know. Oh, Lacey, it was awful."

"He abducted you, did he not?" I asked. "You did not go willingly."

"Of course he did. You guessed that, did you? From the stupid letter he made me write?"

"That very polite letter in which you call Grenville *Lucius*? You'd never have written words so deferential to me if someone hadn't forced you to do it."

"Do not make me laugh—it was dreadful." Marianne drained her glass, stared at it in regret, and set it aside. "I've been frightened before, but never quite like that."

"Dunmarron has sealed his fate, then," I said grimly. "You need tell me no more."

Marianne lifted her head. "I want to. I wish you to understand everything." She took a breath. "I did not lie when I said Dunmarron had been wooing me a long time. When I was on stage, he would wait for me, try to convince me to give up acting and become his permanent mistress. He is rich and a duke, but I never liked being near him. He's unsavory. I put him off, and once Grenville made his interest known, he vanished. I thought that was that." She spread her hands on the tablecloth. "But some days ago, Dunmarron managed to corner me when I was out. I was buying ribbons, of all things, in Oxford Street. He told me he wanted me to leave Grenville and live with him in a little house in Portland Place—and to come with him on the moment. I could send Grenville a letter, he said, and tell him I'd left him. I managed to walk away from Dunmarron with my nose in the air, and I pushed the encounter from my thoughts. Gentlemen are always suggesting such things to me, and it's best to ignore them. They only want Grenville's leavings, the same as they'd keep a snuffbox he discarded as a souvenir."

I gave her a frown. "Do not compare yourself to a snuffbox, Marianne. Grenville does not."

"A horse, then." She shrugged. "In any case, I forgot about it. But then Dunmarron cornered me again at the theatre—when I was there with Grenville. Grenville did not see, as I had left the box to go to a withdrawing room. Dunmarron frightened me.

He is a large man and insistent on getting his way. He wanted me to flee with him right then, became adamant. There was a crowd, and I managed to slip away from him and back to Grenville's box. He was gone by the time we departed. I didn't dare tell Grenville, who might do some damn fool thing like call him out. But I hated to keep it from him all the same. The next morning, when you came calling, I decided to speak to you about it. You are acquainted with a few brutes who wouldn't hesitate to put fear into a man, even if that man is a duke. When I ventured out to meet you at Egyptian Hall, I took every care, but Dunmarron had men watching me. They nabbed me when I wasn't a few yards from the house, blocking the view with carriages precisely at the right moment, so that no one saw to help me."

"He has very definitely sealed his fate," I said, my mild tone belying my fury. "Kidnapping is not done."

"I hope you *do* pot him," Marianne said. "But I haven't told you the worst. It isn't *me* Dunmarron is after at all. It's Grenville."

"How do you mean?" I asked. "To humiliate him, you mean? He tried, but Grenville has brushed him off at every turn. It is Dunmarron who has been made to look an idiot."

"No. Listen." Marianne clasped her hands around her empty goblet as though needing to hold on to something. "Dunmarron and his bullying lads took me to his house in Portland Place. Dunmarron sat me down in his parlor and told me I had to obey every command he gave, or he'd make sure Grenville came to harm. He drew a knife and played with it, describing how he'd cut Grenville's face so he wouldn't be handsome anymore, maybe cut out his tongue so he couldn't speak the golden words that made everyone like him. Dunmarron's look, his smile— horrible." She shivered. "I knew he'd do it. He told me to write the letter to you to tell Grenville I'd left him. If I didn't, he'd find Grenville that night, pop out one of his eyes with his knife, and bring it to me in a box. He put the tip of the blade to *my* eye, and laughed."

who had become a friend, and lay the case before *him*. Again, though, there would have to be proof beyond Marianne's word.

However, I knew a man who did not fear any gentleman, no matter his station in life, a man who made it his business to keep others under his control. He might refuse to act, but I could ask.

At this point, I realized I'd never be cleared of my debt to Denis, but so be it. Dunmarron could not terrorize my friends and get away with it. If I went after the duke myself, as I longed to, I'd end up in Newgate alongside Mr. Floyd—with Mr. Floyd's chances for freedom being far better than mine.

"You will soon be able to go home," I said to Marianne. I took a sip of coffee, which was quite good, though I was barely able to enjoy it. I pushed the cup back toward Freddy.

"If Grenville will have me." Marianne's voice held a note of sadness I'd never heard in her before. "I have put him through hell."

I reached out and clasped her hand, squeezing it gently. "I think you have no worry on that score, my friend."

Tears filmed Marianne's eyes. "Dunmarron never touched me. Please tell *him* that. He was more interested in going on about what he'd do to Grenville than in having any lustful designs on me. Laughed about it."

I gave Marianne's hand another squeeze. I promised her I'd find a way she could go home soon, and rose to take my leave.

Freddy accompanied me to the door, his Methodist footman nowhere in sight. "I'll keep her safe," Freddy assured me in a low voice. "Poor thing. I believe Mr. Grenville ought to take her to Paris and indulge her incredibly after what she's been through."

"I agree." I reached for the door handle to let myself out and hesitated. "There was a large, rough-looking man with ham fists in your street. I hope not sent by the duke, as I will have led him straight to your door."

Freddy's brows rose. He stepped past me to open the door and peer out, then he withdrew with a sigh of relief. "No, that's Rollo. He'll leave you be or answer to me."

My brows went up. "Who the devil is Rollo?"

"A bad fellow. He's for sale, you see—puts himself for sale, that is—and sometimes beats that fact into his reluctant customers. He won't touch me or those I vouch for, so have no worry."

"A nice place you live. And you say Marianne is safe?"

"My dear Captain, it is this way all over London. Rollo is only a bit more obvious, which will land him in the dock one day and get him hanged." Freddy shook my hand again. "Do not worry. I will look after her."

I thanked Freddy, but before I could withdraw, he squeezed my hand. "I don't believe I expressed my gratitude to you for introducing me to Mr. Derwent, Captain. He and I have become quite good friends."

He released me, and I felt my cheeks warm. Leland Derwent, a young man I once thought had been innocence itself, had admired Freddy and was pleased to meet him. Freddy had been kind to Leland, bolstering his spirits after Leland had gone through a tragedy. I was happy Leland had found someone to help him assuage his grief, but I did not want to imagine their relationship beyond that.

Freddy burst out laughing. "No need to blush, Captain. We are friends only." He gave me a significant look. "But I live in hope."

He laughed again, a loud, hearty sound, and sent me out the door.

My appointment to meet Grenville and Brewster was in one hour's time—I knew I'd never ride to Curzon Street, state my request to Denis to warn off Dunmarron, and make it back before the meeting. I settled for walking to Grimpen Lane, letting myself in the door Brewster had somehow locked—he had no key, so Mrs. Beltan must have obliged—and sat down to write a letter.

In the missive I outlined my disgust at Dunmarron and asked whether the fear of God could be put into him, or at least whether he might be persuaded to retire to his country house and leave Marianne and Grenville alone. I explained what he had done

to Marianne and his threats to Grenville, and how he'd sent his
ruffians to abduct Marianne after stalking her like prey.

My anger grew as I wrote but at the end I laid down my pen
and threaded my fingers through my hair, leaning my elbows
on the desk.

If I sent this missive to Denis, providing he did not simply
ignore it, there was no telling what he might do. I was asking
Denis to terrify a peer of the realm to satisfy my outrage and
gain rough justice for Marianne. There was nothing to say Denis
wouldn't simply have the man killed. Denis might also keep this
letter as a safeguard in case he or his thugs were caught, to show
my hand in the matter. If Spendlove needed evidence of my col-
lusion with Denis, it was in this letter.

I sighed, crumpled the paper, poked up the fire Brewster must
have built in my absence, and thrust the letter into the flames.
I wish I could say I did this because my conscience would not
let me bring about the death of or assault on another human
being, but I more worried about the consequences to my family.
I would simply speak to Denis directly.

My next letter was much shorter, asking Denis leave to call on
him. Then I began a third letter, addressed to Sir Gideon Derwent. In it I again outlined what had happened to Marianne and
laid the crime at Dunmarron's door.

Sir Gideon was a reformer and a genuinely kindhearted gentleman who had the respect of the most powerful people in Britain.
His disapprobation could greatly shame a man, duke or no, to
the point of ruin, all without a single blow struck.

I went downstairs to ask Mrs. Beltan to send out my post with
hers, and by that time, Grenville had arrived, Brewster with
him. The two descended at the end of Grimpen Lane, the road
not wide enough to admit a coach, and made their way toward
me, both speaking as soon as they reached me.

"I couldn't lay hands on him, guv," Brewster said, but Grenville's voice broke through his. "You found Marianne? Where is
she? What happened?"

Brewster interrupted Grenville firmly. "Sorry, guv. This won't wait. I couldn't find Billy, Captain, though I hunted high and low. But I have a message to ye from Poppy. She wants to see yer. *Now*, she says."

CHAPTER 21

GRENVILLE'S COACHMAN DROVE US ACROSS the river to meet with Poppy. On the way, I told Grenville exactly what Marianne had told me about Dunmarron.

"He will meet me," Grenville said immediately. "Be my second, won't you?"

"Of course," I answered without hesitation. "But I have put other irons in the fire as well, so perhaps Dunmarron will turn tail and flee."

Grenville scowled when I did not elaborate, and fell silent. If neither Sir Gideon nor Denis could help, however, I would not dissuade Grenville from calling out Dunmarron for what he'd done to Marianne. Grenville was a dead shot, so I did not worry about his survival. In my opinion, he had the right to fight for his honor and hers, even if the law technically disagreed.

We did not return to the Ox's Head to meet Poppy, somewhat to my relief. Brewster instead guided us through Southwark to a pawnbrokers, which held a desultory jumble of items from old keys to worn stools to brass boxes to old books. I glanced at the books out of habit—one never knew where one would find a treasure.

No one was in the pawnbrokers, not even a proprietor, and Brewster led us through the shop to the back room, which was empty of all but a table and a few chairs.

Poppy sat at the table and a large man, not unlike those employed by Denis, lounged by the window. She again was making notes, this time on a large sheaf of paper, and didn't look up until she was finished scratching. I wondered whether she and Denis had met in person and if she'd learned the trick of making her visitor await her attention from him.

At last, Poppy laid down her pen, turned the papers over so we could not see what was on them, and rested her elbows on the desk. She folded her hands, again in beaded black gloves, different ones this time.

"Yes, gentlemen?" she asked.

Brewster cleared his throat. "You asked to see *us*, love."

Poppy furrowed her brow, and then pretended to look enlightened. "So I did." Her gaze moved past Brewster and me to Grenville who stood a pace behind my right shoulder. A smile spread across her face. "Now, *you're* a handsome gent. Step up and let me have a look at you."

Grenville raised his brows and did not move. Brewster coughed. "This here's Mr. Grenville, Poppy. He's not one for taking orders."

"I know who he is." Poppy ran a slow gaze from the top of Grenville's head to the tips of his boots. "I must say you'd brighten up any lass's day. I have a cartoon of you, you know, Mr. Grenville. Done a few years ago, a very nice drawing of your legs all the way down to your ankles." She craned over the table to take in the legs in question.

Grenville flushed a berry red. "Good Lord."

Poppy chuckled, the warmest sound I'd heard from her. "You can't blame a woman for admiring you, love. If you don't want me ogling, you should shave off your hair, rub your face in mud, and wear sackcloth." She cocked her head. "Might not work even then, though. Now then, gents, Tommy tells me you're looking for Billy."

"We are indeed," I said before Brewster could reply. "I am growing worried about him."

"He's tough, is old Billy. I haven't heard a word from him for days, so I can't help you with that." Poppy finished another once-over of Grenville and leaned toward us, her eyes growing cool. "But you came to me before, asking about a certain house, and things that had gone missing from it."

I gave her a nod. "And we believe Billy might have been making copies of these things."

Poppy's face did not change. "I heard word of an auction at the end of the week. Two days hence. If any of the items are to turn up, I wager they'll turn up there."

Grenville started. "An *auction*? Not at a reputable establishment, surely."

"'Course not." Poppy's gaze pinned him again, she making no secret that she liked looking at him. "It's private, only for those who know of it. But no one would stop *you* from going, Mr. Grenville. The world knows your passion for art." She emphasized the word *passion*, and Grenville's face went redder.

"Where is it?" I asked impatiently.

"Surrey." Poppy turned unblinking eyes to me. "A house near Epsom. Grand place but no one lives there. Built by a nabob who went to die at his sister's in Berkshire years ago but hasn't quite managed to yet. He hires it out to those who want it, and this Saturday, whoever hired it is having an auction. You might want to run out and have a look."

Interesting. Poppy gave the information in a neutral tone but her expression indicated she knew bloody well the stolen items would be there.

"Why tell us?" I asked. If Poppy was in on the thefts, why help us find the loot? Or perhaps the thief was a rival, she happy to expose him.

Poppy contrived to look amazed. "Well, I ain't telling ya for free, am I? That information will cost you ten quid. Which you will pay me now."

"Ten!" Grenville exclaimed. "That's a princely sum."

"Well, it's a princely take, ain't it? Don't think about turning around and rushing out of here without paying. I am not alone, and I have plenty what will bring you back to me." Her face creased with a smile that was rather gruesome to see. "Although, if you want to stay with me, Mr. Grenville, and make it up to me, I'd take that."

"Ah." Grenville slid his hand into his coat and pulled out his purse. He opened it and glanced inside then shrugged and set the entire thing in front of Poppy. "No offense to you, dear lady, but we are in a great hurry. Ten pounds will have to do."

"Pity." Poppy made no move to take the money. "Good luck to you, gents. Now, I'm in a bit of a rush, so off you go."

I didn't move. "You seem to be very well informed, madam."

Poppy flicked eyes to me that were hard and cold. "Nothing happens in London, that I don't hear about it. I decided that interesting bit would be worth ten quid to you, so I sent Tommy to bring you back. You run off to Surrey and find your treasures. They'll be there."

"You are also confident," I said. "How do you know we won't bring Bow Street to the auction with us?"

Poppy regarded me steadily. "That's your affair. I am only passing on what I've heard. Do not ask me who stole the bloody things in the first place, because I do not know."

She looked frustrated enough that I believed her. I held the rest of my comments in check, aided by the scowl Brewster was sending me, bowed, and thanked her.

As we left the room, I heard the clink of coins as Poppy drew her riches to her. She had read us well, and reaped her reward.

On our way out, I glanced at the books in the pawnbrokers again, and spied a battered pocket copy of Plutarch's *Lives*. I left a shilling on top of the pile of books, took the small tome, and departed with Brewster, who was frowning with impatience.

Before we set off for the nearest bridge, I asked if Jackson, Grenville's coachman, wouldn't mind taking us to Southwark and the *marché ouvert*. Once we arrived, I wandered the aisles until I spied the woman with wiry hair from whom I'd bought the statue of Theseus and Antiope.

"Evening, gents," she said as we paused in the cold, darkening air. She obviously remembered me but gave me no greeting. "See anything else you fancy?"

I cast my eyes along the jumble on her table but saw very little of value—broken watches, tarnished silver chains, cheap necklaces, books half gone. "I wondered where you obtained the statue I bought."

I posed the question mildly, but the woman's eyes widened in alarm. Brewster stepped beside the stall to block her only way out, and Grenville took a stance square in front of it, in case the vendor decided to leap over her table and flee.

"You're in no trouble," I said quickly. "I am only curious. Whatever you tell us will remain our secret."

"There was nothing wrong in it," the woman babbled, jamming her hands in worn gloves together. "They do this sort of thing all the time."

"What sort of thing?" Grenville asked in a kinder voice. He reached into a pocket and produced a silver crown—I suppose he kept several purses about his person. He dropped the crown on the flat surface of one of the broken books.

The woman shrugged and snatched up the coin. "Gentry cove sold I to me, saying he didn't want much for it. Thought I'd flog it. Why not?"

"What gentry cove?" Grenville asked. "Did you know him?"

The woman shook her head. "Naw, what do I have to do wiv them? He comes to me, says he has this statue he wants to sell, would I give him a coin for it? I do, and sells it to you a day or two later." She nodded at me. "Gents do that sometimes. Grow tired of a thing and want rid of it. No questions. Or it belongs to their wives and they've quarreled with her. Eh?" She grinned at me, showing broken teeth.

"I suppose it happens," Grenville said. "Can you describe this gent?"

Another shrug. "They're all the same to me, ain't they? Looked like you." She waved a hand at Grenville, fingertips sticking out of holes in her gloves red with cold. "Muffled up to the ears with linen and collar, chest stuck out like a pigeon. You look better than most." Another wave at Grenville. "Gent like that shouldn't stay long 'round here." She gave Grenville a pointed look.

"Thank you," Grenville said. He handed over another half crown. "We are much obliged. Had you seen him before?"

"Never," the woman said. "And I never did again. Now then, madam, some nice joolry over here. Won't cost ya much, love." She turned to a middle-aged woman with a basket who'd paused to examine some of the chains. We weren't purchasing, and so the woman was finished with us.

"She describes half the dandies in London," Grenville said in a pained voice as we made our way out of the market.

"But a gentleman," I said, my heart beating faster. "Not a servant or a laborer or a tough. I have to wonder where this gentleman obtained the statue."

Brewster shrugged. "Could have bought it from the thief or the forger. Realized it was a fake, tossed it to the market stall to have a few coins back and be done."

Grenville said, "I'd think a gentleman who'd paid hundreds of pounds, if not thousands, for that statue would be incensed when he found it was a copy. I think he'd find the man who sold it to him and try to bash his head in." Grenville halted, his walking stick hitting the pavement, and he gaped at us. "Good Lord, you don't think this gentleman killed Mr. Higgs, do you? And *Higgs* sold him the copy?"

"No," I said slowly. A soft rain was beginning to fall, and people shoved past us, hurrying to be out of it. "I do believe Higgs was aiding those who were stealing the artwork in getting it out of Carlton House and the copies back in. I don't believe the second statue was meant to be put on a market stall for me—or anyone else—to find. That was a mistake. One, I think, that led to Higgs's death."

Grenville watched me, his curiosity alight. "Do you know who did it then?"

I shook my head. "Not yet. But I believe I can piece together what happened." I sighed, pulled my greatcoat closer against the rain, and walked on. "We need to find Billy. Quickly, I fear. And make ready for a journey to Epsom on Saturday."

Try as Brewster might, he could find no sign of Billy Boxall. I had confessed to Poppy I was worried about him, and my worry escalated as the week went on. I feared that when we finally found him, he'd be dead.

I discussed my theories with Donata and Grenville. I conjectured that the thieves who'd robbed Carlton House passed Billy the originals, which he would copy. The thieves would then retrieve the copy from Billy and return it to the house, leaving it in a different place so the things would be thought of as mislaid instead of stolen, as I'd concluded before.

The thieves took only one piece at a time, because Billy would need days to produce a skilled copy. Higgs aided the process by knowing which items were safe to take and how to keep the house's servants from speculating about the piece's absence.

Perhaps Billy had decided he might as well make more than one copy of the Theseus statue and had given both copies to the thieves, saying one was for replacing in Carlton House and one was the original. Likely the thieves couldn't tell the difference. Then Billy had turned around and tried to sell the original himself.

The thieves must have found out that the statue Billy claimed was the real one was a copy, and they'd rid themselves of it in a haphazard way before *two* wealthy buyers both believed they had the original and started to make a stink. Perhaps they'd then gone after Billy, and Billy was either hiding from them, or they'd found him, and Billy was dead, as I feared.

Or, perhaps the gentleman who'd bought the copy from the thieves, believing it the original, had tossed it to the market in a fit of temper when he'd discovered it was fake. That gentleman couldn't go to the bailiffs or a magistrate, because he would have knowingly tried to purchase stolen goods. A nice scheme, if true.

Billy would know, and he had to be found.

Meanwhile, I would go to Surrey on Poppy's hint and see what I could discover. Grenville would accompany me, and Donata, upon hearing the tale, insisted she go as well.

I hardly wanted Donata near a secret auction of stolen items in an empty house, but I also knew that if I left her behind, nothing would stop her from following. If she went with me, at least I could keep an eye on her.

I remained home for the few days before the auction, going about my usual routine—riding in the morning and again with Peter in the afternoons, visiting with Anne, reading to Peter when he went to bed, taking meals with Donata when she was at home.

I scoured my post for a reply from Denis to my request to meet with him, but none came. I resolved to finish the business in Surrey and then go to him unannounced.

Marianne remained safely with Freddy, and Grenville commenced his own routine, which involved being seen as much as possible out at night, dressed in his finest, Mrs. Froehm or Donata at his side. He'd promised me he'd avoid Dunmarron for now, until I spoke to Denis about him. I worried what Dunmarron would do to Grenville if they met—he'd set up Marianne's abduction well. What was to say he would not plan something equally villainous for Grenville? Dunmarron remained reclusive, however, Grenville and Donata reported, not appearing at any gathering or the theatre, reportedly burying himself in his chambers at his club.

Though Denis had not written, Sir Gideon Derwent had, expressing his distress at Dunmarron's treatment of Marianne. He promised to have a word with those who would condemn his behavior. Perhaps that was why Dunmarron had retreated.

The one sour note in the blissfully uneventful days before the auction was Spendlove tramping in while I was finishing my breakfast one morning, announcing with a snarl that Mr. Floyd had been released.

"Bloody solicitors got the magistrate to reconsider his decision to go to trial. No evidence, they said." Spendlove threw his gloves, which he'd been clenching in his hand, onto the table. "There's no evidence, because you, Captain Lacey, haven't brought me any."

"Because there is none to find," I said coolly. I put aside my plate and rose, signaling Bartholomew, who'd followed Spend- love in, to withdraw. Bartholomew did not look happy, but he went.

"Of course there is evidence," Spendlove began, but I held up my hand.

"I don't believe Mr. Floyd is guilty. I think he was handed to you when the thieves learned that a Runner was coming to investigate. He even wrote to Mr. Higgs some months before you were called in, worried that someone was stealing items from the prince's collection. He'd found what he thought was an identical copy of one of the Regent's paintings in Amsterdam."

I stopped as I said the word. *Amsterdam.* I remembered the surgeon when he'd sent for me, apologizing—or at least explain- ing—that he hadn't spoken to me before because he'd been in Amsterdam.

Oh, Good Lord, was Denis involved in this after all? With the aid of Higgs, smuggling out the originals after Billy copied them, sending them abroad with his agents, like the surgeon? The surgeon was obviously able to get into and out of England without anyone being the wiser.

Denis had denied having anything to do with the thefts, but why would he tell me the truth? I remembered Brewster saying to me that Denis did not confide all to everyone who worked for him—they did not always know what one another did. Denis considered *me* his agent now, and he would not feel the need to impart every scheme he had to me unless I needed to know.

But, no. I halted my spinning thoughts. Why should Denis send the *surgeon* to sell a painting in Amsterdam? Why send him to do anything at all—and once the man had been on the Con- tinent, why on earth would he come back? No, the surgeon's journey there had to be for another reason. Many Londoners went to Amsterdam on business, as it was near, and it was a port with ties to the entire world.

Spendlove, not noticing my stillness, plunged on. "If not Mr. Floyd, then who? Mr. Higgs? Convenient he's dead, eh? He can't stand trial now, can he?"

"I believe that was the idea," I answered. "A dead man can't confess and give away his compatriots. I believe Higgs died because those compatriots feared he'd talk. He'd already spoken at length to Grenville and me, showing us a list of what had gone missing as well as the things that had moved. Perhaps his confederates concluded he was having a fit of conscience."

I stopped again, picturing Carlton House and the easy way I had come and gone on the day of Higgs's death. I'd also moved without restriction during the soiree, the servants caught up in keeping us all supplied with food and drink. No one watched to see what we did.

Brewster had told me that a way to rob the place was to be part of the staff, someone admitted to the house without question. I agreed with him. The prince liked to show off, and so many people had walked through the chambers in Carlton House over the years, admiring all within.

Spendlove took a step toward me. "I need a man to answer for this, Captain. The Regent is growing impatient, and his retinue are threatening *me*, and the magistrate, and all the way up past him." He gestured as though the administrators of the law were stacked up in my dining room. "The Regent doesn't want it in the newspapers—the magistrates wish to announce the incident only after the criminal is caught." He pointed at me. "So bring me a culprit, or I arrest *you* for being Mr. Denis's accomplice. The magistrates want to see Mr. Denis brought down, but most are afraid to act against him. You, on the other hand, will do nicely as an example of why one does not want to become tangled with criminals."

My chest went tight as he spoke, knowing Spendlove was right. If he arrested me, the magistrates Denis had under his control might be happy to see me hang to alleviate their own shame in being bought by him. Denis *might* step in to prevent this—then again, he might not. Thinking over the number of times I'd angered and exasperated him in the last three years, I thought perhaps not.

"Please leave my house," I said to Spendlove. "Bartholomew!"

I did not have to raise my voice. Bartholomew opened the door in an instant—I knew he hadn't gone far. "Yes, sir?" he asked eagerly.

"See Mr. Spendlove out," I said. "And do not admit him again."

Spendlove snatched up his gloves. "When I do come back, Captain, I'll have my patrollers with me, and you'll be marched off. Don't matter what your lady wife has to say about it." He stalked to the door but turned back to deliver a parting shot. "I won't be long."

"I hope to have a culprit for you by Monday," I told him. "If I am lucky."

Surprise flickered across Spendlove's face, but he hid it with another growl. "Hope that you are," he said, then departed. Bartholomew followed close behind him to make sure he went.

Early Saturday morning, Donata and I took our coach south to Surrey. Grenville journeyed on his own in his phaeton, pretending to be doing nothing more than enjoying a drive in the country.

Donata and I rode side by side, she swathed in a rich brown velvet redingote over a gown of fawn cashmere and silk, I in a plainer suit of black under my greatcoat. My ivory silk waistcoat held the watch Donata had given me last New Year's. This New Year's we'd contented ourselves with the gift of our daughter.

Donata's silk-lined bonnet was topped with ostrich plumes which I continually pushed out of my face when she turned her head. I didn't mind one bit.

I'd been to Epsom with Grenville before, when we'd visited the grieving father of a young man who'd been killed in London. I remembered the sadness of that occasion, the quiet grief of his father. The young man had been a fop and a bully, but his father had loved him.

The memory made me squeeze Donata's hand, and I thought of little Anne's face when I'd kissed her good-bye this morning. Also of Peter manfully trying not to cry when we'd left him. Whatever we discovered today, I'd give the information to Spendlove and tell him to leave me the hell alone. Then I'd lock myself in my house with my children and wife and shut out the world.

Grenville had managed to find out exactly where the auction would take place—apparently gentlemen of the *ton* weren't above attending covert auctions, or at least sending an agent to bid for them. Grenville said his cronies seemed surprised he hadn't known about it already.

The mansion Hagen drove us to was well out into the country, far beyond Epsom Downs where we'd watch the racing in June, to a house isolated by a sweep of hill and mile-long drive. Tall trees lined the drive like living columns, and in the woods around the house, I glimpsed what might be a folly, an outdoor building made to look like a ruin.

The house itself was fairly new, its facade speaking of John Nash, and probably designed by him. If this nabob Poppy told us about had wealth he would make certain his home looked as aristocratic as he possibly could. Interesting that the man had finished it then rushed to live with his sister the moment he felt unwell. I supposed we all return to our places of comfort in the end.

The doors of the house were shut, the windows muffled with curtains. Wherever the auction would be held, the house was not a welcoming place.

As Hagen slowed the carriage, Grenville came around the side of the house on foot and waved for us to follow him.

"Round the back," he shouted up at Hagen. "There's a sort of Petite Trianon in the woods," he continued to us through the window I'd let down. "Very extravagant. The auction is being held there. They start in a quarter of an hour."

I reached to unlatch the door for him, but Grenville grabbed the bar on the back of the coach as Hagan started the horses and swung himself to the footman's perch. We'd brought no footman with us—Matthias and Bartholomew were following discreetly in a cart with Brewster.

Grenville hung on as well as any experienced lackey as the carriage moved forward. He risked mud on his elegant riding clothes, but then, he'd driven down here in an open phaeton. Grenville never succumbed to his motion sickness when driving himself, which was why he hadn't journeyed with us. He'd wanted to arrive fresh and with his wits about him.

Apparently motion sickness did not bother him when he clung to the back of a coach, either. When we stopped, he dropped off and cheerfully opened the door for us.

"Watch your step, guv'nor," he said in a false working-class accent. "M'lady."

He gallantly helped Donata descend, and she gave him a roll of her eyes and a dismissive laugh. Grenville steadied me to ensure I didn't topple over, and then Hagen, once we were down, guided the horses toward a grove of trees where coaches and coachmen had gathered to wait. I wondered what conversations the coachmen would have about the insanity of their various masters.

The buildings before us indeed reminded me of the Petite Trianon of Versailles, one of the fabricated villages to which Marie Antoinette and her ladies had retreated to escape the tension of life in the palace. This village had been designed in the classical style, more like a lane of miniature Greek temples than a rustic French village, but the principle was the same.

The auction was taking place in the largest building, a stone box with a deep Greek portico. This porch was shielded by thick columns topped with Corinthian capitals studded with plaster leaves. A pediment rested over it all, the architects determined to fold every facet of Greek architecture into the miniature structure.

The portico led to a door with a fanlight above it, which opened to a wide room filled with artwork and people.

However secret this auction was reputed to be, a good many of London's finest were in attendance. I recognized plenty of men I'd met at White's, Brooks's, and every outing Donata had taken me to; plus two of the regimental gentlemen I'd spoken with at Carlton House. Along with them were earls, barons, and knights of the realm, and very wealthy gentlemen with no titles but plenty of family connections. There were ladies as well as gentlemen—I suppose a gathering like this did not have as many social rules attached to it. As long as the winning bid could be paid, it did not matter who made it.

The artwork resting on easels and tables around the room was stupendous. I was dazzled by paintings of landscapes, still lifes, and beautiful portraits; sculptures in bronze and marble; objects d'art in gold and silver; miniature paintings, watches, and exquisite music boxes; tiny furniture made by a cabinetmaker in exact replication of full-sized counterparts; and an alabaster inlayed sewing box that contained alabaster handled scissors.

As I browsed the tables, I came across an item that made me halt in shock. On a cloth of black velvet lay one of the miniature paintings by the talented Mr. Cosway that had been so well described on Higgs's list of missing items.

"Oh, how lovely." Donata was beside me, her ostrich feathers tickling my chin as she bent over the portrait. The lady in it was in the act of lifting a flimsy garment from herself to bare her breasts. She smiled at us from under her upraised arm, her face surrounded by ringlets of pleasantly mussed hair.

"Very pretty," my wife said with admiration. "And a bit naughty. I believe I will bid on it." She smiled at me, daring me to try to forbid her.

I could hardly argue that the picture might be evidence of theft and fraud with so many others packed around us. I remembered reading in the *Hue and Cry* at the Bow Street office that two such miniatures had been pinched from a market stall. I wondered if this was one of them, and what had become of the other. This might be a copy as well.

Donata was waiting for my response, but I only shrugged, my indication that she could do what she liked. Donata would do so anyway. My wife was hardly a cowed woman.

A rumbling voice caught my attention. I looked up, my anger rising when I beheld the Duke of Dunmarron. He stood in the row of tables behind us, his cropped hair making his head look small on his large frame. He hadn't noticed me yet, or Grenville. At the moment, he was holding a clock identical to the one by Vulliamy in the prince's library, with its gilded sphinxes and malachite stone.

"What are they playing at?" Dunmarron said loudly. "This ain't real. It's a copy. The original is at Carlton House. Do they think we're fools?"

A rustle and murmur spread out from him like ripples. Through those ripples a small man hurried, followed by a larger man, trying to quiet the duke.

"What is he doing?" I murmured to Donata. "He'll turn this crush into a rout if he's not careful."

"It is called *rubbishing the stock*," a cynical male voice came from behind me. "One does so when one wants to prevent others from bidding up the price on a piece. The rest of us will disdain the item, and he'll buy it for a song."

I turned to see Mr. Floyd a few steps away from me, dressed in a plain black suit, his hair neat in its queue, his bruises having faded somewhat since the last time we'd met. Not far behind *him* stood his true employer, James Denis.

CHAPTER 22

DENIS'S GAZE MET MINE, HIS blue eyes cool. He gave me a faint nod and Donata a more polite one. "Mrs. Lacey," he said.

Then, without pausing to exchange pleasantries, he turned and walked away from us, heading purposefully to a row of paintings on easels. Mr. Floyd remained behind, as though apologizing for Denis's abruptness.

"Well met," I told him. "You are looking more hearty than at our last encounter."

"Yes, a rest has done me good," Mr. Floyd said, and bowed to Donata. "My lady."

"May I present my wife? Mrs. Lacey," I said, never tiring of saying the name. "This is Mr. Floyd."

Floyd gave Donata another bow. "I am honored to meet you. A bit far to drag a lady, I'd say, Captain, to make her stand in a drafty outbuilding and gape at artwork."

Donata answered, "Not at all, Mr. Floyd. I find it quite entertaining. Is Dunmarron correct? Are these pieces from the prince's collection copies?"

Floyd gave me a look that showed surprise my wife knew all, but he answered without a blink. "No, my dear lady, I believe they are the originals. His Grace rubbishes it as I've said, to keep down the price so he can have it. Mad collectors will do anything to obtain something special at a bargain."

I flicked my gaze to Dunmarron, who stalked to the next

object, a gold cup, and glowered at it. I'd begun forming the idea that Dunmarron was in on the plot to empty Carlton House of its treasures. Now that Marianne had told me what horrific threats he could make, I easily imagined him bullying and cowing Higgs to commit the thefts for him.

I could also envision Dunmarron killing Higgs when the man began confiding in Grenville and me, and frightening Billy Boxall into hiding, or killing him for making more copies than he'd been commissioned to. Dunmarron wouldn't need the money from the thefts, but both Spendlove and Donata had told me Dunmarron liked to collect art, even it he wasn't the best judge of it.

On the other hand, if he had stolen the pieces, why not simply keep them instead of letting them go to auction? Unless he hoped to make a profit from selling the smaller things to buy something more grand. There were plenty of items at this auction that were *not* part of Carlton House's inventory—whether they were stolen, or quietly sold by their owners who did not want to let on they needed money, or loot from the wars I likely never would know.

At the moment, Dunmarron's acquaintances, Lord Lucas and Rafe Godwin, flanked him and tried to get him to remain quiet. I looked about for Grenville, a bit alarmed when I couldn't see him. I feared that if he drew near Dunmarron, Dunmarron would be left bleeding on the floor, Grenville carted off for the crime.

I heard the soft chime of a hand bell, rung to gain everyone's attention. As we quieted, the auctioneer, a tall, reed-thin man with a head of thick gray hair, stood at the front of the room.

"If you will take your seats, ladies and gentlemen."

Donata said a bright good day to Mr. Floyd and led me to seats in the middle of the room. The chairs were soft and comfortable—I wondered if they'd be auctioned off as well.

As we sat down among the cream of London society, I whispered to her, "Do they not know a few of these things belong to the Regent? Surely someone will report this to the magistrates, or to the prince, or at least to his majordomo."

Donata removed her bonnet and set it on her knee, kindly allowing the person behind her to see the front of the room. "They would not have received an invitation if they would," she said quietly to me. "There are very old names here, Gabriel, and most have no love for the Hanoverians."

True, many of the aristocratic families of Britain believed themselves in a far better class than the portly German princes invited to come and play king. The Hanoverians had been fetched because there had been constitutionally no other choice.

All eyes were not on the auctioneer at the moment, however. They were on Grenville, who had stepped to Lord Lucas to murmur into the man's ear. Dunmarron loomed over Lucas's left shoulder, but Grenville calmly continued to speak to Lucas, as though he didn't notice the duke.

Grenville turned his back on Dunmarron once he'd finished his conversation, utterly ignoring him, though Dunmarron's large body filled much of the space around them. Grenville's expression was as cool as ever, nothing at all in his eyes as he threaded his way to the seat Donata had reserved for him.

Whispers and soft laughter flowed around us. Grenville had just given the Duke of Dunces the cut direct, and they'd been there to witness it. The incident would be the talk of Mayfair.

The auctioneer cleared his throat, and his audience reluctantly dragged their attention back to the matter at hand.

The only auctions I'd attended in my life had been as a lad in Norfolk, whenever a bankrupt farmer's personal effects had been auctioned. The farmer went to debtor's prison, while furniture, plows, and animals were sold to try to help erase his debts and whatever taxes he owed on the land. The process was informal, cold, and damp, with goods going for far less than they were worth.

I sat up as the first item went onto the block, interested to watch, though I pondered what to do. Stand up and declare that some of the pieces here had been stolen? Run back to London for Spendlove or a magistrate? Mr. Floyd, employed by the prince, was here, of course, but would he say a word?

I turned my head to look for Denis. He was seated at the end of an aisle in the back, his hands resting calmly on his walking stick. Why he was here I had no idea. Mr. Floyd was not sitting with him—that man had taken a chair behind mine.

The auction began without much preliminary. The first lots were paintings I had not seen on Higg's inventories. They drew many bids, finally selling at rather dizzying prices. I wondered if they too had been purloined and from where. The bidders seemed unconcerned about the paintings' provenances and quietly lifted hands or nodded at the auctioneer, who was skilled at keeping the bidding straight.

The bidding continued for the better part of an hour, pieces coming up and being sold fairly quickly. I heard nothing from Mr. Floyd, and another glance at Denis showed him sitting like a stone.

Grenville likewise said nothing. The auctioneer occasionally shot him a hopeful look, but so far, Grenville showed no interest in any of the items. Lord Lucas and Rafe Godwin whispered together—or at least Rafe whispered and Lucas listened with a pained expression. Dunmarron, standing in the back, bid on two paintings, neither of which had come from Carlton House as far as I knew. He won one of them, extremely pleased with himself.

"Next, a miniature painted on ivory depicting a pretty young lady. Done thirty years ago by the talented portrait painter and tastemaker, Richard Cosway." The auctioneer's assistant held aloft the painting of the saucy young woman Donata had admired. "I ask ten guineas to start. Do I hear ten? Ten guineas from the lady in the middle." The auctioneer nodded at Donata. "Thank you, madam. Do I hear fifteen? Fifteen guineas for this lovely young woman to carry in your pocket. A welcome respite from a hard day of sitting, gentlemen."

Titters sounded, and a man raised his hand. Donata immediately put hers up for twenty.

The bidding climbed—twenty-five, thirty, forty. Donata continued to lift her fingers serenely as it went on. The gentlemen bidders looked upon Donata at first with indulgence, then in annoyance as she continued, the price climbing. The auctioneer seemed reluctant to let things finish with her bid, sending encouraging looks to the gentlemen. I could have told him he wasted his time. When Donata was determined, nothing short of a catastrophe would stop her, and even then it would only slow her a little.

Finally, the last gentleman dropped out at a hundred guineas, and the auctioneer pointed at Donata. "Sold for a hundred and ten to Mrs. Lacey."

Donata sat back, a smile on her face, her cheeks flushed. "Gracious, that was quite exciting. I won."

"You won the obligation to pay over a hundred and ten guineas," I pointed out.

"You are a wet blanket, Gabriel. I quite enjoyed that. I can see how it can be compelling."

I shook my head. "Do not, I beg you, force us to give up the South Audley Street house and shiver together in my rooms in Grimpen Lane."

"Nonsense." Donata's eyes sparkled. "I am not so silly as that. If you realized how much I wager at whist you would think this a trifle." She turned her impish smile on me as I flinched. "You are so very easy to tease, Gabriel," she said, and the auction went on.

Her win had drawn attention. I turned to see Dunmarron's gaze fix on her, then me, his anger evident.

Bidding continued, item after item coming up and being knocked down. I saw no move from Denis until the auctioneer's assistant held up a small painting that reminded me of the one in Denis's house of the young Dutch lady. This was of a young woman in a blue kerchief, who turned her head to look at the viewer, a simple earring dangling from her earlobe.

The auctioneer started the bidding at five guineas.

I felt movement behind me. Mr. Floyd had lifted his hand for the auctioneer's attention. "Thank you, Mr. Floyd," the auctioneer said. "Five guineas I have. Who will make it six?"

A few people bid but it was rather desultory, no one knowing much about the painting or painter. Mr. Floyd continued until it was twenty guineas. At that point, there was a rumble from Dunmarron.

"Fifty," he said.

The auctioneer's eyes widened. "Fifty guineas I'm bid. Who will make it sixty?"

Irritated, Floyd nodded. Dunmarron raised his hand for seventy, Floyd for seventy-five. They went on, back and forth, up to a hundred, then a hundred and fifty. The rest of the room went silent, transfixed as Mr. Floyd and Dunmarron battled it out.

When the bid sat at two hundred, Floyd glanced at Denis. Denis made the barest twitch of his forefinger, resting on his walking stick, from side to side.

Floyd, looking disappointed, shook his head at the auctioneer and studied his lap. Dunmarron laughed in triumph as the auctioneer said, "Sold to His Grace for two hundred guineas."

I kept my eye on Denis, who looked unbothered. I knew he had a fondness for Mr. Vermeer, who'd done the painting that hung in his staircase hall. Denis had once told me he did not purchase everything for its monetary worth, but in appreciation of beauty and skill.

He remained motionless as the auction continued. Dunmarron gloated a while, and his friends drifted from him as though a pool of mortification spread from his vicinity. Grenville stoically ignored him.

Not until the Vulliamy clock came up did Grenville say a word. Dunmarron's loud declaration that it was fake had done no good—the bidding soared quickly, and Dunmarron's frantic answering bids made it rise to sickening heights. When it was at five hundred and fifty, with Dunmarron in the lead, Grenville said quietly, "One thousand guineas."

There were gasps. The other bidders shook their heads in surrender. Dunmarron growled his displeasure. "One thousand five hundred," he countered.

The auctioneer broke in. "One thousand, five hundred I'm bid. It's with you, sir." He gazed at Grenville. "Do you care to raise? One thousand, seven-hundred and fifty?"

"Two thousand," Grenville said calmly.

"Bloody hell, man." Dunmarron's face was red with rage. "Nothing you want is worth that much."

The insult to Marianne was clear. Grenville never flinched, his color never rose. He only nodded at the auctioneer to get on with it.

"It's with you, Your Grace," the auctioneer said reluctantly.

As Dunmarron opened his mouth to counter, I saw Denis twitch his fingers again. Mr. Floyd drew a breath and announced, "Three thousand guineas."

The gasps turned to cries of amazement. I stared at Denis, wondering if he'd lost his mind. The clock was pretty, but hardly worth that. Yet, he'd let a painting he truly wanted go to Dunmarron for a relative pittance.

Grenville, his lips twitching, shook his head. "No more from me."

The auctioneer gazed at Dunmarron, excited once more. "It's with you, sir." His tone was much happier.

Dunmarron growled. He raised his hands, sending Denis a glare. "Damn and blast the lot of you." He finished these words by whirling about and stalking out of the room. A sweep of cold air filled the space for a moment, cut off when he slammed the door.

A smattering of applause and laughter greeted this display. The audience was enjoying the drama.

"Well, now," the auctioneer said. "Shall we continue with act two?"

More laughter. I noticed as the bidders settled down again, waiting to see what the assistant would hold up next, that Denis had risen and gone. There must be a rear door, because I never saw the front one open and close after Dunmarron's departure, but Denis was no longer in the room.

I rose, excused myself to those in the row I stumbled over, and slipped behind a Chinese folding screen that hid a portion of the room's wall. A door indeed opened to the outside from there, and I departed through it, closing it quickly before the wind could slide inside in my wake.

Denis was strolling in the direction of his coach. As usual, several large men, including the one called Robbie, followed him at a discreet distance. Denis set his tall hat upon his head as he walked, and turned to look at me when I caught up to him.

"Captain," he said without inflection.

"Why on earth did you bid three thousand guineas for that clock?" I demanded. "It can't be worth a tenth that."

"It is not." Denis paused his stride, and halted to face me. "I know you will continue to ask me until your curiosity is satisfied, so I will explain. I will offer the clock to Dunmarron in exchange for the painting."

"Ah." I thought I understood, but frowned. "But you'll be paying three thousand for a small painting, when you could have obtained it for little more than two hundred."

"I will be obtaining more than that," Denis said, meeting my gaze squarely. "I will be obtaining His Grace."

I blinked once, twice. "You will buy his obligation with a clock stolen from the Prince Regent?"

"No, with a copy of the clock. The prince already has the original. I returned it to him this morning."

CHAPTER 23

ISTARED AT DENIS, DUMBFOUNDED, WHILE many thoughts spun through my head. "You had the original clock because the forger gave it to you," I said. "The forger, Billy Boxall."

Denis gave me a nod. "Mr. Floyd, upon his release, told me of your conversation with him and shared his speculation that Billy had done the Carlton House forgeries. I knew where to put my hands on Billy and so removed him from the game."

"Is he all right?" I asked in alarm.

"Mr. Boxall is quite well. He had been hiding the original clock in his room at his boardinghouse, waiting to sell it to a man in Amsterdam for a tidy sum. I returned the clock to the palace and to a grateful prince."

"Who is now also in your debt."

"Possibly. The Regent is rather fickle and not prone to great loyalty."

"What about Billy?" I asked. "And his customer in Amsterdam?"

"I am certain I can sell Billy's customer something else, or else the customer can be disappointed. Billy has worked for me on occasion, and he knows when I am the lesser evil."

"He was not working for you on this occasion, however," I said with conviction. "You had nothing to do with the thefts from Carlton House."

"No." Denis's eyes took on a touch of humor. "As I told you. I sell to the Regent to satisfy his obsessive need for artwork. I prefer him to be a satisfied client. I do not need to steal from him."

"Billy was doing the forgeries for the thieves," I went on, trying to set everything straight in my head. "Then he decided he could make quite a lot of money selling the originals and giving the thieves another copy. He was robbing the robbers."

"Not at first," Denis said. "Once Higgs was killed, Billy decided to sell the originals, yes, but previously, he'd been returning them to Higgs. Higgs was feeding the originals back into the prince's collection without the thieves' knowledge and discreetly getting rid of the forgeries."

I stared in bafflement. "Higgs was *returning* them? Good Lord." I rearranged a few of my ideas. "So Higgs *did* have a crisis of conscience, or thought of a way to confound the thieves. But why would Billy tamely hand the originals back to Higgs once he'd copied them? Surely Billy could see he stood to make a fortune selling them himself."

Denis lifted his shoulders in a smooth shrug. "Higgs was paying him to give the thieves a second copy and hide the originals. According to Billy, Higgs had indeed been forced into helping the thieves, and was quite upset about it. What they threatened Higgs with, Billy never knew. Billy decided to help Higgs, whom he liked—and as I say, Higgs paid him a nice sum. Easier money than trying to sell stolen artwork and not be caught. One by one, Billy gave the true artwork back to Higgs, who would then return them to Carlton House and destroy the copies."

I leaned on my walking stick, ignoring the icy breeze that blew from the Downs and froze my bones. "And then one night," I said, "the thieves caught on to what Higgs was doing. Perhaps someone to whom they tried to sell what they thought was an original told them it was a fake. The thieves stormed back to Carlton House and killed Higgs for it." I felt ill.

Denis watched me, his countenance as bland as ever as I worked through my conclusions.

"Billy did not tell you who the thieves were, did he?" I asked him.

Denis shook his head, the wind stirring the tails of his greatcoat. "He said it was more than his life was worth. I will wear him down eventually." Denis's lips twitched, as close to a smile as he ever came. "Or *you* could tell me."

For some reason, I felt more comfortable going through my speculations with Denis than anyone else. I knew he would not disparage me if I got it wrong and encourage me to think until I reached a conclusion.

"I had thought Dunmarron," I confessed. "He is a collector, and arrogant, and a bit of a dolt on top of it, but he can be terrifying and a little mad." I remembered Marianne shivering as she described how Dunmarron vowed he'd cut up Grenville's face, all the while pressing the knife to the corner of Marianne's eye. "He could have easily cowed Higgs. I imagine it was Higgs's idea to make the forgeries to replace the originals, so the thefts wouldn't be discovered right away—Dunmarron would not have thought of something like that. Dunmarron, who is famously a misanthrope, came to London for the first time in years this Season. I cannot believe it was simply to abduct Marianne and humiliate Grenville. Interesting how Dunmarron approached Marianne very soon after the Regent noticed the oddities in his household and summoned Grenville to help him. As though Dunmarron wished to divert Grenville's attention."

"And yours," Denis pointed out.

"I do not believe Dunmarron thinks much of me," I said. "He sees me as Grenville's hanger-on. His second. To him, I am not a man of much consequence."

"Nor am I," Denis said, his eyes glinting.

"Dunmarron is not the most observant of men," I continued. "Which is why I've decided against him as instigating the crimes. He might have helped for his own reasons, but he truly is a slow-witted man. Donata calls him the Duke of Dunces, and my wife is a fine judge of character."

"She is," Denis agreed. "Why suspect Dunmarron at all? Except for the fortunate coincidence of his diverting Grenville as soon as the Regent sought his help?"

Denis did not ask me in order to aid my reasoning. He wanted to be certain he had all the facts before he dragged Dunmarron before him and made whatever use he wanted of the knowledge.

I could save Dunmarron from Denis by shaking my head and admitting I had no proof. But I remembered the fear in Marianne's eyes, her terror not only for herself but Grenville. Dunmarron was responsible for that—he was not a guiltless man.

"The Regent enjoys giving large entertainments," I said, spinning out my thoughts. "When I attended his soiree, I noticed his guests rambling the house as they willed. I also noted that a person can walk in and out of the ground floor doors without hindrance. The servants are buried in their duties and cannot possibly watch every corner." I paused a moment but Denis said nothing, so I went on.

"Brewster speculates that the best way to rob the house is to work there," I said, "smuggling out bits at a time. I realized one could do the same as a guest—wait for a moment when attention is elsewhere, and help oneself to pieces easy to pocket. Or else move them to the library so Higgs would know which pieces to give to the forger. Any guest who is invited to Carlton House could steal from it—including me. I am going off the idea of Dunmarron simply because he hates London, and must rarely visit Carlton house, if he is invited at all. He was blatantly not present the night I attended the Regent's soiree. Dunmarron was likely not in London when the things began to be stolen and copied, which your Mr. Floyd noted in October." I paused. "Mr. Floyd told me you had him working for Carlton House to keep an eye on what the prince had purchased through you."

"Indeed," Denis said without hesitation. "Mr. Floyd carries in his head a catalog of all the artwork in Britain and Europe. If the prince wants something, he tells Mr. Floyd, who tells me, and I obtain it for him."

"Keeping the commission for every single thing the Regent wants for yourself," I concluded.

Denis gave me a shallow bow. "One must make a living."

He was enjoying himself. "Dunmarron would have bungled the thefts in any case," I said. "He certainly behaved like a fool today. A cooler head must have been at the helm."

As a name drifted into my thoughts, Grenville walked briskly from the auction room, holding his hat against the wind. I saw the anger buried in his dark eyes, a cold rage that seldom came forth, as he stopped and spoke to us, tight-lipped.

"Lucas and Mr. Godwin will be calling on you, Lacey," he said. "To set the appointment to meet Dunmarron. I believe I will ask Freddy to be my other second. He's been kind, and seeing a well-known *travesti* standing on the green might flummox Dunmarron's aim."

"I will be honored," I said quickly. "However, I believe Rafe Godwin might be the thief we are searching for. Dunmarron is the bull, but Rafe has been his driver."

"Rafe Godwin?" Grenville stared at me in amazement. "He's an annoying little toad, but I doubt he could think of such an elaborate plot as the one to rob Carlton House."

"A simple one," I said, and explained to him what Denis and I had been discussing. Grenville listened, his anger fleeing as his interest surged. "Dunmarron and Godwin between them have connections to sell the things to the Continent or to men in Britain who are not bothered by scruples. Look how many gentlemen have turned up at this secret auction today."

"What about the statue you bought?" Grenville asked. "Why did it end up in that market? If the thieves discovered it was another copy, why not toss it into the Thames?"

"Because it might be found by a waterman or the river police, which would draw attention to the thefts at Carlton House," I said. "Once they found out Billy had betrayed them, one of them—probably Rafe—sold the copy to the vendor at the *marché ouvert*. They assumed some punter would buy it and put it on his mantelpiece with no one the wiser. Which one did. Their bad luck it was me."

"And that woman, Poppy, told you to look there," Grenville pointed out. "She must have known all this, and about Billy."

Denis broke in. "Poppy is not a woman who would direct the watch or the Runners to the thieves. But she could direct *you*,

Captain. And she's fond of Billy. If the thieves had threatened him or hurt him, she'd want her revenge. She sent you here today, did she not?"

I studied him. "You know much about her."

"She is my eyes and ears south of the river," Denis said, inclining his head. "I am happy she assisted you."

"You would have told her to," I said. "She knew who I was before I ever met her."

"I do occasionally tell my agents what they need to know." Denis settled his hat as the wind picked up, the first drops of rain falling. "Mr. Grenville, I must ask you to please not kill Dunmarron before I get that painting from him."

"Is it truly worth that much?" I asked, though I knew the answer. Denis did not waste his time on trifles.

"It is," he said. "Good afternoon, gentlemen."

He turned and walked toward the carriages, his guards falling in behind him.

"Bloody hell," Grenville said. "I must add to Denis's wish that you do not give Dunmarron and Godwin over to the Runners before I've had satisfaction." He shivered in the suddenly icy wind. "I believe you about Godwin disposing of the statue in the market. The stall owner did say he looked like a pigeon, and Godwin's suits run to the excess. But who would have garroted Higgs? I cannot see Godwin doing that. He is extremely missish about anything to do with fighting. Not that he won't second Dunmarron, as long as he does not have to soil his lily-white hands."

"No, I put the murder down to Dunmarron. But ..."

Again my thoughts ran around my head, chasing one another like hounds after a fox. "A man would have to have a cool head indeed to creep up behind another and throw a cord around his throat. The cosh on the head must have been to make sure. A cruel man would have done that. Dunmarron *is* cruel—and he might have struck the blow. I can imagine him doing it." I saw it clearly—Dunmarron with his small eyes full of rage and triumph, lifting the bronze equestrian figure and bringing it down on the dead Higgs. The cold began to cut at me. "But Dunmarron does have a calm, collected friend, and I do not mean Godwin."

Grenville's eyes widened. "Oh, good Lord, Lacey, I know what you are thinking, but no. I've known him forever. He's an old friend of Donata's. They played together as children."

"Yes." My heart began to beat faster, my body, which had fixed in place while I thought, woke with a flow of energy. I'd left Donata alone in the auction room. With Lord Lucas.

And plenty of other people, I told myself, as I began moving swiftly back toward the Greek-style building, then trying to run, damn my leg. She'd be all right. She was surrounded by people she knew. And still, I ran, holding my walking stick out of my way.

"Lacey!" I heard Grenville call, and then suddenly Dunmarron was before me.

"What were you saying to him?" Dunmarron thrust himself in front of me, leaning down to bellow into my face.

I did not stop, trying to push past him, fear lodging in my throat. My wife was inside that room with a man who thought nothing of deliberately garroting another.

Dunmarron slapped his big hands onto my shoulders, forcing me to halt. "What were you saying to Denis? I'll kill you, I swear it. And him."

"Was it you who struck Higgs?" I demanded, uncaring of who heard. "After Lucas killed him?"

Dunmarron's face went scarlet. "You cannot know that. You weren't there."

He released me but only to slam his hands to my throat. Dunmarron was strong, big, like the bull I'd compared him to. I grabbed his wrists, trying to yank them apart. The air left my lungs as he squeezed, his lips spreading into a hideous smile.

But he'd forgotten Grenville. Etiquette dictated that a gentleman who'd called out another did not speak to him until they met with pistols to settle their honor. Dunmarron must have thought it meant Grenville would leave me to my fate.

Grenville, however, was a seasoned fighter, a man who'd traveled into dangerous corners of the world and emerged unscathed. He knew when to follow etiquette and when to abandon it.

He came up behind Dunmarron and laced his arm around the man's neck, jerking him backward. Dunmarron's hands slipped, and I was able to throw off his hold. I brought up my walking stick and slapped him hard in the stomach with it.

Dunmarron swore and choked, trying to dislodge Grenville, who hung on, rage flaring in his eyes. Etiquette had gone to hell.

"Go, Lacey," Grenville said in a hard voice. "I'll deal with the rubbish."

Dunmarron bellowed and smacked his big arm into Grenville's middle. Grenville grunted, mouth opening for breath, but he did not let go. Grenville glared at me when I hesitated a step, but he was right. He could hold his own, and I needed to find Donata.

I ran to the auction room, barely noticing the pain in my leg, and in through the back door and around the screen that hid it. The auctioneer was holding up a painting of a still life, another masterpiece from the Low Countries, depicting lemons among glasses of clear water.

Donata's chair was empty. She and Lord Lucas were nowhere in sight.

I raced through the room, pushing aside those who tried to stop my disruption, lords and ladies staring at me in disapproval and anger. I hardly cared. I rushed out the main door and across the portico, down the steps to the mud the carriages had churned up, searching everywhere.

Nowhere did I see Donata and her ostrich-feathered bonnet, which had not been on her chair. Nor did I see Lord Lucas, with his well-bred, fashionable air that had deceived me into thinking him a kind and sensible man.

Donata would have gone with him without worry if he'd suggested they step out of the auction room. The two had grown up together, had been friends since they were in leading strings, and she was fond of his mother. She could not know Lucas was a killer. I had been fixed on Dunmarron and had not warned her.

My lungs burned as I slipped and slid through the mud, panic gripping me, my gaze darting everywhere. She was gone. My breath choked me, my inhalation more of a sob.

Dear God, if I lost her … I did not give a damn about having sons, heirs, estates, wealth—none of that meant anything if I did not have *her*. Because of Donata Breckenridge, my life had turned from something distasteful and barely livable to one I looked forward to every day.

Each morning I awoke knowing I was in her house was all I needed. A look into her room to see her dark hair tangled on her pillow, her face creased with sleep, her eyes fast closed, made my life worth living. The fact that she would not wake for any reason whatsoever until noon at the very least amused me. When she did rise, she'd glide about her chambers in a clinging peignoir, something lacy in her hair, being indescribably beautiful, then drawl at me that she was hardly fit to be seen.

She was more than fit, and I had demonstrated my opinion in this regard many times since I'd married her. I'd banish her maid and shut the door, and then show Donata just how lovely I considered her. Donata would always flush in surprise and pleasure, as though the fact that I loved her astonished her every day.

My acerbic, witty, kindhearted, shrewd, and hard-headed wife, a woman who'd survived her first marriage by sheer resilience, had saved my life. I could not lose her.

She was with a cold-blooded man who covered his deeds by murdering others. How soon would he have killed the Duke of Dunces, who blundered about, ready to give away the game? I had no doubt that Lucas put up with Dunmarron because of his riches—Donata had mentioned that Lucas was skint. How angry it must have made Lucas to watch the profligate Prince Regent flaunting the paintings and other artwork he bought right and left while Lucas had to rely on the charity of his friends.

Lucas must have decided to take what the Regent had and make him look a bit of an idiot in the process. Only he'd not counted on Higgs doing his best to restore what had been stolen, or Billy being loyal to Higgs rather than Lucas. Billy either had honor of a sort, or else he'd feared Denis's wrath for his part in depleting a collection Denis had helped build.

Higgs had not only spoken to us and to Spendlove, but he'd duped Lucas and Dunmarron. They would have been furious at him for his betrayal and also feared he'd say too much. And so, he was silenced. Higgs, definitely honorable, had given his life for the sake of the artwork he so admired.

I couldn't find Donata. I halted, trying to breathe, trying to think, every part of me aching.

Silence surrounded me. I'd run into the woods at the edge of the estate, remembering that I'd seen a folly, or thought I had, on the way in. I imagined it was part of the faux village but it was set apart from the others, another piece of bizarre architecture dreamt up by a man who could not decide what to do with his money.

It was there, among the trees, a round stone building with the inevitable Greek columns, crafted to make it look like a ruin. The building could not be more than ten years old, yet it had a tumbledown appearance, with vegetation growing up against it, so it would resemble the ruins in paintings by Claude Lorrain.

I stumbled over brush and pushed aside tree limbs, rainwater showering through the woods to soak my hair and coat. My hat had fallen off somewhere, but I hadn't noticed.

I rushed up the steps of the folly without bothering to assess the area, looking for weaknesses or danger. I only knew I had to find Donata. All else was immaterial.

I grabbed the door's well-oiled handle and slammed it open. The door swung back easily and crashed into the wall, and I rushed inside.

Lucas was there. So was Donata, her bonnet on the floor at her feet. Lucas stood close against her right side with his arm around her waist, his head lowered to kiss her shoulder, while he held a knife at her throat.

CHAPTER 24

I STOPPED. DONATA LOOKED AT ME, her eyes round with fear but also anger, vast hurt at Lucas's betrayal, and apology.

"Lucas wants me to send for my carriage," Donata said, trying to sound calm, but her words quavered. "He wishes me to take him to the Continent."

Lucas raised his head. His gaze met mine with an expression that was naggingly familiar but I could not place it just now. "You've crashed in at the right moment, Captain," he said in a mild voice. "I was trying to persuade her, but Donata has always been stubborn. But I can better persuade *you*."

The tip of his knife drew a tiny drop of red from Donata's throat.

I took a step. "If you hurt her, Lucas, it will be the last thing you ever do."

He must have heard something in my tone, because he eased the knife from Donata's skin. "Call your carriage," Lucas said. "Accompany us to Dover, and she will not be hurt."

"*I* will accompany you. Donata goes home."

"Gabriel, no." Donata gave me a fearful look—she did not believe she'd ever see me again if I departed with Lucas.

I fully expected he would try to kill me once the carriage reached its destination, but I did not intend to let him.

"You murdered Higgs," I told him. "Because he decided to cease helping you. He knew you weren't worth hanging for."

"He was upset because we had caused Mr. Floyd to be arrested,"

Lucas said impatiently. "Mr. Floyd knew nothing about what we were doing, and therefore could not betray us. But Higgs weakened. Then I discovered he'd been giving us copies to flog to people we'd promised would own pieces of the Regent's collection. He made us look like simpletons, and swindlers. And then he began talking to you. Therefore …"

Lucas shrugged, like an amiable dandy sorry he'd had to expose a man for cheating at cards.

"Therefore you killed him," I said. "Brutally. Dunmarron hit him with the bronze, didn't he?"

"Dunmarron is a halfwit," Lucas said in disgust.

"You told him to abduct Miss Simmons to upset Grenville."

Lucas nodded. "Which worked very well. Grenville ceased caring about the Prince Regent and his petty problems. You didn't, though." He sighed. "You should not be so persistent, Captain. It will be your downfall."

His expression was calm, his eyes holding nothing but determination to escape to wherever he thought would be safe for him. No remorse, not even much anger, only a touch of irritation that Donata had not instantly obeyed him, and now I stood in his way.

I realized where I'd seen the similar look. The surgeon had gazed at me with the same focus Lucas took on now—he was a man on his own path, whether he saved lives or took them along that path did not matter. The surgeon was a man without a conscience, I had decided. Lucas was another.

I swallowed, my mouth dry. "If you release Donata, I promise you will make it to Dover and a boat. I have the means to see to this. Donata can go home. You've been friends with her for years—let that mean something."

"She could have married *me*, you know." Lucas tightened his arm around Donata's waist. "When Breckenridge got himself killed, she could have turned to me for comfort. I encouraged her to. But did she? No. She had to run to a nobody, a captain clinging to Grenville's coattails, and give him all that lovely Breckenridge and Pembroke money. You're her whore, Captain.

She straddles you and then she pays you. What sort of a man does that make you?"

Donata could do whatever she bloody well pleased with me, so the disparagement did not have its intended effect. A man without a conscience might not understand that.

Lucas could babble insults and filth all he wished. I did not care as long as he moved that knife away from Donata.

I took another step forward. Lucas again stuck the point of the blade to Donata's throat. "Do not, Captain."

As I froze, Lucas drew the knife downward, cutting a shallow tear in Donata's velvet redingote. The ripping sound whispered in the silence, and then Lucas rested the blade at Donata's abdomen. "I don't have to kill her, you know. I can hurt her instead, perhaps ensure she never gives you sons."

Donata's eyes flicked up, meeting mine. We shared a look, understanding so deep words did not need to pass. Lucas could not know, would never know, that he'd stirred a profound pain that made this danger seem trivial.

She did not need to nod. Neither did I.

Donata, who'd remained very still in Lucas's grasp, suddenly twisted to her left, her momentum pushing Lucas's knife hand out, enabling her to take a step away from him before he slashed. She leaned down, swept up her bonnet that had fallen to the floor, and slammed the ostrich feathers across his face.

At the same time, I lunged, and while Lucas batted at feathers, I took him down to the floor.

Now I had to battle. Lucas was younger than I was by about ten years, and he was strong. I had an injured knee, and he had a knife. We rolled and wrestled, Lucas seizing my throat with one hand, pressing his thumb into my windpipe, while trying to jab at my face with his blade.

I saw Donata's skirts whirl by us and her foot kick into Lucas's hip. He grunted but continued to try to get on top of me and hold me down. Donata took up my walking stick and smacked Lucas across the back with it.

The impact made Lucas lose his hold on me, which allowed

me to grab his knife hand and squeeze it hard. The knife clattered to the stone floor, but this only meant Lucas could use both hands unimpeded. He punched me, wrapped his hands around my neck, and pressed his knee to my groin. He performed all this without changing expression, a man simply doing what he must in order to get himself away.

We rolled back and forth so rapidly Donata could no longer get in a sure blow. She ran outside, the wind and rain gusting in on us, and shouted. "Help! Help! He's killing him!"

I do not know if anyone heard. Donata's cries continued, and then were suddenly silenced.

Fear pounded through me. I shouted my rage at Lucas as he pinned me down, and heaved myself mightily. I dislodged him for a moment but he was right back on me, the two of us grappling, each trying to gain mastery. Lucas fought vehemently, and we ended up against the open doorframe, the edge of the door digging into my shoulder.

Lucas had the knife again, which he'd swept up somewhere along the way. He stabbed it at my face. I saw the blade coming down, where it would go through my eye and into my brain. I desperately turned my head, even knowing the move was useless—the knife would slide through my temple into my skull.

Lucas suddenly rose straight into the air, ripped from my grasp, the knife clattering down beside me. Bones crunched, Lucas screamed, and then his limp body fell back through the door and slid to the floor.

A giant's beefy hands reached down and pulled me to my feet. "Like I told you, guv," Brewster said, setting me down. "Ye get into far too much trouble left on your own."

James Denis's men held Dunmarron between them. When I hobbled out of the woods to the clearing in front of the auction house, Dunmarron struggled between Denis's pugilists. He wasn't threatening, however, or saying a word. His face was covered with abrasions, his lip split, but there was fear in his eyes when he looked at Denis. He might cow much of the world because of his high position, but Denis did not care, and Dunmarron knew it.

Grenville's greatcoat and frock coat were both off and lying in the mud, his waistcoat torn, his cravat bloody, but he had a triumphant look in his eyes. He had his arms folded over his stomach as though trying to catch his breath, but his smile was satisfied.

That smile fled, however, when he saw me stagger from the woods, supported by Brewster and my wife.

"Good Lord, Lacey, are you all right?"

"I'll mend." The words came out a rasp. "You don't look much the better for wear either."

Grenville hurried to us. "I have come to the conclusion that dueling with pistols is far too tame. Beating Dunmarron to a pulp was exhilarating. I believe I'd have gone on beating him if Denis's men hadn't pulled me off."

Bartholomew and Matthias, who'd arrived with Brewster, now came into the clearing with Lucas's body balanced over Bartholomew's left shoulder.

"Where do ye want him, sir?" Bartholomew asked cheerfully.

Denis broke in. "A good question. What do you want done with these men, Captain?"

He asked as though the decision was entirely mine. Denis was a man who could do almost anything he liked, whether I wished it or not, and yet he was leaving the fate of these gentlemen up to me, politely. If I told him to take Lucas and Dunmarron to the middle of the English Channel and dump them in, throwing Rafe after them for good measure, he'd see that it was done.

Dunmarron understood that. The look he gave me was one of pure terror. If Lucas showed no remorse, Dunmarron had all sorts of it, or at least he had fear of the consequences.

"Give them to Spendlove," I said. "He is so insistent on finding a culprit for this crime, we'll hand him three. Godwin is not guiltless, so he'll go too."

Denis only studied me. He knew my anger, but I made myself *not* ask Denis to disembowel Dunmarron and Lucas to exact vengeance for Donata and Marianne. It was a close-run thing, but I held my tongue. I am ashamed to say my decision had more to do with the fact that being hanged for their murders would take me away from my family than any sense of morality or duty.

I would have to let Spendlove and the magistrates do their jobs. Dunmarron would probably be let off. He was a peer, he had the money to pay for an eloquent barrister to help him, and he had not actually killed Higgs nor done many of the thefts himself—he'd provided the funds for the enterprise, I imagined. He might even decide to turn on Lucas.

Lucas would face a jury in the common courts. His father was a marquess, but Lucas would not be a peer until his father died, and so he'd have the same sort of trial as any of the rest of us. His father would no doubt attempt to intervene, but Spendlove could be merciless. Lucas would probably hang, which he should for killing Higgs, and most of all for endangering my wife.

I had a feeling Donata would enter the witness box and cheerfully tell the jury every sordid thing Lucas had done and said to her today. She would take the view that *Lucas* should be ashamed, not her. Donata was that sort of person.

"Let Spendlove have them," I repeated to Denis, not looking at either culprit. "And Godwin, if he hasn't run like a hare. May God have mercy on their souls."

Denis met my gaze, understanding. He, at least, had a conscience, no matter how often he'd had to bury it to survive. I now understood the difference between men like Denis and men like Lucas and the surgeon.

Denis gave me a curt nod, signaled to his ruffians, and turned to his carriage. How he'd get Lucas and Dunmarron into the Bow Street magistrate's house without Spendlove trying to clap Denis himself in chains I did not know, but I did not much care at the moment.

His men seized Dunmarron, who surprisingly didn't protest, and carried him along, Bartholomew following with Lucas dangling from his big shoulder. Brewster walked close to Bartholomew, keeping a sharp eye on Lucas's inert body.

Once they were gone, I sank into Donata, my legs no longer supporting my weight. Grenville held me up from the other side. A fine trio we made, torn, bleeding, and exhausted. The crowd from the auction had come out to see what all the fuss was about, and now they stared and jabbered. We'd be in the newspapers for a long time.

Matthias helped us to Donata's carriage, driven toward us by a worried Hagen, and assisted the three of us inside. There we collapsed, Donata and I on one seat, Grenville on the other. We rode, dazed and weary, back to London.

When I was next sensible enough to think, I lay in a comfortable bed enclosed by green silk hangings, and I was curled around my wife. Morning sunshine poured through the window, the rain abated for now. The day would be clear and crisp, perfect for riding, but I found I could not move.

Donata slept next to me, her hair tickling my nose. I was not certain exactly how we'd come to be in the house and fallen into bed, but I know we'd sought each other in the dark, celebrating the fact that we were both alive, whole, and safe.

I vaguely recalled Hagen driving off with Grenville, promising me he'd take him to Great Wild Street rather than home. I was dimly curious about what had happened between him and Marianne when they met, but not curious enough yet to seek out Grenville and ask.

As I lay entwined with Donata, enjoying her warmth, she opened her eyes and looked at me. "Good morning," she mumbled. "If it is morning."

"If you are awake, it must be past noon," I said, kissing her hair.

"Tease." She snaked one hand from under the covers and touched my nose. Then she groaned. "Oh, I am growing old. I am sore and stiff and unwilling to rise."

I brushed a strand of hair from her face. "You were exuberant."

Donata, who was usually quite nonchalant about her appetites, flushed. "As were you. I was very glad that I did not have to watch you die."

"Likewise," I said fervently. "Why on earth did you let Lucas take you to that folly?"

"*Let* is not the word, Gabriel." Donata's eyes flickered with remembered fear. "I tried to leave the auction room to find out what you were up to, and Lucas intercepted me outside. Told me he was terribly worried about something, and would I help him. It was not until he steered me out of earshot of absolutely everyone that I knew to be afraid. Then he began berating me, telling me I had to help him because I owed him for not marrying him. I was to instruct my coachman to take him to Dover and pay for his passage to France or the Low Countries. When I tried to evade him and run back to find you, he drew the knife and took me into that folly to, as he put it, talk some sense into me. He was quite mad."

"I know." I kissed her hair again, trying to comfort her. "But he's finished. Spendlove badly wants a conviction for the thefts and Higgs's murder, and Lucas will do. Even if Lucas's father gets him off, he'll be ruined and forced to flee England. We won't see him again."

Donata buried her face in my shoulder. She shivered, my brave wife, and I grew angry at Lucas all over again. The sight of Lucas with his arm around Donata, the knife at her throat, had filled me with dread and grief, the same I'd felt when she'd lain in her father's house, close to death while bringing in Anne. Two men with no emotions had stepped into her life—Lucas to try to kill her, the surgeon to save her.

I held Donata close. Comforting each other segued into something more, and afterward I slept again.

When I next opened my eyes, it was to see, through the half-open bed curtains, Bartholomew setting a tray on a table. He twitched the curtains all the way open, letting in bright daylight. I groaned.

Donata, on the other hand, blinked and yawned. "Good afternoon, Bartholomew. Is that coffee? You are a splendid lad."

Donata and I were bare under the covers, but valets saw their masters and mistresses in all sorts of situations. I kept the blankets firmly under Donata's chin as Bartholomew poured coffee into porcelain cups and set one on the night table on Donata's side of the bed, one on my side. Then he pointed at the tray of covered dishes.

"There's eggs here, and sausages, ham, and beef. Toasted bread oozing butter as you like it, Captain. More coffee here, your newspapers, and oh ..."

Bartholomew lifted a small package wrapped in paper and laid it next to Donata's cup. "For you, my lady. Delivered not an hour ago."

"From whom?" Donata started to sit up in spite of my efforts to protect her modesty. She ignored me, holding the sheet to cover herself as she reached for the package.

"Not certain," Bartholomew said turning back to the tray. "Big man brought it. Looked like one of Mr. Denis's."

The rustle of paper crowded his words as Donata broke the plain wax seal that held the package together and unwrapped it.

An oval fell into her hand, from which a lady with a bare bosom smiled up at her. Donata sighed in delight.

"I do like her," she said. "So cheeky."

I plucked up the card that had lain on the paper beneath the painting and read its few words. *With my compliments. J.D.*

"He went back for it," Donata said. "How very splendid."

Bartholomew, who had glanced hastily away when he'd seen the nude in the painting, now held up a newspaper. "It's all in here, Captain." He opened to a page and pointed to the middle column.

> *Brawl in Surrey, in which several Prominent Gentlemen were arrested for Theft on the Highest Order and a Marquess' son is accused of Murder.*

Instead of handing me the newspaper, Bartholomew set it down again. "But they have most of it wrong. I was there at Bow Street when they were taken in."

He had carried Lucas to Denis's carriage, I remembered. I'd

seen nothing of Bartholomew after that.

Donata made a noise of exasperation. "Do tell us, Bartholomew. I know you are craving to."

Bartholomew looked pleased and cleared his throat. "Mr. Denis, he asks me to come with him to London to help make sure his lordship and His Grace don't get away. He said he needed strapping lads to hold them down. Me and Mr. Denis's men did that all right, and so did Mr. Brewster. Mr. Brewster enjoyed it a little too much, between you and me, sir. They was already down, wasn't they? Didn't matter—he'd give them a cosh every once in a while. But, he was like that when we was out in Egypt, wasn't he?"

"Mr. Brewster comes from a different world, Bartholomew," I said. "I, for one, am not unhappy that he made his disapprobation known. Pray continue."

"Well, it was the maddest thing, sir. Mr. Denis had his coachman drive straight to Bow Street. Mr. Denis gets down from the carriage himself, takes Lord Lucas over his own shoulder. Lord Lucas is awake now and yelling. Mr. Denis walks inside the Bow Street magistrate's house, spies Mr. Spendlove and Mr. Pomeroy, strides over to them, and dumps Lord Lucas in front of their boots. *The man who's been stealing priceless artwork from His Royal Highness,* he announces. *And his accomplice,* he adds, as me and Mr. Brewster and one of his other men drag His Grace in between us. Mr. Denis looks at Mr. Spendlove, *and* the magistrate who's come down to see what is happening, bows to them, turns on his heel, and walks out. Not too fast, not too slow, no arrogance. He just goes. He climbs back into his coach, signals his driver, and he rolls away. The rest of us had to scramble to grab on before we was left behind. You should have seen it, sir." Bartholomew ended on a note of admiration.

Donata's delight had grown as she listened. "Mr. Denis knows how to put on a performance, I will grant him that. I do hope that is the last we see of Mr. Spendlove."

I agreed, but remained skeptical. Spendlove was nothing if not determined. But perhaps such a conspicuous arrest for an audacious crime would keep him mollified.

Bartholomew, pleased he'd held us enthralled with his tale, left us to our breakfast. Donata and I devoured the meal hungrily, I feeling decadent for lolling in bed while breakfasting.

We tried to get on with our day as we usually would—Donata dressing and making calls, I reading, riding, meeting with acquaintances, spending time with Peter and Anne—but neither of us could put much interest into it, other than our time with our children. We'd both had a bad fright, and we would not recover for a while.

I made myself ride in Hyde Park, avoiding the fashionable areas and seeking less-traveled paths. Donata resolutely put on her finest feathers and went out for her calls, but I could see her tremble as she briskly requested her carriage. She'd go to Lady Aline's first, she told me, before she kissed my cheek and departed. I imagined she'd linger there, letting Aline's kindness and no-nonsense ways comfort her.

I read the newspaper accounts of the arrest of Lord Lucas and the Duke of Dunmarron, noting that Bartholomew was correct to say their accounts were not the same as his. The newspapers reported that it was the Runner, Spendlove, who'd made the arrests and discovered what these shameful aristocrats had been up to. Lord Lucas was in Newgate now, sent there by the magistrate, awaiting trial for murder.

His Grace of Dunmarron, as I'd suspected, did not fare the same. He loudly put the blame of the murder on Lucas, claiming he had not known quite what Lucas was up to in regard to the thefts. Dunmarron had been released by the magistrate but told to remain at home until the trial. The newspaper had gone on to talk about the other things Dunmarron had done, both rude and foolish—the man would not be able to lift his head for a while.

Rafe Godwin, apparently, had got off completely. He'd virtuously announced he knew everything Lucas had done but denied any part in it. He'd been shocked and scandalized, but too afraid of what Lucas would do if he told. For lack of evidence against Godwin, he'd also been told to go home until called as a witness in Lucas's trial.

Dunmarron and Godwin had been let off far too lightly, I thought in anger. But then I remembered the vast fear in Dunmarron's eyes when Denis had calmly asked me what I wanted done with him. If anyone could keep His Grace cowed and tamed, it was Denis.

I contemplated this as I rode in the sunny park, letting the outing soothe me. My name had not been in the newspapers, or Donata's, though Grenville had been mentioned as bringing Dunmarron to justice with his fists. However, my part and Donata's in this would be known by few, to my relief.

When I returned from my ride, I found Brewster at the house, as well as a letter in the post from Freddy Hilliard. I snatched up the letter, ready to break the seal, but Brewster, who'd come up the back stairs as I'd entered by the front door, placed himself before me.

"His nibs wants to see you."

My brows rose. "Are you running errands for him again? I thought *I* employed you."

Brewster shrugged. "I'm giving you my notice. Mr. Denis wants me back with him."

I felt a pang of disappointment. I'd rather liked the camaraderie we'd been forming. "And you wish to be? Do I not pay you enough, Brewster?"

I said the last in jest, but Brewster shook his head in all seriousness. "His nibs will pay what I ask, but it ain't blunt I'm worried about. Truth to tell, it's a bit more restful working for Mr. Denis than for you. In *his* house, I know what I'm about."

Whereas here, he had to put up with my unpredictable comings and goings, as well as the snobbishness of Donata's servants.

"I understand," I said. "It must be trying to work for me."

"It is, guv. Never know what you're going to take into your head to do, such as go after a man armed with a knife without fetching me first. If I don't work for ye, and ye get yourself killed, it won't be my fault."

"It will be entirely mine, I know. But I did not wish to go in search of you while a man was threatening my wife. However, I do thank you for your timely arrival."

Brewster studied the ceiling. "Almost *wasn't* timely, if you know what I mean. A second later, I'd have been explaining to Mr. Denis why I hadn't looked after you proper."

"Well, I hope he does not assign you to other duties," I said sincerely. "I count you as a friend, Brewster, and I'd hate to lose your company."

"Oh, he wants me to go on watching you," Brewster said heavily. "But that ain't a reward, trust me. We'd best go, guv. Mr. Denis ain't one for patience."

CHAPTER 25

DENIS WAS WRITING A LETTER when Brewster and I entered his study. He kept his attention on the page, his pen scratching, as I took a seat, and Brewster stood by the fire, warming his hands.

After a few moments, Denis laid down his pen, blotted his sheet, and slid the papers aside. Only then did he lift his eyes to me.

"Did you teach Poppy that?" I asked before he could speak. I waved my hand at the letter. "Writing or making notes before deigning to speak to those you've summoned?"

Denis's expression did not change. "No," he said. "She taught me."

This took me aback. "I see," was all I could think of to say.

"You very likely do not. I called you here to apologize, Captain."

Not at all what I'd expected. I blinked a few times before I said, "That isn't necessary. I thank you for taking care of Lucas and Dunmarron."

A faint twitch of lips. "I enjoyed it. No, I apologize for the threats I made to your family." He spoke as calmly as ever, as though going through a formality. "I warned you off, you see, because I did not want you to simply give anyone you could put your hands on to Spendlove in order to pacify him. I did not know who was committing the thefts, which annoyed me, and I wanted to find out before you turned people over to the magistrates. When I heard you'd spoken to Mr. Boxall, I worried for him. He is a man who is useful to me. Poppy too, is useful."

He said *useful*, but I saw the pained look on his face. Denis did not employ people he did not trust, and he did not trust many.

"Did you know Billy was faking things from Carlton House?" I asked. "Until you interrogated him, I mean?"

Denis gave a faint shake of his head. "Not until I saw the statue you'd purchased and the copy in Carlton House. I suspected it was his work, and Mr. Floyd thought the same when he was released—I had not had the opportunity to consult with Mr. Floyd after his arrest. I was puzzled. When I found Billy, it became clear—he told me everything except, as I said, the identities of his employers—and I feared you were up against dangerous men. He said that the thieves were using private auctions to pass the things to buyers, which was wise, as they could enter the items under a false name and collect the proceeds afterward. I pried from Billy where the next auction would be held—they often had him deliver the pieces himself—and I told Poppy to pass the information to you. I did not communicate with you directly, because I did not want the thieves to know I was involved. I decided they'd betray themselves more quickly if it was put about that I was *not* assisting you, and in fact had told you to keep out of the matter."

I remembered my rage when he'd threatened to use Marcus to keep me away from aiding Spendlove, and I was still angry about that. Denis had hinted that Marcus's resemblance to me would be *useful*—he liked the word. I would have to write to Marcus or make the journey to Norfolk to explain to him exactly what sort of man Denis was, and what he could do.

"I am not sure why Dunmarron was interested in bidding for the clock when he and the others had put it into the auction in the first place," I said.

"That I have not discovered. He either knew it was a copy and wanted to have it before a buyer claimed it was a fake, or he'd been promised the clock but Lord Lucas did not give it to him. Whatever the case, one or more of them attended the auctions themselves to make certain the pieces sold and that they were paid. They'd bid on other things as a blind, to appear to be collectors who did not much worry about an item's original ownership. I knew if you went to an auction you'd find some of the stolen pieces and likely the thieves as well. I sent my men to be in place to capture them."

"And turned up yourself," I said. "To make sure all went according to your plan." I spoke with my usual cynicism, but I could not be too angry at him, and he must know this. His men and Brewster had ensured that Donata and I were today alive and well.

But Denis was shaking his head. "Not at all. I'd heard that a painting I wanted would be there. The auctioneer delivered it to me this morning—I settled up for Dunmarron yesterday and had the auctioneer send him the clock in exchange for the painting. He'll remember our encounter whenever he checks the time. I do not believe he will be causing any more trouble."

"Is the painting worth that much?" I'd asked this before, but I was trying to understand why he'd go to so much effort and expense for it.

"It is worth a good deal more," Denis said without inflection. "I had it at a bargain." And now he had a duke as well.

"You'll sell the picture?" I persisted. "For a hefty profit, I imagine."

"No, indeed. I will hang it on the wall and admire it. Mr. Vermeer is a favorite of mine, and one day the world will agree. I will keep the painting." He gave me a pointed look. "What will you do with the Theseus?"

"Clean it off and set it on a table. I rather like it. Even if it is a fake, it was well done. Donata likes it—and she thanks you for the miniature."

Denis acknowledged this with a nod. "Your wife is a lady of fine taste."

"What happened to the real Theseus statue?" I asked in curiosity. "Higgs obviously had not had the chance to get rid of the false one, and the thieves put the second one Billy made into the *marché ouvert*—what happened to the original?"

"Billy has it," Denis answered. "He'll tell me where he put it when he's finished being afraid to face me."

"Will you return it to the prince?"

Denis regarded me steadily for a long time. "Of course," he said. He drew another sheet of paper toward him and picked up his pen. "I have much to do this afternoon, Captain. Mr. Brewster will escort you home."

I walked to Donata's house as I'd walked to Denis's, the day being fine and the way not far. Brewster lumbered beside me, saying nothing as usual. I found him restful.

I had Freddy's letter in my pocket, and as soon as I reached the foyer of the South Audley Street house, I opened the missive and read it. I was folding it again, musing on its contents when Donata stepped out of her coach and entered, her footmen and maids swarming around her to relieve her of her wraps.

"I thought you'd be out all afternoon," I said, then stopped in concern. Donata looked tired, shadows beneath her eyes.

She shook her head as she went up the stairs, first one flight then the next, all the way up to her private rooms. I followed, entering her boudoir as she dismissed her maid then collapsed onto the divan and flopped her hands to her sides.

"It is too exhausting," Donata said. "Talking and smiling, trying to make witty observations when one's heart is not in it." She sighed. "Aline suggested I made a quiet night of it, have a rest. She is being motherly."

"I agree with her. We'll have a fine supper here, the pair of us." I drew out the letter. "This might cheer you." I began to read it out loud.

> *To my dear Captain and his lovely lady wife,*
> *Mr. Grenville arrived in great furor yesterday, as you must know by now. Our Miss Simmons, while she had been vowing to me she did not want to see him, flew up and at him when he stormed in, she crying like a flood. Mr. Grenville caught*

*her up, and they held on to each other so tightly ... Well, I am
unashamed to admit it brought tears to my eyes. They were
weeping and kissing, both trying to talk at once. I tiptoed away
and left them to it.*

*I had to depart for the theatre after a time and called out to
them that they could stay as long as they liked, but from the
noises issuing from my sitting room, I rather feared I'd have to
find another place to bunk for the night. The theatre was full
and the audience lively, and when I returned home, all was
quiet. They'd retired to my spare bedchamber, much to Henry's
relief, and were both fast asleep.*

*This morning, they departed. Mr. Grenville has taken
my advice and carried Marianne off to Paris. I do not know
whether he allowed her to gather her things, or if they ran off
like a pair of ne'erdowells with her still in her breeches.*

I wish them luck, and thought you ought to know.

God bless you, Captain, and your lady as well.

Yours ever,

Frederick Hilliard

"Good," Donata said when I finished, some of her spirit
returning. "They need time together, away from the stuffiness
of London."

I set the letter aside and sat down beside my wife, my thigh
touching her rich rose silk skirt. I kept my voice even as I spoke.
"It will also remove him from my temptation to call him out.
I said nothing while he was having so many troubles, but he
will have to answer for placing that wager about your virtue in
Brooks's betting book. Though I will likely only try to wound
him, since he declared you would have no affairs at all."

I spoke in jest, because I had no intention of saying anything
about the matter. Grenville had no doubt been trying to throw
cold water over the gentlemen sullying my wife's name by showing that he, the most influential man in London, believed in her
loyalty.

Donata only stared at me, her cool look stealing through her warmth, then suddenly she threw herself back on the divan and burst into laughter.

She'd laughed almost as much when I'd told her about dumping Dunmarron's beef and port onto his lap, and her peals of joy were the same. "Oh, Gabriel," she said when she could speak. "How delicious. I nearly believed you. But if you *must* call out the person who proposed the wager, I would be happy to meet you on Hyde Park green. However, I will insist our duel is not at dawn. Such an unseemly hour. And you will have to lend me a pistol."

I gazed at my wife in perplexity—her flushed face, her starry eyes, her wicked look. "What are you talking about?" I asked with a touch of irritation.

Donata raised her brows and sat up, recovering her aplomb. "You said you wished to call out the person who placed the wager about my virtue. In that case, you must face *me* over pistols, because it was I who had the idea. I bade Grenville enter it for me, under his name, of course." She lapsed into a smile, looking vastly pleased with herself. "I won three thousand guineas."

The way I gaped at her must have been comical, because she was off again. "All my effort was worth seeing that look on your face, Gabriel. You do look upon life so very seriously."

"Bloody hell, Donata."

She only regarded me with her warm smile. "I knew there would be speculation when you left me alone so long, and I decided to cut straight through it. I had Grenville make the wager, and I won it, blast them all." Donata subsided, leaning back on the divan. "I was swollen like a melon most of the time, unable to do anything but sit and read. And miss you."

The last phrase was wistful. I took Donata's hand, kissed it. "Perhaps we too need time from the stuffiness of London."

Donata took on a contemplative look. "Perhaps. My mother's gardens are quite restful. Peter would be glad to have room to roam a bit. And you so like the country."

"I do," I said. "But I admit London has grown on me."

"Well, we won't rusticate in Oxfordshire forever," Donata said, sounding a bit more like her lively self. "We must be back in April, when Gabriella arrives. Now that she's out, there will be many, many things to be done. Aline and I must have her engaged soon or she'll be pitied as a spinster. Now, do not look so alarmed, Gabriel. She is a sensible young woman, and Aline and I are wise guardians."

I let out a long breath. "Thank heavens I do not have to worry about Anne for another eighteen years."

"Sixteen," Donata corrected. "She should not leave it too late."

"Eighteen," I said firmly. "Sixteen is a child."

Donata turned her head on the cushion to study me. "*I* was out at sixteen."

"And I met the man you married. Eighteen."

We frowned at each other. Donata shrugged, but I knew I had not won. "We will have a few years to argue about it. But I know what will bring both of us out of our doldrums."

Without waiting for me to ask what, she rose, took my hand, and led me out of the room and up the stairs.

The sun was setting, and the nursemaid was readying Anne for bed. Peter had just finished his evening meal, his face grave as he studied the Plutarch I had found at the pawnbrokers.

Donata beckoned Peter over as she sat on the sofa, and the nursemaid handed Anne to her. Donata's face changed as she held her daughter, every bit of sharpness falling away.

I sat down next to Donata and Anne and lifted Peter between us. He was reluctant to put aside his book, so I read it with him, looking over his shoulder, marveling anew that he'd grown another few inches while I'd been in Egypt.

Presently, Donata gave Anne over to me. I looked upon this miracle of a child, who regarded me sleepily with her mother's eyes.

"A bit of time in the country," Donata said, pressing a kiss to the top of Anne's head, and ruffling Peter's hair. "Yes, I believe that will suit us well."

End

AUTHOR'S NOTE

IT WAS A CHALLENGE TO write in detail about Carlton House, because of course it no longer exists. In 1826-27, on the advice of John Nash, who declared the building structurally unsound, Carlton House was demolished. Much of the interior architecture (fireplaces, columns) and many of the furnishings found their way to the Brighton Pavilion and Buckingham Palace, the latter of which George IV turned into his primary London residence.

The famous rooms of Carleton House were no more. The artwork and sculptures were dispersed among the other royal residences, and the house torn down.

Fortunately for us, ladies and gentlemen of the Regency enjoyed looking over the interiors of the rich and famous as much as we do now. From 1816 to 1819, W. H. Pyne published *The History of the Royal Residences* in installments, which were collected into one volume in 1819. The *History* contained one hundred color engravings of rooms from Carlton House, Windsor Castle, St. James's Palace, Hampton Court, and more. The color plates, done by various artists, are detailed, beautiful, and quite a boon for the historical researcher.

Carlton House was born in the early 1700s as a private home of one Henry Boyle, who was later made Baron Carleton (the correct spelling of the title). Boyle's heir's mother sold it to Frederick, Prince of Wales (father to George III) in the 1730s. The house was bestowed on our Prince of Wales (George III's son) in 1783 when he reached his majority. The prince quickly began the house's complete renovation and invited his friends, the so-called "Carlton House Set," over for nights of decadent revelry.

As I researched, I marveled at the amazing artistry of Carlton House's interior, notably the conservatory and the Blue Velvet Room. While a bit over-the-top, the décor nonetheless shows a master hand at proportion and coordination. The Prince employed only the best (and paid lavishly for it).

The artwork I describe in the novel—the bronze of Theseus and Antiope, the miniature paintings by Richard Cosway, the Vulliamy clock and inkstand, the Rembrandt that hung in the Blue Velvet Room—are real (in Pyne's book, the engraving of the Blue Velvet Room shows the Rembrandt quite clearly). The pieces can be found in the royal collection to this day, and were procured for or commissioned by George IV.

The royal collection can be browsed online if you are not fortunate enough to be able to travel to a royal residence, and is full of stunning paintings, statuary, and objects d'art. We will assume Mr. Higgs and James Denis managed to return the true versions of the pieces to the collection long ago.

I very much enjoyed following Captain Lacey through London and exploring new facets of it. The next book will remain in London and England, as Lacey settles in with his growing family and finds new problems to solve.

I am thankful every day I've been able to take this incredible journey with Captain Lacey, and very happy to be able to continue it. I especially appreciate all the letters and emails I receive asking for more of the good captain.

Best wishes,

Ashley Gardner

ABOUT THE AUTHOR

USA Today bestselling author Ashley Gardner is a pseudonym for *New York Times* bestselling author Jennifer Ashley. Under both names—and a third, Allyson James—Ashley has written more than 90 published novels and novellas in mystery, romance, and fantasy. Her books have won several *RT BookReviews* Reviewers Choice awards (including Best Historical Mystery for *The Sudbury School Murders*), and Romance Writers of America's RITA (given for the best romance novels and novellas of the year). Ashley's books have been translated into more than a dozen different languages and have earned starred reviews in *Booklist*. When she isn't writing, she indulges her love for history by researching and building miniature houses and furniture from many periods.

More about the Captain Lacey series can be found at the website: www.gardnermysteries.com. Stay up to date on new releases by joining her email alerts here: http://eepurl.com/5n7rz

47138882R00174

Made in the USA
San Bernardino, CA
22 March 2017